THE FUND

H. T. NAREA

A TOM DOHERTY ASSOCIATES BOOK   NEW YORK

FC
Narea

To my three Kates: Francesca, Nicole, and Connie

THE FUND

A Forge Book
Published by Tom Doherty Associates, LLC
175 Fifth Avenue
New York, NY 10010

www.tor-forge.com

Forge® is a registered trademark of Tom Doherty Associates, LLC.

ISBN 978-0-7653-2890-8

First Edition: May 2011

Printed in the United States of America

0 9 8 7 6 5 4 3 2 1

ACKNOWLEDGMENTS

I am indebted to many people for getting this book into your hands:
Jason Wright and Kathy Lacey Hoge, who acted as godparents
to my manuscript; my agent, Lynn Nesbit, who took me under her
wing and so graciously sprinkled her magic dust on the manuscript; the entire team at Tor/Forge: publisher Tom Doherty, edi-
tor Bob Gleason, marketing guru Linda Quinton, publicity rocker
Patty Garcia, and the unflappable Katharine Critchlow, for their
professionalism and care in teaching this banker how the book
business should be run; Maria Campbell for her thoughtful advice
and guidance; Nelson DeMille, Paul Farrell, Thomas Fleming,
David Hagberg, William Martin, Douglas Preston, and Whitley
Strieber for so generously lending their precious time away from
their own keyboards to read my manuscript; Judy Sternlight for
her masterful editing eye; Peter Krogh, Emile Heredia, Sharon
Kristjanson, and Robert Svensk for their early feedback and en-
couragement; all my good friends at the Mystery Writers of America, who welcomed me so warmly into their community of writers;
Denise Hale for her support; Ambassador Diego Arria for his many
truths; Fredric King and his team at Fountainhead Creative for their
critical visual perspective; Professor Ross Harrison for inviting
me into the Georgetown University academic community, thereby
granting me access to its fantastic research facilities; the many dedi-
cated journalists who report from every corner of the globe, providing fodder for storytellers like me; Paul Erdman for paving the
way and allowing me to marry his eldest daughter, the love of my
life; my parents, Hernán and Isabel, for braving that difficult cultural crossing all those decades ago; my daughters, Nicole and Francesca, whose pursuit of excellence in their daily lives inspires me;
and finally, my wife, Connie, who encouraged me to write, read my
words countless times, and from inception, thought this little dream
of mine was much more than just remotely possible.

This book, which is set in the future, is entirely fictitious. Though a few real names have been used for purposes of verisimilitude, the author does not intend to suggest that these persons, governments, companies, or institutions have acted or will act in the way described in this novel.

...أيّها الناس، أين المفرّ؟ البحر من ورائكم، والعدوّ أمامكم، وليس لكم والله إلا الصدق والصبر

O People! There is nowhere to run away! The sea is behind you, and the enemy in front of you: There is nothing for you, by God, except only courage and constancy.

> —General Tariq ibn Ziyad
> to his troops at the Pillars of Hercules,
> right before the battle that laid the foundation
> for the Caliphate of al-Andalus
> April 29, 711 A.D.

Endless money forms the sinews of war.

> —Marcus Tullius Cicero
> Roman author, orator, and politician
> (106 B.C.–43 B.C.)

PROLOGUE
⊸┼┼┾⊸

DECEMBER 10

THE CORRODED METAL OF the car's undercarriage could not hold up intact for many more long journeys. After a two-day mud-splattered trek, maybe its last, the SEAT Panda automobile from the 1980s sat idle on the upper level of the airport parking garage. The commercial jetliners crossing overhead in the blue morning sky were only visible through the two interlaced half moons cleared by the front windshield wipers. Caked mud hid the edges of a once-brilliant silver chassis, making it stand out from the modern, cleaner cars parked alongside it. It was clear that the car's owners couldn't claim very much for themselves in this material world, and any future journeys in their fragile lives would require other means of transport.

Inside, a man and a woman, he in his mid-twenties and she just breaking past her teens, sat on the front seat searching for just the right words to say good-bye. She didn't want to. He knew he had to.

The young woman's large round eyes, outlined in thick black, held the hint of a tear. She tried to catch his gaze, but his focus was on the red backpack next to him. He hadn't shaved in two days. Dark stubble framed his face, and his bare head was starting to show the faintness of returning hair. She began to whisper some words, but the sound of another large jet, its engines at full take-off throttle, made it difficult to hear her.

From the sadness swimming in her deep hazel eyes, though, he knew the words her lips were softly forming. "Please don't go. . . ."

The roaring jet engine diverted her attention long enough to glance into the backseat. The young boy was still sound asleep. He lay there curled up in a fetal position, safely wrapped in a blanket, his closed eyelids hiding his deep hazel eyes. The young woman was relieved to see that neither the loud aircraft nor the rising tension of the adults in the front had caused him to stir.

"Please stay with us," she implored. "We need you. I need you." She spoke in short breaths, like her life depended on it; like *his* life depended on it. "Please . . ."

She fought hard not to release the tears. No helping it. Her eyes began to glisten like two precious cut stones. He reached over and gently coaxed her brown scarf to fall from her head onto her shoulders and used the edge of it to wipe the tears from the beautiful, round curve of her cheek. That gesture of emotion, however kind, was the last he could allow himself to show her.

In the past few weeks, something had drastically changed inside of him; he no longer had appetite for matters of the heart. Instead, a feeling of invincibility had taken over. He was ready to make his mark on the world. And for that, he just didn't need her. His mind refocused on what he needed to do. He grabbed the red backpack next to him on the seat, held it close to his torso, and opened the car door to get out. A clump of dried mud cracked off the bottom of the door and dropped onto the pavement. He stepped on it with his left foot, crunching the particles of mud into the sole of his black leather boot. Dirty boots didn't matter where he was headed.

The man took a final look at her and the boy through the window. From very early on, it seemed they had always understood each other without the crutch of words. That's how it had always been. Even now, she could see resoluteness in his eyes and knew that he had reached a point of no return. Without uttering a word, he was saying good-bye and telling her not to come looking for him—he was on a different path that didn't include her. An immense feeling of pain rose from the depths of her stomach all the way to her throat.

She sat motionless, watching his worn black leather jacket and red backpack disappear into the sea of parked cars. He did not look back. Now, all the tears she'd kept in check these past few days ran down her face. She felt emptiness wrapping around her as she realized how different life would be for them without him. She buried her face in the scarf, trying to muffle her sobs.

Another aircraft took off from the runway, an Iberia flight. She followed its rise in the sky through the half moons of the windshield. It took her mind off her tears for a moment, allowing a ray of hope to bubble up in her breast. I can still change his mind, if I can just speak to him, she thought. Casting aside the burdens of logic and doubt, she decided to run after him. She looked at the sleeping boy and knew that her only choice was to leave him resting. She rolled down her window slightly and locked the car. She expected—no, she hoped—to be back in less than twenty minutes. It pained her to think of him waking up alone, but she knew that he would be safe here—certainly safer than with her in the terminal.

THE YOUNG WOMAN FELT THE CRISPNESS of the winter day but also smelled the waft of gas exhaust from the airplane traffic in the air. She looked at the signpost, made a mental note—fourth floor of the parking garage—and then ran toward the elevator bank, almost bumping into a man walking in the opposite direction. For less than a second, they glanced at each other, she with a preoccupied look and he looking startled. She noticed something familiar about him. Maybe it was the scar on his face, above his right eyebrow.

She had no time to wonder, though, as the elevator door was closing. An elegant-looking middle-aged traveler held it open for her. He couldn't help but stare at her youthful beauty, her thick brown hair pulled back in a long braid, her large hazel eyes outlined in black, now marred by her tears, and the skin of her angular face flushed with color by the urgency of her pace.

She caught his stare, but then immediately remembered herself. She turned away in embarrassment and, in the manner of all her short adult life, wrapped the brown scarf around her head, covering everything but her eyes.

She turned back around again, now more confident, her face covered, but revealing her true self. She was Fadiyah, a Berber Muslim from North Africa, whose face could only be seen by men who were family members. The embarrassment now passed to the man in the elevator, who quickly moved to the opposite side of the elevator and turned his gaze to the illuminated floor numbers above the doors.

After a few moments, which seemed like an eternity for both of them, the elevator opened onto the first-level walkway leading to Terminal 2 of the Madrid-Barajas International Airport. She rushed out and made her way to the terminal. Bathed by the bright morning sun, it was crowded with locals en route to domestic flights throughout Spain, many seeking climates that were warmer than the capital at this time of year. The departure hall was chaotic, full of laughter and shouting, as Spanish families gathered for a winter break.

Fadiyah couldn't immediately spot him in such a large crowd, so she raced about the terminal looking for him. Her full head scarf and swift movements in the departure hall made her stand out—lost and out of place amid the crowd of more relaxed travelers dressed in their beach pastels.

In her halting Spanish, Fadiyah asked a group of women, "Have you seen a man with a black leather jacket and red backpack?" The women were struck by the panic in her eyes; it frightened them. They quickly turned away, rejecting this young Muslim woman with the frantic smudged eyes peering from behind her head scarf. This made Fadiyah even more agitated and she rushed to approach the next group of travelers, this time pleading in Arabic, "Please help me!"

This growing commotion didn't go unnoticed by two officers of the Guardia Civil. Standing outside the security entrance to the departure gates, the two officers in their green and black uniforms began to follow her movements in the large main hall of the terminal.

Fadiyah looked down at her watch. Fifteen minutes had passed and she still hadn't found him! In desperation, she finally yelled out, "Won't anyone help me, please?!" At this point, the two Guardia Civil officers became alarmed and started to walk toward her, not sure if they should be helping or arresting her. It all depended on her reaction to them.

The young Muslim woman stopped for a moment to study the long line of passengers that stretched in front of check-in desk number 1109, for an Iberia flight bound for Gibraltar. Directly across was a kiosk selling newspapers, gum, and *lotería* tickets. This weekend there was a big national lottery jackpot, so many travelers were

lined up for tickets, hoping for some luck before going through the
security checkpoint to board their planes, making this part of the
terminal even more crowded.

One man in a worn leather jacket with a red backpack and dusty
boots was not standing in the *lotería* line. He seemed to be thumbing
through the latest issue of *¡Hola!*, but in fact, he was barely glancing
at the magazine's pages. Every time he flipped a page, his eyes nervously darted to his watch, as though he were worried about missing
a flight. He saw that he only had a few minutes left. A bead of sweat
formed on his brow and dripped onto a photo of Spain's Crown
Prince Felipe de Borbón greeting Penélope Cruz at her latest movie
premiere in Madrid. This broke his concentration long enough for
him to look at the crowd around him. He noticed the two officers,
who were a mere ten paces away from him. Have I been spotted? he
wondered. His mind began to race. Are they following me? But then
as the guards walked right past him, he caught his breath again.

His relief, however, was short-lived when he realized whom they
were approaching. His gaze locked onto the object of their attention: it was his younger sister, Fadiyah, peering with desperation
from under her veil. He wanted to warn her to run far away from
here now.

She stared back at her older brother, now frozen in her movements, knowing that there wasn't much time left. The two officers
closed in on her, blocking his path of vision. They asked if she needed
help. Fadiyah started to run toward her brother but was held back
by the now alerted officers.

"Sajid!" His young sister's scream pierced through the noise of
the crowd. "Come back!" she yelled in her native Arabic.

The officers now finally understood what, or rather whom, she'd
been looking for. They looked at Sajid. With Fadiyah tight in their
grip, they made their way with forceful steps to where Sajid was
standing, thinking he might be able to answer questions about this
woman's outbursts in the airport this morning, or at least take her
home.

As their attention focused on her brother, Fadiyah found the
strength to break free for an instant and race toward Sajid to make
her final plea. Acting on pure instinct that something was wrong

with the scene playing out before their eyes, José, the younger guard, raced ahead of his older partner, Rodrigo, as they all now tried to reach where Sajid was standing. Concern heightened around them, and the crowd in the departure hall moved away, leaving a path for the rushing trio.

Sajid hadn't wanted it this way. It was supposed to be just him. He looked at his watch: 8:45:50 A.M. There was no time left. He glanced at Fadiyah and tried to remember her before all of this began, as a little girl playing in the sand on the sun-drenched beach in their native city of Ceuta on the North African coast. That was the very last thought that ever crossed his brain.

BACK IN THE CAR on the fourth floor of the parking lot, the boy was beginning to stir in his sleep. There was a new driver in the front seat: the man with the scar above his eye. He had his cell phone open, waiting for the right moment. At exactly 8:46:00 A.M., the man pushed the programmed code, and in an instant, he heard the explosion that rocked the terminal at check-in desk 1109. That was this new driver's cue to start the car. The boy in the backseat was now fully awakened by the sounds of both the explosion and the revving engine. He stared at the back of the driver's head as they left the airport parking lot. And somehow, despite his short life, the events of the last minute didn't alarm this boy. It was almost as if he'd been forewarned that this could happen.

AT THE MOMENT OF DETONATION, Sajid's precious cargo of explosives and its intended shrapnel, nails and bolts, ripped through the red backpack and shredded his body into pieces that were flung across the terminal. The force of the explosion hurled his sister's body against the wall, fracturing her skull. Only her brown veil seemed untarnished by the violence, floating to the ground and landing—as if by design—on what remained of her brother's torso, the epitaph of the short bloody episode.

The waiting area was littered with the remains of others who had been unlucky that day, only in their choice of flight departure time. The slowness of Rodrigo, the older Guardia Civil officer, had saved him from the full force of the explosion that killed his young partner. Dazed and dripping with bloody cuts, Rodrigo managed to stand up amidst the death, mayhem, and police sirens.

WITHIN MINUTES, REPORTS SPREAD ACROSS the Internet about the bombing.

BOMB BLAST AT MADRID AIRPORT

POSTED: 4:08 A.M. EST, December 10

A bomb has exploded in the domestic terminal of Madrid-Barajas Airport, several dead and many injured among the travelers.

There have been immediate reports of deaths and injuries from the blast, which occurred shortly after road traffic coordinators received a telephoned warning from a man who claimed to be a member of ETA, the paramilitary Basque nationalist organization, the reports said. The ETA has carried out four decades of violence aimed at creating an independent Basque state in the north of the country.

However, in a disturbing reference apparently to the 9/11 attacks in New York, the bomb blast occurred at 8:46 A.M. in front of check-in desk number 1109; the exact time of the first plane hitting the World Trade Center and the Spanish order of date notation, day followed by month, 11-09. The Iberia flight being checked in at gate 1109 was bound for Gibraltar. Direct service from Madrid to the British overseas territory was reinstated several years ago, after a 30-year gap, following a series of agreements between Britain, Spain and Gibraltar.

A police officer who was approaching the suspected suicide bomber was among those killed, in addition to a woman reported to have been an associate of the bomber, who was being questioned just before the blast.

The blast sent a plume of dark smoke high into the skies and resulted in bloody chaos in the large crowds of travelers waiting to check in to their flights. Flights in and out of Terminal 2, mostly domestic, have been halted, and there is chaos at the other terminals, officials say.

1

OLD TOWN, ALEXANDRIA, VIRGINIA
DECEMBER 10

THE MORNING WAS NOT GETTING off to a good start. The phone, not the alarm clock, woke her up at 4:20 A.M. She raised her head, opened her eyes in the pitch dark bedroom just enough to see the time, and then rolled over, hoping it was a wrong number. She buried her head back in the warm soft pillow, her chestnut hair tangled in all different directions. The answering machine picked up but she wasn't happy with what she heard. It was a familiar voice.

"*¡Mierda!*" Shit! she muttered under her breath, her head now hidden under the duvet. As a rule, she only swore in foreign languages, so that those around her wouldn't know of her transgression. Not that there was anyone in her bed to hear her swear; she'd been waking up alone in that bed for longer than she cared to recall.

Katerina Molares—Kate to her friends and colleagues—could never get used to waking up for work when the moon was still high in the sky. It was another cold, gray December morning in the Washington, D.C., metro area. She had planned to go to work a little late today, to ease back in after four days of a lazy beach vacation. No such luck. Those types of plans never seemed to work out right.

"Why should anyone have to get up at this god-forsaken hour?" she said to herself. All around the Beltway, countless other sleepy souls wondered the same thing as their early drives took them to the CIA, the White House, the FBI, and in the case of Kate, to the Defense Intelligence Agency—DIA for short. The rest of Washington— the legislators, the judiciary, the executive branch, and those that lobby them—all began their days early, yet in comparison, their hours were much more reasonable.

That familiar voice started leaving a message. "Rise and shine, Kate." It was her boss, Bill DuBois, using his best cheerful voice almost like a taunt. If he called her at home, something was up.

She fumbled for the phone next to her bed. "Hey, Bill . . ." Her voice was groggy. "A little early for you to be making the rounds, isn't it?"

"Not my choice. I'm sitting here in pj's, making wake-up calls. Another hour of sleep would've been just fine by me, too, believe me. The SecDef woke me up ten minutes ago on my secure line. Seems like there's been an 'incident.' So skip the jog this morning, Kate, and get to the office, pronto. Turn on CNN in the meantime. It'll give you the gist of today's agenda." Kate grabbed the remote by her bed and turned on the TV. Since they weren't on a secure phone line, Bill couldn't give any further details. The jogging comment had been a joke, as he knew that she didn't do anything before 9 A.M., other than drink coffee.

"Funny, Bill. Okay, I'll see you there at five." She jumped into the shower as soon as she hung up the phone.

In the small nucleus of D.C.'s high-level intelligence professionals, Kate certainly stood out. Her mother was American and her father was from Venezuela, a country that wasn't always the most politically stable or on the best of terms with her employer, the U.S. of A. Her parents had met as PhD students at Georgetown University in the 1970s—he in Economics studies and she in International Security studies. From there, they'd both landed assignments at the United Nations in New York City, where Kate was born thirty years ago.

Kate was their only child and had benefited from their undivided devotion. She had an olive complexion like her father, and her eyes were deep green, like her mother's. Her slender face, accented by strong cheekbones and a chiseled nose that reminded some people of a young Meryl Streep, was framed by thick straight dark chestnut hair, which was usually tied in a perfunctory ponytail. Her quick smile always put others at ease.

Kate exuded an easy natural beauty and style that was all the more charming because she was mostly unaware that eyes turned to stare at her when she walked in a room. She had been a swimmer through her college years and still maintained her athletic frame. Her style of dress was simple but feminine, favoring tailored slacks with silk blouses, which—depending on how hard the wind blew—showed off more or less of her healthy figure.

She looked in the bathroom mirror. Given the ridiculously early hour, with her hair sticking out in several directions, and groggy eyes, her natural beauty had not yet emerged to greet the day. She wondered how, in the few short hours following her vacation, she could already look like hell.

Kate brushed her hair with one hand and fumbled through her closet with the other. She grabbed the simplest thing possible because she wasn't in the mood for fussy today: slacks, blouse, and jacket.

Kate stared at the TV as she brushed her teeth, watching live reports from Madrid's airport. Not a pretty picture, she thought, and now she understood why Bill had woken her up. She figured everybody had been called into the office earlier than usual so they could spend the next couple of hours sifting through the megabytes of info traffic that poured in from every U.S. embassy around the world. The real headache would start when they had to figure out exactly which parts of all that data should be included in the President's security briefing. A double shot of caffeine was definitely in order for the commute this morning.

As she left her apartment, images from Madrid flashed through Kate's mind, prompting her to ask the same question that every other U.S. intelligence officer was thinking this morning, at this very same hour. *Could this have been prevented?*

2

━╋╋╋━

CANTON OF BASEL, SWITZERLAND
DECEMBER 10

THE SILVER BMW 760LI with European Union plates traveled down the Swiss A2 autobahn at 90 mph, which was not unusual in and of itself, since most traffic on this road traveled at a minimum speed of 75 mph. Today, however, the rain was coming down at a steady pace; enough to make it dangerous for most travelers to maintain that speed. But this particular sedan was not out for a leisurely family drive through the pastoral valleys of the Canton of Basel. A skilled observer might have noticed that all of the vehicle's windows were made of aluminum oxynitride, the most bullet-resistant glass, which U.S. military forces thought only recently was exclusively available to them. Obviously, the occupants of this particular BMW were expecting to run into more than just *Braunvieh*, the famous Swiss brown cows.

The driver, Hasani, a heavyset, bald Egyptian in his mid-forties, had an Austrian Glock 22C semiautomatic revolver snugly packed in his shoulder holster. His muscular frame didn't leave much room for maneuvering in the front seat. His seatmate looked like his twin, dressed in an identical white shirt and dark tie, only his name was Asar. Both men were residents of Milan's growing Muslim community and, not surprisingly, neither spoke a word of Italian.

Their passenger, Nebibi Hasehm, was of a slighter physical stature. He was draped in his customary attire: an Armani suit with cashmere sweater—all black. Nebibi was five feet nine inches and weighed only 165 pounds, all of it taut, lean muscle. Growing up, he'd been the fastest runner, bar none, and he combined this agility with weight training and martial arts to fill out his frame. Now, at the age of thirty-four, his reputation for physical prowess meant that the two larger men in the front seat wouldn't dream of messing with him. Nebibi was known as an uncompromising and swift agent, always ready to execute all directives of his superiors. Those who knew him well—a select few—realized that the name chosen for him by his parents had been quite prophetic: *Nebibi* was the Egyptian word for "Panther."

Despite his birth in Milan, Nebibi the Panther considered himself, first and foremost, a Muslim; second, an Egyptian; and only in a very distant third could he identify with the rest of the Milanese, which was most apparent in his choice of suits and his weakness for *cotoletta di vitello alla Milanese*—veal Milanese. His immigrant Egyptian parents had raised him and his older brother in the Muslim enclave of the city.

Like so many Muslim immigrants across Europe, Nebibi was an outsider to the world he was raised in. He was ostracized by Italian society, which was predominantly Catholic and not so eager to accept foreigners of different faiths. So instead, he had spent all his free time at the Milan Islamic Cultural Center, where he was trained in Arabic, the teachings of the Qur'an, and the five daily prayers to Allah.

The particular mosque frequented by Nebibi had a faction that was isolated from the rest of Muhammad's peaceful religious followers. And it was through this sect's auspices that Nebibi received the financial means to attend the best schools that money could buy. He completed his university studies at King's College at Cambridge, where he read history, and then he returned for further religious training at the mosque in Milan. It was there that the next stage of his life was determined through the guidance of the mullah and his elders. It was decided that Nebibi would complete an MBA at INSEAD, Europe's leading business school, just outside Paris. The study of money and its movements from a Western perspective would assist in his first calling in life: *to help his Muslim brothers change the path of Western financial history.*

FOR MOST OF THE TRIP from Basel this morning, the traffic on the A2 had been light, except, of course, for the usual backup at the St. Gotthard Tunnel. Now, after almost two hours of driving, the car neared its final destination—Lugano in the Swiss Canton of Ticino.

The interior of the sedan was covered in soft Italian cream leather. The backseat was equipped with all the amenities favored by Nebibi. Pull-down trays revealed a Bloomberg terminal and two overhead television monitors, one tuned to the Arab Al Jazeera network from Doha, Qatar, and the other to CNN International from London. Both monitors were muted and except for the occasional taps on Nebibi's keyboard, there was silence in the car.

Nebibi always kept his copy of the Qur'an—the Wahhabi edition, with an intricately carved leather cover—next to his seat. Muslims believe the Qur'an was revealed by God to the prophet Muhammad in the seventh century, and because of that direct transfer from God, the words of the Qur'an cannot be altered. However, the Wahhabi edition includes additional explanatory text, which some Western scholars will argue directs more militant interpretations. And this, the one favored by the Islamist extremist minority, was the only version Nebibi ever read.

At exactly 9:46 A.M., Nebibi picked up his iPhone, waiting for a message. At 9:47 A.M., he received a call from Madrid. In the background, sirens were blaring. The man on the line simply said the word *Andalus*. This was all Nebibi needed to hear. He hung up without speaking and knew that the first half of today's historic mission had been completed. Now he turned his focus to the second half—settling some accounts long overdue.

"How much longer?" Nebibi's voice was rarely raised in either elation or annoyance. He noticed that CNN was beginning to report the incident at Madrid's airport. The world was now finally getting the news of something he had known about for months. He turned up the volume to listen to the live reporting. A slight grin of approval hovered on his lips.

"Five minutes, sir. We're very near Lugano now." Asar answered in a military fashion, like a lieutenant responding to his general on the battlefield. As it should be, since this was indeed their battlefield.

Nebibi saw the markets reacting on his Bloomberg screen: volatility in London, Tokyo, and Frankfurt, and oil was up slightly, as he had expected. New York markets weren't open yet. He typed a few instructions on the Bloomberg terminal and cashed out of positions that yielded just the right level of profits on that oil price volatility. Not extraordinary profits, as that would have raised suspicions. But attractive nonetheless, especially in comparison to the measly $75,000 that was used to pay off the suicide bomber and his family in Ceuta. Not a bad investment at all. A perfect dry run, he thought as that slight grin returned to his face.

Nebibi's phone rang again. He looked at the number. A 202 area code. Washington. Quite early for someone to be calling from there, he thought; nonetheless, he answered it. "Hello."

A man responded in short elevated breaths. "It's me. Need to make this quick. The CNN reports this morning concerned me. Someone zeroed in on those money transfers, and I don't know how long I can keep them under wraps. You need to cover your tracks right away. Neither one of us needs them breathing down our necks."

"Don't worry. The last leg will be cut off before you finish your Starbucks. Keep your cool. You have much at stake."

"If you want to keep me here at your beck and call, *you* need to cover your damned tracks!" The man hung up the line. Nebibi was not concerned. He was certain that his contact would call again. After all, Nebibi still held the key to the man's big payoff.

Nebibi looked outside and gazed at the view as they passed over the Dam of Melide in Lugano. In a blink, they had officially crossed the border of Switzerland and entered Campione, a small Italian town. Surrounded by Swiss territory on all sides, the town exists in a sort of limbo, neither entirely Swiss nor Italian. Campione's three thousand privileged residents enjoy Swiss efficiency in matters of banking, postal service, telephone, and Internet, in a legal atmosphere of less efficient Italian jurisdiction regarding matters at the Casinò di Campione.

The sedan made the next right onto Via Belvedere, which took them up a mountain. Nebibi looked out at the ever-more-impressive views across the lake to Lugano, nestled in between Monte San Salvatore and Monte Brè. The sun shone down upon the town, which at this hour had stirred to full activity, cars traversing the main road and people sitting down at the many picturesque cafés facing the lake.

As they pulled up to their destination, an electronic eye scanned the car, and the imposing gates swung open. The driver continued on a private road hung with dormant bougainvillea vines, following a series of twists and turns up the hill until they reached their final destination.

Asar and Hasani quickly exited the sedan, donned their suit jackets, and opened the door for Nebibi. The earlier rain had ceased but the air was thick with humidity, signaling more showers to come. The house was an old stone structure with red tiled roofs, a Mediterranean villa amidst the Alps. The surrounding grounds were covered in pristinely manicured grass, like an expensive shag wool carpet, edged with carefully pruned shrubs. This didn't stand out in this neighborhood, as the region was home to many wealthy Italians, a smattering of international jet-setters, and the occasional movie star.

Nebibi and his bodyguards were expected, so as soon as they stood at the front entrance, the door swung open and a man equal in physique to the Egyptian twins welcomed them in, Nebibi first.

"Good morning, sir. Good to see you again." With a nod of his head, Nebibi acknowledged the greeting.

Their shoes clicked on the highly polished white marble floors of the double-story foyer. The circular staircase they passed had an intricate beaux arts wrought-iron banister leading to the second-floor living quarters.

This was the home of Abdul Rahman bin Omar, a central figure in the Muslim Society, a loose community of fund-raising organizations for Islamic causes, the most prominent of which is al-Qaeda. Officially, the Society does not support violence, however its ruling credo is

Allah is our objective.
The Prophet is our leader.
Qur'an is our law.
Jihad is our way.
Dying in the way of Allah is our highest hope.

In the last twenty years, the Society had expanded into a global network of organizations in more than fifty countries. With such breadth, it is easy to see that their credo could have different interpretations on the use of violence in different pockets of its membership.

Abdul Rahman's role centered on finance. This is how he'd managed to spend his golden years in quaint, comfortable Campione as opposed to some dusty outpost in the mountains between Pakistan and Afghanistan. His work on behalf of the organization focused on creating vehicles that could legitimately funnel the funds donated by Muslims worldwide to where they were needed, on the front lines of the jihad. This was a reverse money laundering—legitimate money being pressed into service for less than legitimate purposes—at least as far as the U.S. government was concerned. In the process of assisting his Muslim brothers, Abdul did not forget to charge impressive fees that would be the envy of the bankers and lawyers across the lake in Switzerland.

Nebibi and the Egyptian twins were escorted through a long hallway with twelve-foot ceilings and walls displaying many antique ceremonial sabers. Nebibi didn't stop to admire the display, since he had been to this house many times before. At the end of the corridor was a doorway leading to a large dark-wood-paneled boardroom. On one side was a wall of floor-to-ceiling glass looking out over the lake. The opposite wall was covered with a row of six large flat-screen monitors.

The large oblong oak table had room to seat twelve people comfortably. Today, only two of the chairs would be necessary. Arranged on the table were two water glasses, a large bottle of Sanfaustino water from Umbria, a cigarette box, an ashtray, and a lighter encased in a heavy Baccarat crystal sphere. Also, in the very unlikely event that someone would feel the need to take notes at this meeting today, there were two writing pads arranged with a selection of pens.

Nebibi sat down at one of the large leather chairs facing the wall of video screens. The twins posted themselves by the door, along with the man who had greeted them at the entrance.

Once all were in position, the door opened and the eighty-year-old Abdul Rahman made his entrance. He was no longer the vibrant physical figure that had guided many on a path supporting the mission of the Society. In fact, following his MBA, Nebibi had been one of those who received early tutelage in real-world finance from Abdul. So when he approached Nebibi, Abdul anticipated a certain deference that a teacher, an able one at that, could expect from a former student, however brilliant he had been in learning his lessons. Abdul was surprised when Nebibi did not rise to greet him.

"*Asalaamu alaykum*—peace be upon you, Nebibi." The old man did not betray his disapproval, or his suspicions of what possibly lay ahead for him in this meeting. A cool demeanor was what had seen him through pressures in surreptitious transactions in the past, and today would be no different.

"*Wa alaykumu asalaam*—and upon you peace, Abdul Rahman." It was difficult to interpret Nebibi's monotone. Was it cold professionalism, or a lack of deference for his old teacher?

With brief formalities over, the old man, his back slightly hunched, slowly moved to his place at the table. His doctor had recommended a cane for walking, which Abdul refused. Instead, he steadied himself against the edge of the table. His assistant finally came over to help him sink into the chair, next to Nebibi. He immediately reached for a cigarette and the lighter. After all, it had been five whole minutes since he'd puffed his last one. Nebibi shifted slightly, to avoid the smoky trail of Abdul's fragrant Turkish tobacco.

Abdul raised his hand with the lit cigarette between his fingers and waved to his assistant, who was now seated in front of a flat computer monitor at a side table. On that command, the assistant flicked a switch on the wall next to him and then tapped some commands on the keyboard in front of him. Immediately, large glass windows facing the lake went from transparent to cloudy opaque, hiding the room from any prying eyes. In the same instant, the flat-screen monitors that spanned the opposing wall lit up with several faces. All seemed to be sitting in similar white rooms that could have been in the same building but in fact were at different locations around the globe: Zurich, Dubai, Caracas, and Bilbao.

"Have you all followed the protocol as instructed?" Abdul knew that this "protocol" was the only way clandestine global communication could occur without having the Internet equivalent of nosey neighbors listening in on their very private discussion. Though he didn't really understand exactly how the connection protocol worked, he nonetheless asked the question in an authoritative voice.

The "nosey neighbors" in this case would be the combined intelligence forces of the English-speaking world—the U.S., U.K., Canada, Australia, and New Zealand—and financial issues were a priority for these formerly robust economies. Their intelligence surveillance system, known as ECHELON, can capture radio and satellite communications, telephone calls, faxes, and e-mails nearly anywhere in the world. All *except* those secure connections based on the latest quantum cryptography, that is, the "protocol," recently developed at the University of Geneva for the European Union. The reliably neutral Swiss, of course, also made it available to Nebibi and his circle of friends, in return for a hefty honorarium to certain members of their underpaid research team.

Each of the nodding heads on the large screens confirmed that they had indeed taken advantage of the Swiss research. All set. Now the annual meeting of the board of directors of Banca di Califfato could commence.

Decades ago, Abdul had founded the bank quite legitimately in Lugano with charitable contributions of wealthy Muslims across the Middle East. Some of the bank's profits funded political causes, such as the election of Muslims to the Egyptian parliament, educational programs in "new" territories in Europe, such as Milan, and the building of new mosques like the one on East Ninety-sixth Street in Manhattan. However, another portion was covertly funneled to support more ancient methods used by religions to turn people's hearts and souls. The modern equivalent of swords and sabers. *Terrorism.*

Abdul stared at the live screens. He recognized a couple of new participants, but they were not a part of the bank's regular brain trust. What was Nebibi up to? He opened his mouth to speak. But before he could utter a word, he was interrupted by Nebibi, who stood up and took charge of the floor. The ease of the younger man's physical movements underscored the difference in age of the two men seated at the table. "We have gathered you here today for our annual, and regrettably the *last,* meeting of our Board."

Abdul tried to straighten his shoulders, which he accomplished only halfway. He sat there frozen in a partial slump, astounded that this young upstart had dared to interrupt him, let alone close his bank. The bank was his old age pension, after all. He didn't notice that the burning cigarette he held in his trembling hand had dropped ashes on the wooden table. "Why is this our *last* meeting?

I demand to know why you are shutting down the bank without my knowledge. And who are these new faces I'm looking at? They haven't even been introduced, and this is a closed meeting." Abdul raised his voice in anger, but his old age betrayed him and it came out weak and pleading instead.

Towering over the old man, Nebibi turned to him and said, "You didn't really expect that the illicit activities of the bank would go unnoticed forever, did you?" Nebibi was slowly inching toward the kill.

Abdul tried to take a moment to regain his composure. He smashed his cigarette in the ashtray and poured himself a glass of the Sanfaustino. His hand was still unsteady, a result of his anger combined with his frail physique. He took a sip, ignoring the few drops of liquid that fell on the table. He was feeling more control flow back to his body. Now he was ready to speak.

"We've had many years of providing support for our shared activities, and yes, we've had some close calls with the Swiss authorities when they've had weak knees in facing the American inquiries. But we've always managed to find the right type of friends." Abdul was referring to the eager Swiss attorneys who could always accomplish miracles, for the right price. Abdul felt calm again and was ready for another cigarette.

"Yes, my friend." Nebibi's voice was drenched in sarcasm. "For the most part, that's covered. But my sources in Washington tell me that it'll be increasingly hard to get away with simple bribes. We need to cover our tracks. The international arm of U.S. regulations is getting longer and has even reached your little Canton of Ticino. We need new ways to achieve our goals without attracting attention."

Abdul's anger returned, causing him to drop the heavy crystal lighter he was holding. It hit the wooden surface with a thud but didn't crack. Instead it rolled to the end of the long table, where it remained. His assistant scurried to his side to light his cigarette. He took a deep puff and exhaled a large swath of the fragrant smoke. He knew it bothered Nebibi.

"The attention can be controlled!" The old man shouted, thinking he could veer from the path of this approaching Panther.

Nebibi didn't flinch. "We can't risk the Vereinten Kantonalbank making a deal with the Americans. If they dig any deeper, they'll find too much sensitive information on our donors. So as of today at 17:00 hours, we will cease operations of Califfato. Our lawyers filed the necessary papers yesterday with the Swiss authorities and our clients have been notified that a new entity will take its place. Tomorrow, we are also launching our new vehicle, The Milestones Fund." Nebibi's attention once again focused on the faces on-screen. None of this was news to them. Nebibi had spent the last few days getting each of them used to the new strategy.

The significance of that name did not escape Abdul. *Ma'alim fi al-Tariq*—*Milestones*—was a book, first published in 1964, that called for a reawakening of Islamic ideals and the creation of an Islamic world based on the Qur'an. Nebibi's new fund was a way for Islamic loyalists to put their money where their mouths were. Put up or shut up.

"Today, we are introducing new equity partners, Venezuela and the Basque Country." Nebibi had managed to gather seemingly disparate forces at the same table. The men in Caracas and Bilbao smiled for the camera. Each had an interest in creating political instability in the world for the benefit of their unique regional causes. The Venezuelans wanted to keep the Americans occupied in any place other than Latin America for as long as possible. And the Basques continued to seek complete autonomy for their ancient homeland in northern Spain.

"Their investments will be managed through shell companies registered in Grand Cayman so as not to attract undue attention. We believe that the structure of the fund will allow us to operate in a more opaque manner with respect to regulatory authorities in Europe, the U.S., and elsewhere. Any questions?"

Nebibi's question was for the screen participants, *not* Abdul, who was sitting in his chair trying to understand the impact of all these changes. The hand that didn't hold a cigarette was under his jacket, rubbing a spot on his chest, where he was feeling a burning sensation.

Abdul's mind was racing. He quickly tried to assess the significance of the two new entities that Nebibi was bringing into the fold. The Venezuelan Bank for Trade and the financial arm of the Basque Nationalist Party, even as new, minority partners, could send U.S. and Western European intelligence operations into a frenzy of activity trying to determine the implications of such new partnerships of non-aligned nations; that is, if they ever found out about its true intentions.

As had been the case with ancient Rome, a world dominated by the unilateral hyper-power of the U.S couldn't last forever. And everyone, including Abdul, knew that the global economic crisis had seriously dented the U.S.'s hold on that power. He wondered what his role in the new fund might be. Even a diminished role could be very lucrative. But would he have a role in this new Milestones Fund, or was Nebibi pushing him aside?

"Finally," Nebibi continued, "because of our underlying mission, The Milestones Fund will be *Shari'ah* compliant, and only focus on activities allowed under the teachings of the Qur'an. Therefore, we won't invest in the prohibited sectors of tobacco, liquor, and entertainment, and will not make money from charging interest." He glanced with disdain at Abdul, who was still puffing away.

The men on the flat screens were all aware that an Islamic fund would be a relatively new type of entrant in the upper echelons of the multi-trillion-dollar global funds market. The Milestones Fund would be an attractive haven for wealthy private citizens in the Gulf States and also their governments' investment arms. All within the limits of the law, but intended, in the end, to help pay for the spread of Islamic political organizations throughout the world, through whatever means available.

"This is an exciting phase for our organization's growth, particularly with the addition of our new partners in South America and Europe. I want to thank you for joining us in this new launch. As most of you know, the initial size is targeted for $25 billion, but I can tell you that we already have subscriptions of $20 billion. It's clear that our target will be reached, if not exceeded.

"Now to old news." Nebibi turned his attention to Abdul. "In performing our audit of the accounts of Banca di Califfato, we found certain troubling discrepancies in the last five years of accounting reports. A few percentage points are reasonable to support the infra-

structure you and your staff require to perform these services for us."
Nebibi looked at the screens for reaction. The faces remained stoic.

Abdul began to shout, "These proceedings are invalid—!"

Nebibi cut him off. "There is no point objecting; the audit trail
is quite clear. You've been paying yourself far more than we agreed
on. By our account, it seems that $750 million has vanished over
the past five years, presumably at the bottom of Lake Lugano.
And this is a second, very important reason why we must cease
operations of this bank."

Abdul's throat felt dry. He finished the rest of the water in his
glass.

What Nebibi did not let on was that he had known about these
discrepancies since day one of their mutual dealings. For years, he'd
kept this knowledge hidden until more convenient methods to finance his organization's activities could surface. Now, with the
potential noose of the international regulators tightening on Swiss
banks and the changing landscape of alliances—namely the significant addition of allies in South America and Europe—that day had
finally come. The days of Banca di Califfato had dwindled to zero.
And Nebibi knew that the head of the snake must be cut off first.

Abdul started touching the knot of his Hermès tie. It felt tight
around his neck, and that pain in his chest seemed tighter. With a
shaky hand, he reached for another cigarette to calm his discomfort. He suspected that his ongoing livelihood would be cut off.
The question was whether or not he could manage to keep his
$750 million golden parachute, which was not, in fact, at the bot-
tom of Lake Lugano. In truth, it was squirreled away in an account in Andorra. Safely hidden, so he hoped.

Abdul had selected the Principality of Andorra, a small landlocked country sitting between Spain and France, because of its tax
haven status and, more important, because it was one of the select
countries in the world *without* an extradition treaty with the U.S.
Its strict bank secrecy laws imposed stiff criminal penalties on
bank employees who dared to release any client information. The
citizens of Andorra enjoyed the world's longest life expectancy—83.5 years, to be precise. The principality was Abdul's Plan
B: his old age retirement home where he could, quite comfortably,

live off his golden parachute. But now, he wasn't sure if he'd even reach Andorra's long life expectancy.

"Gentlemen, if there are no more questions, I move to a vote by the shareholders of Banca di Califfato. On the table is our proposal to close down the bank and transfer our $5 billion in assets to The Milestones Fund. All those in favor, say *aye*." Nebibi scanned the monitors and saw that each partner was nodding his head in approval and that all were in unanimous support of the proposal. He didn't bother looking at Abdul.

"Our business here is done. We look forward to the future success of The Milestones Fund." All the faces on-screen signaled their approval to Nebibi and then signed off one by one.

3

KATE TOOK SIPS FROM HER large coffee cup as she drove her red Mini Cooper to the office. She had her iPhone plugged into the car dock and was listening to Rufus Wainwright's version of "Across the Universe." His melancholic voice was just shy of a yogi chant, and she began to sing along to the part she knew by heart.

Her mind wandered as she looked at the small stream of headlights on the Capital Beltway. Since her duties centered on Latin America, she wondered why she was included in this early-morning drill on a 9/11-tinged Basque terrorist attack in Europe. But the world since 9/11 was not the same; dots had a way of connecting themselves in the most unexpected patterns.

She tried to recall everything she'd been working on before vacation. There was that country briefing for the new ambassador to Chile, a report on the sale of Russian military jets to Venezuela, and an analysis of the security implications of the hostile takeover of that development bank in Panama by China's sovereign wealth fund. Kate figured that most of these projects would be back-burnered now.

Thanks to her wandering mind, she almost missed the exit for Bolling Air Force Base. She made a sharp turn to exit, and some of the coffee spilled over on her slacks. "¡Mierda! Perfect start to a perfect day!" she yelled at herself. She set the coffee back in the cup holder and with one free hand tried to soak up the mess with a few tissues.

Across the river, she could see the runway lights of Reagan National Airport, while ahead of her stood the imposing steel-skinned headquarters of the Defense Intelligence Analysis Center, the DIA's major operational arm. She showed her badge to the guard at the front gate while her car chassis was scanned. Two army personnel checked under the belly of her car and, finding nothing unusual, waved her through. "Good morning, Ms. Molares." She waved back at the guards as she passed through the checkpoint. She always felt secure behind a garrison of military personnel.

After parking in her assigned spot, she made her way to the main entrance. Two army officers were raising the American flag at the tall flagpole in front of the building. She usually managed to get in to the office *after* this morning ritual. Today she hadn't, so for the next few minutes she stood at attention in the brisk morning air as the national anthem played on the loudspeakers. Just another day at the office.

Inside the building, after passing through a retinal scan, Kate finally headed into the inner sanctum of the DIA. As she walked down the unadorned gray halls, there was more activity than usual this morning as other specialists hurried through the corridors.

About two-thirds of them wore uniforms from various branches of the armed forces—the remainder, like Kate, were the privileged civilians who had passed rigorous screenings on their areas of expertise, and background checks for the highest security clearance levels in the U.S. government. Kate's access was, like everyone else's at Bolling, "top secret." Without it, you couldn't even go to the bathroom by yourself in this building or get close to anyone's classified garbage cans. Given her father's foreign nationality and their circle of international diplomatic friends in New York, Kate's initial security clearance had taken months longer than normal, after which she was squeaky clean and allowed to travel the building unaccompanied, including, thankfully for Kate, the bathroom.

The DIA staff collected and analyzed military intelligence data that would be seen by only a handful in the executive and legislative branches. They also performed the more mundane country briefings for newly appointed ambassadors. In a nutshell, the DIA ran the full gamut of intelligence, without the baggage of the CIA's bad reputation with governments around the world.

A lot of that intelligence now came from digital sources—the

Internet, electronic currency movements, and telecommunications. Some argued that too much came from these sources, which is why even in the twenty-first century, the human element in intelligence collection was not only present, it was crucial.

For this reason, the DIA had a major component, the Defense HUMINT Service, staffed by experts who obtained and analyzed critical pieces of the intelligence puzzle from sources around the world, often gathering information that was not available from technical collection alone. And this is where Kate had found her calling. After finishing her undergrad studies at Georgetown in International Relations, she completed an international MBA.

A year later, after a European "adventure," she was back in the U.S., at the age of twenty-four, looking for a way to make her living. Not knowing any better, and feeling the need for a cash flow to pay off student loans, she jumped on the first offer that came her way, the trading floor of the now-defunct Bear Stearns. It was a short-lived career of only a couple of years, as she had quickly figured out that she didn't belong in an environment where everyone relied on screens of data points to make a living. The firm's eventual demise gave her the chance to find a different sandbox to play in.

Kate opted for a career in intelligence. She signed a short-term sublet on a basement apartment near Capitol Hill and launched a networking assault on the nation's intelligence community.

Within three weeks, she managed to get an informational meeting with Bill DuBois, the Latin America Section Head at the DIA. He immediately homed in on what Kate could deliver: her enthusiasm and financial experience. Bill had the foresight to understand that her background in finance, in particular, would help his agency cover more intelligence angles than purely military ones. That, coupled with the fact that one of his analysts had just departed for a higher-paying position at the NSA, made for excellent timing. So Bill brought Kate in for more extensive interviews and championed her application up the chain of command. Within a month, she was offered the position of analyst on his team, with the portfolio of Andean countries and regional responsibility for all financial-related issues.

A year into her new career, she discovered her passion for finding

out about things that weren't in textbooks or on computer databases or even in the news, but instead uncovered through fieldwork with her growing network of international contacts. She loved
how that knowledge could be harnessed to make the world a safer,
more sustainable place. She was one of the good ones in a career
that, by definition, is filled with murky situations and even murkier
characters.

KATE'S CUBICLE WAS HOUSED with all the Latin America specialists, in a
section wedged in between the larger and more prominent NATO/
Europe and Middle East teams. Arriving at her desk with a fresh
cup of coffee, milk no sugar, she tried again to blot away the recent
coffee spill, but a damp dark spot remained on her slacks. Kate sat
down in front of her desktop looking through the various reports
coming in about the bombing, with a certain focus on any financial implications. Shares on the London, Frankfurt, and Paris stock
exchanges opened slightly lower, in line with the Bolsa de Madrid.
Some widening on credit spreads. Oil prices spiking. All to be expected with news of terrorism.

Global dynamics had certainly shifted. The U.S. government, like
its European counterparts, was now a direct owner of large chunks
of the country's banking system. In the last two years alone, a thousand community banks had failed, and all of America's resources
were devoted to keeping the economy on a sound recovery track.

Kate walked over to her boss's corner office, small in comparison to those she'd been in during her Wall Street days, but large
nonetheless in government circles. There was a dark wooden desk
on a diagonal facing the door, with an in-box piled high with an
overflow of classified folders, and a computer monitor next to a
keyboard littered with phone messages.

Bill was just hanging up the phone when Kate arrived.

"Thanks a lot for the wake-up call," she said with a smirk on
her face. "So what's all the commotion about?" Kate settled into a
relaxed slouch in a chair facing his desk. She noticed he'd cut himself shaving this morning and a fresh spot of coffee had dribbled
down his tie. She smiled, knowing that she hadn't been the only
one with a rough start this morning. Even a career officer like Bill
could be thrown by sudden events.

Bill had been around the block a few times in the intelligence world, and despite his meek physical stature—a five-foot-eight runner's body—he was still a force to be reckoned with. He'd taken undercover postings in various Latin American capitals: Lima, Panamá, Bogotá, and Brasília. In the process, he'd married and sacrificed two wives to divorce. After twenty-five years in intelligence and multiple marriages, Bill DuBois had more or less seen it all.

He was long past the stage in his career where he wanted to conquer the world of intelligence. Now he just wanted to make it intact to his early retirement age of fifty and settle down on his horse stud farm in Arkansas full-time. Two more years and he'd be baling hay for those prized horses of his.

Kate was okay in his book as long as she delivered airtight security analysis, did her quota of mundane ambassador briefings, and followed the intelligence rule book without sloppy mistakes. If she managed to keep her nose clean, he'd consider her for that promotion to deputy section head. He knew she had the verve for it, but still questioned whether she had the self-discipline to follows that rule book.

"I caught the CNN report after you called," Kate said. "Looks like our friends on the Mideast and Europe desks are going to be pretty busy in the next few weeks. . . ."

"Yep, they really have their work cut out for them on this one. The President's made it clear all the way down the food chain that the White House wants answers and wants them fast. Remember, he's scheduled to go to Spain in March on the anniversary of the 2004 Madrid train bombings, and they're planning to make a big speech about how the world is safer today."

Bill's voice was infused with the certain sarcasm that comes from having access to privileged classified information that paints a less rosy view of the current global outlook. Because of the troubled global economy, terrorist cells were breeding like cockroaches in all corners of the globe. About the only completely safe thing to do these days was brush your teeth in the morning, assuming you made your own toothpaste.

Bill continued. "And today's bombing, which by all indications, points to an alliance between al-Qaeda and the Basque, is anything but a 'safer world.' On top of that, the bomb went off in front of the check-in desk for a flight bound for Gibraltar. . . ."

"So what's the significance there? . . ." Kate leaned forward.

"Not really sure if it's related yet, but we're supposed to be a major player at the Gibraltar sovereignty talks."

Kate racked her brain for everything she could remember about this upcoming event. It had to do with the ongoing discussions between Spain and the U.K. regarding the terms of the 1713 Treaty of Utrecht in which Spain, under duress, handed over full sovereignty of Gibraltar to the British. In the past centuries of naval-dominated warfare, Gibraltar had always been a highly coveted military stronghold for global superpowers, thanks to its strategic location between the Mediterranean and the Atlantic. Now, after close to three hundred years of British rule, Spain had decided it was time to revisit the terms of the treaty, despite the fact that many Gibraltarians would find it difficult to give up their British passports. So talks continued, in the hope of removing the single most contentious issue in Anglo-Spanish relations, namely who owned the deed to that famous Rock of Gibraltar.

"Any way you look at it," Bill added, "we're on high alert here and abroad. And you know what that means: every crackpot in every embassy is feeding us every friggin' jackass story from the last six months. We need to go through these in a period of hours, not weeks like we should be doing around here to avoid mistakes. We're back on the defensive again. Damn it, I just don't think that's the way to run intel." Intelligence insiders like Bill knew that their top secret world had ballooned almost out of control since 9/11, making it difficult to gauge its effectiveness in protecting the homeland. The National Security Agency alone intercepted 1.7 billion phone calls each and every day.

Bill started shuffling the papers on his desk, like he was searching for something.

"Ah, there it is." Bill held up his favorite pen. "So, have you seen any impact on the markets?" Pen and pad now in hand, he was ready to take notes.

"European exchanges opened lower. No surprise there. Since there haven't been any further bombings, I suspect any downturn's gonna be short and sweet. Actually, by the time New York opens, I'll bet we'll start to see things settle back and recover some of those early-morning losses in Europe. I guess everybody's pretty much desensitized to the economic impact of terrorism. . . ."

"Yep, unfortunately, Kate."

"Anyways . . . so why did you call me in early? Did you need me to do a little pinch-hitting for the guys on the Europe desk? I could help them on the ground in Spain, if you think that's a good idea." If she had to do temp work taking orders from the Europe staff, Kate thought she might as well angle for a short trip to Madrid for some tapas and a new pair of shoes.

"Yeah, I know you're always angling for fieldwork. We may need you in Spain later on, but no, for the moment, I actually need you to go south—to Caracas."

Kate's eyes opened wide. What could Caracas have to do with a Basque Islamist-tainted bombing in Madrid that might be linked in with the Gibraltar sovereignty talks?

Bill smiled at her puzzled expression. "It seems our friends in Caracas continue to diversify the beneficiaries of their oil-funded largesse. We think they're spreading their wealth outside of their Latin American neighborhood. Here, let me show you."

Bill got up from his desk and motioned for Kate to join him in front of a large monitor on the office wall that was connected to the DIA's computer mainframe. The screen was blank except for a rotating 3-D image of the DIA's seal.

Bill touched the screen with his index finger. The multi-touch inter-action technology popped up a password dialog box. Bill tapped in his security code to access the mainframe. Now logged in, he tapped again and folders appeared. He touched the one that had a map of Spain on the cover, and the contents spilled out in front of them, like pieces of paper scattered on a desk. There was a picture of a dollar on one, which he tapped, uncovering a map of the world. With both hands he drew an imaginary box around a particular seg-ment of the map. The map now showed fund movements around the globe.

"See this? It's the thread of data from our Treasury Department that surfaced last week while you were out." The screen now showed a wire transfer notice for $25 million which was debited from accounts controlled by the Venezuelans at the Vereinten Kantonalbank—VKB, United Cantonal Bank—in Switzerland, and transferred to the Banco Central de Cuba's accounts at that same Swiss bank.

"Who got this at Treasury?"

"It's that deputy assistant, what's his name?" Bill had a sour look on his face.

"You mean the one that came over from Lehman a few years ago? Bernard something? . . ." Kate recalled something from an interagency meeting last month; the man's embroidered initials on his shirts stood out among the other less stylish government employees. ". . . I think his initials are BOG."

"Yep, that's it! Bernard O'Donnell Galbraith. He was still sitting on it over there, until we forced his hand on it. Now look at this, Kate. . . ." Bill pulled up another image showing the subsequent $1 million wire transfer from the Cubans to a small Swiss bank in Lugano, Switzerland.

He pointed to the screen and said, "And on the same day, another small amount, $75,000, went from that Lugano bank to an obscure money order payment house in Ceuta in North Africa. After that, the trail goes cold. If it did go to the group responsible for the airport bombing, then that last leg was delivered to them in cash via that last bit of the money in Ceuta." Located on the North African coast across the Strait of Gibraltar, Ceuta was officially Spanish territory, but if you asked the Moroccans, they thought this city rightfully belonged to them.

Kate sat back in her chair and looked at Bill's map of the money trail. Her job was to find holes in analysis, and so she began. "That's a mouthful, Bill. First of all, what makes you think these transfers have anything to do with events this morning?"

"We know that this Lugano bank has ties to the Islamic world. They claim it's all aboveboard: Muslim charities, education, that kind of thing. But that's *their* version of the story. We've never really gotten close enough to investigate."

"Okay, but that just leaves a question mark there, not an answer, right?" Kate got up and used an index finger to trace the transfers in and out of Lugano on the map.

Bill leaned against the side of his desk, also studying the screen. "The problem is that piece that went to Ceuta. Since that's officially Spanish territory, it puts them into the bucket of our investigation for this morning's airport bombing. Anything that comes up positive *both* in terms of Spain and Islam is now a lead that we need to look into. So the NATO/Europe guys are coordinating with Treasury on the VKB info and we need to see if we can get info at the source in Caracas. Got it?"

"Okay, okay. But are these guys at the VKB even within our reach?"

"You tell me," said Bill, as though he were testing her.

"You're kidding me, right?" Kate crossed her arms. "You seriously want me to put on a little show for you? Come on, I already did that memo on them six months ago. . . ."

Bill just nodded back, insisting on his one-on-one briefing.

"Alright, alright. So let's see. We know that VKB steers clear of U.S. business and the U.S. Patriot Act, so that it can go on acting like Swiss banks used to, secret numbered accounts and all. For most other foreign banks, U.S. regs have forced them to be watchful of every transaction that goes in and out of their U.S. accounts, which means that murky deals are a lot harder to do." Kate paused to ask with a subtle mocking tone, "Any questions so far, fearless leader?"

"Does that mean the Patriot Act works just like it was intended?"

"I said murky deals are *harder* to do. I didn't say they were impossible. Most global banks, the Swiss included, think twice before giving up their big profits from U.S.-based operations and when push comes to shove, they play nice with our regulators. Those guys at VKB, however, are another issue altogether. . . ." Kate's tone was now serious, recognizing that Bill's questions were zeroing in on where to go on this investigation.

Bill stood up again and tapped the location of Zurich on the global money trail map, popping up the Web site of VKB.

"Yeah, you're right. They've managed to sidestep our banking regs, but that doesn't stop us from sitting them down for a 'friendly' Q and A session. We might not be able to strong-arm them directly through regs like other foreign banks, but I'm sure they wouldn't be too happy if we let some confidential info on these kinds of transfers leak out to the press."

Kate stared at the picture on-screen of their headquarters on Zurich's Bahnhofstrasse. "It's amazing how these guys stay clear of our laws just by not having a single thread of U.S. operations. Remember when I ran into some of their senior folks at the IMF/ World Bank meetings last year?"

Bill nodded, recalling her debriefing at the time.

"They didn't even give out their business cards on U.S. soil. It's like they were never here."

"Damn right, Kate. They used to call Swiss bankers the 'Gnomes of Zurich.' I think maybe a better name for these guys is the 'Phantoms of Zurich.'"

Bill returned to his screen. "Look. I think these VKB phantoms picked up the questionable deposits that other Swiss banks won't touch anymore and are making quite a nice little business for themselves." He tapped a link on VKB's Web site, opening a new window. "This is the list of VKB's correspondent banks from their own Web site. Now let's compare it to another list."

Bill opened another dialog box with the U.S. Treasury Web site right next to it. "And there you go. Every country that is officially under sanctions by the U.S. Treasury also conveniently happens to be on VKB's list of correspondents. I tell you, these guys have got a global monopoly on questionable accounts."

Seeing these virtual images side by side on the screen was very compelling in the case of VKB, but Kate was still not convinced of the link with Venezuela. This was one of her countries of responsibility and she hadn't seen a single hint in the intelligence traffic that the Venezuelans were starting to fund operations outside of Latin America—and more important, terrorism. Granted, Hugo Chávez, their president, had been a thorn in America's side for years. But this was exclusively a war of rhetoric and influence peddling with other countries in Latin America.

"Okay, so some of those VKB accounts are worth asking about. I'll grant you that. But, Bill, could they *really* have something to do with Madrid?"

"That's what I need you to find out. We need supportable assessments. You know as well as I do that anything that smells like

sloppy intelligence work is gonna get shot down in flames, and the
analyst along with it. We can't be cowboys shooting from the hip;
we need airtight intelligence work." That horse farm in Arkansas
weighed heavily on his mind. . . .

"Here's the counterargument," said Kate. "Why would Chávez
risk the negative attention?" Kate was just not convinced that Venezuela's president would seek to endanger his historical legacy, not
to mention his life, to help out some Islamist extremists, thereby
creating havoc in the countries of his OPEC partners. Still, she
didn't want to argue too persuasively—a trip to Caracas to quietly
investigate was actually very appealing.

Bill's phone rang. He yelled out the door, "Sam, can you see who
that is?"

Moments later, Bill's secretary, Samantha, all six strapping feet
of her, stood at the doorway of his office. "Bill, it's some guy from
Little Rock. Says he's got to talk to you about a filly you wanted to
buy. Want me to pass the call through?" She continued chewing
her gum loudly, waiting for Bill's response.

"Shoot. Damn." He looked over at Kate, and he knew that they
hadn't wrapped up yet. "Can you just get a number? I'll call him
later."

Kate looked over at Bill, amused by his conflicting priorities. As
the statuesque Samantha left to deal with the man on the phone
about the filly, she winked back at Kate. "Good to see you back,
hon."

Bill leaned in, clearly eager to wrap things up. "So where was I?"

"The issue about Chávez? . . ."

"Right. The issue is that there's intelligence noise out there and
we need to get a handle on where it leads or doesn't, no later than
yesterday, if you know what I mean. Let's face it, he wouldn't be
the first leader to do stupid things and flush his legacy down the
friggin' toilet." Bill's wry comments indicated that he hadn't voted
for the previous administration that was now retired to that little
ranch in Texas.

"So for argument's sake," said Bill, "why would Chávez pal
around with terrorists?"

Kate pondered the question. Chávez's moment in history was
coming more into the fore of the region's politics. He'd taken the

region's aspirations for unity, added a dose of Castro's populist socialism, sprinkled in the requisite spice of anti-Americanism, and wrapped the whole enchilada with his petrodollars. Correction, *arepa*. They eat enchiladas in Mexico and Texas, but in Venezuela they eat the cornmeal bread called arepas. And Chávez's arepa was a meal hard to resist on a continent that usually got leftovers.

"Well," she began, "with the price of oil at these levels, he doesn't have a lot of extra cash to keep buying influence like he used to—either in the slums of Caracas or the rest of Latin America. But why would bombing Madrid bring money in? By elevating oil prices?"

"Keep in mind his latest proposal, Kate. That business with SATO. You know that's not sitting well with any of our friends at the Pentagon. They'll do anything to make sure it doesn't get any traction, which is another reason we can't wait for the guys at Treasury to get their act together on this."

SATO, the South Atlantic Treaty Organization, was Chávez's latest brain wave, dreamed up as a counterpart to NATO with one important difference: it didn't include the U.S., not even as a simple observer. Bill tapped his screen to log off and the rotating DIA seal returned.

"So how would terrorism—and we're talking about *state-sponsored* terrorism—help the cause of SATO? This is the kind of stuff people around the Beltway have been dying to pin on him and he knows it. Why would he take the risk, Bill?"

"Because he thinks he can get away with it, without any friggin' interference from us. So the only quiet way we can counter him is by piecing together the threads of evidence that can tie him to this morning in Madrid. Simple rule, Kate: No money, no terrorism. Remember that."

Kate took a big gulp of her coffee, though her adrenaline was doing just fine without the added caffeine. "Okay, okay. Chase that money trail."

Bill added with a stern voice, "And no sloppy stuff. Follow the rule book on this one. I don't want to read about some loose operative of mine in *The Washington Post*. Got it?"

"Got it, loud and clear." She feigned a salute.

As she walked out of Bill's office, Kate could overhear the beginning of his next conversation. "So how much did you say you wanted for that filly? . . ."

MARKETS KNEW FULL WELL OF VENEZUELA'S desire for higher oil prices, as Kate reminded Bill via the following cutout from the day's *Wall Street Journal*:

Oil Price Nudges Slighter Higher
By Steven Reston, Commodities Correspondent

Published: December 10 09:45 | Last updated: December 10 09:52

This morning's Madrid bombing caused oil prices in European markets to spike, prompting policymakers to again warn about the potential danger of rising energy costs to recovering economies.

Brent crude oil, the most widely used measure of global oil prices, rose to an intra-day high of $89.56 a barrel, with profit taking later pushing it back down to $85.24.

In its last quarterly meeting, the Organization of the Petroleum Exporting Countries (OPEC) rejected calls from Venezuela's President Chávez for "concerted reductions" in production, to increase prices above his country's budget breakeven level of $90 a barrel. They also rejected calls from Chávez to change the currency for OPEC price quotes from the U.S. dollar to the Euro.

Goldman Sachs, the U.S. bank holding company that has emerged as the leading lender to the energy sector, warned prices could surge again within 12 months if OPEC follows Venezuela's recommendations at its next quarterly meeting.

Sources indicated that today's increase was greeted favorably by the Venezuelan leader, but in the long run these levels will be insufficient to cover his government's budget deficit.

4

VIA BELVEDERE, CAMPIONE
DECEMBER 10

ABDUL RAHMAN SAT IN STUNNED SILENCE as the last screen image went blank. His eyes carefully followed Nebibi as he got up and took over the technician's spot in the corner, punching in a few keystrokes committed to memory. A new live feed came up on-screen; this one seemed a bit fainter, with a lot of static cutting through the image. After a few seconds, the image stabilized. A man in his late thirties, not of Middle Eastern heritage, appeared. It was Ted Morton, better known in these circles as Murad the American, the most famous recruit of the al-Qaeda network.

A born-and-bred American raised as a strict Methodist, Murad had discovered Islam through the Internet. He frequented a local Islamic Cultural Center in Lodi, California, and had eventually garnered the trust of the local mullah, who sent him abroad for further training in a *madrasah*.

Once outside the U.S., Murad quickly latched on to the more militant factions of international Islam; eventually, he had reached the core operations in Afghanistan. There, he worked his way up the ladder to become ever more useful to the inner circle of al-Qaeda and, because of his ease with English, took the natural role of international spokesperson. He was usually in the group's grim video releases and was the architect of its technology and Internet outreach. Al-Qaeda's own Bill Gates and Michael Moore combined. As Murad often explained to his fellow *mujahideen*, the media was as important to the global jihad as a storehouse filled with AK-47s or handheld rocket launchers.

And it soon became apparent to most senior level al-Qaeda leaders that the Internet was critical to their future success. Their master plan for building the future Caliphate, a Muslim Qur'an-ruled society, relied on an international organization bound together through the tentacles of the Internet—a "virtual" Caliphate. Through it, they could more effectively reach each disaffected youth—Muslim and non-Muslim alike—in all corners of the globe; the al-Qaeda youth outreach program. And Murad was at its forefront.

The backdrop behind Murad's image was a white sheet used to protect his true location. *"Asalaamu alaykum."* Murad's Arabic was flawless.

Nebibi and Abdul both responded, the latter with more hesitation in his voice, as he knew that Murad's involvement in today's discussion did not augur well.

"Abdul, we are gathered here today to pass judgment upon your actions in accordance with *Shari'ah* laws of our people." As soon as Murad said those words, Abdul knew the true purpose of the visit by his former pupil and he also knew his fate. His hand holding the cigarette started shaking again and, to cover it up, he tried to put his cigarette out. His trembling hand missed the mark of the ashtray in front of him, and so instead he squashed the burning cigarette butt onto the polished wood surface.

"You have been judged to have stolen the property of others. You have stolen $750 million from our Society." Murad passed the solemn judgment.

Well versed in the punishment befitting this crime, Abdul nervously wrung his hands under the table.

"As required by *Shari'ah*, we have two able male witnesses to the crime of theft and you are judged to be of able mind. We can also attest to the fact that you did not steal this money out of hunger and that you took the money knowing that this property belonged to others," Murad uttered in a monotone voice.

The thing about *Shari'ah* is that it is not set completely in stone. Different judges take either a more lenient or stringent view of crime and its related punishment. A more lenient punishment indicates a desire to reform the criminal. The court gathered today, Nebibi and Murad, to pass judgment on Abdul did not look like it wanted to reform anyone. Just silence him.

Abdul saw that the road to Andorra had grown dark and full of dangerous curves. But he had survived many such curves in his eighty years. Just one more is all he asked of his almighty Allah. Maybe if he repented and told them where the money was, he could manage to live.

Nebibi tapped a few more keystrokes and the second screen flashed an online bank statement. Abdul recognized it as his principal account in Andorra. He looked over at his assistant, who had joined Nebibi at the computer. The man diverted his eyes away from Abdul's stare, and at that moment the old man knew that his assistant had betrayed his trust, giving Nebibi access to the accounts. The balance as of this morning read zero. Abdul had lost his only leverage.

Before the old man could consider the cost of his dwindling options, the final judgment was passed. "Abdul, for your crime of theft, you will be punished."

One of Nebibi's large Egyptians walked out into the long hallway of sabers and picked one commensurate with his size. Abdul could hear the Egyptian's footsteps on the marble floor of the hallway, now coming back into the room. Silently, the bodyguard took his place behind Abdul with his long saber ready to execute the sentence passed by this court. *Shari'ah* justice was swift.

The other Egyptian took hold of Abdul. "No!!" He tried to struggle, but his feeble body was no match for the heavyweight muscles of the Egyptian twin. The pain in his chest grew stronger, almost unbearable.

The Egyptian held his left hand firmly twisted behind his back to the point of almost dislocating the old man's shoulder. Abdul's other arm was held tightly on the surface of the oblong table, his shirtsleeve rolled up to expose his bony arm. The air gave the man goose bumps up along his bare skin. The twin holding the saber looked at Murad on-screen and asked a somewhat improbable question: "Short sleeves or long sleeves?"

Nebibi studied Abdul's face as Murad coldly proclaimed a most severe interpretation above and beyond the realm of the Qur'an. "Short sleeves."

The blood drained from Abdul's face; a bead of sweat fell across his brow. His eyes caught the glint of the saber positioned above his arm, and that finally made him realize how real this was. He pleaded, "Please have mercy! I'm an old man. Please, by the grace of Allah, I beg for mercy!"

The Egyptian with the saber no longer saw a man, but instead pictured a lamb in front of him, ready for a ritual slaughter. Abdul was still screaming when the Egyptian, in one swift movement, brought down the saber with all his force, slicing Abdul's arm just above the elbow. *Thud! Short sleeves.* Abdul let out a deathly moan. Blood gushed from the exposed flesh, forming a puddle on the table, and then by force of gravity, started dripping down onto Abdul's Italian wool pants. The tremors of his hand now were rocking throughout his entire body, his system's response to the saber assault. He collapsed forward onto the table, his head knocking the Sanfaustino bottle over and spilling the remaining water over the notepads.

Abdul would have preferred a bullet in his head. Worse yet, his other hand was still attached to his body, meaning that he'd have to endure the punishment all over again, except this time he'd know exactly the measure of pain coming. His eyes raced about the room like a frantic mouse that had succumbed to the temptation of illicit cheese but instead found its torso caught in the vise of a steel trap.

The Egyptian firmly held that hand down on the bloodied and dented oak table. He rolled up the sleeve of the shirt, blocking out the old man's continued, but now much weaker, pleas for mercy. Again, the saber struck the man's arm right above the elbow. *Thud!* This time the cut was not final and a second blow was required. *Thud!* The second cut pushed Abdul over the edge of consciousness.

The rounded Baccarat crystal lighter teetered close to the edge of the table. The force of the last saber cut finally made it roll over the edge and crash to the hard marble floor, where it shattered into little pieces. Abdul wouldn't be smoking anymore today. *No lighter. No hands.*

He was left slumped backward in the chair. His head was contorted to the side and his eyes were frozen in a look of shock, staring blankly up at the ceiling. The stumps of both his arms bled profusely and the puddles of blood below his chair continued to expand on the marble floor. At his age, his feeble heart gave out in

a mere sixty seconds, causing a final spasm of his body. The lamb
had been slaughtered.

Murad saw the entire scene play out on the video monitor from
his end. He could report to his superiors that the weak link in Campione had been severed. Literally.

The screen went blank.

The Twins and Abdul's assistant sanitized the room, replacing the
damaged and bloody table and removing all signs of the meeting—
from cigarette ashes to fingerprints and computer memory boards.
Nebibi had trained them well to search and destroy any threads of
incriminating evidence. His reputation to the outside world remained
stainless and, one could say, completely legitimate.

The task of disposing Abdul's body fell to his previously trusted
assistant. The recommendation was, of course, the very bottom of
Lake Lugano.

Within thirty minutes of the final cut, Nebibi was back on the
road to Milan. In the backseat, he stared down at his shoes, making sure he didn't have any red speckled souvenirs of his short visit
today in the hills of Campione.

The rain had managed to hold off in this part of Europe today.
A bright sun shone through the dark windows of the sedan. For
the rest of the ride back to Milan, Nebibi shut down his monitors
and surveyed the Italian countryside, simply enjoying the neat
rows of Lombardy poplars. It had been a heady month of intense
preparations leading up to this moment. Much had been accomplished and set in motion. His mind wandered to an earlier time
when life was about getting up, saying his prayers, and getting
something to eat. Back then, he still dreamed of one day building a
family. No longer. For some time now, Nebibi had recognized that
his life path did not lie in following tradition. Instead, he was destined to create a world in which new traditions could take root
and grow.

THE NEXT DAY, THE NEWSPAPERS, Lugano's *Giornale del Popolo* and Zurich's *Neue Zürcher Zeitung,* carried brief news of the closure of the
Banca di Califfato. Another seemingly unrelated item announced
the launch of The Milestones Fund. In addition, the Lugano paper
briefly mentioned a break-in and robbery on Via Belvedere, which

fortunately took place while the resident was away. The Italian police stated they would be adding more officers to cover the area in case the robbers had ideas about starting a crime wave. The well-heeled residents of Campione felt reassured by these statements. *Case closed.*

5

◄┼◆┼►

H E STARED IN THE MIRROR. Freshly shaved, with his teeth brushed and mouth rinsed with mouthwash, he was all set for the world. He squinted a bit and looked in the mirror again. Much better. Now, he could make out the face of Simón Bolívar staring back at him. Yes, that would be Simón José Antonio de la Santísima Trinidad Bolívar y Palacios, otherwise known as the liberator of Venezuela, Colombia, Ecuador, Peru, Panama, and Bolivia from Spanish colonial rule. Mr. Bolívar, who died in 1830, had been for a time President of Bolivia, Colombia, Peru, *and* Venezuela. His dream had been to create a South American nation of many states, like the U.S. in North America. That dream died and had remained good and buried with him since 1830; that is, until this moment in history.

"*Con permiso, Señor Presidente.*" It was the majordomo of La Casona, home to the modern-day President of Venezuela.

The voice outside the bathroom in his bedroom suite interrupted the mirage of the mirror. The face staring back at him was once again that of Hugo Chávez, current President of Venezuela, the self-proclaimed inheritor of Bolívar's dream, leader of the nation that had come up with the idea of the OPEC cartel, and the largest supplier of oil in the Americas.

"What do you need?" The slight displeasure of being interrupted in his morning routine was evident in his tone.

"I am very, very sorry, *Señor Presidente*. The finance minister has come to see you. He says he has urgent news for you and insists that I interrupt you." The majordomo knew better than to interrupt

His Excellency at this hour, but Minister Alarcón had been quite insistent.

"Alright, alright. Tell him I'll be with him in a few minutes." The President smiled at the mirror a last time. "Give me the strength to carry your dream forward today, *mi hermano*." Bolívar, in his full early-nineteenth-century military garb, which resembled that of Napoléon, smiled back at him. Chávez was crazy like a fox; the only person he really listened to had been dead for almost two centuries.

PRESIDENT CHÁVEZ STEPPED INTO THE LARGE bedroom suite to find the minister sifting through papers on the coffee table. After ten years in office, surviving in the face of multiple coup and assassination attempts, the President had finally grown accustomed to his exalted position and the profound deference paid to him by all who surrounded him. By hook or by crook, he would figure out a way to be president for life; he felt he had earned that right. The only real question that remained was how much longer he could be president, and if his eventual demise would come at the hands of one his countrymen or some stealth operative hired by the U.S.—or both? Until that future fateful moment, he intended to fully wrap himself in the history and privileges of his hard-earned position.

"So, Alarcón, what is so urgent? I give my all for our revolution, but prefer to do so after six a.m." The tone of a superior speaking to his underling was evident.

"Yes, I'm very sorry, *Su Excelencia,* but you asked me to tell you the minute news came with respect to our project. And we received word this morning from our contact in Europe that a first candidate has succeeded in Madrid."

"Oh, yes." His interest quite obviously spiked on this particular topic.

"We have news that a bombing at Madrid's airport was carried out by one of their operatives. After six months of training, he carried out his duties successfully." The minister made an effort to push aside the qualms he'd felt when reports on television showed the number of innocent civilians killed.

"Well, that is excellent news. I mean, of course, the success of the operation. Were many killed?" The President asked the question not really wanting to know the answer. He knew they had entered difficult terrain from which turning back was impossible.

"*Su Excelencia,* I have seen reports that at least twenty *inocentes* have been killed." He lowered his head as if in prayer for those unfortunate souls. This sordid assignment was not sitting well with the minister.

Reading the mood of his lieutenant, the President framed their involvement. "Alarcón, I know that this is difficult for you. For us. Our goal is not to murder innocent people, but you and I both know that we must work to complete our revolution here in Venezuela, and also help our *hermanos* in Latin America to rediscover their passion for revolutions. And the only way we can be free to forge our own path to the real and lasting liberty and prosperity that Bolívar wanted for us is to be left in peace and alone. It's time the U.S. stopped engaging in one misadventure after another here in our lands.

"The world, the U.S., needs to have something else to focus on. First, there was Iraq and then the economic crisis caused by their banks. These planned diversions in the Middle East and Europe are what we need right now. It will give us time to further our work, like setting up SATO and giving us the cash we need to finance our initiatives. So chin up. This will not be a long involvement, and then, our role is purposely indirect. We are only helping to finance certain operations; we don't direct them, and we can't even assume that they will be successful. No one will know of our involvement, our partners have made this very clear. In the process, we will help our friends in the Islamic world to reclaim what was theirs so long ago, while we get what is rightfully ours."

"*Sí, Su Excelencia.*" The minister was not quite convinced by the President's arguments, but at the same time, he knew exactly which side his arepa was buttered on.

"Alarcón, come here." The President walked over to the glass doors facing the city of Caracas and stepped out on the Presidential Balcony. The skyline held its share of high-rises funded by the country's oil richness, not in any architectural master plan but loose and unwieldy, like a salsa dance. In the distance, he could see the twinkle of lights in Caracas's poor neighborhoods that still shone despite the hint of daybreak.

"See those lights at the homes of Bolívar's children? All of them are blue."

The bluish incandescent lights had been an energy-saving program instituted by Chávez a few years earlier with the help of his mentor, Castro. More than forty-five million of these lights had been handed out by Chávez's government. Besides their energy efficiency, these lights also signaled to all whose side you were on. With or against Chávez's Bolivarian revolution.

"Not a single one of those old white lights. The people are with us and look to us to light their way to a better future." Chávez didn't look at polls. All he had to do was look at the blue light emanating from the slums—and the international price for Venezuela's crude oil exports.

6
⏤◆◆◆➤

S U PASAPORTE, POR FAVOR," said the check-in clerk. It was 7:30 A.M., and Kate was taking the first flight out of Bogotá bound for Caracas. She had traveled here from Washington, D.C., the evening before to avoid flying directly from the U.S. to Caracas. No need to alert the Venezuelans that someone from D.C. was in their midst, let alone someone from U.S. intelligence.

Kate fished through her purse and dug out her burgundy red Venezuelan passport. Given her background, she legally had the option of three passports: Venezuelan or either of her two U.S. passports—the normal one or the official diplomatic one. Her clear objective on this trip was to lie low and attract as little attention as possible, so before leaving she'd selected Venezuela as her nationality for the day.

"*Aqui tiene, señor*—here you are, sir." Kate's accent in Spanish could have identified her as a resident of Caracas.

She walked to the boarding gate and made a quick call on the way.

"Hello, Dad."

"Hi, Kate. Where are you? Or am I not allowed to know that?" Her father was by now accustomed to being kept in the dark about her job and her travels. He had only forced a requirement on her that she needed to check in when she was going to be out of D.C. It was a rule even more firmly enforced after his wife had died a few years earlier. He didn't speak very often about his wife, not even with Kate. The pain of her death was still raw just below the surface. And now that it was just the two of them, he knew he couldn't take another loss like that. So he worried.

"I'm going to Caracas," she said.

Her father could only guess that this trip involved some new security threat, but he knew better than to ask about that. "Try not to draw attention to yourself, okay?"

Now, there was the fatherly concern she was looking for. "Don't worry. Got to board now. Bye."

"I've heard that before. Maybe you can stop by and see—"

BEFORE HE COULD FINISH, she'd already hung up. He stared out his office window, seeing the top of the low buildings and bare trees of tranquil Greenwich. He couldn't hide worrying about Kate. It's not like they didn't let Americans into Venezuela, but anything that smelled of intelligence missions would not be welcome by Chávez and his government.

KATE SIPPED HER SECOND CUP of *tinto*—strong black Colombian coffee. Looking out her window through scattered clouds, she could see her destination below. Though the city dated back to the late 1500s, Caracas's skyline was overgrown with skyscrapers built by Venezuela's oil wealth. She could see the city's outline, a long valley going east to west surrounded by hills. On one side, the slope was green and uninhabited; the other side was sprinkled with dwellings. A road wove through the hills, leading toward the ocean. The jet banked right, aiming for the seaside location of Simón Bolívar International Airport.

After landing, she was welcomed with open arms because of her Venezuelan passport. As Kate walked out of the air-conditioned terminal, she immediately felt the warm local temperature. It had been six years since her last visit here, and a lot had changed in her life since then. She knew from the intelligence traffic how things had changed in Venezuela, but she was still anxious to see those changes at ground level, with or without any involvement with the Madrid bombing.

She scanned the gaggle of waiting people, finally spotting a sign that read: HOTEL TAMANACO.

"*Buenos dias, señor. Yo soy* Kate Molares."

"*Señorita* Molares. *Con mucho gusto*—It's a pleasure. Welcome back to Caracas. Let me take your bag. My name is José Antonio." The driver was a man in his early fifties, neatly dressed in dark slacks and a white short-sleeve shirt.

He led Kate to a late-model American car, the type that seemed to cover half an acre, the antithesis of a "green" hybrid model. This was the luxury of living in a country that was the continent's largest exporter of oil. The local price for oil was usually about 95 percent *less* than the price paid by consumers in the U.S. and Europe. This explained why the parking lot was lined with the largest SUVs made by man, and late-model tanklike cars. Only here and in the Arabian Peninsula could these cars be considered "fuel efficient."

The Hotel Tamanaco was only fifteen miles from the airport, but the road was usually backed up with traffic, in spite of winding through the green uninhabited mountains surrounding Caracas.

"*Señorita* Molares, is it alright if we take a secondary road? The traffic ahead looks very bad."

"*Por supuesto,*" she responded.

José Antonio made a right, which took them through even more winding roads, where cars were driving at breakneck speeds, presumably to make the trip go quickly. However, the real reason was that this road traversed Caracas's most impoverished, and therefore dangerous, sections.

Kate looked at the scene outside her window. She saw many children running barefoot on unpaved sidewalks that were strewn with garbage. Sprinkled among the ramshackle homes were new schools and medical clinics run by world-class Cuban doctors. Clearly, Chávez's government, in partnership with his Cuban *hermanos,* was making strides in combating poverty and providing crucial services in these slums. But they still had far to go as measured by the weekly death toll from violent crimes in these poor neighborhoods.

Ninety minutes later, they arrived at the hotel—safely. José Antonio received a well-deserved tip from Kate, and she asked him to be available for the duration of her visit. Looking at her generous tip, he was more than happy to oblige.

She walked into the lobby, which was the antithesis of the slums she had seen. This hotel was the first of Caracas's luxury hotels, and despite competition from newer hotels, it managed to stay as the preferred choice for travelers who knew their way around Caracas, and the lobby was full of them. Despite Chávez's rhetoric, the country's attractive oil economy continued to attract foreign business. Checking in here, Kate felt at home and blended right in.

AN HOUR LATER, A FRESHLY SHOWERED Kate sat in the back of José Antonio's car.

"*Por favor,* José Antonio, let's go to El Centro Sambil." Soon they were on Avenida Libertador in front of South America's largest shopping center: five stories, five hundred stores, and thousands of shoppers by the minute. The throngs of people entering the center reminded her of a tide of salmon swimming to spawn. All the more because of the Christmas shopping season. American consumerism had taken hold a long time ago in Venezuela. Perfect, Kate thought, she could easily disappear in this crowd.

"Please come back for me in an hour. I'll meet you there by the taxi stand."

"*Sí, señorita.*" To him, it seemed to be a short time for a woman to shop, but then again, he was beginning to guess she wasn't a typical Venezuelan housewife.

She found the largest of the four bookstores in the mall and searched for the shelf with the books on Simón Bolívar, neatly placed next to several tomes on Hugo Chávez. She looked at her watch and was pleased she was just on time. Her rendezvous was set for 1:00 P.M. She picked up one volume, titled *El Libertador—The Liberator*, and started thumbing through it.

A man in his mid-thirties approached the same shelf and picked up a book on Chávez instead. "*Este es el futuro libertador.*" This is the future liberator.

Kate took a good look at the man and grinned. He had a tanned complexion, and was about twenty pounds over his ideal weight, and with dark, wavy hair that was beginning to recede. He was wearing a white shirt, blue blazer, and pressed gray slacks. In other words, he looked the part of any other Venezuelan husband seeking refuge in the bookstore while his wife shopped.

"*Cómo estas?*" They embraced warmly. This was no stranger; it was Kate's contact, Alejandro San Martín, the government insider who could hopefully shed some light on the puzzle of Venezuelan involvement in the airport bombing. He'd been a student with Kate at Georgetown, and they'd forged a friendship that was initially based on their common Venezuelan heritage and, later on, because of their parallel government careers.

After paying for their books, they strolled the corridors of the mall, catching up on their lives and exchanging vital information in Alejandro's mother tongue.

"Still single, Kate? There must be dozens of suitors trying to sweep you off your feet. I still remember that guy you brought to Caracas a few years ago. It looked like you were crazy in love. But I guess—"

Before he could finish his sentence, she replied. "No, it didn't work out in the end. I had my heart broken, and even though I date now and then, my heart belongs to my career at the moment. It's safer that way."

Alejandro shook his head. "Oh, you modern young women. I'm glad you didn't meet my wife before I proposed to her. You might have talked her out of it."

"Hey," said Kate. "Not everybody has the life partner thing figured out by high school. Some of us lose the man of our dreams and have to spend the next few years trying to find another guy who matches up." A bit shocked at her own candor, Kate swiftly changed the subject. "Can we talk about why I'm here?"

Alejandro grinned. He knew that he was lucky to have found his wife, Isabel. He just hoped that he could keep his family safe while he treaded this turf of international information trafficking.

"Okay, talk to me, Kate. What's going on? Do your people really suspect that Venezuela had something to do with the Madrid bombing?" They both stood in front of the display window of Zara, the Spanish clothing retailer.

"Large amounts were funneled from your Central Bank's account in Zurich to Cuba's account at the same bank. At the same time, a smaller amount took that same route to Cuba; from there, it was sent to a bank in Switzerland, which we're looking into. That bank might have ties to the Islamic world. We just haven't figured out yet if those ties are with good Islam or bad Islam. Too much of a coincidence, though. Within twenty-four hours of that money arriving in Lugano, there's a transfer out of that account for the same amount to Ceuta."

They entered the Zara Store and Kate gravitated toward a rack of colorful blouses.

"How much money are we talking about here?" Given Alejandro's senior level at the Ministry, he didn't have intimate knowledge of every transaction that passed through their government's accounts, but he was on the distribution list for the daily report prepared by a junior payments clerk, which showed any transactions that totaled more than $10 million.

"How would this look on me?" Kate feigned an interest in a light blue silk blouse, and then answered Alejandro's question. "The first transfer that stayed in Cuba was for $25 million. Maybe a drop in the bucket for those fund managers in New York and London, but a lot of money when it hit the coffers in Cuba. The second was smaller, $1 million. Since the transfer instructions went out in quick succession, there's a good chance that whoever ordered the first transfer also ordered the second one."

Alejandro's eyes flinched. He remembered this transaction, and the size of it had struck him as odd. So odd, that Alejandro had requested more information from the clerk that prepared the summary report. Could he really have hit upon a trail that led to funding for terrorism? he asked himself.

"What? . . . Do you know what I'm talking about?" Kate could see that Alejandro was troubled by her question.

A saleswoman hovered over them, too close for comfort, which prompted Alejandro to suggest, "How about we go to another store?"

As they rejoined the masses walking in the mall, Kate returned to their conversation about the money trail. "Is it possible that the first transfer relates to doctors from Cuba? It could be paying for their services here in the slums, like I saw on my way in from the airport."

"Could be, Kate." Alejandro remembered the details of the transfer, and one aspect made that theory unlikely. He was hesitating, trying to figure out the impact of that information before divulging it.

Kate noticed his discomfort. "Alejandro, if there's a chance that Venezuela is sponsoring terrorism in Europe, then I think it's probably better that we know about it and try to stop it. It would be terrible if the conflicts born in another part of the world were brought back here to Caracas. Don't you think?"

That last point stuck with Alejandro. She was right, he thought. Better to nip any of this at the outset before it completely sucked their country into conflicts not of their own making. On the other hand, what might the U.S. do to his country if they thought they were working with terrorists? He trusted his friend Kate to a point. But he didn't trust the people she worked for.

"You're right. I'm hesitating because this isn't definitive. It's just that I saw that transfer and wondered about it as well. And now that you're asking about it, it makes me think that there was something more to it."

"Okay, go on."

They stopped in front of an ice cream stand, Gelatería Parmalat. Alejandro looked at the available flavors. "I'm going to get the *avellana*—hazelnut—do you want one?"

"Sure, same for me. Thanks." There wasn't any organized line, just a mob of parents with their children clamoring to pick out just the right flavor. And very much like any ice cream stand in any other part of the world, there was a chorus of loud pleas on the part of the children that would soon try the patience of their parents.

Cones in hand, they walked away, with the sound of screaming children fading in the distance.

"I recall that the large amount, the $25 million, went to the Ministry of Science in Cuba," said Alejandro.

"Okay, so that's to pay for all those doctors that are sprinkled all over Venezuela, then? . . ."

"That was my theory. But the odd thing is that the money didn't go to the Ministry of Health, which is the Cuban government's arm that pays for the education and salaries of all their doctors. So it doesn't seem to fit neatly into the puzzle. Unfortunately, there wasn't anything else describing that transfer. Just who the payee was."

"What about that other $1 million? Did that just flow out?"

"Normally I wouldn't see an amount of that size in the report that I get every day. But the junior person who prepares the report must have dumped the $1 million piece in because both transactions originated through the same payment order. So whatever the large one was for, this smaller one was related. I think the report listed some bank in Italy. . . ."

"Maybe you're thinking of the Banca di Califfato in Lugano?"

"Yes, that's it. It wasn't Italy, it was Switzerland."

"Alejandro, this is very helpful." The money trail was still a bit murky to Kate, but at least she had info on the Venezuelan link without letting on that U.S. intelligence was looking for it. No alarm bells raised so far, she thought. But then she remembered her boss's dictum: airtight intelligence.

"Alejandro, can I get a copy of those money transfer orders?" She knew she was pushing it with Alejandro, but it was worth a shot. The more physical evidence she had, the stronger her briefing would be.

Alejandro closed his eyes for a second, not responding, a picture of his wife flashing through his mind. Handing over physical evidence to the Americans was a more active role than he bargained for, coming out of this simple stroll through the mall. He'd have to more fully weigh the pros and cons before making any promises. "Let me see what I can do, Kate. Okay?"

"Sure, I understand." Kate knew she was asking him to take risks, not only for himself but also for his family, all of which could go beyond merely getting a slap on the wrist at the Ministry. But she also knew that if Chávez was in fact starting a program to fund terrorism abroad, it wouldn't end well for the rest of Venezuela, Alejandro and his family included.

AS KATE AND ALEJANDRO made their way out of the mall, neither of them noticed the man who had been trailing them for the past hour. On the surface, he fit in with the rest of the mall's shoppers, but Alejandro should have recognized him as the Minister of Finance's loyal driver. Alejandro's inquiries on those money transfers had been noticed and reported up to the minister. The driver's surveillance work today had uncovered one of two worthwhile facts. Either Alejandro was having an affair, or this mysterious woman was on the receiving end of information, possibly related to those money transfers Alejandro had started inquiring about at the Ministry.

IN THE CAR RIDE BACK to the hotel, Kate considered her options. She wanted to call Bill and tell him about her findings, but she didn't have any secure way of telling him. A call could be traced and she wanted to retain the option of coming back to Caracas undetected. She would have to wait till she was on more friendly turf. But meanwhile, she could call Cuba. No alarm bells there.

"Hello, Inge? It's Kate."

"Kate. Hey, how are you? Where are you?" Inge Johanssen was another one of her closest friends from Georgetown. She was Swedish and worked with the U.N.'s office in Havana. They had been fast friends since being thrust together as roommates their freshman year.

"I'm in Caracas right now, on business. Since I'm so close already, what if I stop over for a visit?" A Venezuelan passport would not present a problem at Havana's airport.

"That would be great, Kate. It's never busy here at this outpost of our global empire. When can you come?"

"I could take a flight tomorrow."

"Great, the Aeropostal flight arrives here about seven o'clock. I'll wait for you at the airport. I'll tell customs you're here on official U.N. business so you can sail through on arrival."

"Perfect. See you then. And thanks." Kate felt better now that she had a plan for getting to the bottom of that $25 million. Only thing was that she was flying solo now. Havana was not on that original itinerary and, since the Bay of Pigs, it was a rare stop for U.S. intelligence.

Bill's words flashed through her mind. A U.S. operative caught in Havana was definitely not in that unwritten rule book. I can't screw this up, she thought. But there just wasn't any choice if she wanted to get to the bottom of the money trail. Bill would surely agree. She was just another private Venezuelan citizen, visiting a friendly neighboring country. And that's exactly what she'd tell anyone who asked her along the way. What could be the harm in that? she tried to convince herself. If anything did go wrong, however, dealing with the Cubans would be far easier than dealing with Bill's reaction back at the office. Of that, she was certain.

BEFORE HAVANA, KATE HAD ONE MORE visit to make in Venezuela, one she made each time she was here. After a quick stop at the hotel, she and her driver, José Antonio, were on the road again, this time to San Felipe, a small town west of Caracas, nestled in a fertile agricultural valley.

In the outskirts of town, Kate directed José Antonio onto a dusty road that led to a thousand-acre sugarcane farm. An old wooden gate served as the principal entrance, with a sign in need of some repair swinging loosely overhead. It read HACIENDA MOLARES. This is where Kate's father was born and where her grandfather still lived.

The main house was a white stucco building with a red-tiled roof and a terrace made of thick wood, weathered by age, which wrapped around the entire house. As she got out of the car, the first thing that caught Kate's eye was that all the windows and doors were boarded up.

She started to walk around to the back courtyard, but then heard a car driving up. It was another large old American model, and as it approached she was relieved to see a familiar face. The head caretaker of the farm, Roberto Gonzáles, stepped out with a broad smile.

"*Señorita Katerina,* how good to see you." Roberto's face beamed at the sight of Kate, remembering her as a lively toddler. Except for more gray hair and weathered skin, Roberto looked the same: same smile, despite the six years that had passed since her last visit. He'd been employed by Kate's grandfather for most of his adult life and in that time had become the most trusted steward of the family's land, particularly after Kate's father opted for a career in the U.S.

"*Don Roberto,* how have you been? How is my grandfather?" She noted a certain look in his eyes—defeat—uncharacteristic for him.

"He's doing as well as can be expected, given his age. I'll take you to him. Your driver can follow us."

"So how are the crops?" Kate asked, sitting alongside Roberto in his car. She already had an inkling; the passing fields, which should have been planted in neat rows of cane, lay overrun with weeds.

Roberto shook his head. "With Chávez, the workers have gotten different ideas. Many local farms have been taken over by workers, and the government is encouraging their squatting, even setting up schools in some of these settlements. A local owner was killed last month and then the squatters took over. The remaining private farms, like your grandfather's, are struggling to hang on. Most are looking to sell and leave Venezuela. But what sane person would buy into this mess?"

They drove another ten minutes, finally arriving at the small wood-frame cottage that Kate remembered as Roberto's house. They got out of the car and walked to the front door. Roberto took off his worn straw hat and ran his fingers over its frayed edges.

"Like I told your father last week, your grandfather just doesn't want to leave. I'm worried about the violent clashes around us. This is why we're staying in my cottage, away from the main house, so we don't attract attention. Your grandfather was always very fair with all his workers, and out of respect for him, they've stayed away from his lands—so far."

"Roberto, we owe you a great deal for what you've done all these years. When the time comes, if you need help, you know we will be there for you." Kate reached out and placed her hand on his shoulder, knowing that all these years he'd been much more than an employee, or even a friend, to her grandfather—he was a second son.

Kate opened the door and saw her grandfather, Rafael Molares, a small figure asleep in an oversized leather chair. He was finally succumbing to his eighty-six years. The turmoil around him was taking its toll on him, she thought. The Molares Hacienda was one of the largest privately owned properties in the region and, without doubt, it was already a target of the government's forced land redistribution program.

She reached over and gently touched his shoulder. His eyes opened slowly, just expecting Roberto there, but then lit up when he saw this morning's visitor. The old man's arms reached up to hug her, and despite the frailness of his limbs, Kate once again felt like that little girl who had spent many summers on this hacienda.

"*Mi querida,* Katerina, what a wonderful surprise."

"Yes, *Abuelo,* I came to make sure you're not overexerting yourself in those fields."

"No such luck, Katerina. Roberto keeps me out of trouble."

Kate tried to decipher her grandfather's mental mood. Maybe he was forcing himself to ignore everything around him, so that he could stay here. "Why don't you come back to the U.S. with me? You'd be safe with us there," she said, stroking his wiry hands.

"What would an old man like me do there? I'd just get in everyone's way. No, I'm better off here with my people and my land. *Our* land." The old man wanted to change the subject, but his voice came closer to pleading than a command.

She could tell he wanted to live in another reality, one where he tended to his crops as in the old days. Her father had been trying for years to change his mind, to no avail; the old man's will was still strong.

"And how is my son? Is he keeping busy?"

"He's very happy working in the private sector, on top of which he's making more money than he ever made at the U.N."

"I'm glad it worked out for him. He was worried about leaving the U.N., but I told him it was time to take some chances. You understand about that, taking risks, don't you, Katerina? You're just like your grandmother Teresa. She would always say to me, 'Without risk, where's the fun in life?'" The years of happiness with his wife shone again on his face.

Kate's grandmother had died when Kate was a young girl. She had been the love of Rafael's life and he never remarried, despite many offers. His legacy was one son, who in turn had one daughter; and she reminded him of Teresa, both in looks and tenacious spirit.

"I definitely understand that, *Abuelo.* Problem is that everyone likes to remind me that it's better to take the safe road."

"Don't listen to them, even if it's your father telling you that. My body is old, but inside I'm young, still ready for whatever challenge God still wants to lay at my doorstep." He coughed several times,

as if that fire inside him were trying to escape his weak body. Kate
handed him a glass of water, and after a few sips, he continued.

"So what ever happened to that young man you brought here
the last time you visited? Or was that one of those college flings
that your generation has?"

Kate's eyes wandered at her grandfather's question. "Yes, *Abuelo*,
just a fling."

"Don't worry; I'm sure you'll have no problem finding another.
I'm just wondering when I'll have a great-grandchild to visit me
here."

Kate was impressed that he could look to the future; so very few
his age did. She made a point of savoring her hours sitting with him.
They talked about when he was a young man on the hacienda and
the fears he had for the future of his beloved country.

"It's true that most of our leaders since Bolívar have been corrupt in one form or another. . . ." Her grandfather's voice trailed
off and his head fell slowly to one side. The excitement of the
morning had been too much for him. He drifted into sleep, which
was the signal for Kate to leave.

As she left the room, she looked back at her grandfather, asleep
in his chair. For a second, she felt sad to be leaving, but decided
instead to focus on the joy she had felt as a child each time she
came to visit.

A vivid memory came back to her from those days. It was an
early morning in the dry season. The air still held coolness from
the night before, and the cane was growing, but not yet ready for
harvest. As was her daily habit, her grandmother, Teresa Molares,
rose before the rest of the household and set out for her walk to
pick up fresh milk at the cow pasture on the property, near the
entrance to the hacienda. She had many servants who could do this
for her, but it was something that Teresa enjoyed doing herself,
giving her a sense of accomplishment first thing each day.

That morning, Kate remembered forcing herself to wake up
early so she could go with her grandmother on her venture. She
remembered walking along the farm's dirt roads hand in hand
with her, their shoes covered in the loose agricultural soil. When
they reached the barn, the cowhand had two glass liter bottles
filled with the morning's warm milk.

Usually, Teresa would turn around and head back to the main house, one warm liter in each hand. Today, because Kate was with her, she took a detour. They walked another few hundred yards, stopping at the front gates of the hacienda. Far beyond these gates lay an entire universe that Teresa only wondered about, and despite her years, she still craved visiting those places one day.

She looked at her granddaughter's smiling face and told her, "*Mi Katerina,* we're the rebels in our family. And one morning, we're going to walk on this very road, right past these front gates, and we're going to keep walking till we've seen every part of the big world out there. We'll face every new thing with wonder and every danger head on. Just you and me, you'll see."

Her grandmother never made it outside those gates, but Kate did. And tomorrow, she was going to another place outside those gates, as her grandmother would have wanted.

7

THE BARE TREES OF CENTRAL PARK were only slightly visible from the main conference room of Milestones Capital Partners. Their newly minted offices were on the fortieth floor of the General Motors Building, which took up the block of Fifth Avenue between Fifty-eighth and Fifty-ninth Streets. And the conference room's long expanse of windows overlooking the park was a significant factor in that address's stratospheric rent. Outside, Manhattan was in the midst of another gray and overcast winter Monday morning.

The cream-colored walls blended with the soft white leather chairs and blond wood table at the center of the rectangular room. There were plasma screens on one wall, which in their current idleness slowly flashed photos of desolate desert scenes at sunset. In one corner was a serving cart packed only with bottles of Voss water. The choice of refreshment seemed to have been made for aesthetic reasons; these sleek cylinder bottles complemented the rest of the modern décor. The only deference to another time was an ancient saber displayed on the wall. Its size was impressive, making it difficult to imagine that a soldier could have held it high in combat, let alone carry it while galloping on a horse.

The investment banking team from White Weld & Co., the world's largest investment bank, newly spun off from Bank of America, was gathered at the far end of the room, admiring this relic of ancient wars. Clifford Cheswick, the most senior team member and head of Middle East business, was in town from their London office. At the age of fifty-four, he was enjoying the final stage of his career in the banking business, with dreams of a quieter time with his books at his eighteenth-century farmhouse in Provence. Unfortunately, those plans had been forestalled when his vested pension was eviscerated in the economic crisis.

Today, in his emphatically British striped blue suit and fine linen pocket square, he held court over his retinue of managing directors, each of whom possessed a specific expertise: debt, M&A, regulatory, and proprietary capital. They were on the verge of completing one of the largest and most innovative deals of the year, and all of them had already impaled the right sides of their cerebrums with a year-end bonus number. Nothing could stand in the way of getting to cash such a check, certainly not after several years of government-imposed salary caps. If necessary, they'd even get on a horse and pry that saber from the wall.

At exactly 10:00 A.M., the bankers' concentration on things ornamental was broken by the opening of doors at the far end of the boardroom. There stood the lone figure of their client, Nebibi Hasehm. His usual black Armani suit enveloped a white French cuffed shirt and black tie. Everything about him was crisp, fresh, and reeking of cash. The White Weld crowd admired that type of client. Bonus numbers flashed across their brains again.

Clifford made a beeline to Nebibi. "Hello, Nebibi. Trust you had an uneventful trip over from Milan."

Nebibi shook the senior banker's hand. "Yes, thankfully one of our limited partners made his private jet available to us. So the trip allowed me some needed rest."

"We were admiring your saber over there and wondering if you've ever used it on one of your bankers?" Clifford's question generated a hearty chuckle from his team.

"No, but I did ask them to mount it so that it can easily be taken down." Nebibi's response caused an even heartier laugh from the group. They had no idea that their client was merely speaking the truth.

Nebibi got right down to business. "So are we all set for tomorrow?" He eyed the bankers around the room, and all of them nodded their heads in affirmation.

"Why don't we sit down and do a last run-through?" Clifford was eager to demonstrate his firm's knowledge and grasp of what they were embarking on.

Nebibi understood things quite differently, however. He had in fact engineered the entire transaction from thin air. He had devised the structure and had even identified the source of the funds. White Weld was only providing the overlay of paperwork necessary to lend an air of legitimacy to the entire deal. Nonetheless, he would allow them to go through the exercise of today's meetings because it was all part of the formalities required to cement the Fund as an important and new kind of *legitimate* player in the global equity market.

Nebibi took his jacket off and sat down in the middle of the long table with the impressive vista of Central Park behind him. He did this purposely, finely attuned to the art of Kabuki theater in business. The group of bankers sat opposite him, all men except for one woman. As he crossed his hands in front of him on the table, they all noticed the small silver saber cuff links on each wrist. He was ready for battle.

Clifford led the presentation, which was now displayed on one of the plasma screens in Nebibi's direct line of vision. The first slide was the tombstone ad that had appeared in the *Financial Times*.

"We think this will be an important event in our markets. The Milestones Fund will be the first *Shari'ah*-compliant fund of this magnitude. There have been others, but those were minuscule, none reaching more than $500 million. Here we've managed to amass not only our first tranche target of $25 billion, but also upsized that by another $5 billion. Clearly, there's an appetite for more, despite the fact that Western markets are still licking their wounds."

He pointed at the chart up on the screen. "As you can see, this places Milestones within the top echelons of funds management. Well done." Clifford's brain flashed that bonus figure again, causing a dribble of saliva to form at the edge of his mouth. He took out his white hanky to wipe it away.

Nebibi knew that there was more money from where that came. The last $5 billion had come from Venezuela through various shell companies in Grand Cayman and the investment arms of the House of Saud and the Kuwaiti royal family.

The major part of the funds, however, had originally come in the form of, shall we say, an endowment of sorts from the U.S. government. Back in the early days of the U.S. invasion of Iraq, the U.S. government had allocated close to $40 billion for reconstruction. A large portion of this was flown over to Baghdad on C-17 transport planes that were loaded up with literally tons of greenbacks in the middle of the night at Andrews Air Force Base in Virginia. Each night flight carried about $2 billion in shrink-wrapped dollars.

The Coalition Provisional Authority never fully managed to account for a quarter of those shipments, about $10 billion, bound from the U.S. to Iraq. Add another $20 billion that was on hand in Iraq on day one of the invasion, thanks to the U.N.'s Oil for Food Program, and you have some interesting sums of dollars unaccounted for. Suffice it to say that many of those shipments, occurring in the midst of air-to-ground missile fire, fell through the cracks of the mortar shells. A portion had landed in the hands of eager Iraqi citizens acting as brokers. But the lion's share of the lost billions was funneled back to support the insurgent movements associated with al-Qaeda.

The money was cleansed through various deposits, much of it landing in the coffers of the now defunct Banca di Califfato. In turn, following another cleansing round through trading companies registered in Grand Cayman and several banks in Uruguay, those billions were accumulated as the anchor investment that was helping to launch the new Milestones Fund. And now the money was back in the U.S.; the free and clear round-trip ticket provided by the astute banking team from White Weld & Co. The thought that their own government's funds would be used to promote Islamist causes around the globe always brought a slight grin to Nebibi's lips. Ignorant of this fact, Clifford took this as a sign his client was pleased with the course of his briefing.

Next in line for the presentation was the debt guy, who got up and walked to the monitor. At the tender age of thirty-two, he looked a little rumpled and worse for wear, thanks to way too many late nights looking at computer models. There was a tinge of jealousy in him, sparked by the fact that his client, the sole manager of the new multibillion-dollar fund, was only a few years older than he. The young banker excused it by concluding that Nebibi must have started with good connections in the business. If he only knew . . .

"Debt liquidity hasn't recovered to the high levels we had pre–mortgage meltdown. However, because your investments will be

Shari'ah compliant, we've been able to raise debt for the fund at a very attractive ratio of three to one from Middle East banks."

He clicked to the next slide, which showed a list of some of the debt syndicate investors. "So every dollar of equity investment in the fund is matched with three dollars of debt. Since the fund is now at $30 billion, your total buying power will be significantly higher, $120 billion to be exact."

Nebibi stood up to stretch his legs, still somewhat stiff from his multiple cross-Atlantic trips over the past few weeks. "And the terms for the debt, are they compliant with Islamic finance rules?"

Of course, you little shit. How fucking stupid do you think I am to present you terms that wouldn't be *Shari'ah* compliant?— that was what the thirty-two-year-old banker wanted to tell his young client, Nebibi. But instead he replied, "Good question, Mr. Hasehm. We've structured the debt component to sit alongside the equity in a preferential arrangement, utilizing the *Shari'ah*-compliant instrument of *ijara*—leasing. The fund will sell a portion of its holdings to a trust that will in fact be owned by the lender group. They in turn will *not* charge interest, in conformity with *Shari'ah* law, but instead will charge lease payments on the assets, the level of which will provide them an attractive rate of return."

"And this has been approved by our religious scholar?" Nebibi was walking around the room, which was making his bankers a bit on edge. Similar to a tennis match, they tried to keep their eyes on the moving client.

Again with the fuckin' asinine questions, thought the young banker. "Yes, of course. We enlisted the assistance of your Islamic scholar in Dubai, Mr. Hasehm."

"Good. Who's next?"

"I'll go next, Mr. Hasehm." It was Ted McCree, an ex–New York Fed bureaucrat, responsible for regulatory matters. He was on the far end of the table, wearing a suit, shirt, and tie with the least natural fibers in the room, and with a full head of jet black hair that, regrettably, no longer passed as natural. Ted had spent his entire career earning a government salary, trying to impose regulations on his more astute and far better paid counterparts in the private sector. When White Weld & Co. offered him a position a few months before, he jumped at the opportunity to finally make some real money advising clients, like Nebibi, on how to *avoid* government regulations. By the looks of Ted's beaming face this morning, he was clearly savoring the opportunity to be in the limelight and prove his worth today.

"We've reviewed all possible regulatory angles, and all issues will be cleared this week. The new financial regulatory regime in Washington may make it difficult for your fund to stay outside its purview." He scratched an itch near his neck, which made his colleagues wonder if Ted was nervous about the increased fervor of U.S. regulators. But in fact, it was only the man-made fibers irritating his pasty skin.

Nebibi interrupted him. "But I asked your firm to concentrate on *offshore* registration. . . ."

Ted kept scratching his neck, now looking up at Nebibi's stoic face. "Yes, yes, of course . . . ," he stammered. "Offshore tax havens. Clifford tells me you're focused on Gibraltar, but we wouldn't recommend that—"

Nebibi's raised his left eyebrow at being contradicted. "Why?" he asked, cutting Ted off midsentence.

"First of all, Gibraltar is a much smaller offshore financial center, with much less experience on this type of matter. In contrast, Ireland or Grand Cayman would offer you—" His colleagues could see a bead of sweat forming near Ted's dark sideburn.

"Other locations are of no concern to me or my investors. Gibraltar is the only place we wish to consider. I thought I'd made myself clear on that." Nebibi looked past the nodding faces, motioning for Clifford to meet him at the far end of the table, under the mounted saber. All eyes were still locked on Nebibi's cuff links as he got up and slowly walked to the other end of the room.

With his back to the rest of the team, Nebibi spoke in a low tone to Clifford. "I don't have time to negotiate with your deal team on these matters. You either get them to do what I want or I get Goldman over here this afternoon. Understood?"

Clifford shot a cold stare at Ted over Nebibi's shoulder; he wasn't about to let go of that potentially fat bonus check because of some poorly dressed ex-bureaucrat. "Certainly, Nebibi, I'll take care of it. Why don't we take a two-minute break?"

"Just make it fast." Nebibi headed out of the conference room, all eyes still focused on him, Ted's more so than others'.

When Nebibi returned, the White Weld team was short one member. Ted had been summarily sent back to the office, his time in the limelight of client interaction cut short, and those who remained planned on doing whatever the client asked.

"Our apologies, Nebibi, but our colleague Ted was summoned on a personal matter of utmost urgency. However, he did brief me before he left. He actually supported your selection of Gibraltar because of their attractive tax incentives. And since they're so small, their regulators will bend over backward for your business. Given the sunny climate, I'd be pleased to perform any on-the-ground review." Clifford ended with a big grin, sensing he'd just saved his bonus check from the clutches of Goldman.

Nebibi adjusted his cuff links. White Weld is signing off on Gibraltar, so the regulatory part was a breeze, he thought to himself. He looked up to find the team staring at him, actually at his silver sabers. "Alright, what's next?"

Clifford broke his concentration off those cuff links long enough to move the meeting along. "Now mergers and acquisitions."

The forty-year-old alpha male in charge of M&A had bright suspenders peeking under his Paul Stuart suit jacket. He spoke loudly—a habit that made most people assume he was partially deaf. "We're finally starting to see some real M&A volumes, though not anywhere as high as the 2006 peak. There are sizable deals to look at, with less competition than we've seen in the past, which is excellent for a new entrant, like The Milestones Fund."

As the M&A guy wound up his presentation, Nebibi's phone vibrated. A short message had come through from a nondescript Yahoo e-mail account:

Zurich. Tuesday. Usual spot. 10 A.M.

Good news, thought Nebibi. It meant his D.C. "friend" was ready to collect his payoff in exchange for the classified information Nebibi was waiting for. He quickly tapped an e-mail to his secretary down the hall to reserve his usual room at the Baur au Lac in Zurich. He looked up and saw that all eyes were focused on his tapping. "Continue," he said, not looking up and without apology.

"Of course, onto proprietary capital. Your turn." Clifford was looking at his female colleague, Margaux Bretz, who had not taken her eyes off Nebibi since he'd entered the room. She represented the side of White Weld that made investments using the capital of the firm's senior partners. She was an attractive blonde, divorced and in her early forties. A single cougar. No children. No boyfriend. *Yet.*

"Thanks, Clifford." Margaux stared directly at Nebibi, but her mind was racing. Forget the view of the Park behind him. Shit! No one had thought to mention that their newest client was such a piece of eligible young ass. Black hair, slicked back. Fine chiseled features. Deep, dark eyes. From his fitted shirt, she could see that he worked out a lot. A helluva lot.

For a second, she pictured herself giving him her presentation dressed only in her latest purchase from Victoria's Secret. She wouldn't mind being his "easy leverage." Get a grip! she reminded herself. Margaux, the cougar, filed away the picture of her bedroom for later and brought herself back to the boardroom. She adjusted her gray silk suit jacket, touched the Mikimotos on her triple-strand necklace, and proceeded with her comments.

"We consider this a monumental transaction for the market and will look to support it with strong participation from our firm's proprietary capital. I'm happy to report that we are prepared to commit $500 million as part of the *Shari'ah*-compliant structure." She relayed this with a voice of firm competence in the matters at hand.

And that voice of competence was saying that White Weld's senior management thought that The Milestones Fund would make a killing and they all were clamoring for a piece of the action. For Nebibi, the cover of legitimacy was complete and absolute. Now, even the chairman of White Weld was on the hook. He flashed a quick smile at the thought of the growing snowball of legitimacy granted upon his mission for Allah, and Margaux's pulse went through the roof.

"So in summation, my dear friend, Nebibi"—of course, he was Clifford's new favored, very rich, and mightily powerful friend—"by

tomorrow, at close of business in New York, your Milestones Fund
will have all the capital horsepower to be on the front lines of major
investments in the global economy."

"Thank you, Clifford. I must say, you've all done excellent work
and I trust you'll each receive kudos for this transaction both
within your firm as well as from your competitors in the marketplace."

At that very instant, the silver saber cuff link on his left wrist
caught the first glimmer of sun shining through a clearing in the
clouds. Each and every banker in that room, Margaux included,
made a plan to buy a set of those cuff links when that bonus check
came in.

8

◄+ + +►

THE SMALL AEROPOSTAL AIRCRAFT from Caracas circled over Havana before landing at José Martí International Airport. December is part of the dry season in the Caribbean, so it was a clear, hot day in Havana. At customs, Kate presented her Venezuelan passport and was summoned to a special agent. Now what?! wondered Kate.

Kate didn't frighten easily, but given her employer, she was definitely in enemy territory now. After a few tense minutes of questioning, she was welcomed to the República de Cuba. She exited the customs area and was relieved to find Inge waving at her. Kate felt more at ease now, having passed through Cuban security and seeing her friend's smiling face. They embraced with kisses on each cheek.

"It's so nice to see you, Kate. You're looking good." Inge knew full well what Kate's line of work was and who her ultimate boss was. So, in arranging the special U.N. visa, Inge had entered dangerous territory. But she also knew that Kate wouldn't chance this kind of trip unless there was a damn good reason for it. So Inge had put herself on the line for her old friend Kate. They shared too much history to let a little thing like the decades-old U.S. Cuban Embargo stand in the way of this visit.

There would be time to talk about the real purpose of her trip when they were in a more private setting. For now, in the taxi ride to the city, Inge gave Kate a tour of Old Havana. As this was her first time in Cuba, Kate looked out the window, trying to take in the largest metropolis in the Caribbean. There was a bustle in the street as people headed home, many on bicycles. The double-length buses, called camels by the locals, were packed more tightly than any subway in Tokyo. And yes, the roads were packed with pristine-looking mid-1950s cars. The scene of human traffic was framed by a backdrop of magnificent beaux arts buildings in a general state of disrepair, which added to their charm.

After an abbreviated tour, they headed to their destination, the Hotel Nacional de Cuba, Havana's premier hotel. Built in 1930, it has a unique history, having hosted the likes of Hemingway, the Duke and Duchess of Windsor, and many other luminaries.

"This is a good place to sit down and catch up quietly without a lot of people interrupting and trying to sell us boxes of second-class cigars," Inge said. They drove up the impressive palm-tree-lined oval driveway of the art deco hotel, which was situated on a hill overlooking the harbor.

They strolled through the lobby with its intricately tiled floors, tall ceilings with dark wood beams and chandeliers, all from a by-gone era. Inge led the way to the Galería Bar, which was on the pillared veranda facing the hotel's inner courtyard. There, they found cushioned wicker sofas arranged in a corner. The lush, tropical inner garden was peaceful and comfortable—no cigar vendors to be seen. At this hour, only about half of the available tables were filled.

"*Dos mojitos, por favor.*" What else could Inge order in Havana but the island's inspired contribution to the global cocktail hour? Lime, sugar, mint, and Cuban rum crushed by an expert hand.

Kate took her first sip of the best *mojito* she had ever tasted. "So, how is it going here?"

"It's a real challenge at times, the living situation and all. I share a house in the old part of Havana with another U.N. rep; I have the second floor and he has the first floor. The house is just like most things in Havana, turn-of-the-last-century style. The plumbing is ancient and always in need of repair. Somehow 'central planning' doesn't think that fixing my plumbing is central to the management of this economy so, most days, there is no hot water and no pressure to speak of. I don't expect to take a real shower until my next vacation back in Göteborg.

"Then there's the dating thing. Not much to choose from, so I doubt I'll find the love of my life here, but you never know. Let's just hope he doesn't turn out to be Cuban. I don't look good in green fatigues." This was the second year for Inge in Cuba as part of the small local staff for the United Nations Development Programme, the UNDP.

"Inge. You'd look good in anything, fatigues included."

"Just like you, Kate. What can I say? We certainly did drive those freshmen crazy back at school, huh?" Inge was the stereotypical blond Swede. Twelve years ago, the pair had been an attractive and seemingly unattainable duo for most freshmen.

Today, as they sat in the courtyard engaged in their animated discussion, their effect on the opposite sex had not diminished. All the waiters' eyes were on the attractive pair in the corner alcove. And each young man took a turn coming to their table to get a closer look under one guise or another. And here was another one. "May I get you another round of *mojitos*?"

Before Kate could object, Inge answered, "Absolutely." She eyed the waiter as he walked away. "Maybe I should ask him out on a date; haven't seen anything better in the diplomatic corps here. . . ."

"You're too much, Inge," Kate laughed.

"So, have you found the man of your dreams yet?"

Kate sighed. "Why does everyone bring up my lackluster love life?"

Inge shrugged in sympathy. "I guess you haven't been with anybody serious since that guy after graduate school?"

"No, nothing serious. Just like you, concentrating on my work. Trying to have some fun, though. A fling every now and then doesn't hurt. It's just that the guys I meet in the military are either already long married or there's something seriously wrong with them." Kate's memory of recent dates swirled through her mind.

"Our time will come, Kate, at least that's what I keep telling myself. Until then, I try to convince myself that our careers will keep us sane and out of trouble, though the second part may be slightly more difficult in your line of work. Which brings us to the subject of what you're up to, Kate? I'm sure you thought long and hard before coming here."

"It's about Madrid . . ."

"*Ja,* that was pretty nasty. I think more so because we were getting comfortable with a quieter environment." Inge drained the bottom of her *mojito* glass, where the sugar and mint had settled.

"My end of this is the money trail. I was in Caracas looking

into some money transfers: large ones that went from the Venezuelans to the Cubans. We heard that some of it ended up in
Ceuta. That's where it gets a bit funny. If you ask my eager colleagues, their knee-jerk reaction is to say that the money went
from Cuba to Ceuta and eventually ended up on the wrong side
of the bombing in Madrid. And then they start those drum-
beats. . . ."

"We know where that goes. Another messy global episode."

"Yep. So I need to figure out whether or not the Cubans and
Venezuelans are really involved with all that."

"Chávez and the Cubans setting off bombs in Madrid—that's
pretty out there, isn't it, Kate?"

"I know it sounds far-fetched. That's why I'm here. Really to
just prove that assessment wrong. Frankly, I'd rather find that the
money went to pay for Cuban doctors working in Caracas. The
world would be an easier place to manage if that were the case. If
it isn't, though, it means that there are some mighty funky plans in
the works that could explode on several fronts all at once."

"Okay. So let's break this down. How much are we talking
about and do you know who was on the receiving end of the money
here in Cuba?"

Kate leaned forward and lowered her voice. "$25 million and it
was the Ministry of Science. What I'm stuck on: if that money was
for paying doctors, then it should have gone to the Ministry of
Health, right? That's my problem."

Inge raised her empty glass, motioning to the group of waiters
staring at them. They all scrambled to get the new order to the pair
of women at table five. "Any more transfers?"

"There was another $1 million sent from here to Lugano." Kate
had now reached the bottom of her glass as well.

"I could probably help you out with the large piece. I have a lot
of contacts in both ministries because of my work on HIV/AIDS
issues. The interesting thing about my work here is that we don't
do much outreach through education to stop the spread of AIDS.
The Cubans have one of the lowest occurrences of AIDS in the
world." The lucky waiter was delivering the next order of drinks
to the table with a big grin on his face. Both women looked up at
him and said in unison, "Gracias."

"May I get you anything else?" The waiter was going to stretch this for as long as possible.

"Why don't we get something to eat, to cut all this liquor? These *mojitos* taste good but I have a feeling they pack quite a punch." Kate was already feeling the power of just two of these small drinks, and now a third was sitting in front of her.

"Certainly. How about a selection of appetizers for you, misses?"

"That sounds perfect." Kate watched the waiter walk back to the kitchen. She looked around the lounge area and noticed that several more guests were now sitting around the patio. At the loudest table sat a group of Chinese men.

Inge noticed them as well. "That's the Chinese Ping-Pong team. They're here on a goodwill tour of Latin America. It's been splashed all over the paper for days; Even Chávez hasn't gotten as much ink this past week."

"Does that mean a slew of government programs for table tennis training here? . . ."

"Exactly, Kate. You're getting the hang of how things operate."

"So back to the AIDS issue, how's it possible that they have such a low infection rate?" Kate asked.

"It's the way they treat the disease. Anyone diagnosed with AIDS is immediately locked away for a three-month stay in a sanatorium, where they're trained on how to stop the spread of their infection. It's really unique and incredibly effective. The rate of infection here is about sixty times less than their neighbors in the Caribbean. From a civil liberties point of view, though, the approach is a bit radical. But still, we need to study them and their approach, rather than vice versa," explained Inge.

"That's impressive. That alone would seem to make their doctors worth more than $25 million. . . ."

"The Castro brothers have paid a lot of attention to that sector. The little cash they could muster when the Soviets cracked was spent on creating a medical welfare net. That's how Cuba ended up with not only world-class doctors that they've exported to places like Venezuela, but also a vibrant medical research industry. In the past few years, the Cubans have patented several drugs that are selling in international markets, in spite of the U.S. embargo, and even contributed profits to the economy."

"So you think that the $25 million from Venezuela was paying for drugs and research, all in the name of humanitarian efforts?"

Inge looked pensive. She wanted to be very careful in voicing her assessments, or rather suspicions, about something peculiar that she had seen. If she led Kate down an incorrect path, she just might end up starting another military fiasco, and this time the U.S. would make sure it was successful.

"The thing is, Kate, there is something very strange that I came across recently. I didn't think much of it at the time, but now, with the questions you're asking, I can't help wondering if it might be part of something bigger than AIDS research."

"What was it?" Kate asked.

"Maybe it's nothing and it's just my suspicious Swedish brain taking over. . . ."

"Inge? . . ."

"Okay, okay. In my work here, I'm in contact with just about every researcher working in Cuba on all types of diseases, especially AIDS. It's a big industry here. In Havana alone, there are more than fifty scientific research institutes, and the most respected one is the Bermudez Institute of Tropical Medicine." Inge was referring to the secluded campus outside of Havana that was under strict twenty-four-hour security with close ties to the U.N.'s World Health Organization in Geneva.

"They're working around the clock, trying to beat out the rest of the world in finding a cure for AIDS. We know their people very well and we encourage their ties with similar facilities around the world. Science can be a very healthy way to cut through the nonsense of politics."

"Okay, but all that sounds pretty normal so far. . . ."

"*Ja.* I know. Just wait. Last year, I met one of their senior researchers, Dr. Mirella Martínez. She's our age, and we started hanging out in Havana. She was pretty open with me, taking me on tours of their facilities and doing the same for every UNDP official that came through here."

Two waiters came with a tray of local appetizers, from little *empanaditas* to sausages and olives. Both women started picking at the platter right away to counter the effect of the liquor.

Inge waited for the waiters to retreat and then continued. "About a month ago, I had the big honcho from UN headquarters in New York here, and I took him for the usual round of site visits, capped by a meeting with Dr. Mirella. We start going through the normal tour of the research lab. I've pretty much memorized the inside of that place. Well, anyways, we're on the second floor where the animal testing takes place. All of a sudden, a pack of lab animals runs from the direction of a corridor that has never been part of the tour. All of them cats. Are you still with me here? . . ."

"Yes . . ." Kate took a bite of a sausage. In the background, a cheer rose from the Chinese table tennis team. They were evidently enjoying their moment of relative freedom from intense training, helped along by a third round of *mojitos*.

"Well, these cats, they weren't running *away* from something. They were running *toward* something. They were chasing a large dog and trying to catch him. It's like they were fearless against their natural predator. Next, there's a slew of lab technicians in their white coats trying to catch this pack of aggressive cats.

"I stood there totally speechless. Never seen such a thing in my entire life. I asked Mirella what that was all about, but she just clammed up. I never got a straight answer about it. I called her a week later to schedule a tour for a visiting Swiss pharmaceutical company executive and was told that she had been transferred to another research facility, no forwarding number. I called her house, but the line was disconnected. Pretty strange, huh?"

"Sounds very odd, just not sure if what you saw was $25 million worth of cats," Kate said before taking a sip of water, trying to slow down her intake of the deadly *mojitos*.

"Maybe not, and you're right, if they were just regular cats. And frankly because it sounds a bit absurd, I would have left it at that. Another forced relocation of a trained professional like Mirella in a centrally planned economy. Stuff like that always happened in places like the USSR and China, right?

"Problem is that a week later, I was walking down the *Malecón* along the water and one of those guys selling cheap cigars comes up to me. He practically accosts me, but he doesn't do the hard sell on me, instead he looks me in the eye as if he knows me and then slips a note into my hand. Before I could talk to him, though, he disappears into the crowd, trying to hawk his cigars to some other tourist. The note was from Mirella. In it, she warns me to stop asking for her at the clinic, not to look for her at her apartment, and that she would be in contact with me when it might be safer.

"So there you have it, Kate. Pretty strange stuff. I'm not sure how it fits in with the money angle, but I suspect the fact we've separately stumbled upon two disturbing events unfolding at the same time with respect to Cuba's medical community is no coincidence."

Kate turned to the waiter. *"Dos mojitos mas, por favor."* Two more *mojitos,* please. As her mind tried to make sense of this crazy cat story, she decided that another round of Cuban liquor was definitely in order.

9

⊸+✦+✦+⊷

A LEJANDRO SAN MARTÍN SAT in his small office staring at a folder on his desk. He opened it slowly and laid its contents, two sheets of paper, side by side. They were photocopies of the payment orders that Kate had asked about. The clerk in the Ministry's payments area had been reluctant to give him copies, but Alejandro insisted and felt confident that he'd managed to convince him he was acting on the orders of the minister himself. So now Alejandro sat there trying to decide what his next step should be. He glanced over at the picture of his wife, Isabel, on his desk. What would she want me to do? he wondered.

Just then, his middle-aged secretary barged into his office. "The minister's secretary called. He wants to see you right away." She was out of breath, not only because she was forty pounds overweight, but also from the urgency of the message she was delivering. Alejandro quickly threw the papers back into the folder.

"Did they say what it's about?" Alejandro rarely had one-on-ones with the minister.

"No, but maybe it's about that senior position that's open. Wouldn't that be wonderful?" The secretary was thinking about her own possible elevation as much as his.

"WOULD YOU LIKE SUGAR WITH THAT?" Alejandro's concentration on the portrait of Chávez over the minister's desk was broken by the question from the minister's able driver, who hovered over a small silver tray.

"Oh, yes, sugar please." It should have seemed odd to Alejandro that the driver was serving coffee, but his mind was more concentrated on anticipating what the minister wanted with him today.

As the driver carefully stirred the small espresso brew, the Minister rushed in. The driver placed the small china cup in front of Alejandro and, with a nod to the minister, left the office.

"*Hola,* Alejandro. Sorry for my delay. The President kept me longer than expected." The minister was a slight man, displaying more nervous energy than normal. He looked preoccupied with matters other than the underling sitting in front of him.

"Of course, I understand, *Señor Ministro.*" Alejandro took a sip from his coffee. It had a slight bitter aftertaste, which made him think that he should have asked for more sugar.

"You're probably wondering why I asked you here? . . ."

"Well . . ." Alejandro's voice trailed.

"I've been noticing your extra initiatives. Your critical questions and oversight on matters outside your day-to-day responsibilities."

"Is this related to my questions regarding those funds transfers? I was just—"

The minister cut him off. "Yes. That's exactly the kind of initiative we want to encourage around here."

Alejandro wanted to give himself time to react to the minister's words, so he took two quick gulps of the remaining espresso. The bitter taste caused him to cough as a way to clear his throat before responding to the minister. "Thank you, *Señor Ministro.*"

The minister winced a bit, but then he composed himself, saying, "Just keep up your good work, Alejandro. There will be many more opportunities for you to shine here. I'll make sure of it."

ALEJANDRO LEFT THE MINISTRY that evening feeling very comfortable about his future. Unfortunately, though, the small particles of cobalt-60 radioactive material that the minister's driver had sprinkled in his espresso would soon ravage his body. Alejandro's descent into a physical hell would come quickly, leaving local doctors little time to misdiagnose and treat his malady. His real disease was too much knowledge about sensitive money transfers, and without a correct diagnosis, a certain female intelligence officer could also be afflicted.

10

ZURICH, SWITZERLAND
DECEMBER 16

A MIDDLE-AGED MAN WITH DISTINCTIVELY BUSHY eyebrows fidgeted in his chair on the second floor of the Confiserie Sprüngli. All around him, the locals sipped their coffees accompanied by delicate Swiss breakfast breads. The man's dark suit made him fit in with the other bankers, though his passport was American. He seemed to be staring at the menu, but in fact, his eyes were singularly focused on the street traffic below, specifically on the double wooden doors across the Paradeplatz that marked the entrance to the Vereinten Kantonalbank.

The man kept one hand parked firmly on the slim black leather valise that rested on his lap. He was risking everything to be here today and his senses were on alert. He looked at the antique Swiss clock in the corner. 9:55. Every minute brought him closer to his payoff, or so he hoped, as his fingers tightened their grip on the leather.

His line of vision was blocked by a belt and white shirt. It was the waiter, asking in his singsongy Zurich dialect, "*Gu-ëte morgë*— Good morning, what may I bring you?"

"Just a café au lait and a croissant for now," replied the man as he leaned over to keep his eyes locked on the bank entrance across the street.

As soon as the waiter walked away, the man caught a glimpse of what he'd been waiting for: the slim figure of Nebibi in his dark wool coat stepping out of the Vereinten Kantonalbank. He watched the figure step quickly across the square.

By the time the waiter was back with the café au lait, Nebibi was approaching the table.

"Good morning," Nebibi said to the man as he slipped his leather gloves off. He didn't extend his hand. Instead, he just sat down with his coat unbuttoned. This would be a short meeting.

The man reciprocated in a curt, purely business tone, "Good morning."

"Is that it?" Nebibi motioned to the valise.

The man responded only with another question: "Is everything taken care of across the street?"

"The account is arranged. I transferred $5 million this morning on delivery of the sample information. The remaining $15 million after you deliver the balance of the data."

"Good." The man felt a sense of elation; he was so close to that finish line. It had been two years since he had lost his retirement nest egg in the Lehman bankruptcy, followed by the fleecing of his remaining assets in a messy divorce. He'd managed to land a government job but knew that at his current salary range, he'd never recover economically. Now, thanks to the man sitting across from him, he stood to gain a multiple of that nest egg. The man pulled a sheet of paper from the valise and slipped it across the table to Nebibi. "Here you go. That should be worth your time and money."

Nebibi stared at the page without touching it. He could see the stamp TOP SECRET on one corner and the seal of the U.S. Treasury on the other. It was exactly what he needed and worth far more than the $20 million he would pay the weasel in front of him. Nebibi pulled out a folded paper from his coat pocket.

"It's what you came for," Nebibi said as he slid the paper on the table in front of him. It was an account statement emblazoned with the seal of the Vereinten Kantonalbank. It showed a zero opening balance and one wire transfer from a Banca di Califfato account at a bank in Andorra. The balance as of this morning read $5 million. Nebibi pulled out another piece of paper on which he had handwritten the access codes for the account.

The man reached for the pieces of paper, all the while trying to maintain his composure. He felt his fingers tingle as he took the papers, folded them neatly, and placed them in his suit pocket. Without saying a word, he took a sip of his café au lait, stood up, and grabbed his coat, purposely leaving the valise with the sample data for Nebibi. He extended his hand to Nebibi. It was the least he could do to acknowledge the man who had just put him firmly on course to replenish his pension.

11

BOLLING AIR FORCE BASE, D.C.
DECEMBER 17

KATE WALKED INTO THE ORANGE-COLORED CAFETERIA at the DIA earlier than usual so she could begin to file her intelligence reports. At 7 A.M., the cafeteria was already in full swing with a line of military staff waiting at the grill. Kate stood in line just behind an air force colonel who was in charge of logistics analysis. If you needed to bomb a country, she could tell you the capacity of the airfields all around your target. In front of Kate was an army officer assigned to the medical research unit of the DIA, the Armed Forces Medical Intelligence Center. He was the guy to fill you in on the latest innovations in bioterror. "Good morning, Colonel Sherry, Lieutenant Khoury."

Hit with a voracious hunger after all the nervous energy from her travels, Kate ordered the full military breakfast from the mess hall private behind the counter: "Two eggs over easy, two slices, no make that three slices of bacon, and two pieces of whole wheat toast, please." She poured herself a large glass of fresh orange juice and a large cup of coffee, milk, no sugar. She was not a dainty eater. When she was hungry, she dealt with it head-on. That should do it, she thought to herself. Kate's metabolism was such that she needed to be sure to eat enough, so as not to lose too much weight. Lucky her.

She sat by the window looking out toward Reagan National Airport with the stack of unread *Financial Times* that had piled up on her desk from before vacation and started to scan the headlines. Given her security clearance and the fact she was inside a secure location, she could have used this time to catch up on some classified reports. But, she knew herself all too well, and didn't want to risk leaving some classified folder in the cafeteria. That would be tantamount to treason in her line of work. She could stand accused before a panel of her intelligence community peers on her lax handling of intelligence data; big black mark on her human resources file. It had already happened twice before, and the third time would not be pleasant.

She dug into her breakfast with every intention of finishing in fifteen minutes. She wanted to file all of her reports by the end of the morning. After the last bite of bacon, she got up for a refill of coffee to take back to her cubicle. Lieutenant Khoury stood behind her waiting to get his refill, which made Kate think about one of those reports.

Lieutenant Khoury was just a couple of years older than Kate and had enlisted in the army to escape the projects of Detroit right after high school. His Muslim Lebanese family had settled there when he was five. The army had given Lieutenant Khoury a free education. Now he had a master's degree in biology and chemistry, and had survived two deployments in Iraq. He was celebrating his tenth wedding anniversary next week and was the father of two healthy toddlers. Military life was good, and a far cry from his childhood in the projects. It was not hard to foresee that he would be a lifelong career officer. And he was a good example of what some in the Pentagon argued was needed for more Muslim officers in their ranks.

"Lieutenant, I need to ask you a hypothetical question. Do you have a minute? I'll walk down with you." Lieutenant Khoury's desk was on the same side of the building as the Latin America area.

"Sure, no problem, Miss Molares. Let me just get some cream and sugar." In his mind he knew enough to question the hypothetical part. That's how things always seemed to start around here. Next thing you know, jet fighter planes are on secret reconnaissance missions right and left.

"Are those your newspapers over there, by the way?" The lieutenant noticed the stack of the pink *FTs* sitting at the table by the window.

"Oh yeah, thanks." Slightly embarrassed, Kate rushed over,

grabbed the pile of unread *FT*s, stuffed them under her arm, and carried her full large coffee with the other hand.

"Were you away? I haven't seen you around for a while," he asked.

"I was on vacation, and then came back the same day as the Madrid bombings. When all hell broke loose around here, I was sent on a cat-and-mouse chase down in South America. What about you? Are you involved in any angles on this Madrid thing?" The crazy cat story was working on Kate's subconscious.

"Nothing for us at the moment. All quiet in the bioterror part of this. Seems like it was just your good ole standard bomb-in-backpack sort of thing."

"That's a small favor at least. I'm sure your wife's happy to have you at home on a normal schedule," she said.

"Yeah, it's good to be home before the kids go to sleep. So tell me about your 'hypothetical' question."

"Right. So hypothetically, let's say you're walking down the street near your home on the base and all of a sudden you see two animals chasing each other. Nothing unusual, right? But what if you saw a small cat chasing a large dog?" Kate ventured, slowly and deliberately.

"Maybe that was an anomaly. Maybe they had been raised together since birth and so they were just playing." Given his scientific background, Lieutenant Khoury would try to find a clinical reason for this.

"Okay, I can see that. But what if instead of only one cat, there were twenty like that, all chasing this large dog? Wouldn't that be strange to you?"

"Well, yes, if I saw that on my street, I'd do a double take. Did you see this on base?" Lieutenant Khoury tried to imagine such a scene in his mind.

"No, not exactly. I just want to know if there is anything that might cause such weird animal behavior."

"Hmmm. Off the top of my head, no. But let me give it a think. I'm assuming we're keeping this all in the 'hypothetical' world for the moment?" Khoury resisted an impulse to ask Kate if she'd been reading too much Stephen King lately, but something told him not to make light of her question.

"Yeah, just hypothetical. And thanks." Kate tried to come up with the scenario that could take this story from the hypothetical to the very real, but nothing was coming to mind.

KATE PLOPPED THE *FTS* ON her in-box and sat down in front of her computer monitor. Later, she'd have to catch up on the news that everybody else was reading. Right now, she needed to get cracking on the news that only a select few read. She booted up her desktop.

Not for the first time, Kate marveled at the whole phenomenon of the Internet, and the crucial role that the U.S. military had played in developing it. Their goal had been to create a network that connected computers in distant locations to allow for secure transfer of data, particularly in the event of a nuclear holocaust. That made them early funders of the RAND Institute's work that created the first network of computers connecting four universities in 1969—the Internet's first baby cry.

As the infrastructure of connectivity grew and stabilized, it created more opportunities for socialization of newly connected individuals on the network. The military adapted to this by introducing the IntelWiki in 2006, which works like the online encyclopedia, Wikipedia, available to the global public. This version, however, is available only to the intelligence community with only the highest security clearance at the likes of the DIA, CIA, and NSA. In turn, these intelligence officers can create articles that are instantly shared across the highly secure intelligence network.

However, despite the growing volume of reporting, the WikiLeaks debacle had slowed intelligence assessments, as there was once again less sharing peer-to-peer across agencies. More than three thousand government and private contractors worked on counterterrorism issues in about ten thousand locations in the U.S. alone. That was a lot of intelligence to sift through to get to that one useful nugget.

Once her system booted up, Kate logged on to the IntelWiki to draft and post her reports. Before directing her browser to the Latin America tree, she caught up on the other information coming out of Madrid. Thousands of posts were coming in from all directions. Once a topic is established, in this case, *Madrid Bombing,* anyone on the network can edit or add to the original posting, and they frequently add hyperlinks to related articles posted in the secure space. The network was very, very busy on the Madrid topic.

Kate was impressed with the flow of traffic. Five hundred edits in the last hour alone; seemed like she wasn't the only one already at her desk this morning. She could see that they had a lot of loose threads of data, but nothing definitive. The only live piece of intelligence seemed to be the call from that ETA guy and the remains of the two dead suspects. She wondered if the Spanish were analyzing the remains for any clues. So she posted a question on that:

1. Is Spanish Intelligence performing an analysis of the bomber's remains?
2. Will we be getting a sample for our own analysis?

Forensics wasn't Kate's specific area of expertise, but given her high security clearance, she was one of the select few who could view reports across a broad swath of the network.

Kate moved over to the Swiss page to see if there were any developments with the money transfers. Nothing new there either. Nothing from CIA or Treasury. So that's where she decided to insert herself.

She started typing a new subtopic:

Country:	Spain, Venezuela, Cuba
Topic:	Madrid Bombing
Subtopic:	Background on Venezuelan Source and Direction of Money Transfers.
Filed by:	72689/D.I.A./BollingAFB
Source:	HUMINT
Classification:	TOP SECRET/N.F.D.

NFD stood for "no foreign dissemination," making her report available to only the highest levels of security within the U.S. intelligence infrastructure. It could not be shared even with America's friends and allies. She continued typing.

Finding: Performed site visit to Venezuela and made contact with
government official on an unidentified background basis.
Have confirmed that both the $25 million and $1 million
transfers were initiated by the Central Bank of Venezuela by order of the Finance Minister for the account of
the Central Bank of Cuba at the Vereinten Kantonalbank
in Zurich.
$25 million was earmarked for the further credit to the
Cuban Ministry of Science. Purpose of the payment
unknown. Possible hypothesis (unconfirmed) is payment
for Cuban medical staff presently in service throughout
Venezuela. Payment may have also been earmarked for
medical research at the bequest of Venezuela. Scope of
such medical research unknown.
$1 million is confirmed to be transfer initiated simultane-
ously to larger transfer. Transfer did not stay in Cuban
Central Bank account at the Vereinten Kantonalbank.
Same day funds made available at Banca di Califfato in
Lugano. $75,000 transmitted to money order house in
North Africa.

Two days of travel boiled down to a couple of paragraphs, and in
an instant, it could be linked to the main topic and available for her
superiors from here to Langley, Virginia, and highly secure locations for U.S. personnel around the world. She was about to click
on the POST command when a thought flashed through her mind.
She hadn't briefed Bill yet. There'd be hell to pay if she posted this
without telling him first, particularly because of her unscheduled
Havana stopover.

She walked down the hall to Bill's office, trying to come up with
the best possible way to position why she took her side trip to Havana. She was two doors away when she could overhear Bill's
secretary, Samantha, speaking on the phone. Kate wasn't ready, so
she turned around and headed back to her cubicle, thinking about
all the possible ramifications if she had been caught in Havana.
The Cubans would have made a big splash about it in every global
media outlet. Thankfully, she thought, no harm done since this

was all hypothetical. Satisfied with that route, she turned back around toward Bill's office.

"Bill, you got a minute?" She popped her head in his doorway.

He looked up from his papers and smiled. "Glad to see you made it back in one piece. When'd you get in?"

Kate stepped into his office, but stayed only a step away from the door. "Pretty late last night . . ."

She paused, took a deep breath, and then recounted for Bill the events of her trip in rapid-fire sentences. Bill stood up from his chair at the mention of Havana, but Kate didn't stop until she was finished with that last untidy thread about the crazy cats.

"So what do you think?" she finally asked.

"I . . ." Bill was about to get into it, but then changed track. He walked over to close the door behind Kate and then pointed at the chair, saying to her in a terse tone, "Sit down."

Not going as planned, thought Kate. She sat down, her hands firmly clasping the notebook on her lap. She was wearing her hair down today, so Bill couldn't see that the edge of her ears were turning red, bracing for what was sure to be a reprimand.

"Did it ever occur to you for a god-damned second to clear your little Havana expedition with your boss? What the hell were you thinking? What if you'd been caught? I told you I didn't want to hear about your trip in *The Washington Post,* didn't I?" Bill was in no mood for explanations and wasn't letting Kate get a word in until he was finished. "I should fire you for this crazy move, you know?"

"Just let me explain, Bill—"

He cut her off. "What kind of lame explanation can you give me to justify the risk of creating a major international incident? Were you looking for some ex-President to go and bail you out— was that your Plan B? Jeez!" Bill shook his head in disbelief.

"But *you* told me to follow the money trail—and that's exactly what I did."

"Yeah but . . . but, I didn't mean for you to go and have a *mojito* with Castro!"

"You didn't tell me *not* to. . . ." Kate continued holding her notebook firmly. "As far as the DIA is concerned, I traveled there on personal business, using my Venezuelan passport. And you know I couldn't even call you from Caracas. Besides, my trip to Havana is taking us to a whole new level on this. . . ."

"You're not seriously telling me that those cats are a credible part of this whole thing? I should write you up for friggin' bad intelligence, if nothing else." Bill's voice went up a couple of notches again.

"I know, I know, Bill. I need to get more evidence on that. But hear me out. If I hadn't gone, we'd be left with just that Ceuta angle on this, and now I'm convinced that *your* instinct was right. Chávez is up to something here, just not sure what that is yet."

"Cats, Kate?" he asked skeptically, not taking the bait of her backhanded compliment.

"I know it sounds crazy. But it's crazy enough to turn out to be a real lead. I just need to get some more evidence, and my friend is trying to get hold of Mirella, the research doctor. She can be the key to this whole thing."

"Okay, Kate, I don't want to hear any more. Here's the deal. First off, you were wrong to go off on your own to Havana, risking an international incident. That's just too big for me to ignore. I have no choice but to cite you for that infraction, and you know what that means. . . ."

"Not the Intelligence Review Panel again, Bill." This wouldn't be her first time. In her first year on the job, she had carelessly left her notebook in the ladies' room after a meeting at CIA headquarters, something one just doesn't do when handling intelligence. Fortunately, the review panel found that the notebook only held nonclassified information, so she didn't end up with a black mark on her record. And then there was the time she forgot to properly classify her garbage. Those two security infractions were nothing compared to Havana. The guys at CIA would have a field day with that one.

"You know the rules, Kate. They're going to judge whether or not you created an intelligence breach. And before you complain, my hands are tied on this. It's rules and protocols. There's no way that you can explain an unauthorized trip to Cuba. Fortunately, you got in and out without drawing attention, and that may be your only saving grace in this. But on something as serious as this, their decision could go as far as booting you out of intelligence."

Kate let out a large breath of air as she fell back into the chair, facing the prospect of the end of her intelligence career. This was definitely not going according to plan.

"And that cat story, forget it. Because you have no evidence, it's just gonna weaken your case with the review panel."

Kate opened her mouth to speak, but Bill cut in before she could say anything. "Listen, Kate, I believe in you; I always have. If not, I wouldn't have hired you. But in this case, I'm way disappointed in how you handled this whole thing. You let your hunger for intelligence get ahead of your brain. And that's why you're in this hole. I'll still fight for you, but I just don't know if that's gonna be enough. Suggest you keep your head low for the moment. File your report—without the cats—and stand by for further instructions from me."

"¡MIERDA!" KATE MUTTERED UNDER HER BREATH, staring at her report on screen. Not a single cat mentioned, just like Bill wanted. She was angry at herself for not thinking through her Havana trip beforehand, but was even angrier at Bill for not recognizing how she helped move the investigation forward by going there.

Kate was convinced there was something to Inge's story, but she needed the good Doctor Mirella to quickly surface a credible lead. She bit her bottom lip, realizing this wasn't only about the Madrid investigation anymore. Now, she needed some breakthrough to save her own skin in front of the Intelligence Review Panel.

Just then, an appointment reminder popped up on her screen. She had an hour to get to the working interagency lunch at CIA headquarters in Langley. Hopefully there was no traffic. Nothing worse than stumbling in late to a lunch with her collegial competitors at the CIA, particularly now that some of them might be called to sit on her review panel.

She locked down her desktop, made sure there weren't any stray pieces of paper with notes anywhere. She found one. Dumped it into the classified garbage. It was Friday and after the working lunch and the long week, she didn't plan on coming back to Bolling AFB. She'd promised her father to catch the 4:40 P.M. US Airways flight from Reagan National to Westchester County Airport in New York. He had told her to bring something nice to wear; they would be heading straight to dinner on her arrival. Given the day she was having, dinner with her father might be the only medicine.

She was almost outside her cubicle, but she stopped to look back one last time, just in case there was a stray piece of classified paper she'd missed. Then she spotted them—those *Financial Times*. She stuffed them in her bag to read later on her flight and rushed out.

DESPITE ALL HER PLANS TO CATCH up on her *Financial Times,* Kate fell asleep as soon as they hit cruising altitude. It certainly had been a long week. Since she never managed to get through even the first section of the day's *FT,* Kate missed the following item that appeared on the front page of the second section of the paper.

Milestones Fund Hits Record
By Robert Handels in New York

December 18 2009 23:04

The appeal of alternative structures to global investors was highlighted on Thursday when Milestones Capital Partners, the European-based private equity group, raised a record $25 bn fund for deals conforming to the principles of Islamic finance.

The new fund, Milestones' first tranche, sold strongly in Middle East investor markets.

While the flow of private equity money from that part of the world is smaller than other markets such as Europe, it has been growing strongly, and with the advent of this new "milestone," is expected to open up to more volumes.

Clifford Cheswick, a senior managing director at Merrill Lynch, who acted as advisor in the launch of the fund, and who is in charge of its Middle Eastern business, said: "There continues to be strong demand from Middle Eastern institutional and high-net clients for investment vehicles focused on the U.S. corporate market. The Milestones Fund's unique *Shari'ah*-compliant structure has opened a new highway for that capital to flow. As an indication of the capital interest, we launched at $20 billion and closed at $25 billion in less than a week. There is more where that came from and our firm expects to be on the forefront of such activities."

The new fund's manager, Nebibi Hasehm, originally from Milan, was not available at press time for comment. Market sources advise that the fund will focus on special situations in the U.S. market and that many deals are being discussed.

12

⏤✦✦✦⏤

THE TRAFFIC WAS HEAVY HEADING north out of Manhattan at 5:30 P.M. This wasn't a problem since the stretch silver Mercedes was packed with every possible amenity save a bed, though for one of the passengers, Margaux "the Cougar" Bretz of White Weld & Company, that would certainly have been a welcome addition. She had made damn sure that she was the one designated to escort Nebibi to tonight's special event and she had taken great care to coordinate things.

Tonight, Margaux had dressed in her favorite hunting attire: the latest St. John's Couture black cocktail suit paired with silver Manolo Blahnik heels. The signature zipper of her jacket revealed a very low-cut knit dress. It's what she liked about St. John's. She could be ready for any kind of celebration. *Zipper up. Zipper down.*

Following the successful closing of The Milestones Fund earlier in the week, the Chairman had called his other favorite client, Sam Coldsmith, who managed one of the most successful funds in the country, Royal Lane Advisors. Once a year, Sam opened up his palatial Greenwich estate to industry notables for his annual holiday gala.

An invite to Sam's estate was highly coveted on the Street because of his consistent success despite the volatility of the past few years. Actually, he had thrived on that very volatility and chiseled his way up to number 302 on the *Forbes* global billionaires list. That, coupled with Sam's reclusiveness with the press, made his annual gathering the place to be. Besides, after the last couple of years of tenuous recovery, the market was ready to party.

Always on the lookout for making the right kind of news, the Chairman told Sam he wanted to introduce him to his latest successful client, Nebibi, and snagged him an invitation for the reception this evening. On top of which, in between the eggnog and hors d'oeuvres, there would be many deals to be set in motion for the first week of the New Year, hopefully with White Weld as the chosen advisor.

News had already spread among those invited that Nebibi would be there. So, both out of curiosity and thinking they might be able to skin some of that newfound bounty of cheap Middle East money for their own firm's deals, many were making the trek up to Greenwich.

After their meeting earlier in the week, Margaux had confirmed that Nebibi was neither currently nor ever married to one or more wives. She pictured quite a nice little future with him. In subsequent meetings that week, Margaux's knees trembled whenever she was close to him; all the more when he took his jacket off to reveal that physique through those Italian-cut shirts. And first and foremost, there were all those millions he was set to make. He was the total package in Margaux's book. No surprise then that she was quick to volunteer, in the interest of White Weld, of course, to accompany Nebibi to this evening's reception.

The only thing she wasn't too sure about was his religious zeal. A religious scholar she wasn't, but it seemed to her that Islam would frown on what she wanted to do with, or rather to, Nebibi in that car ride up to Greenwich today. The more traffic, the better as far as she was concerned; he looked liked he had stamina to spare. In her mind, they were a match made in heaven, or wherever it was that his religion told him nirvana existed.

What she didn't know about Nebibi is that he had long ago crossed the line of what his religion required with respect to the opposite sex. Beginning with a long affair in graduate school, he had seen every detail of a woman's body, which, for a true Muslim, should have been hidden from him under a chador until marriage.

Nebibi had an appetite for the company of women, and long ago figured out that they found him attractive. However, all that was secondary to a disciplined focus on his mission.

Margaux stared out the window, gauging how much time they

had before their destination. They passed under the George Washington Bridge and, assuming no traffic, they'd be at the Coldsmith Estate in fifty minutes, more or less.

She worked out in her mind how much her bonus should be this year. Based on the number of deals she'd brought to the firm, she expected a minimum of $10 million. And now that they were no longer subject to the government's salary restrictions, she'd get it.

As her eyes traveled the line of the frigid Hudson River, her mind wandered beyond thoughts of deals and bonuses and started playing out another scene of what she'd like to be doing right now in this limo.

She'd start by pressing the button to close the partition with the driver and then inch herself closer to Nebibi. Very slowly, she would lower that zipper on her jacket, all the while looking at him, her Chanel-lacquered lips open just enough to see a flash of white with the edge of a smile in one corner.

She'd then put on a no-holds-barred performance for Nebibi, pulling her dress down below her shoulders and then opening the front snap of the 40D-cup black lace bra to reveal her pink nipples. His large manicured hands would reach out and touch her breasts, their softness telling him they're real. The touch of his fingers massaging her nipples would bring them to life. Soon they'd be the size of two fat Tic-Tacs standing on end.

Margaux's head rocked back and her mouth opened wider, letting out a soft moan, "Ahhh . . ."

"Are you alright?" Nebibi asked, wondering if she'd fainted.

"Huh? Oh . . . no. Yes, I'm fine." Margaux immediately looked down, relieved to see that her jacket zipper was still closed. She tried to put on the airs of a composed financial executive, which she usually was, though her flushed cheeks were evidence of a very intense daydreaming session. Concentrate on winning the business, and those bonuses, first, she reminded herself. Then, and only then, comes carnal satisfaction.

KATE RUSHED OUT OF THE TERMINAL and spotted her father's old black Jaguar. "Dad!" Tomás Molares had bought the car at the insistence of his wife, and he would never think of replacing it, no matter how many times he had to take it to his mechanic.

"Kate." Her father got out to greet her with a warm hug. His daughter had always been precious to him, but ever since his wife's death, she was all the more so.

Tomás beamed at the sight of his daughter. She was wearing simple winter white: straight wool slacks with a loose cashmere turtleneck cinched with an ostrich leather belt that had been a gift from her mother. Her jewelry was equally understated: yellow citrine earrings from Brazil and an 18K gold pre-Columbian pendant hanging from a simple chain. For additional warmth, she wore a cream cashmere wrap. She had let her hair fall down freely. For Kate, style was effortless and never found in the mall or mail-order catalogs.

"That's a beautiful pendant. I guess you did have free time on your trip to Caracas after all." He recognized it as the artisanship of Galeria Cano of Colombia, and knew they had a boutique in Caracas. They took gold artifacts from pre-Columbian indigenous lost civilizations and painstakingly reproduced them using the same ancient methods.

"Actually, if you can believe it, it's a gift from a previous admirer, long gone."

"Did I know this mysterious admirer?" Tomás's interest spiked.

"It was soon after Mom died, so no, you didn't get to meet him. We took a trip to Venezuela together about six years ago." This had been a difficult time for Tomás; he was not much in the mood for anything, let alone meeting suitors of his only child. She, on the other hand, had been searching for ways to move beyond the grief, and the affair kept her from falling apart. Though the relationship didn't last, she kept the pendant and held on to the happy memory of that time.

"Okay, then, let's see if we can find you a handful of acceptable *new* admirers this evening." Her father was in a mood to celebrate. It made her happy to see him smiling. Working with Sam Coldsmith must be agreeing with him, she thought.

They both got in the car, and Kate asked, "Did you make reservations somewhere?"

"No, we're going to my boss's house for drinks and dinner."

"This isn't that same party you've been trying to get me to go to, is it?"

"Yes, it is. Just do this for your father. You never know, maybe you'll meet the love of your life there. On second thought—not sure I really want that."

"I sincerely doubt that will happen," Kate reassured her father, picturing those bright suspenders from her Wall Street days. The truth was, a party might just be what she needed to take her mind away from those cats and the review panel, at least for one evening.

IT WAS 6:45 P.M. by the time the silver limo finally turned off at the Lake Avenue exit. Both passengers noticed that they were now off the highway and into more leafy terrain. Half a mile down the road, the car made another right, onto Royal Lane, and there came upon the jewel of backcountry Greenwich real estate—in fact, of the entire area within a hundred-mile radius of Midtown Manhattan.

Over a two-year period, Sam Coldsmith had accumulated adjoining properties, one by one, through various anonymous trusts, and before anybody had wised up, Sam had amassed a mini-principality of one hundred acres of prime Greenwich real estate, in the same stealth moves that would normally lead to a hostile take-over. He purchased smaller individual lots at a slight discount as other, less astute buyers didn't realize that there was only one buyer behind all those disparate purchases. The local zoning commission looked the other way; actually more likely, it stood in awe of Sam's endowment of the town's new cancer research hospital, which rivaled Sloan-Kettering. The town finally balked when he wanted to build an airstrip on the property; so Sam was forced to park his two Boeing aircraft at Westchester Airport like all the other poorer slobs.

He knocked down all the structures on his hundred acres, taking the land back to its pristine state. In the center, he built a forty thousand-square-foot mansion, with every imaginable amenity. Sam had also added his very own eighteen-hole golf course, designed by Tiger Woods.

If that wasn't enough, he had built an aquarium, rivaling the one at Monterey Bay, with a main viewing window fifty feet wide and twenty feet high, and filled with a million gallons of seawater. Sam's favorite fish, sharks, were the predominant species in the tank. Part of the show this evening would include the ritual feeding of the sharks. Given the Wall Street crowd that would be munching on canapés on the other side of the twelve-inch-thick Plexiglas, it was anyone's guess about which shark-feeding show would provide the most entertainment this evening.

Inside the limo, Margaux was freshening her lipstick and checking that every hair was in place, as usual. She looked over at Nebibi and smiled, making a mental plan of playing out that daydream in reality on some future limo ride.

Business first, though, she remembered. She would be sure to tell her chairman how excited she was to enter this next phase of fostering a close, very close, working relationship with this client. And she also hoped the chairman would understand that she wouldn't be as available for those private limo rides with *him* going forward.

"So, Nebibi, may I call you that?"

"Of course."

"You'll find this a worthwhile event. Many people will want to meet you this evening, but I'll try to limit your time to those who matter most—those who can help bring deals to you to jump-start Milestones' deal pipeline."

"Feel free to direct these introductions. I'm not intending on staying here long. I don't need a new circle of friends, just deals."

Margaux's mind kept ticking, making future plans, realizing the man she was lusting after was, like her, all business. She thought, We can go far, you and me, Nebibi.

The door on Nebibi's side opened. He stepped out and then extended his hand to help Margaux out of the limo. She took hold of his hand and emerged one leg at a time in a wide, revealing stance, making sure to give him a show, as the hemline of her St. John's Couture inched way up her thigh.

Before them was the grand entrance to, for lack of any more exact description, a replica of the White House. It was so exact a copy that it seemed Sam had simply written a big ole check to the Federal government and the Presidential mansion had been loaded on a trailer at 1600 Pennsylvania Avenue and plopped down here in the middle of backcountry Greenwich. The only difference, of course, is that *this* White House had far greater acreage than that of the President.

A retinue of butlers in formal white ties stood ready on a long red carpet to welcome the arriving guests. The majority of these hundred guests were being led down the path that would take them to the shark tank for the first part of the evening. Upon identifying themselves, Nebibi and Margaux were instead led inside to the main ballroom and from there, outside to the south portico, where a smaller number had gathered ahead of the larger masses that would follow after the shark feeding. The outdoor heating lamps were on at full force, turning the December air to the level of a comfortable fall day.

The Chairman of White Weld & Co. was there, as well as the CEOs of the top five Fortune 500 companies, the Mayor of New York City, and a retired former governor of the New York Fed. Everyone was hoping that the coming year would finally put some distance between the market debacle and a sustained economic recovery.

Holding court at the center of the group was a very lively Sam Coldsmith. He was a large man, six feet two inches, and judging by his girth, he was a fellow who did not refuse seconds at the dinner table. In fact, he enjoyed life. Why shouldn't he? He had built a financial empire from scratch and now, at fifty-nine, was ready to enjoy the fruits of that lifelong labor.

"Ah, Nebibi." It was the White Weld chairman, their top shark. "Allow me to introduce you to some of our friends. Gentlemen, this is Nebibi Hasehm, who'll be teaching us all about how business in the Middle East is truly done." The White Weld shark gave a slight knowing nod to Margaux, and felt the Viagra pill in his breast pocket. He was looking forward to having her ride back to the city with him. The other men had been watching with interest the development of The Milestones Fund, and were now very interested in meeting this financial innovator, Nebibi, who had made them all take a closer look at the growing Islamic finance market.

"Welcome, Nebibi." Holding his Davidoff cigar in one hand, Sam Coldsmith stretched out his other one to Nebibi.

"Thank you for the invitation to your magnificent home." Nebibi knew he needed to get close to Coldsmith; he held a smorgasbord of corporate acquisition deals in his hands, and this Panther was ready to eat. "Allow me to introduce Ms. Bretz."

"Oh yes, of course, we know Margaux. Good to see you again."

Margaux looked around, measuring up this small exclusive gathering. She was the only woman in the bunch, which pleased her enormously. She needed to get Nebibi alone in conversation with Sam so they could cut that first deal. She had heard that he was working on something big and Milestones needed to muscle in on that.

What Margaux could not see was that another female was entering her territory at the far end of the ballroom. A butler was leading Tomás Molares and his visiting daughter to the same portico. As they neared the door to the portico, Margaux's ears perked up at the sound of heels clattering on the marble floor of the ballroom. There were certain sounds that Margaux's ears were particularly attuned to, predator heels being an important one. She looked behind her to see if her exclusive zone of influence was about to be broken. No matter, she'd fought off wives, girlfriends, and even mothers before in her mating pursuits. Bring 'em on, she thought.

Sam Coldsmith saw that his trusted advisor, Tomás, was approaching. "Excuse me for a second." He left Nebibi, still flanked by Margaux in her Praetorian Guard stance, along with the former governor of the New York Fed.

"Tomás, good you could make it. And I presume this is your lovely daughter. He does nothing but brag about you around the office, and finally, after three years, I get the pleasure of meeting you." He kissed her on both cheeks. He reminded Kate of the doting uncle she'd never had.

"The pleasure is all mine, Mr. Coldsmith. Sorry we're late. I couldn't get an earlier flight from D.C. this afternoon."

"Tomás, old man, you should have told me. We always have a spare plane. We could have sent it down to D.C. to pick her up. And Kate, call me Sam, everybody does." Okay, make that the doting, charming, and very, very rich uncle she never had. "Now, let's introduce you around here. Tomás tells me you work at Defense, keeping the world safe for people like us. That's exactly what I like to hear young people doing."

Sam led them back to the small group around Nebibi and began introductions. "This is my chief international strategist, Tomás Molares. He was a bigwig at the U.N. when we convinced him to come over to the dark side of finance. After three years with us, I can promise you that his talents were being wasted at U.N. Plaza. And this is his lovely daughter, Kate, who's keeping the world safe for the likes of those sharks standing next to the tank outside."

Nebibi's head turned in the direction of Tomás, but his eyes were firmly locked on Kate. Nebibi shook Tomás's hand and then extended it to Kate. "It's good to see you again, Kate." His voice had a softness that had not been present for six years.

Kate touched his hand. She felt a tingle run up her arm and wondered, Is he as surprised as I am?

Margaux the Cougar caught the focus of his eyes, and she was not pleased with the sight of this young creature. "Do you know each other?" she asked.

Kate let go of Nebibi's hand, noticing that she had held on longer than a simple handshake called for. "Yes, we do. We met in graduate school." Kate was going to be tight-lipped about anything else in this crowd of strangers.

Kate studied Nebibi's face for clues of how he was feeling about their chance meeting. His lips were pursed slightly, accentuating his defined cheekbones, and his eyes, a piercing brown, still had that slight Asiatic quality to them. His left eyebrow arched slightly, divulging his curiosity. A few strands of his straight black hair had fallen on his upper forehead. All in all, attractive as ever, thought Kate, but he's playing our past together as tight-lipped as I am.

Meanwhile, this development was making Margaux uncharacteristically fidgety. She smelled something more than study partners here.

"Kate, I don't remember you telling me that you knew Nebibi," Tomás said with a fatherly tone.

"I didn't know that we would be running into him here tonight. I mean, how long has it been, Nebibi, since we last saw each other?" She knew perfectly well how long it had been, almost to the day. Here was the man who had broken her heart, and no one had been good enough for her since. So she asked this question to see if their relationship had meant anything to him.

"Six years, as of last month," he responded with a slight smile. He was staring at her pendant.

Kate bit her bottom lip, thinking—Okay, so it did mean something to him, so why'd he disappear on me?

Margaux noticed that Nebibi looked at Kate's pendant, and thought it might be a good diversion from going down memory lane. "Darling, that's a beautiful pendant. Where did you find it? Bendel's?"

Kate looked down, embarrassed. Of all nights to wear this, she thought. "It was a gift. Actually, you would have a hard time finding it here. It's a limited reproduction of an original from the—"

"—Gold Museum in Bogotá. I believe the original dates back a thousand years to the pre-Columbian culture of the Zenú people on the Colombian coast. Right, Kate?" Nebibi was showing more than he intended, but he had been struck that Kate still had this memento he'd purchased for her during their last day in Caracas.

"That's right, Nebibi." Her heart was pumping a bit faster, but her brain was telling her to slow down. Remember, he vanished before, he can vanish again.

"And what are those animals on there, cats?" Margaux was grasping at straws to stay in the middle of this little repartee.

"No. Actually, they're two jaguars facing each other but separated by a shaman, the religious leader of the Zenú." Kate looked at Nebibi as she answered.

"So that's like a lion, then?" Margaux was not letting go.

For Kate, this woman now held the record for the number of stupid questions that one could possibly ask about a pendant. Kate was definitely tiring of her, and wondered, Who's she here with anyway?

"No. It's the Latin panther." Nebibi took up the charge on Margaux's question, and she, having succeeded in getting back his attention, stopped asking any more. Lost to all others in the conversation, Kate knew the meaning of Nebibi's name, as he had explained it to her the day they came across the jaguar pendant in Caracas.

Tomás was zeroing in on Nebibi, the "mysterious admirer" who now stood right before his very eyes. Tomás could tell there was more to this story, but present company didn't allow for those types of questions. He would have time later to ask his daughter more about this Nebibi. Tomás chuckled to himself about his comments earlier in the evening—here he was, joking that she just might meet the love of her life tonight. He just didn't think it would be in the first five minutes.

Sam finally took charge of the conversation. "So, Nebibi, you're telling me that you and this young lady were study pals? Well, now isn't the world just a damn small place? That just makes you practically family, so we're just going to have to do some deals together."

Sam was no slouch. He knew Nebibi's Middle East sources could boost the leverage components of his deals, and help keep him making those impressive returns for himself and his investors. He placed his hand on Nebibi's shoulder and led him to a quieter corner of the portico, where the shark and the panther could circle each other.

As they walked away, Nebibi asked, "So where did you say Kate worked? . . ." Not far behind them trailed Margaux, just then feeling a most unwelcome icy chill, a winter evening breeze that caught the edge of her St. John's dress and rode up between her legs.

In the distance, one could hear the roar of the other guests outside the shark tank. The ritual feeding had begun.

13

⊰+◆+⊱

I T WAS 8 A.M., AND KATE sat at the kitchen counter in her thick bath-robe and warm fuzzy slippers watching her father make their morning coffee. They were in the rambling house Kate's parents had bought on the cheap twenty years ago in Old Greenwich. Over the years, they had made some improvements, but the house was modest compared to the McMansions around them.

In the winter, the house never seemed to get warm until noon, except in the kitchen, where the morning sun shining through the large windows gave the temperature an extra boost. The walls also added to the feeling of warmth, painted in a light shade of yellow that matched the outer edges of a sunflower. The house was like her father's Jaguar: not the most up-to-date model, temperamental and slow to get up and going. But for Kate, the house's charm was far greater; happy memories wrapped around her like a comfy bathrobe.

"We didn't get much time to talk last night. How was your trip?" Tomás Molares asked in general terms, knowing that his daughter's line of work didn't allow for much detail to be disclosed.

"It was fine." Kate wanted to talk to her father about the mess she was dealing with at work, but knew she couldn't go there.

"I did see Abuelo, though. He looked frail, until I suggested he move here. Then all his pent-up feistiness came out."

"Believe me, Kate, I've tried. I do worry about him. He blocks out the reality of the situation around him, but at his age, he deserves whatever happiness he can get. Being there with his land is what keeps him happy. So we just need to accept that." Kate could see from his face that her father had not easily arrived at this decision, but was resigned to it.

Tomás opened a new bag of Peet's Major Dickason's Blend from San Francisco, Kate's favorite, and poured the roasted beans into the grinder.

"So, did you have a nice time last night?" Tomás started another line of questioning quite innocently, though he was hoping to reel in some details about his daughter's connection to Nebibi.

"Actually, I did." She knew her father was fishing for more.

He waited till he had finished grinding the beans so he wouldn't have to shout over the noise. "So I guess I finally had the pleasure of meeting your mysterious admirer? Hey, can you grab some milk out of the fridge?"

"Yep," Kate replied, her green eyes taking on a distant look.

"Great, thanks."

"No, I mean yes, you finally did meet the mysterious admirer. It was Nebibi. And yes, I'm getting the milk."

Tomás knew that the soft, disinterested approach always worked with Kate. "He seemed like an interesting fellow and I'd say pretty accomplished on top of it. I haven't seen Sam work so hard to ingratiate himself with anyone before. Your friend must have a fairly compelling business going there. . . ."

Kate remembered their brief, intense exchange at the outset of the evening. And then just before she was leaving, Nebibi tried to engage her in a conversation, but she quickly excused herself, saying she needed to head home. Kate wasn't ready to have a tête-à-tête with him last night, certainly not in such a public setting. Now she was second-guessing herself, wondering if she'd been too quick to make her exit. What must he be thinking? she asked herself.

"Yep, sounds like he's doing okay for himself. Though I didn't get to talk to him much. That woman from White Weld kept interrupting, introducing him to everybody in the room. What was she, his bodyguard?" Kate asked.

"As I understand it, his firm just closed the largest Islamic finance fund ever raised. That's quite an accomplishment, bringing such a traditional form of Middle East financing to U.S. markets.

It's why Sam was so taken with him. Sam was really interested, which means this is something pretty big."

"Sounds impressive, but I just know him as Nebibi, the graduate student with a passion to argue about global politics."

"Is that the only thing he had a passion for in graduate school?" Tomás asked with a grin.

Kate blushed. Not the kind of discussion she wanted to get into with her father. She took a long sip of coffee to avoid answering, but then the ringing phone interrupted that train of thought. She looked at her father, who seemed perplexed to be getting a call at this hour.

"Hello?"

"Hello, Mr. Molares. This is Nebibi Hasehm. We met last night at Sam Coldsmith's house."

"Oh, yes. Hello, Mr. Hasehm. How are you?" Tomás then covered the receiver and mouthed over to his daughter, "Do you want to talk to him?"

Nebibi kept talking. "I hope you don't mind me calling at this hour on Saturday morning, but Sam Coldsmith was kind enough to pass me your number. I was hoping to catch Kate there."

Kate nodded "yes" to her father.

"No, she's still here. We were having some coffee. Let me get her on the line. By the way, I hope I'll be seeing you at our offices in the near future. I'm looking forward to hearing about your fund." In truth, Tomás was just as interested in sizing up this Nebibi and gauging his intentions toward his daughter.

"Thank you, Mr. Molares. I look forward to that."

"Hello?" Kate spoke into the receiver as she walked to the living room with her coffee mug and settled into an old sofa. One entire wall of the room was floor-to-ceiling bookshelves packed with everything from Aristotle to Howard Fast novels to Jacques Pépin cookbooks. On the other side were windows looking on to the blue spruces in the backyard.

"Hello, Kate. Hope I haven't called too early."

"No, not at all."

"I guess I was the last person you expected to see last night."

"It certainly was a surprise." But now Kate was even more surprised that he had tracked her down.

"I was looking forward to catching up last night, but we didn't get much time to talk because of all the interruptions. . . ."

"Yeah, who was that, anyways?" Kate was referring to the intrusive Margaux.

"Oh, Margaux, you mean? She's part of the White Weld gang they have trailing me. She was going to make a deal happen last night if it killed her."

"And did she? I mean make a deal happen?" And is she still alive? she wanted to ask him, as sarcastically as she could muster, but didn't.

"She did. Actually, one of the introductions last night resulted in us getting in on a deal."

"Not to worry. It was a business event and I was there as my father's official escort, so I had to do my share of 'meet and greet' with his business associates as well."

"Kate, when we quickly spoke last night, you brought up a very good question. I thought we should talk about it in person, if that's alright with you. Can we meet for lunch today in the city?"

Kate pondered his question for a second: In the city? Let's see. He disappeared last time around. Make him work for this, if he's really interested. "That's too bad. I can't make it into the city today, because I promised to have an early dinner with my father in Greenwich."

"Oh, that is too bad."

She didn't want to completely close the door on him, so she met him halfway, trying to see if he would take the bait. "How about we meet in Greenwich instead?"

Nebibi wanted to see her again, and there was no hesitation in his response. "That'll work. Where?"

He's interested, she thought. "I'll make a reservation for noon at a restaurant called Méli-Mélo. It's in downtown Greenwich. You can take the train from Grand Central."

"Okay."

"See you at noon. Bye," replied Kate, pondering what she was embarking on. She decided that the best approach was to expect nothing. Just two old friends having a meal. Her career was front burner now.

"I'm meeting him for lunch at Méli-Mélo."

"Pretty fancy, Kate. Trying to impress your friend?"

"It's just lunch with an old friend. No expectations. No pressure. Can you drive me there earlier, like at ten? That way I can get some laps in at the Y before lunch. Haven't had much time for exercise this week."

"Sure. After I drop you off, I'll head over to my office and catch up on some e-mails. Just walk over to the office after lunch. I'll wait for you there." Tomás's office was right in central Greenwich, in fact, right across from the commuter train station. Sam Coldsmith had gotten a good deal on the lease from the previous tenant, Long-Term Capital Management, after its prized financial modeling engines had been clogged by a vicious little bug called Russia.

FRESHLY SHOWERED AND EXHILARATED by her swim, Kate walked into the restaurant a few minutes ahead of schedule. She knew exactly where she wanted to sit today. "Is the table by the window available?"

"It's your lucky day, mademoiselle. Everyone's still in their Christmas shopping 'zone.' So you're going to have a peaceful lunch." Kate's chosen table was nestled next to the large window overlooking the bustling holiday scene outside. She sat and ordered a glass of dry sauvignon blanc. Soft snow had started falling, and as usual, no matter the season, cars were vying for limited parking spaces.

Kate saw a limo pull up in front of the restaurant and wondered if, maybe, it was one of the local celebrities. She'd heard that Diana Ross used her driver when she shopped on the Avenue. She leaned over to make sure she got a good view of whoever emerged from the limo. The door opened and she saw a man's figure dressed in a black sheepskin coat. The man turned in the direction of the restaurant's door, and in that second she knew this was no local celebrity but rather her lunch date.

A minute later, Nebibi stood next to the table. "Hello, Kate."

She extended her hand to him. He took it, but instead of shaking it, embraced it with both his hands. Kisses on both cheeks, like old friends, would have felt strange for both of them because at another time it would have led to greater intimacy. Therefore, somehow the handshake was a more comfortable acknowledgment of their past history.

"Hi. Any problems in finding the place?"

"No, not at all."

They sat down, but there was a bit of awkwardness on both their parts. Both were wondering where to begin. Many years had passed, and a cloud of unfinished business hovered over them.

Nebibi took a first stab at conversation. "You're looking very well." She still had that infectious open smile he remembered, and when he touched her it had felt like the last time, six years ago. He would certainly be leading a different life today if he had stayed with her. No loneliness, but no Panther either.

"Thanks, so do you. And from the fawning I saw by White Weld, you seem to be doing quite well in business, too." She stared more closely now at his face. It looked more chiseled, like he'd been through a lot and was trying to put on serious airs for the rest of the world. His eyes looked the same to her, that same hint of sadness almost seeking to be rescued. Kate had to remind herself that it wasn't her job to save him.

"Money talks, and since they see a lot of fees coming because of me, I'm their new favorite son." Nebibi's posture was softer than usual.

Nebibi saw her move her hand to play with her ponytail. It was a nervous habit she'd always had. It was charming before and it was having the same effect now.

Kate buttered her bread. "So what happened to that fiery guy I knew in graduate school who thought the world was being sucked dry of its dreams and aspirations by the capitalists of Wall Street? Now you seem to be right in the middle of them; actually, you're one of them." Kate remembered their many political discussions, which always left her feeling like she, because of her American passport, was to blame for everything that was wrong with the world. But now she didn't ask the question in anger. Given her present job, she now knew that the bad guys were everywhere. Every side had its good guys and bad guys. Nothing, and maybe no one, was purely black or white, good or evil.

"You're remembering our intense political arguments from school. Yes, to an extent, you're right. I've probably become one of them. Difference is—and it's a big one, mind you—who or what I am making profits for. My hope, my plan, is to funnel our profits back to support Islamic causes. From there, it's up to them to build their own dreams."

Kate took in his words. Their dreams, not his. That sounded like an odd way of putting it to her. His outlook seemed more mature, not as fiery, though there was still some of that there. But definitely more sure of where he was headed.

"So what about you, Kate? Where did life take you after school?" Nebibi was walking a tightrope between his public and private personas; between the overt Nebibi and the clandestine Panther.

"After school, I hunted around for a job. And I needed to get my mind focused on different things."

She had wanted to say, *get my mind off of you,* but she held back. Her eyes strayed to the snowy scene outside the window for a moment. Larger flakes were falling now. "Looks like it's coming down stronger. I hope you won't have problems getting back to Manhattan. . . ."

"I'm sure it'll be fine . . . ," he said.

"Anyways. The guys at Bear Stearns took a chance on me and I jumped into the fray of Wall Street, without really thinking it through."

"Which part of the firm did you work in?"

"I was in sales for the derivatives desk, calling corporate treasurers and convincing them to buy structured protection plays. . . ."

"Really? . . ."

"Why? Is your fund heavy on derivatives?"

"Not at all. It's hard to fit derivatives into the requirements of *Shari'ah* law. They definitely cross into the arena of financial gambling. Even your Greenspan knows that now."

"So you're not a gambler?" Kate asked.

"Not on financial matters, and I bet a lot of people now wish they had been more prudent in their bets. That whole market of derivatives grew a lot faster than people's understanding of them, including regulators. Problem is, there are still chinks in that system, no matter how much people want to think otherwise."

The waiter interrupted, refilling their water glasses and asking, "Have you decided what you would like today?"

They looked at each other. They hadn't even opened their menus. Kate responded, "Can you give us a few more minutes?

"After Bear fell, I started looking at things back in D.C. and ended up at the Defense Department. Nothing too exciting. I cover political and economic goings-on in Latin America and I brief some of the ambassadors. Wish it were sexier than that. Most people think that this is the world of James Bond and Jason Bourne, but the truth is that those are just good movie plots. Real life is a lot more boring than that." She had practiced and used this speech often. Her top secret security clearance required her to be as circumspect as possible about the more interesting parts of her office duties.

"I guess we're both in the same mundane boat, then. I just source capital from the Middle East to invest in productive sectors of the U.S. with the hopes of making a respectable profit for those investors. Pretty straightforward stuff." Nebibi wondered if he should believe that she was just a lowly pencil pusher at DIA.

Without admitting to it, they were each setting the groundwork for any possible future engagement: You don't ask details about what I do, and I won't ask details about what you do.

A beeping sound. They both reached for their respective iPhones. "It's mine." Kate looked at her screen and saw that it was "caller unknown." She decided to answer it. "Hello."

"Kate? It's me, Inge. Did I catch you at an okay time?" Kate now knew that it *was* important. Good thing she'd taken the call.

Kate looked at Nebibi and said, "Sorry, this will just take a minute. It's a friend from overseas." Nebibi gave a good-natured shrug and turned to stare outside at the snow.

Kate turned her full attention to Inge on the line. "Hi. How goes it? I am just about to sit down for lunch with an old friend from INSEAD."

"Is that *the* friend from INSEAD? That's a surprise. And there we were, just talking about him last week and now a flash from the past in the flesh. Oh gosh. You're not lying there in the flesh with him right now, are you? That would be an awful time for me to be calling." It was comforting for Kate to know that they could revert to their eighteen-year-old personas when life called for it.

"No, no. Oh no, not at all. I'm in Greenwich, visiting my father." Kate's cheeks flushed a little remembering the last time they did lie together in the flesh.

"Oh, okay. So you're in Greenwich. Perfect. I need to see you as soon as possible. My friend came by to see me yesterday and had a gift she wanted me to give you. It's special, so I need to do it in person. Can you meet me in New York on Monday for lunch at our usual spot? I have to be there for a conference all next week. This couldn't have worked out better from my end."

"Sure, I can do that. See you there at noon." She purposely didn't mention places or day, given her company across the table. If lunch didn't go well today, no need to have him know that she would still be in town on Monday.

"Great. See you then."

The entire call took less than two minutes, but in their short-hand, a lot of information was passed. Including the news that Mirella had appeared and that Inge had some important news update for Kate. Now, she refocused on her lunch partner. "Sorry about that. It was a friend who's coming to the States. So where were we?" Kate kept her explanation short, wanting to get the conversation back on track, but then was interrupted by the waiter, who had re-appeared.

"May I take your order?" the waiter asked them. Kate and Nebibi looked at each other, thinking the same thing. Even without Margaux, one interruption after another today.

After ordering, Nebibi interjected quickly, "I think we need to take advantage of this momentary lull in interruptions. So what do you say we deal with issues straight on and take it from there. For old times' sake, Kate?"

"Okay. Head-on is probably best in this case. So here's the deal as I remember it: We met. You asked me out, which I had wanted. We went on that first date and it led to twelve great months to-gether. A lot of good memories overshadowed by one bad one. I never really got why this thing between us didn't work out. It was such a big mystery to me, since you just got up and disappeared." Kate realized that was somewhat harsh. True, but harsh.

Nebibi clasped his hands together. "You're right. I can't explain it perfectly, but you have a right to some kind of explanation. If it helps, I can tell you that no one before or since has affected me the way you did. No one. It's as simple as this: I figured out that I had a big responsibility to my family and to the people who gave me the opportunities to get an education so that I wouldn't end up in some menial life. I owed them a commitment to work for the cause of Islam. At the time, I just didn't know what form my contribution would take. Now I do. And . . ."

Alarms went off in Kate's head. Oh God, has he been converted into a fanatic? she wondered.

"That's a mouthful to digest, Nebibi. So here's my question for you, then. Are you a believer in Islam or Islamism?" Kate had hit squarely at the turmoil within the Muslim world. Islam is the religion, whereas Islamism is the religion plus a political governing system. Nothing secular about that government model. Those who believe in Islamism also believe in Islam, but the converse is *not* always true. And it was this internal conflict that usually overflowed into patterns of violence.

"Insightful question, Kate. My short answer is, both, which makes it all that much harder for me to live outside my religion."

"So what you're saying is that the religion thing stands between us? Just like the shaman separates the two jaguars on my pendant?"

"Yes, just like that pendant. . . ." He looked out the window at the falling snow and for a moment paused to wonder if his life could have followed a different path. He started to continue, but was interrupted by another question from Kate.

"But do you think extremists are justified in their violent methods, suicide bombers and all?" Kate had the Madrid investigation squarely on her mind.

"Do you think that I would, Kate?" That was Nebibi talking, not the Panther.

"Well, no, certainly not the Nebibi I knew. But I want to understand. . . ."

"What I do want you to know is that I never intended to hurt you."

Kate paused to think about Nebibi's words and then responded. "I guess when you're young and finding your place in the world, you think you can change society and turn it topsy-turvy, ignoring any rules. Problem is that some of those rules date back centuries and it's going to take more than one generation to shift that tide. But what kind of religion is it that doesn't allow you to be happy, allow you to fulfill your potential as a human being, as a husband and even as a father? That's the part you lose me on . . . ," Kate said, arriving at the crux of the matter for her. Why pursue a religious belief that doesn't believe in you?

"Islam does allow for that. That's not the issue with me."

"Okay, so then what is it, Nebibi? Would it have made a difference if I'd put on a veil?"

He smiled, trying to picture Kate with her face covered by a *hijab*. "Oh no, not at all. You are who you are and that's your beauty. The issue's on my end. I wouldn't have been allowed by my elders to marry outside my faith, and I couldn't impose that much change on you. You have your own destiny and I can't ask you to live only through mine."

"That, I can appreciate. I'm not completely inflexible, you know, and I would've been willing to make some adjustments. Just not enough to make me unrecognizable. I can't lie, though: I think the *hijab* would've been the deal breaker." She smiled as she said this.

Nebibi was thinking far more than he was verbalizing. In his life as the Panther, he couldn't have a "loved one." It would make him weaker and susceptible to making decisions that weren't in the best interest of his people's goals. The life he chose was the solitary one of a soldier. That's why he had disappeared six years ago.

"Well, that has to be the best and worst rejection of all time." Kate could see a glimmer of something deeper in his eyes. She also thought he was involved with some serious religious fervor and hoped he wouldn't lose himself completely in all that stuff. She wanted to warn him not to drink the Kool-Aid, but also knew that wasn't her job anymore.

So what's the score here? she thought: Islamism 1; Kate 0.

FOLLOWING LUNCH, KATE WALKED DOWN the avenue toward her father's office, a few blocks away. On the way, the sound of children playing made her stop in front of a small park set in from the street. At the far end of the park, she saw children beginning to build a snowman. It was the idyllic winter scene she needed to stare at right now, so she decided to sit down on a bench under a barren tree in a quiet corner of the park. The snow was beginning to come down stronger and the temperature was perfect for it to stick. The children's snowman was beginning to take shape.

She tried to make sense of the lunch she'd just finished and realized that it represented the last entry in the book called Nebibi. She mourned the cutting of that thread she had held on to for six years. A wave of melancholy came over her, thinking of a time when matters of the heart seemed easier or, at least, didn't cut as deeply. She needed to let some quiet tears flow down in the privacy of this little corner of this very public space.

A snowflake broke her concentration. It fell and landed on the bridge of her nose. And since sadness was not an emotion that stayed long with Kate, she got up, wiped the melted snowflake from her nose, and made her way with a purposeful pace to her father's office down the street. Remember, Kate, she said to herself, no expectations. Time to get yourself together. *Onward and upward.*

14

H E WATCHED KATE WALK DOWN Greenwich Avenue. She said she was headed to her father's office, a few blocks away. In that brief moment, Nebibi allowed himself to imagine how his life would have been if they'd stayed together all these years. Married? A family? All possible, but that was in the past now, he reminded himself.

When he saw Kate turn into a park down the block, he called his driver. "This is Mr. Hasehm. Meet me a block above the restaurant on the Avenue."

Back in the limo heading to Manhattan, he turned his attention to the present. He trusted she was satisfied with his explanations and that she continued to think of him as the graduate student she fell in love with and who fell in love with her. But *not* someone who could be even remotely related to events that took place in Madrid last week.

However, what Nebibi had omitted in his conversation was as important as what he had actually said to Kate. The reason for his so-called disappearing act was much more involved than he had let on. His mind wandered back to that time, years ago, when he'd received a frantic call from his mother at home in Milan, a call that had put him on a different path.

NEBIBI'S MOTHER SHOUTED INTO THE PHONE, "Rashidi, Rome, my Rashidi!..." The rest of her screams were unintelligible. She feared the worst for her son because she knew that Rashidi was most definitely not on a religious pilgrimage to Rome, or least not one that would be welcome by the Catholic Church.

Nebibi's brother, in attempting to escape the confines of the Milan Muslim ghetto, had come in contact with radical Islamists. The frustrations of second-generation Muslim immigrants throughout Western Europe were strong fodder for minority extremist factions. As children of immigrants, they grew up largely as foreigners in countries of their birth, be it in the Pakistani neighborhoods of London, the North African community in the far northern suburbs of Paris, the Muslim Satellite City area of Amsterdam, or the relatively newer Muslim ghetto of Milan.

Despite having an Italian passport, Rashidi felt like a foreigner in Italy, except when he was in the local mosque, where he became a convert to the most extreme factions of Islam. Nebibi later learned that Rashidi's role took him to Rome to train for an important battle in the global jihad. He was part of a six-man underground terrorist cell that spent its days casing and planning for its eventual strike: setting off a bomb in St. Peter's Square in the Vatican. They lived in a cramped apartment in the Muslim neighborhood of Rome. Rashidi was chosen to be the one who would finally deliver the bomb at one of the Sunday Masses led by the Pope. It was a duty his brother took as an honor both for himself and his family.

"ALLAHU AKBAR, ALLAHU AKBAR, ALLAHU AKBAR—God is great." It was Thursday, December twelfth, and Rashidi Hasehm was leading his five colleagues in the fifth and final prayer of the day in Rome. Right after Rashidi finished his call to prayer, the men, kneeling on their prayer rugs facing Mecca, heard a loud thud, and the door to their apartment was knocked down. Seconds later, the apartment was swarmed by fifteen members of the recently minted CIA paramilitary force, Task Force 8-27, dressed in black from head to toe, with dark visors on their eyes, acting under direct authority of the American executive branch. Each one of them had the musculature of a linebacker and one was indistinguishable from the next. They acted in complete silence, taking hold of each of the extremists.

"Do not say anything! Praised be Allah!" Rashidi yelled in the scramble of the ambush.

IN THE WEEKS FOLLOWING his mother's initial frantic call, this was all that was known of Rashidi's fate that day, pieced together from eyewitnesses in the apartment building. It was never confirmed, but after a few months, his family came to accept that Rashidi was most probably dead, killed by the Americans.

At the time, Nebibi was ignorant of both the extent of his brother's involvement in extremist plots and the terrorist factions in Milan and Rome that had prompted him down this path. After all, Nebibi was to be the son who, following successful studies abroad, would return to raise a family and take care of his parents in their old age—the normal life of a good Muslim son.

But the evening that the CIA thrust the door open on Rashidi in that small apartment in Rome was also the day that the CIA thrust itself into the life of Nebibi. And it was this event that had been the true defining moment of his conversion from just being Nebibi, the dutiful Muslim member of society, to Nebibi, the Panther seeking punishment, violent punishment, for the infidels that had taken his brother from his family, and for any who stood in his way.

And now, after seeing Kate again, Nebibi knew that his conversion was complete as the last vestiges of an earlier life were now gone. He was completely free of emotional ties to pursue his life's mission.

This Panther, like those in the wild, hunts alone.

He picked up his iPhone and scrolled for a contact. He rang the number. The person picked up on the second ring. "Hello." It was Margaux of White Weld. She'd recognized his number. "Glad you called. I had an idea for another deal for your fund. It's a company in the manufacturing sector, kind of under the radar screen, so far. When can we sit down to go over it in more detail?"

15

◄–+–+–+–►

NEW HAVEN, CONNECTICUT

DECEMBER 19

A T THIS HOUR OF THE EVENING, all the regular employees of the Wright Nuclear Structure Laboratory had long gone home. Located on the Yale University campus, the lab was entirely funded by the U.S. Department of Energy, and all its research was classified as top secret.

"Hey! Who's there!?" A voice cut through the darkness down the hall.

Juan Ernesto, a twenty-six-year-old Guatemalan immigrant, stopped dead in his tracks. He nervously stuffed the piece of paper he'd been looking at in his oversized jeans and turned around. He could see the guard's flashlight moving toward him down the hall.

As he got closer, they recognized each other.

"*Hola*, Joe," Juan Ernesto said, trying to make sure his voice didn't reveal any apprehension.

"I didn't see you come in, buddy. I was making my rounds on the other side of the building," said Joe, the fifty-eight-year-old African-American guard.

"I was late at my other job, so I didn't get here on time. Don't tell the bosses, okay?" Juan Ernesto had another day job unloading cargo at the docks.

"No problem, amigo. We little guys have to stick together. Listen, I've got to go check the floors upstairs. I'll let you get started and meet you for coffee later at nine o'clock. Hey, where's your cleaning stuff?" Joe finally noticed that Juan Ernesto, whose job was to clean the lab's offices, didn't have his usual bucket of cleaning supplies; instead, he just had a backpack slung over one shoulder.

"Oh, um, it's in the office I was just cleaning. I came out to check when I heard noise down the hall." Juan Ernesto's first duty tonight was not going to be cleaning.

"Okay, buddy. See you in an hour." Satisfied with the explanation, the older man went back to his security rounds.

Juan Ernesto waited to hear the elevator doors close before pulling out the piece of paper again. As he walked down the long corridor, he studied the names on the office doors. He was looking for the office of Marco Erin. On the third door, he stopped and compared the name on his piece of paper. The sign on the door read Marcus Herring, and Juan Ernesto decided that this was probably the one. Juan Ernesto had just simply written it as it sounded to him, *Marco Erin*. He took out the keys, given only to the researchers with top secret security clearances and, conveniently, the cleaning staff. He found the right one and opened the door.

He flicked on the light switch. In the center, there was a desk piled high with folders and papers, a sign that the current occupant clearly fell in the category of absentminded scientist.

Juan Ernesto turned over his piece of paper to recall what he was supposed to be looking for. It read: ^{60}Co. If he found it and delivered it to the gringo that had recruited him, he would get the impressive cash sum of $1,000.

The gringo was a student at Yale who had told him that these medical research products could get a hefty price on the black market. Juan Ernesto couldn't figure out what anybody would want with this sort of stuff, but the gringo told him it was for finding a cure for cancer. To Juan Ernesto that made all the sense in the world. Anything that paid $1,000 made complete sense to him.

^{60}Co is the scientific notation for cobalt-60, the radioactive form of the common metal cobalt. Each atom of ^{60}Co has a nucleus of various subatomic particles: protons, neutrons, and electrons. The inner nucleus of ^{60}Co is so unstable that the electron particles race out of the atom at a speed equal to hundreds of millions of miles per hour, creating deadly radiation. This eventually decays the atom, leaving behind relatively stable remnants, which instead become the atom for the plain metal nickel.

The half-life, or rather the time that it takes for half the nucleus of the ^{60}Co to decay into nickel, is 5.271 years. In that time, persons coming into unprotected proximity to the ^{60}Co will experience various degrees of radiation sickness depending on the length of exposure, distance from the source, and whether or not it was ingested or inhaled. In the right dosage, it is known to cause cell deformities leading to cancer in humans.

The center at Yale creates ^{60}Co as part of its research into the metal's more beneficial applications, such as food sterilization, treatment of brain tumors, and industrial measuring devices used in the oil-drilling business. The gringo, however, was not seeking the material to sanitize apple shipments, but rather for far more nefarious activities being planned by his terrorist cell.

Following the gringo's instructions, Juan Ernesto looked for a metal cabinet. He remembered it was behind the desk and crouched down to examine the combination lock dangling on the door. No problem, he thought to himself. Juan Ernesto reached in his backpack and pulled out a metal V-cut wedge he had fashioned from a piece of aluminum can. He slipped the V-cut wedge in between the metal loop and the locking mechanism. With one swift pull, the lock was open, all for the cost of a can of soda at the vending machine.

Juan Ernesto opened the metal door and saw what he was looking for: a tray of rounded metal cylinders no larger than a small bottle of aspirin, each labeled ^{60}Co. He doubted these little pieces of metal could be worth $1,000. But then, that wasn't his problem.

He put on leather gloves, which he had stuffed in his backpack, and carefully took out each of the twelve metal pellets from the tray, placing them in a plastic Target shopping bag. That $1,000, the beginning of the American dream for this young immigrant, was as good as in his gloved hand now. And those leather gloves would certainly avoid any fingerprints, he thought. Unfortunately, however, Juan Ernesto was very misguided in thinking that what he was involved in was mere petty theft. The true danger he faced was this: if any of the pellet casings broke, leather gloves would be woefully insufficient to prevent the onslaught of cancer in Juan Ernesto's body in a few weeks.

THE TERRIFYING THEFTS OF DANGEROUS MATERIALS from loosely watched research facilities across the U.S. and Europe were more than the International Atomic Energy Agency, the nuclear "cop on the block," could keep up with. They already had their hands full keeping the world's rogue nuclear states at bay and containing the loose nukes in the former states of the U.S.S.R. The likes of petty thieves like Juan Ernesto fell right through the cracks, which made radioactive and biochemical products available in relatively bountiful numbers.

The "gringo" said he was from Amsterdam and, indeed, that's where he was born twenty-five years ago, to first-generation Libyan immigrants. By birth, however, he held a valuable gift from that long-standing U.S. ally: Dutch citizenship. For U.S. Customs, it's one thing to flag a Middle Eastern passport at JFK, but it's a whole 'nother kettle of fish to flag the passports of travelers from every Western European ally. The Dutch citizen of Libyan descent—the "gringo"—was essentially below the radar screen of the U.S. government, which should have had an interest in watching his moves. And it would prove to be a costly mistake.

THE "GRINGO" TYPED AN E-MAIL in his native Dutch on his laptop using the Yale University servers. It read simply:

Dear Parents,

Studies are going well. I have all the materials I need to focus on studying when school starts again in January. E-mail me back with any updates.

Bye for now.

He hit SEND and off went this seemingly innocent e-mail to his parents. Problem is that his immigrant Libyan parents didn't have a computer or e-mail address, let alone know how to read Dutch. Also, since he had purposely reduced his workload this semester to only one course, just enough to continue to qualify for his student visa, there wasn't much to study in the spring semester. Instead, he was actually spending all his free time making contact with the likes of Juan Ernesto and Marcus Herring. Now that all his preparations were set, all he had to do was wait for his school term to begin and for any updates from his "parents."

THE INNOCENT CONTENTS OF THE "GRINGO" 'S e-mail left the Yale University servers and raced around the world. The e-mail was picked up by his contact in Amsterdam, who immediately translated the simple lines into English and forwarded the message to Murad the American, sitting in his secret location in the mountains near Kandahar. He knew who the "gringo" was and his exact location.

Murad was pleased to read the e-mail from the Yale University campus. He was keeping track of various e-mails of this nature, coming in from around the globe. They all started with "Dear Parents" and talked about upcoming "studies." Al-Qaeda was showing its strength as one of the world's most successful youth-recruiting organizations on the Web.

On the wall behind him, the white sheet he used for televideo communications had been removed to reveal a global map with little pushpin markers of various colors, each with its own significance. Blue equaled a terrorist cell that was in place but dormant. Red, a cell that was armed and ready. Yellow, a planned location currently being recruited. And finally, black, a cell captured or killed.

Every continent with the exception of Antarctica had pins on it of one color or another. There were crowded numbers of black pins on Guantánamo Bay in Cuba and in Afghanistan. There were heavy concentrations of armed and ready red pins in certain key locations, such as Iraq, Afghanistan, and North Africa, with new additional sprinklings of red pins in Europe and North America. Latin American and certain parts of Asia had the largest number of yellow pins, whereas North America and Europe had the highest concentration of available but dormant blue pins.

This was their map of troop locations worldwide ready to push forward on the many fronts of their global jihad. This simple map pricked by pushpins was worth somewhere in the neighborhood of $600 billion, or rather the cumulative cost of the U.S. foray into Iraq. One little map, equal to Jeffrey Sach's calculation of the money needed to entirely eliminate extreme poverty throughout the globe for the next four years. Imagine the Einsteins and Mother Teresas that could be spawned by the human race from all corners of the globe in those four years. Instead, there were these deadly colored pushpins.

Murad turned to the young American recruit sitting at a desk in front of him. "Take the earphones off for a second." The blond, blue-eyed twenty-year-old was listening to an Arab language course on his iPod. "Change the operative in New Haven from blue to red. I just got word that he's ready in position. You need to reflect the change on the board and on our Web site." *Web site?* Yes, al-Qaeda had a Web site set up for this purpose. A far-flung military campaign of this nature required real-time coordination on a global scale. And the Web was the natural tool. After all, it had been invented by the U.S. military for use in warfare.

So, taking a page from his American roots, Murad had devised a method for al-Qaeda to hang up a shingle out there in the very public World Wide Web, for anyone to see, as long as they knew exactly where to look. And, unfortunately for a U.S. intelligence community burdened by sheer size, it was the equivalent of looking for a needle in a *billion* haystacks.

16

⟵✦✦✦⟶

THE PANTHER SAT IN HIS MANHATTAN apartment on the forty-ninth floor of Olympic Tower in Midtown Manhattan. Nebibi's residence had ten-foot ceilings and floor-to-ceiling windows. It was sparsely decorated with simple square leather chairs, glass side tables, and recessed lighting, a sign that these were only temporary quarters.

The windows looked down upon St. Patrick's Cathedral. It was an unusual vantage point, since most New Yorkers and tourists were accustomed to looking straight up at the three-hundred-foot spires of the neo-Gothic-style cathedral. Nebibi instead looked down on them, and that was his preference, given his family's history with the icons of the Roman Catholic Church. Each day he looked down and smiled at the view, looking forward to the day when he could finish what his brother had attempted.

It was 6 A.M. Monday morning and Nebibi had just returned from a sprint around the Central Park Reservoir. He stripped off his sweaty jogging attire and jumped in the shower. Still dripping, he walked to his desk and sat down in front of his iMac.

He first checked on market activity, then glanced at his e-mails, and finally he embarked on a little online shopping. Judging from his browsing, Nebibi was in the market for a new bicycle and knew exactly where to look. He typed in: http://www.bicycle tradingpost.com, a site for Italian racing bicycles. The home screen had several expected links, such as a catalog of bicycles and related paraphernalia, suggestions of bike paths around the world, and payment and shipping details. But anyone who clicked on those links would get an error message of "Page Temporarily Not Available. Please Try Again Later."

At the bottom of the left-hand banner, there was a button labeled FOR SUPPLIERS. This was presumably for the business's trading partners, the ones who supplied all these bicycles and spare parts. Different from the rest of the page, this link was in full working order. Nebibi clicked on that button, bringing up a dialog screen for user and password. He entered his user name, PANTHER, and then his password, ANDALUS.

The image took a moment to load. Then it appeared: a copy of the map up on the wall behind Murad's desk, updated with the latest information. There were new red dots blinking in New Haven and Spain. Perfect, he thought. They were very close to being ready. And in a few short weeks, the rest of their preparations would be in order.

The Panther needed to move quickly to position Milestones in concert with the preparations on Murad's map.

17

MANHATTAN, NEW YORK
DECEMBER 20

ATE WALKED ON EAST FORTY-SEVENTH STREET toward the East
River. This was familiar territory from her childhood.
As she neared Second Avenue, she passed her family's
old apartment building, Dag Hammarskjöld Tower,
which faced a small patch of a park stretching the length of the
block, crowded with New York nannies sitting on benches with
their young charges, some more watchful than others.

A couple walked past her with their U.N. ID cards dangling on
chains around their necks. She overheard the older balding man say
with a British accent, "The Secretary General certainly won't go for
that. . . ." In this neighborhood, one couldn't escape the physical
shadow of the U.N. building complex in the distance, but equally,
the conversations of people on these nearby streets were also a signal that one was nearing international territory.

At the end of the block there was a kiosk selling snack items
with several metal café tables and chairs outside. As she passed by,
Kate noticed a woman sitting with a young child no more than
three years old. The young woman was wearing *hijab*, which made
Kate think about life with a Muslim. She questioned whether she
would have really done that for Nebibi—for the sake of building a
life, a family. By the woman's warm laugh, Kate knew she had
great joy in her heart for her child. She looked to be Kate's age,
and she already had a child. But I'm just not ready to have a baby,
thought Kate. I'm way too young for that.

Kate continued walking to her destination. The personal side
would have to wait for another day. Ahead of her was the main entrance to the U.N. Headquarters. The white-slab, thirty-eight-story

Secretariat Building, designed in the 1950s by Le Corbusier, was
an official icon of the Manhattan skyline. In the post-9/11 era, this
added an even heavier security burden that had to be taken seriously. Now, the open esplanade at the entrance to the main building was taken up by impromptu tents housing the lines of visitors
waiting to pass through guards and scanners. As she saw the line
snake around a couple of times, Kate realized this would take a
while. But since she'd seen the intelligence traffic of several threats
per week against one or another foreign delegation or the Secretary General himself, she, more than anyone in that line today,
knew how necessary it was.

ONCE THROUGH SECURITY, KATE HEADED from the U.N. building to the
walled garden. In the dead of winter, there were only a few U.N. personnel strolling past the famous sculptures. Next to the Vuchetich
sculpture, *Let Us Beat Swords into Ploulshares,* Kate spotted Inge
waving at her.

As she walked by, she caught the conversation of two men huddled together. "I think we can get Mauritania to agree with the Liby-
ans on this one. . . ." The man spoke with a Russian accent. This
place was simply crawling with internationalists.

"Funny bumping into you here, Inge." It was a treat for Kate to
see her good friend twice in such a short span. They greeted each
other with a hug and kisses on both cheeks.

"It's been only a week, but I get the sense that we've both covered a lot of ground in the past few days. Who goes first?" Inge
was referring, of course, to her call to Kate in the middle of her
lunch with Nebibi.

"You probably should."

As they walked arm in arm, Inge leaned closer to speak. "So here's
the thing, Kate. A couple of days after we had all those *mojitos,* I got
a message from Mirella to meet her at a bar in Old Havana."

"Okay, so what did she say? . . ."

"She told me what is going to sound like a pretty incredible story,
but hear me out. I tell you, it left me with this gut feeling that it might
have something to do with that money trail you were chasing."

"I'm listening, Inge, go on. . . ."

"It turns out that my friend Mirella started working at the Cuban research center after her brother became a patient there. He was one of those few unlucky ones who was diagnosed with AIDS and was immediately forced into a clinic. Remember what I told you about their system of containment?"

"Sure, sure." Kate nodded, imagining that without a strong voice of dissent to fight for their civil liberties on the island, these patients ended up with few or no rights.

"It seems Mirella went to visit her brother a few times over a couple of months. He was supposed to be there for eight weeks but they kept stretching it out. In total, he's been at the center for twelve months now. After four months there, Mirella told me she noticed that her brother was starting to lose patience and was more aggressive."

"Maybe it was just frustration with his diagnosis? . . ."

"Mirella knows a lot about the disease and she could tell this was more than just that. She asked her brother what pills they were giving him, and some of it didn't make sense to her."

"She is a doctor, right?" Kate was trying to keep up with Inge's story, though where she was heading was not yet clear to her.

"Yes, of course. Highly trained. She was on the team that created that hepatitis vaccine breakthrough. She's well known in Cuba. She's shaken Fidel's hand and received a civilian medal of honor from him. That's why her disappearance seemed so odd to me at the time. It's like those old Soviet times, when luminaries that weren't following orders from above suddenly ended up in Siberia. In her case, she was transferred to a small village in the interior to become the local general doctor; what a waste of her research talent. She's still there, but made the special trip to Havana to meet me."

"Okay, so go on. So she was getting suspicious about the treatment her brother was getting—" A loud horn from a passing ferry in the East River interrupted her.

"Yeah, right. She figured the best way to find out is to work there. So, she arranged for a transfer to the clinic. Given her stature in medical research, they welcomed her with open arms. Long story short, she discovers what she feared. They were using her brother as a guinea pig for experimental drugs."

"But aren't people always volunteering to be test cases for new AIDS treatments?"

"That's right, Kate. But what Mirella discovered was that they were testing altogether unrelated drugs on him. Nothing to do with his HIV status. They just prey on the AIDS patients because they're readily available without any legal protection. That is, until my brave little friend Mirella came along."

Inge led Kate to a small bench to sit down. "I need to give you something." Inge reached in her purse and took out a padded envelope and then carefully opened it so Kate could see its contents. It was a small vial of clear liquid, no more than a couple of tablespoons.

"What is this?" Kate held the vial in her hand now.

"It's good old Mirella's Christmas present. It was inside a box of Cuban cigars she gave me when I saw her last week. It's a sample of the drug they were using on her brother. Before using it on him, they tested it on those cats that I saw escape that day in the clinic. At least now I don't feel like I was crazy to bring up that episode. So it seems they're not only experimenting with cats, but also with humans."

Kate continued studying the vial. "Humans?" she asked.

"*Ja,* humans, Kate."

"Well, in that case, maybe we shouldn't be flashing that vial around. How'd you manage to get this into the country?"

"Hey, don't forget, we're in international territory here and I have special diplomatic status. But better safe than sorry." Inge took the vial from Kate's hand and placed it back in the pouch.

They put it away just in time. A man from the Chinese delegation was waving at Inge from about twenty paces away. It was a Chinese diplomat who until last year had been stationed in Havana alongside Inge at the U.N. office. While they'd shared many a *mojito,* there was still a question mark about this guy. It was rumored that he was actually a colonel in the Chinese Army. Inge got up to greet him. "Give me a sec with this guy. I'll be right back."

Kate watched as Inge was warmly greeted by the Chinese diplomat. In short minutes she was headed back. "Don't ask. . . ." Inge rolled her eyes for effect.

Kate did, but not about the Chinese diplomat. She let loose a litany of questions that had accumulated in her mind. "Did Mirella tell you how this fits in with those cats?"

"Mirella didn't have time to give me an in-depth science lesson, but she said that it's related to something called 'toxoplasmosis.' Supposedly, it's what made those cats aggressive to the point of being fearless. What it does to humans? No idea. But that's why I'm giving you this sample, so you can have those crack guys in U.S. intelligence get to the bottom of this. You know the U.N. doesn't have the resources to investigate this kind of thing. Just do me a favor and keep the U.N. out of it entirely. You didn't get this from me. . . ." Inge handed the envelope to Kate, who quickly put it in her purse.

"And what about that money?" Kate still had that open question.

"Well, I think what you put in your purse is probably worth $25 million to somebody out there."

"Hmmm . . ."

"So now that we're on track to solve the case of the crazy cats, how about that visit with your little friend this week? Are you an item again or is it still old news?"

Kate had no idea how things stood, so she wasn't sure what to tell her friend. "Inge," she said, "I have a feeling that those crazy cats are easier to figure out than one little panther."

Inge looked puzzled, but figured that all would be revealed. Two girlfriends having an innocent chat about the dating scene.

LATE THAT AFTERNOON, KATE SAT at the window seat of the Acela Express train from New York to Washington, D.C. The train was filled with lobbyists going back to their posts on K Street, and Wall Street professionals heading to the Treasury Department to report to their boss, Uncle Sam. She thought about how what she held in her purse might be the break she needed in this messy investigation, and might help repair her reputation in front of Bill.

As the train passed the skyline of Philadelphia, Kate made a quick call to the DIA's biomedical lab. "Hello? Lieutenant Khoury?"

"Yes?"

"Hi, Kate here, calling from a train." She wanted him to know that she wasn't on a secure line. "Remember that 'hypothetical' case we spoke about the other day? Any further thoughts?"

"Oh, hi. Yeah, well, uh, on that issue, not really. It's kind of hard without having the specimens in front of me." Lieutenant Khoury started recalling the story about the cats, which he had filed at the bottom of his to-do list.

"I think I have exactly what you need. I'll stop by your office tomorrow. Will you be there?"

"Like clockwork, Kate. Stop by the lab tomorrow morning. By the way, are we talking about a package with air holes punched in the top?" The lieutenant began to imagine his lab overrun with cats.

"No, but that would be a specimen now, wouldn't it? What I have is better."

"Okay, sounds promising. Definitely bring it over." All of a sudden, the crazy cat story had moved several positions up on the lieutenant's to-do list.

18

NEBIBI LOCKED THE DOOR to his office to avoid interruptions. He pulled out the 100-gigabyte USB drive, the size of a money clip, from his pocket and plugged it into his computer. It contained one file, a very expensive one. The rest of the $20 million price tag was now in that numbered account of the Vereinten Kantonalbank in Zurich.

Nebibi manipulated the massive database file. He had several analysts on the payroll to perform this work, but this data was far too sensitive for any eyes but his to see. In any event, Nebibi wasn't a stranger to databases and spreadsheets. He could find a single piece of data in a spreadsheet the size of a football field.

He was mining a highly confidential list of derivatives transactions of all banks with a U.S. presence. This was the result of Treasury's newly expanded powers. It had finally imposed the unprecedented requirement on financial institutions to provide their entire confidential derivatives exposure, line by line, no matter where they held it. So now, the U.S. Treasury held terabytes of data detailing most of the world's $1 quadrillion's worth of derivatives transactions. Given the potentially lethal impact these instruments had on the economy, the Administration correctly deemed this a matter of national security.

While the government now had the power of a new financial reform law behind it, it still didn't have enforceable rules ironed out. On top of which, money could quickly travel across borders that weren't always harmonious. The devil is in the details, as they say. Regulators' attention was taken up with sticking fingers in each new hole of the weak financial dam, with little time and resources left to truly harness the dangerous beast of derivatives once and for all. The strong countercurrents of market greed were far too powerful for mere bureaucrats to navigate.

Any market participant would kill for the confidential information contained in this file, because it granted the omnipresent power to structure highly profitable trades. At that level, $20 million was cheap. Nebibi, however, wasn't just looking to make billions. He was planning to make a killing.

With several keystrokes, he ran another query and his screen flashed the result. It had taken him all of fifteen minutes to find the weakest link in the global derivatives house of cards. Clearly, he hadn't lost his touch with data mining. As he looked at the answer on the screen, he grinned, whispering under his breath, *"Allahu Akbar"*—God is great.

NEBIBI PICKED UP HIS CELL PHONE and dialed a 202 number. The man on the other line picked up almost instantly.

"I can't talk long. Did you get it?" The man spoke in hushed spurts, all business, as he got up to close his office door. The window behind him looked out onto the gated lawn that separated the Treasury Building from the White House grounds.

Nebibi stared at the database in front of him and responded, "Yes, just what we needed. Your delivery is waiting at the usual spot." A few seconds later, the line clicked off. Nebibi was sure the man was on his way to catch the first flight out of Dulles to Zurich to personally accept his "delivery" at the Vereinten Kantonalbank.

NEBIBI'S CAR SWUNG ONTO West Forty-fourth Street, stopping mid-block at number 27, a seven-story building that featured a large crimson flag out front emblazoned with a single white letter *H*. The doorman stood inside the vestibule, guarding against the December air. When he saw the young man in a trim navy Italian wool coat exit the dark sedan, he immediately stepped out to hold open the door to the Harvard Club.

"Good morning, Mr. Hasehm."

Nebibi checked his coat and made his way into the main foyer. He had his usual uniform on, a black Armani suit, crisp white shirt, dark tie, and sleek Ferragamo tie-ups. And, of course, his saber cuff links. On the left was a staircase with walls painted in Harvard crimson leading to meeting rooms, the library, guest rooms, and gym facilities. As he walked by, people turned and wondered about the striking figure that moved with such purpose in his stride.

Nebibi entered the most impressive room in the club, Harvard Hall, with its forty-foot coffered ceiling, dark oak-paneled walls, worn leather Tudor chesterfield sofas, and two tall marble fireplaces, each with logs aflame on this chilly day.

Several men and one woman spoke in hushed tones, but no one had a cell phone or a business document in hand. It was against club rules for business to be transacted here, but absolutely no one kept conversations solely to the innocent topics of weather and gardening. As he walked by, Nebibi overheard the conversation between two men: "The Administration offered me a position at Commerce, but I'm holding out for Treasury. I've got to take one of them because there's nothing left for me on Wall Street, at least not for the next year or two." Just two Harvard men tending to their gardening.

Nebibi proceeded to the Formal Dining Room, where tables were set for lunch: tablecloths and china with a crimson-colored *H* in the center. His lunch partner sat alone at one of those tables, already munching on the club's fresh-baked popovers. As Nebibi approached, Sam Coldsmith, the Harvard MBA, stood up to shake his hand. He was almost half a foot taller than Nebibi and had a girth twice his size. Sam wore a charcoal gray Paul Stuart suit, somewhat rumpled from sitting in his limo for the hour ride from Greenwich. The fact that he had very little hair left on his head made his face look even rounder.

"Nebibi, good to see you again. Glad you could meet me at my hangout."

"Thank you for the invitation. This is very impressive." Nebibi was stroking Sam's ego. As a graduate of Oxford, Nebibi was a member of the far more impressive Oxford and Cambridge Club in Pall Mall in London.

"I come here all the time. This club is the best reason to go to Harvard in the first place. B-school is just a couple of years out of your life, but this place, you can come back to for the rest of it." Sam beamed, thinking he had impressed the Egyptian from Milan. "How about we order some lunch and then plot some future business?" Sam took out the order sheet and, in between bites of his popover, wrote down his regular lunch menu. "What are you having, Nebibi?"

"Quaint ordering system you have here. I'll have the mesclun salad and the poached salmon." Not quaint, really, just a bit too egalitarian for Nebibi. "Now that we have that out of the way, how about you fill me in on how you managed to survive this crisis. It's been one of your best periods, right?"

In fact, Sam had been one of the select few that remained unscathed by the economic downturn. He owed his grand Greenwich estate and two private jets to the decisions he made in that period of financial turmoil. But Sam also knew that all good things can come to an end, and now he was planning to have Nebibi help him make his next killing.

"Real simple stuff. I believe in fundamentals and don't rely on data that gets spewed out of mega-galactic computer models. I like to kick the tires of things I own." Sam walloped a whole lot of butter on another popover.

Nebibi interjected, giving Sam time to chew. "In Islamic finance, we also believe in, as you say, kicking the tires."

The waiter delivered a fresh basket of warm popovers. Sam immediately grabbed one in his hands before continuing. "Yep, that's exactly what we did before everything went to hell. Back then, things looked rosy, on the surface at least."

Sam waved at the waiter for more butter for the table. "My buddy Schwarzman over at Blackstone joined in the party. He orchestrated a nice little IPO for himself before the crisis. It put him a little ahead of me on that *Forbes* Billionaires list."

Schwarzman was more than fifty slots ahead of him on that list and not a day went by that Sam didn't think about that. He'd been planning to float a third of his Royal Lane fund in an initial public offering on the New York Stock Exchange. But markets had soured and since there was no telling when conditions would be that favorable again, Sam was on the prowl for another way to unlock his fund's value. When he heard about Nebibi's Middle East money, Sam knew that it was his only ticket to liquidity.

Sam continued, "But my gut was telling me something wasn't right. There were too many record-setting takeover bids fueled by cheap bank debt. And let me tell you, that bank debt was so cheap, it was downright floozy, makes that gal from White Weld and Company, what's her name? . . ."

"Margaux, you mean?"

"Yeah, Margaux. That debt was so cheap that it made Margaux look like Mother Teresa." Sam let out a deep laugh as he remembered the many legal covenants, the equivalent of chastity belts for bank loans, that were broken at that time as banks raced each other to cram more debt down their clients' throats.

Nebibi also chuckled, uncharacteristically for him, but he had to admit that it would take a slew of miracles to make Margaux look like Mother Teresa.

Sam continued, "Second thing that worried me was the record level of Wall Street bonuses. Anytime those guys end up with more of the wealth pie for creating nothin', I know we're headed for trouble."

Nebibi was surprised by this, given that Sam had been the beneficiary of such bonuses when he had been head of trading at Goldman Sachs. "There's another example of where you agree with the rules of Islamic finance, making money on true economic activity, not speculation."

"So we see eye to eye on certain things, then. Imagine that, a Catholic boy from the Bronx and a Muslim from Milan being on the same page." Nebibi looked around the dining room, which was now practically full, with red crimson-jacketed waiters darting from table to table. Nebibi could guess that he was probably the only one in the room who had read the Qur'an from cover to cover more than once. A Muslim in a room full of infidels.

"Here you are, Mr. Coldsmith. . . ." The waiter arrived with Sam's oysters and Nebibi's salad.

"Thanks, Ramón." Sam had a broad smile on his face at the sight of the large plate of oysters set before him. "Where's the Tabasco?"

Nebibi turned attention back to business. "So what did you do about those trends?"

"Simple. I took my top guys and formed my own financial SWAT team. We had a damn intense couple of months in the spring of '07, zeroing in on anything that needed fixing. It sure kept us out of trouble, though. I had a real nice summer vacation on the Vineyard that year while my competitors raced back to New York to beg their bankers for financing." Sam salivated as he squeezed some lemon on one of his oysters.

After shucking another one, Sam continued. "But hey, just like everybody else, we bought our fair share of mortgage loans that had been diced, sautéed, smothered in triple-A ratings by those investment banks. They called them CDOs, collateralized debt obligations. By the way, some advice: whenever these guys in their fancy suits come up with a cute name for the stuff, watch out." He wiped some of the oyster's juice that had dribbled on his tie.

As soon as he'd chowed down another one, he continued. "In any case, while the market was still licking up that creamy triple-A sauce, we switched gears and ignored the fancy pitch books. We dug into the underlying industry metrics, and guess what we found? Mortgage delinquency rates had been going up since '06. Those damned pitch books were fucking worthless horseshit. And hey, you didn't need to be a rocket scientist to figure out any of this stuff. Problem was, most guys didn't bother to look, especially the ones sitting in places like Wall Street, Düsseldorf, and Zurich."

Coldsmith's fund had quietly sold out of potentially bad positions and tacked on loss protection in the form of derivatives for the rest. He completely neutralized his portfolio, protecting his capital before the mortgage meltdown hit the front page of *The Wall Street Journal*.

Sam's healthy spa regime in the cuisine of finance didn't extend to real life, however, as Ramón placed a hefty plate of sizzling grilled lamb chops in front of him. "That looks great, Ramón. Hey, where's the A1 sauce?"

Nebibi watched as Sam doused a chunk of his meat and raised it to his mouth, sauce dripping down from his fork. Before Sam could stuff that large piece in his mouth, a female voice interrupted.

"I see you're still on that diet, Sam. . . ." It was Hannah Merton, the CEO of Sam's primary lender and counterparty, WR Shipley & Co., the nation's largest bank. She was a tall woman, only an inch shy of six feet. Her short hair, tinted an even brown, framed a lined face that didn't hide her fifty-six years of age, twenty of which had been spent on her firm's male-dominated trading floor. She wore a simple loose-fitting skirt, a knit jacket, and sensible low heels. She wasn't a fashion icon, but then again, that's not what her firm paid her for.

Sam didn't stop his eating for most people, but Hannah was one important exception. He stood up and greeted her with an expansive hug, like the old friends that they were.

"Hannah, great to see you. Are you here for lunch?"

"No, I was giving a speech upstairs at the Women's Business Enterprise Council. . . ."

"I see. By the way, I missed you at our bash up in Greenwich the other night. . . ."

"Yeah, sorry. I had a late meeting in D.C. with our most demanding shareholder, the U.S. Treasury." She looked down at Sam's lunch partner and, not recognizing him, stuck out her hand. Not a shy one, nor one to stand on ceremony, this Hannah Merton.

Sam corrected himself. "Sorry, Hannah. This is Nebibi Hasehm of Milestones."

Her eyes lit up. "Oh yes, I've heard a lot about you. Too bad my bankers couldn't convince you to go with us for your launch. I guarantee you, we're a far more complete 'one-stop' shop for all your financial needs. Front-office, back-office, even your personal banking needs, we'll have you covered anywhere in the world. Here's my card. Call me when you do a second round." Hannah never stopped selling, and since her bank was crowned one of the few crisis survivors, she had much to brag about.

Nebibi exchanged his card with her. "It will be a pleasure, Ms. Merton."

"Please, call me Hannah." She turned to Sam and said, "I saw on my calendar that we're meeting later. Can we push it back by a half hour? The head of the New York Fed called just before lunch and he wants me on a conference call this afternoon." She rolled her eyes, signaling this wasn't a call she was looking forward to. "I split my time fifty–fifty these days with my regulatory buddies. I can't wait for things to finally get back to normal."

"I'm with you on that. But sure, no problem. See you at two thirty, then."

"Great, thanks. And watch that diet, my friend. I need my favorite counterparty fit and trim." She then turned to Nebibi and said, "Mr. Hasehm, I look forward to seeing you at our bank in the future." She smiled and walked off to rejoin her nervous assistant, who was signaling by the exit, trying to keep her frenetic boss on schedule.

When she was far from earshot, Sam said, "She's not a bad one, that Hannah. It would be worth your while to see her for your next capital raise." Nebibi just smiled at his suggestion.

Sam looked at his chops, no longer sizzling, and waved Ramón over to put them back on the grill. He looked over at Nebibi's plate; a piece of unappetizing cold fish is all he saw there. "Dig in. Mine'll be back out in a sec."

Nebibi took a forkful, but wanted to get their conversation back on track. "Sidestepping the mortgage mess is quite a feat. You certainly earned your fees that year. Is that when you started dealing in derivatives, Sam?"

"Yep. We'd always had some of that, but then made the decision to expand the derivatives desk full hog. We selected companies with big portfolios of sub-prime home mortgages and heavily shorted their stocks. We made a fuckin' boatload." With a big grin on his face, Sam conveniently omitted to mention that his short-selling strategies also contributed to the downfall of both Bear Stearns and Lehman, yielding him hefty profits. By that point, Sam and his fund were practically addicted to the profit potential of derivatives.

"And so you use derivatives for protection on your investments?" Nebibi asked innocently, knowing the answer full well from his $20 million confidential database.

Sam responded, while still chewing. "Yes and no. Sometime after Lehman went under, we started buying up more companies and portfolios in that fire sale. We stayed away from anything involving government bailout funds, though; last thing I needed was Barney Frank breathing down my back every day."

Sam took the last bite of lamb on his plate, savoring it, along with the memories of the deals he had done that year. "Cash was king and we ended up with more risk on our plate than our infrastructure could handle, so we just tacked on more structured derivatives."

Royal Lane's total assets were $150 billion, hedged against risks through heavy use of derivatives. But Sam had gone way beyond that and now used derivatives to make sizable bets on market movements. And those bets placed exclusively with a foreign subsidiary of Hannah Merton's bank, WR Shipley & Co., amounted to more, much more, than Sam's capital base. Someone with a line-by-line knowledge of that bank's exposure with Sam might conclude that it teetered close to the edge of a steep cliff, and that with one push, one or the other counterparty could lose its step and tumble over.

"Always ahead of the curve, Sam." Nebibi knew exactly where his killing was, sitting across the table from him, staring at a slice of cheesecake. "So what's your portfolio composition? Is there anything there that my Islamic scholar wouldn't allow?"

"It depends. We own more than forty companies. What does he look for?"

"Lending, gambling, alcohol, pornography, or weaponry."

"I think we're okay on most of that." Sam then took a bite of cheesecake, against Hannah's advice. After swallowing most of it, he was ready to get down to brass tacks and make a play for his liquidity. "So, Nebibi, have you given any thought to that deal we talked about at my house on Friday?"

"Yes, I have. I'd like to present it to my limited partners. I'm confident they'll follow my recommendation and approve it. I'll have an official response in a couple of days. Would it be alright if I sent my senior analyst for some preliminary due diligence on your portfolio tomorrow?"

"Excellent news, my friend. And yes, feel free to have him come by the office tomorrow, first thing." Sam savored that last bite of the five hundred-calorie slice of cheesecake. His Greenwich physician, Dr. Blumberg, would not be too happy knowing that Sam was putting off dealing with his Type 2 diabetes for another day.

19

—◄─◆─◆─┼─►—

NEBIBI CHECKED IN WITH THE YOUNG, attractive brunette at the front desk office of the Venezuelan Mission to the United Nations. "Good afternoon. I have an appointment with Minister Alarcón. My name is Hasehm."

"*Ah, sí, Señor Hasehm*. The minister is waiting for you. I will take you up to the third floor." The young receptionist-cum-beauty-pageant-contestant from Caracas told the guard to watch the desk while she escorted the handsome visitor.

"Thank you." Despite the teachings of the Qur'an, Nebibi had to steal a second glance at the young woman. She was a product of Venezuela's factory of beauty pageant contestants, which had already produced a world record of six Miss Universe winners. The receptionist, however beautiful, had only come in as runner-up in the Miss Caracas contest last year. So now she was looking for a rich husband, which explained the personal escort service she gave every eligible visitor, Nebibi included.

They took the small elevator upstairs, the young woman putting on her best competition smile for the entire one-minute ride. Ahead of Nebibi, she sauntered in her formfitting pencil skirt like it was the pageant runway and, on reaching their destination, she gave him one last parting photogenic smile.

The minister was sitting at a large desk in the center of the room, and was so engrossed in a telephone conversation that at first he didn't notice Nebibi standing at the door. He was speaking in Spanish, but Nebibi could roughly make out aspects of the conversation.

"*Sí, Señor Presidente. Hare exactamente como usted ha dicho.*"

I will do exactly as you said. The minister was receiving his marching orders from President Chávez. "I will report back to you as soon as I return." As he hung up the receiver, he noticed Nebibi standing there and motioned for him to enter.

"Hello, Mr. Hasehm." The minister walked around the desk and extended his hand to Nebibi. The minister, who stood a few inches taller than Nebibi, was in his mid-fifties. He was tidy in appearance but not comfortable in a suit and tie. Before this high-profile job, he had been a left-leaning economics professor at the Universidad de Caracas. It was not his mastery of economics that had earned him the ministerial appointment, but rather his socialist politics that appealed to his current boss.

"It's good to see you again, Minister. I trust you had a good trip from Caracas?"

"Yes, very uneventful, despite the fact I was flying on American Airlines. Last-minute trip. Unavoidable choice, as all other government aircraft were already allocated. The food they serve just isn't edible."

"Next time, please let me know if you run into such difficulties, as I am certain that our mutual acquaintances would be more than happy to make a private jet available."

"Very kind offer, Mr. Hasehm, which I will definitely keep in mind." Such offers appealed to the former low-paid economics professor. "So, I heard from our development bank that you are planning to have a conference call later this week to report on the fund's progress. Care to provide me with a preview?"

"Certainly. We are fully funded and already have a deal in mind. After due diligence, we'll submit it for formal approval."

"Excellent. And what about the other aspects? Is all proceeding as planned? Have your colleagues on the Pakistani border received the shipments from Cuba?"

"Yes, all has been well received and our agents are ready in the necessary locations. You'll know when we've succeeded by looking at your oil price. I'm sure it will meet your government's needs."

"That is certainly good news. At these levels, our Treasury can't keep pace with our social welfare spending. However, I must again bring up a rather delicate issue. It is of the utmost importance that we are clear on our further involvement. Following this initial phase, we need to maintain a certain distance from, shall I just say, the more 'controversial' aspects involving your colleagues. As I'm sure you understand, Venezuela's sovereignty would be compromised by a battalion of U.S. forces coming across the Colombian border if it were shown that we were involved in anything more than charitable funding of innovative medical research in Cuba, or, as in the case of our funding of The Milestones Fund, pure economic gains on investments. There can be no hint of any other type of involvement here."

"Yes, that was our understanding from the beginning, and nothing going forward will compromise that arrangement. That is a message directly from our supreme commander to your President. I don't expect that we'll be in contact again in the next few months. It's probably best that direct communication be restricted to your representative on the board of Milestones."

"Yes, agreed. A pleasure as always, Mr. Hasehm. *Ojalá* all will go as planned from here on out." The minister had interjected his English with the Spanish word *ojalá,* which is used through Spain and the Americas to mean "hopefully." In the presence of the Arabic speaker, Nebibi, however, it didn't require any translation. *Ojalá* was another often overlooked signal that Islam had at a time been so interwoven in the Spanish peninsula that it remained to this day a normal part of the language. The roots of the word were in the Arabic term *Insha'allah*—by the grace of *Allah.*

Nebibi responded in kind. "Yes, *Insha'allah.*" The two men shook hands and Nebibi left the Mission to head back to his office.

When he was alone again, the minister made a quick call. "*Señor Presidente,* I delivered the message, and all is well. They're continuing with their plans, and our country is simply an investor in that fund of theirs. No more."

"*Excelente, Alarcón.* The next time I hear about any of this, I only want to read about it in the newspapers."

ON FOOT, NEBIBI HEADED NORTH on First Avenue toward his apartment. His mind was cataloging Minister Alarcón's comments into one of the many distinct pockets of closely held information regarding his mission. The Venezuelans wanted to stay far away from future plans. That's fine, thought Nebibi; they've served their purpose of funding the Cubans. As before, it was still up to him to make sure all the other components remained on track.

Though he communicated with Murad regularly, Nebibi was the only one in their organization who knew the details of the entire mission. This gave him great leeway to change course, but also placed on him the final responsibility for the mission's eventual success or failure. And in this business, the implications of one or the other were stark. Success would bestow honor on him and his family, and important, retribution for his brother's fate. Failure, however, would only bring him violent death or capture.

Three years ago, Nebibi had been selected for this mission because of his proven tenacity and training in financial matters. It wasn't that he lacked the capacity for fear or love, as most thought when dealing with him. It's just that he willed his brain to put those emotions aside and only concentrate on the logical sequence of steps necessary to achieve a final goal. Today was no different. He filed away the conversation with Alarcón and stepped forward. No emotion. No fear.

20

BOLLING AIR FORCE BASE, D.C.
DECEMBER 21

IT WAS 4:00 P.M., QUITTING TIME for most of the DIA's early risers, but Kate still sat at her desk catching up on intelligence traffic regarding the Madrid bombing. She was just about to close down the IntelWiki when her secure line rang. She answered on the second ring. "Kate Molares speaking."

It was Lieutenant Khoury, the bio-medical terrorism expert. "We've finished our preliminary testing of the sample you gave us this morning. Can you come over to review the results with us?"

"Wow! That was fast, Lieutenant. Sure, I'll be right over." The gym would have to wait. From the sound of his voice, it looked like Inge's cat story was leading somewhere after all.

"Okay, but meet me in the conference room instead."

On her way, Kate popped her head into her boss's office. "Bill, news came back from Fort Detrick on that sample. Lieutenant Khoury is ready to meet with us now." Kate was referring to the Armed Forces Medical Intelligence Center, the AFMIC, in Frederick, Maryland. The AFMIC, which is part of the DIA, makes all medical-related intelligence assessments for the armed forces, and Lieutenant Khoury was the liaison at the DIA for the extensive resources of its main operations hub at Fort Detrick.

The vial delivered from Cuba via the U.N. fell into the category of bio-material "potentially" vital to U.S. national security. *Potentially* had been the key word that Lieutenant Khoury used earlier in the morning when Kate gave him the sample. Now she would find out if AFMIC would be taking the word *potentially* out of any future description of the sample.

"Okay, hold on. I'll be right there." Bill's attitude toward Kate had changed 180 degrees this morning when she showed him the vial. It didn't matter that she'd taken a sick day to meet her contact in New York. Kate had, in fact, delivered the goods, or so they both hoped that's what the test results would show.

When they reached the conference room, Lieutenant Khoury was there with two colleagues she hadn't met before.

"Ms. Molares. This is Major Longwell and Colonel Youtz. They're my chain of command at AFMIC. Mr. DuBois, I think you know each other." Both men were in their mid-forties, fit and trim beneath their green army uniforms, which were sprinkled with colorful medals. There was a round of hand-shaking in the room, after which all sat down. The postures of the major and colonel looked as starched as their uniforms. Lieutenant Khoury handed out a report with a dark blue cover that stated simply in bold white letters NEED TO KNOW BASIS ONLY.

Kate's heart was pounding. Given the classification of the report and the fact that not *one,* but *two* of Lieutenant Khoury's bosses made the hour trip from Fort Detrick indicated there was definitely something to this cat story after all. Something big.

The lieutenant kicked off the meeting. "I've briefed my chain of command on how you ended up with a sample of this chemical compound. As discussed, Ms. Molares, any references to the U.N. have been redacted from the report. We don't want to jeopardize that potential future source."

"That's good news." Kate was relieved. She smiled at the two starched suits for reaction, but their faces, by training, revealed nothing.

"My commanding officers have also been briefed on the story about the cats at the Bermudez Institute in Havana. Because of that, we decided the best unit to analyze the vial was the animal testing unit at Fort Detrick. They weren't surprised by the story of the cats, since they've been performing similar research. But their research is exclusively on animals, whereas we understand from your contact's story that the Cuban clinic is already testing this compound on humans."

"That's right. The scientist at the Bermudez Institute has a brother who is something of a 'captive' patient there, and apparently he's been receiving dosages. Seems her brother was showing some stark changes in behavior."

Kate noticed that Lieutenant Khoury's eyes shifted in a brief glance toward his superiors. They nodded for him to continue. She wondered what part of the story they weren't telling.

The lieutenant had hesitated because he was not going to tell the full story coming out of Fort Detrick. To begin with, the reason his superiors had been immediately summoned to this case was that the U.S. military had been carrying on similar top secret bio-medical research. Unlike the Cubans however, the U.S. military scientists at Fort Detrick had not yet managed to crack the code that was now obviously in the hands of the Cubans.

"The sample from Cuba is a concentrated form of parasites that causes a disease called *toxoplasmosis* in humans. In its normal oc-currence, it's estimated that up to one third of the world's popula-tion is infected by the parasite called *Toxoplasma gondii*. There is a growing body of research to suggest that harboring this parasite, *T. gondii* for short, may also result in certain neurological changes in humans. The most common host of the parasite, however, is not humans but rather the field cat." Kate felt a chill run up her spine, causing her to straighten in her chair. What looked like a crazy story on the surface was becoming more real by the second.

The lieutenant continued. "*T. gondii* exists in distinct phases. It can reproduce only in felines. In its first, asexual, phase, it resides in warm-blooded mammals, such as rats. *T. gondii* alters the in-fected rat's normal brain function in a very specific and weird way. It makes the rat fearless in the face of its normal predator, the cat. This alteration is so complete that a *T. gondii*–infected rat will not only be fearless in the presence of a cat, it will in fact be attracted to its scent. Instead of running away from a cat, the rat will seek it out. The parasite causes this change for a very specific purpose: it needs to be ingested by the cat in order to reproduce.

"Once inside the cat's intestines, *T. gondii* clicks into its second, sexual, phase, reproducing and eventually making its way out through the cat's feces. And it's at this stage that humans can be in-fected by *T. gondii*—"

"Excuse me, Lieutenant, how's that?" asked Kate.

"Through unwashed vegetables, raw meat, and improper hand-ling of cat litter," Khoury explained. "You may be aware that preg-nant women are advised not to clean out their cat's litter box. This is so that they won't be infected by the parasite and endanger their unborn child. In a healthy adult, the parasite causes mild flu-like symptoms. However, in an AIDS-infected person, T. gondii can be fatal. This is why the Cuban scientist was so concerned about her brother."

"So, if I were to see a cat with a rat in its jaws, are you saying that it is most likely T. gondii hard at work versus the hunting skills of the cat?" Bill remembered the number of times he had seen those feral cats proudly displaying their rodent catch.

"Yes, chances are you're seeing the natural cycle of T. gondii at work as much as the hunting skills of the cat, Mr. DuBois."

"But wait. I'm not clear on something here. What my contact in Havana saw were not rats chasing cats, but cats chasing a dog. How does that fit into this parasite's life cycle?" Kate was trying to make sense of the confusing picture Inge had painted for her of that day at the clinic.

"Right. What your contact saw was outside the expected, cats chasing a dog. It seems the Cubans accomplished quite a feat of medical technology. They've managed to isolate the internal mechan-ics of how the parasite recognizes its current location and clicks itself into one mode or another."

The lieutenant continued, "They've been able to alter the internal levers of the T. gondii parasite so that it is tricked into the wrong phase of its life cycle. So, for example, when it's residing in a cat, the normal T. gondii parasite will reproduce, whereas the altered one will stay in its asexual phase where it instead alters the neurology of the cat's brain. The reengineered T. gondii marches into action to change the way the cat's brain controls fear, resulting in a cat that is fearless of its normal predator, the canine. That's how you end up with cats chasing the dog. They were all obviously injected with a reengineered T. gondii parasite.

"And the vial you delivered is exactly that, a serum composed of concentrated Cuban reengineered T. gondii, we're calling it T. gondii prime. We tested it on a cat at midday, expecting to have any possible effects come up in a few days, but since this is a very concentrated serum, we saw an intense reaction in just a few hours."

"Does that mean you have a cat chasing a dog over at Fort De-trick?" Kate imagined that the sight of such a cat is what probably made the colonel and the major race over here.

"Yes, we do. Honestly, the guys over at AFMIC tipped their hats, though not happily, to the Cuban medical researchers who managed this. This type of parasitic reengineering has far-reaching effects, beyond *T. gondii*. AIDS research can benefit from this, and so can those looking for elusive cancer vaccines."

"So the discovery of new lifesaving vaccines is what they're after, or are there other applications for this?" Kate was still trying to fig-ure out whether it was altruism on the part of Venezuela that had inspired it to fund the Cubans' research of *T. gondii prime*. The lieutenant fidgeted in reaction to Kate's question. He looked over at his superiors for a lifeline.

The stiff colonel decided it was time to interject. "Yes and no, Ms. Molares. While we all like to think we're making advances in solving the mysteries of cancer and AIDS, the truth is that there are other, not altogether beneficial applications of a mind-altering serum."

"And what could that be, Colonel?" Kate was on the edge of her seat by now.

"Imagine having the ability to create an army that is fearless in front of the enemy. This is where we need to consider our country's military security. If our soldiers are facing future enemy ground forces that have increased risk-taking behavior, we need to know about it and plan for it. In fact, we need to match it." That last sen-tence seemed to float longer than intended in the dead air of the closed conference room.

The truth was that the military wasn't just looking to cure dis-eases. It was looking for ways to artificially enhance the combat capabilities of its all-volunteer ground forces, and this was all the more critical now that Cuba had stumbled upon it first. And if Cuba had it, who knew who would get their hands on it next, for the right price.

Kate looked over at Bill to see his reaction. She caught the colonel's last comment and then understood the full ramifications of that little vial of *T. gondii prime* and why it could be worth the sum of $25 million, as Inge had said. Actually, at that price, it was very cheap. Fearless armies racing toward the enemy. No general could ever manage to instill that kind of loyalty in modern-age combat troops, unless they got a little boost from some reengineered parasite delivered in their morning coffee. No wonder the colonel had raced over here, she thought.

Kate chose not to make a big deal about the colonel's last statement. At least, not before knowing a bit more. "So where does that leave us, I mean with this serum?"

"Given the bio-medical aspects here, I think it best that I file the report on the IntelWiki—that is, if you agree?" Lieutenant Khoury and his superiors wanted to make sure they were controlling the future flow of information on the prized *T. gondii prime*.

"Not a problem, as long as we continue to keep the U.N. out of it." Kate was a faithful friend. "And what are the next steps?"

"We'll continue to run tests on the sample with the objective of breaking the code of Cuba's reengineering. Not sure how long that will take." The colonel had already created a large team to work on just that, around the clock. However, what even the colonel's underlings didn't know was that he had already briefed the SecDef on the *T. gondii prime*. They'd decided to create a much smaller team that would be testing the Cuban version of *T. gondii prime* on *humans*. First step was finding the humans, and quite conveniently, the CIA still had some remaining enemy combatants left at its facility in Guantánamo Bay.

"Is there anything else you need from our end on the bio side of this?" Bill had heard enough to know exactly what the next step was.

Kate looked over at her boss. She wanted to keep her hand in this but it looked like Bill was detaching her from "her" find.

"Not for the moment, Mr. DuBois. But we will keep you informed of any developments." The colonel was satisfied to see that Bill understood this was in their hands now.

With that, the meeting adjourned. Kate left the room somewhat deflated. She had expected her involvement to escalate, particularly on this case, which had come close to derailing her career. Now, it looked like her role had evaporated. So much for fieldwork.

AS THEY WALKED OUT of the conference room in the direction of Bill's office, Kate looked over at her boss and let him see her disappointment. She couldn't leave it at that. She started to speak. "What the—?"

Before she could finish her sentence, Bill closed the door to his office behind them.

"Bill, what the hell was that about? I'm the one that uncovered the serum in the first place and you almost fired me because of it. That investigation belongs to me!" Her face was turning red from anger over the issue.

"Kate, now listen to me. That was the best way to handle that meeting, believe me. We're not gonna win by fighting city hall on this one. AFMIC holds the key to any bio-medical intelligence issues—we don't. We have no jurisdiction on those matters. By me not grabbing for territory on that piece of intelligence, that colonel will be more inclined to come back to me with updates."

They were both now sitting around his desk, as Bill kept outlining their strategy. "But at this point, the bio-medical angle is not the big fish we want to catch anyway. The bigger part of this now is the fact that Cuba and Venezuela are in cahoots to create this type of serum. It also begs the question why? What are they going to use it for, to invade Miami? Not likely. You were down there last week, so I'm sure you noticed, it's *already* taken over by Cubans and Venezuelans. The next thing I want *you* to concentrate on is that small piece of pocket change: the $1 million that ended up in that small Swiss Bank in Lugano. I think that just might unlock what this *T. gondii prime* is really for."

"More fieldwork?" Kate's eyes lit up.

Bill nodded. "Yep. First thing tomorrow, I'm going to get you assigned to work with the Europe team. It probably means you'll have to spend some time on the ground over there. I need to figure out exactly where. Let me make some calls around the network. In the meantime, go home and get your travel bags in order. And that's an order from *your* chain of command."

"What about the Intelligence Review Panel?" Kate asked.

Bill reached into the top drawer of his desk and took out several sheets of DIA letterhead. He held them up to Kate. Her brow furrowed when she figured out that it was the official write-up of her unauthorized Cuba trip for the review panel.

"I guess I forgot to file this with the review panel on Friday. . . ."

"Can I read it?" Kate's hand reached out for the document.

Bill put up his hand as if to silence her and said, "As a matter of fact, no, you can't."

"What do you mean? . . ." Before Kate could argue, though, Bill proceeded to put the sheets through the shredder next to his desk.

With a broad grin on his face, he looked at her straight in the eye and said, "If anybody asks, let's just say that I did sign off on your trip and that my approval paperwork got lost in the filing while you were away. And now, it's resurfaced."

Bill held up another form, an approval sheet with his signature on it backdated to before her trip to Cuba. Kate now understood that Bill in fact wavered about filing the report to the review panel, and in the end decided against it.

"Thanks," she said.

"I'm not taking away anything from your good work on the serum, but don't get too comfortable. I don't want to hear about any more maverick moves while you're in Europe. People over there may not be as forgiving."

"No argument from me." Kate had to admit that sleepy old Bill was in fact at the top of his game. He'd been right all along in saying "chase the money" and had backed her up on the Cuban trip, so she just nodded in agreement.

21

⊸+✦+⊶

5:00 A.M. IN NEW YORK AND CARACAS, 10:00 A.M. in London, and 11:00 A.M. in Gibraltar and Bilbao. Nebibi sat in the white conference room of Milestones' New York offices, calculating the start times for the various participants this morning. Hardly a soul traveled on the streets below except for the occasional street vendor pushing a coffee cart and the few taxis that shepherded traders to their posts on Wall Street.

Nebibi's assistant, Eunice Jameson, an African-American woman in her early forties, was the only other person in the office at this hour. Eunice was a statuesque former classical ballet dancer who still had the poise of her earlier, preferred career. Her black hair, streaked with gray, was braided and tied back in a neat bun, accentuating her rose-dusted cheekbones. Her large brown eyes stared out from behind hard-to-ignore, traffic-light red, Alain Mikli frames.

She was busy measuring the exact level of mint leaves for Nebibi's morning tea. In the few weeks she'd worked for Milestones, Eunice quickly surmised that there was no kidding around the watercooler with this one from Milan; at the same time, the pay was good, damn well better than she was used to. All she needed to do, to keep this gig, was follow through on his instructions, with no questions and absolute discretion. But that was always hard for Eunice.

As she entered the conference room, Eunice gracefully balanced herself in her high heels on the plush white carpet, her body trained to float above the floor.

"Mr. Hasehm, here is the folder you requested. And the televideo conference will be up on the screen in a few moments. We're waiting for Mr. Yzaguirre from Bilbao to be connected to the call.

Is there anything else you need right now?" She could see he had that look on his face, like he wanted to get her out of his office quickly.

Without saying a word, he moved the empty teacup over to her.

Eunice forced a smile, tipped her head ever so slightly, and exited gracefully with cup and saucer in hand, closing the double doors behind her.

Inside Nebibi's conference room, the video screens had lit up with faces. Mr. Yzaguirre, a descendant of a long line of Basque nationals, was sitting in his office in Bilbao. He was the finance director of the Basque Nationalist Party. Also on screen was Mr. Rodríguez, the director of investments for the Venezuelan Bank for Trade.

The Fund's London solicitors, Finchley, Emerson, Eggleston & Saunders, were also present. Their acronym was not by design, but their exorbitant legal bills were. The two solicitors charging by the hour on this account today were Hilliard Humphries, from their London office, and his junior partner, Fredric Tarlock, who practiced out of their Gibraltar office.

"Hello. Are you all receiving my signal well?" There was a round of affirmative responses to Nebibi's question.

"Good. Let's get started. Since our last call, we've made significant progress. As you know, we launched Milestones last week with the help of our investment banker, White Weld, and, of course, with the able legal team of Mr. Humphries in London and Mr. Tarlock on Gibraltar. Mr. Humphries, any news to report from the legal end? All our regulatory approvals in place, I assume?"

"Yes, of course. We're up and running as a registered offshore fund in the eyes of the Governor of Gibraltar. The last bit we need to tidy up is the tax exemption for the fund. Don't think that will be a problem, though, you see, that good old chap, the governor, and I went to Eton together. Lovely wife as well. She's fifth-generation Gibraltarian. His son and mine are now going to the same boarding school, carrying on our families' traditions. It's an absolutely brilliant coincidence."

"Very good news, Mr. Humphries." No coincidence here at all. Nebibi had done his research well and knew that Mr. Humphries had exactly the type of connections that no level of bribe could ever achieve. "All looks to be in good order. No need to remind you gentlemen that thanks to your contributions and that of the now closed Banca di Califfato, we have $120 billion to spend and put to work," added Nebibi.

"If I may ask, Mr. Hasehm, are you adequately staffed to analyze new investment opportunities?" asked Señor Rodríguez from Venezuela.

"We poached the corporate finance team from Lazard Frères, all eager to receive their sizable sign-on bonuses. We think they will be adequate to meet our needs for the foreseeable future. Bear in mind, however, that our first transaction may allow us to deploy our capital in a period of weeks, as opposed to months." Thanks to my new "best friend" Sam Coldsmith, thought Nebibi.

"Do tell us, Mr. Hasehm." Mr. Humphries was getting excited about the additional legal fees that any such transaction would generate for his firm.

"Royal Lane Advisors has emerged as one of the remaining healthy investment funds in the market. I've had several discussions with their principal shareholder, Sam Coldsmith. He has large holdings in U.S. corporates, and has proposed that Milestones becomes a silent partner on their portfolio. In order for us to abide by *Shari'ah* laws, his fund would sell 49 percent of his underlying holdings directly to us."

"His reputation is well known, but I also understand that makes him one of the few who is able to attract new financing in these leaner times. Why would he need our help?" Obviously, the Basque finance director was a keen reader of the *Financial Times*.

Eunice sauntered into the conference room carrying a fresh cup of steaming tea. She noticed the odd collection of faces on the video screens, and then remembering herself, set the tea beside Nebibi on the table.

Nebibi nodded his acknowledgment of the tea and then eyed the door, signaling her to leave the room. He took a sip and answered Mr. Yzaguirre's question. "Yes, indeed, he's quite respected. The issue is that Mr. Coldsmith wants to enjoy some of the fruits of his labor and realize some of the wealth that is otherwise frozen in the holdings of his fund. If market conditions were better, he'd be filing for an IPO. So, instead, Coldsmith wants Milestones to generate for him the same exit that an IPO would."

"I see. So what are his terms?" The Basque man was acting like he held decision-making power in this partnership, but in fact he and the Venezuelan were but minority players in this conversation. Nebibi humored their questions in order to maintain a sense of joint purpose for the greater causes he had in mind for Milestones.

"Mr. Coldsmith has proposed that we purchase 49 percent of his fund at the same valuation multiples that Blackstone used when they issued their IPO. His fund currently has approximately $150 billion of assets under management and is leveraged four to one. He's looking to sell at a 1.4 times multiple of current valuation. That would leave Coldsmith with a personal profit of just under $15 billion."

"Mr. Hasehm, with all due respect, isn't that a bit rich, given current market conditions? At today's levels, we should pay about one quarter less than that. That Blackstone IPO was completed at the height of the market." Mr. Tarlock, the lawyer from Gibraltar, was uncharacteristically thinking of his client's interest as opposed to the higher fees his firm could charge for a larger transaction in dollar amount.

Since they were in different cities and he couldn't otherwise get his attention, the senior solicitor, Mr. Humphries in London, was furiously tapping out an e-mail on his BlackBerry to his underling, Mr. Tarlock on Gibraltar:

Bollocks, Tarlock! Don't ask the man any more questions. The more he pays Coldsmith, the more he pays us!!!

"Agreed, Mr. Tarlock. The extra premium we're paying over today's market will give us an option to have a right of first refusal on the purchase of the remaining 51 percent of his fund at a valuation to be determined at that time."

At that instant Mr. Tarlock's BlackBerry, hooked onto his belt, vibrated. He was so focused on Nebibi's words that the vibration caught him off guard, causing him to straighten in his chair. Mr. Tarlock looked down for an instant and read his boss's urgent e-mail, after which he immediately looked up at the screen with a frozen smile on his face, showing his agreement with Nebibi's train of thought. "I see, Mr. Hasehm. That certainly does explain it well, thank you." At that moment, another e-mail and vibration arrived from his boss in London:

> Now put your mic on mute and you'd bloody hell better not utter
> another word on this call!!!

Seeing that Tarlock had stopped his questions, the Basque now took up the charge. "That seems like an interesting transaction, depending on the conditions for the option. . . ."

"No conditions, other than that Milestones receives the 'right of first refusal' on future stake holdings at a price to be determined in the future."

"Who'll determine the price?" The Venezuelan couldn't let himself look shy in this discussion.

"Coldsmith and Milestones will agree on a price at any point between now and the next five years."

"I see," said the Basque. "So in essence, Coldsmith can sit on the sidelines for as long as he wants during those five years and never discuss selling anything, making our right of first refusal basically worthless."

"Yes. Unless market circumstances force him into a corner and he needs to liquidate his holdings."

"And what kind of market conditions could require that? In spite of everything, he seems to be doing quite well." The Basque beat the Venezuelan to the crux of the deal.

"Yes, he's doing quite well. We've performed our initial due diligence on his portfolio. Good investments, all of which we can be happy to own. In terms of potential market conditions, the most obvious one that comes to mind is a repeat of any one of the crises that have hit international markets in the past. Take your pick, Asia, Russia, Latin America, the Internet bubble, 9/11, and of course, the current protracted recession. Any of these would make Coldsmith sell a further portion, if not all, of his holdings."

The Venezuelan, Rodríguez, still had doubts, adding, "But except for 9/11, all these crises were caused by converging unrelated market forces. So, it seems that the option we're getting is the equivalent of a casino bet on those independent market forces once again coming together to create a crisis. And what are the chances of that happening again so soon? It sounds like a very long-shot casino bet to me."

"Unfortunately Mr. Rodríguez, markets always seem to prove us wrong. These crises seem to occur almost with a reliable cadence. There's always the next bubble waiting to burst, don't you think?" replied Nebibi.

"Yes, Mr. Hasehm, but I guess I'm missing something. If the only way we have to recoup our overpriced 49 percent of Royal Lane is to wait and hope for a market crisis, then who is to say that Mr. Coldsmith doesn't manage to once again survive the day, as he's done before? Like they say, 'It never rains on Sam Coldsmith.' "

"Ah yes. There is one point I omitted to mention. A fairly important one, as a matter of fact. Sam Coldsmith's fund has a healthy amount of leverage on it, four times his equity capital of $30 billion, more or less. On top of that, however, he has mortgaged the future of his fund's investment by making bets in the form of derivatives, many times over the value of his fund. He's up to his eyeballs in them, about $2 trillion worth. He's betting his future on the continued recovery of corporates, low oil prices, and a strong dollar." There was a palpable gasp from the London screen. "And most of those trades are concentrated with one derivatives dealer, WR Shipley and Company. . . ." And a second gasp from Gibraltar. At this point, both lawyers made a mental note to check their personal portfolios for any holdings of WR Shipley & Co. stock.

"Of course, our purchase would exclude those derivatives positions, which would stay on his books entirely. And in a moment of market crisis, it will be a house of cards waiting to fall. If markets turn and his directional derivatives gambles go sour, Royal Lane will face a liquidity crunch that would cause him to want to sell his holdings even further. He would initiate the exercise of our right of first refusal."

"Alright, so in a moment of crisis, it finally begins to rain on Coldsmith. That still leaves open the issue of when and how that crisis will materialize."

"Yes, it does, doesn't it?" Nebibi let that comment hang across these Swiss encryption-protected airwaves.

There were a few moments of dead silence in the video conference. Nebibi watched the faces of the Basque and the Venezuelan on their respective screens as they silently realized that Nebibi was not counting on a series of independent market forces to converge. Instead, the scenario wherein Coldsmith would come begging Milestones for needed cash liquidity would in fact be a "market crisis" caused by a well-laid-out plan. More than that they didn't want to know.

This quiet promise of instability would mean rosier times for Chávez's Bolivarian Revolution and the Basques' centuries-old desire for independence from the Kingdom of Spain. And neither the Venezuelan nor the Basque wanted to get in the way of these plans.

"Mr. Hasehm, I think we've heard enough. On behalf of Venezuela, I approve of your proceeding with the proposed acquisition of 49 percent of Royal Lane Advisors, as you have outlined, subject to completion of due diligence on his current portfolio, and confirmation of his derivatives exposure, particularly the ones linked to oil prices. I trust they are as high as you've stated."

"I second the motion, Mr. Hasehm." The Basque could practically taste independence on his lips as he spoke those words.

Nebibi looked down at the papers in front of him. It was the full data dump from his contact in the U.S. government, the man with the bushy eyebrows. It showed the exact detail of Sam Coldsmith's derivatives trade as recorded by his sole counterparty, WR Shipley & Co.

"Thank you, gentlemen, and I assure you that his exposure is exactly like I said, higher than any casino would think prudent." Nebibi grinned as he said this. The four men on the screens signed off one by one and the room was once again silent. Outside, the sun had still not risen on the horizon, but the wind was picking up. Evidently, a storm was brewing.

SITTING BEHIND CLOSED DOORS in his office, Nebibi began to dial a number. He stopped as soon as he saw the door swing open.

It was Eunice, with several phone messages for Nebibi. "Did the video call go well?" she asked.

"Fine. I need to make a call." Nebibi was perfunctory in his response, holding the receiver in his hand.

"May I dial it for you?"

"No, but I do need you to run an errand for me."

"Of course, what is it?" she responded, trying to imagine what kind of errand he could possibly need at 5:45 in the morning.

He pointed to his Ferragamo lace-ups, spotted with drops of dried gray slush.

"I seem to have scuffed up my shoes walking to the office this morning. Can you take them up to the Regency Hotel to get them cleaned and shined? While you're there, treat yourself to break-fast." He needed to be alone in the office for his next call, without the possible snooping of his eager secretary.

As good an actress as she was, Eunice simply could not hide the incredulity written across her face. Shoe-shining was not in her résumé, but then again, the pay was extraordinary, so she bit her lip and replied, "Of course, Mr. Hasehm, I should have suggested it when you walked in. And thank you for the breakfast offer. I'll be right back with a bag for your shoes."

Within minutes, Eunice left with Nebibi's shoes in a Bergdorf Goodman shopping bag, her mind singularly focused on what she would order for her power breakfast at the Regency.

Nebibi walked over in his socks and locked the door to his of-fice. He knew that his entire analyst team was en route to Green-wich for a second day of due diligence at Royal Lane, and now that Eunice would take her time at the Regency, he had the place to himself for at least another hour. He dialed a number that he only carried in his head.

Murad the American answered. "I see that you logged on. So you know the status of our 'suppliers'?" He spoke in coded terms of the Italian bicycle suppliers' Web site he'd created.

"Yes, I see that you have all the 'items' ready for delivery."

"How are arrangements on your end?"

"We have an investment that will fully deploy our capital. The entity in question has a significant speculative exposure, concen-trated with one bank. Should an unforeseen crisis arise, markets would certainly question the solvency of that portfolio and, in turn, that of its primary dealing bank."

Nebibi was counting on some strong winds in financial markets, which would turn derivatives, as had been presaged by the Sage of

Omaha, Warren Buffett, into "financial weapons of mass destruction." And those financial WMDs were already embedded in the balance sheets of major financial institutions, funds, and corporates around the world, waiting for something, or in this instance, some*one* to pull the trigger to explode.

"*Insha'allah.*" By the grace of Allah. Murad didn't need further details. They both knew that other plans related to those "bicycle suppliers" would very quickly serve to tighten market liquidity, if not choke it off completely, and once again create dangerous storm conditions across global markets.

"Assuming we are agreed, our first-stage purchase will require two weeks to document. After that, all we will need to do is wait for 'market conditions' to change."

"I spoke to the Supreme Commander, and he agrees this is the right time to move forward on Operation Andalus."

"*Allahu Akbar.*" God is great.

"*Allahu Akbar,*" Murad repeated after him.

He hung up the line. Nebibi was now ready for the final stage of Operation Andalus, except for one very small detail. He looked down at the floor and said out loud to himself, "Where is that woman with my shoes?"

EUNICE WAS BACK FROM HER JAUNT to the Regency, cold and hungry, with Nebibi's freshly shined shoes. It was too early for the Regency's breakfast, so she had returned grumbling the entire ride back in the taxi.

As she reached to open the door of Nebibi's office, she happened to glance up at the clock in the hallway. 6:35 A.M. She froze and then slowly tiptoed back away from the door. Eunice had made this mistake once before, and after receiving the worst tongue-lashing from Nebibi, she vowed never to do it again. 6:32 A.M. New York time on December twenty-second was the time for the *Fajr* prayer, the one just before sunrise. Nebibi was in the midst of the first of his five daily Muslim prayers. Nothing could interrupt him; the world and Eunice would just have to wait.

22

THE WHITE AND GREEN NAUTAS fast ferry vessel was traveling at top speed across the Strait of Gibraltar on its scheduled seventy-minute journey from Morocco to the port city of Algeciras in Spain.

The vessel had departed Tangiers early that morning under a sky that still held remnants of an overnight storm. The warm Levanter winds from the Sahara and the cool Poniente from the Atlantic had collided to create cloud formations that spiraled upward in the vast blue sky, accented by dark shadows of brewing storms and brilliant pockets of white light from the day's new sun. The Saharan winds were stronger today, pushing the clouds toward the Atlantic, so the rest of the day promised to be clear. The waters were relatively calm, broken only by the waves of passing vessels and the jumps of the bottlenose dolphins that made this area their breeding ground.

The passengers were mostly merchants and laborers, but there were also tourists, who lugged their carpets and other trinkets from their brief sojourn in "Arabia." At the far end of the boat was a group of twenty elderly Japanese tourists from Nagasaki who had just kicked off a tour of Morocco and Southern Iberia. They stood on the bow with digital cameras ready for any action or monument worthy of recording. One of them saw a break in the water and alerted his colleagues. And then a bottlenose dolphin jumped in the air. In no more than half a minute, twenty cameras took five images each of this one sighting. A whole school of dolphins would have caused a virtual tsunami of camera clicks.

This group of elderly Japanese tourists was led by the very able

but harried Michiko, a twenty-six-year-old on her first foray as
tour guide. As an undergraduate, she had studied at the Universidad de Salamanca and in one short year she had embraced the rich
history, language, and culture of Spain, making her the perfect
guide for these retirees and their cameras. She looked at her note
cards and began her tour narrative.

"*Sumi masen.*" Excuse me. "*Kudasai.*" Please, everyone gather
round here. "*Kudasai.*" A thin wire pole with the flag of the rising
sun at her side, Michiko stood with her back against the railing of
the vessel, her short, straight black hair tousled by the strong winds
on deck. The senior citizens crowded in a half circle around her.

"*Domo arigato gozaimasu.*" Thank you very much. She spoke
into a blow horn in order to be heard above the roar of the engines
and breaking waves. "Can everyone hear me?" Her voice now carried through most of the vessel.

"Most honorable colleagues, I will now tell you an interesting
story about a famous warrior who crossed these waters almost thirteen centuries ago." They all paused to listen attentively. "On a very
early morning in April, 711 A.D., an ambitious Muslim general
from North Africa named Tariq ibn Ziyad stood at the bow of his
boat in these very same waters where the warm Mediterranean
meets the cold Atlantic. The Caliph in Baghdad had ordered him
to leave his family behind in Tangiers. He was not sure if he would
return, but was convinced that a glorious future lay in the vast, rich
land to the north. General Tariq looked up at the mountain of limestone known as one of the Pillars of Hercules that jutted straight up
more than thousand feet before him, still illuminated by the moon."

The elderly tour group's attention was diverted for a moment. Another dolphin was spotted in the water and only after another hundred photos could they once again turn back to listen to their guide.

"As he crossed the strait, General Tariq stared at the smooth
façade, and he knew that he, Tariq, *insha'allah*—by the grace of
Allah—must claim this rock for his Muslim people. With him that
morning was a small force of four hundred men and one hundred
horses. Once ashore, he ordered his men to burn the sails of the
boats they had used for the journey, leaving his troops no choice
but to head north to fight the Visigoth rulers of the Kingdom of
Hispania. This made his men fierce in battle, allowing him to claim

a bloody victory over the rock. And so it is, to this day that the rock, the Pillar of Hercules as it was then known, is instead known as his: *Gibr Al-Tariq,* meaning *rock of Tariq*—Gibraltar."

Michiko's audience let out a communal sigh.

"After Gibraltar, Tariq and the Moors went on to conquer much of the Iberian Peninsula. And each victory brought a new wave of Muslim immigrants through Morocco who came to rule Spain for close to eight centuries. They called their new home al-Andalus and their civilization flourished, allowing Muslims, Jews, and Christians to coexist. It was a true Golden Age."

Michiko's tour group clapped in unison. She had done very well in the timing of her narrative, because just as she finished her story of General Tariq's victory, his rock, the Rock of Gibraltar, loomed on the horizon. The tour group once again whipped out their cameras and started clicking. Michiko bowed deeply, showing respect for their approval as their tour guide on this journey.

ENTERING THE BAHÍA DE ALGECIRAS—the Bay of Algeciras, as it's known on the Spanish side—the ferry was now ten minutes from docking at the port. The bay's western coastline is dominated by the Spanish industrial port city of Algeciras, which was founded by the Muslims shortly after General Tariq's conquest of his Rock. Today, it's the largest urban center in Spain's southern peninsula and is a vital transportation link between Europe and North Africa.

The eastern coastline of this same bay is known as the British Overseas Territory of Gibraltar, and the British gave this bay an entirely different name, the Bay of Gibraltar. Gibraltar covers only two and a half square miles, but its location and famous rock, rising 1,400 feet above the water, give it prominence greater than its actual footprint.

The simple, elegant geography of this naturally protected bay has made Gibraltar much prized and heavily contested since the time of the ancient Greeks. And to this day, the broad question of the continued validity of the 1713 Treaty of Utrecht, which granted sovereignty to the British, continues to strain relations between Madrid and London.

At the local level, kerfuffles arise daily as Spanish fishing boats cross back and forth over the invisible man-made lines of respective territorial sovereignty, alongside British naval vessels that stand ready to police every unauthorized intrusion. It was against this backdrop of cool tension between the two European Christian nations that the ferry, from the ancient launching pad of Muslim conquerors across the Strait, made its way to dock.

ONE TALL MAN, WHO WASN'T a tourist, stood at the bow of the ship looking east at the dramatic skyline. As he gazed at Tariq's Rock, the sun emerged behind the iconic landmark, casting a large shadow across the bay. The man was wearing a white djellaba, the traditional dress for men in Morocco. To complete the look, he was sporting a fez, the well-known red felt truncated cone of a hat. The man had one accessory that didn't quite fit the look: white earphones connected to an iPod hidden in the pocket of his djellaba. The ingenuity of Steve Jobs reached far and wide.

To any of the Western tourists on the ferry, the tall Moroccan added to the authenticity of the scenery. In the eyes of the Spanish authorities, he was part of the usual commercial ties with the North African coast first established centuries ago. None of his fellow passengers had detected that he was neither a tourist nor a Moroccan, despite the fact that at six feet three inches, he was taller than most Moroccans, or Spaniards for that matter. And how were they to know that under his dark weathered tan, this man was pasty white with freckles? On close scrutiny, his blue eyes and light brown hair would certainly have raised some questions. But the human eye is lazy and only focuses on the broader external clues, and the man's form of dress hid his underlying secret quite well from those who only gave him a passing glance.

Another man, also dressed in a djellaba, approached the much taller man. He was carrying two cups of hot Moroccan mint tea. The shorter "Moroccan" was older and his skin was a naturally darker complexion. His physique was better suited to the costumes of North Africa. He offered a hot tea to the taller man, who took off his earphones and powered off his iPod, interrupting his Spanish-language instructional podcast. The men drank their tea staring at the Rock, two Muslims eyeing this ancient prize.

Suddenly, a gust of strong wind accompanied by a thundering noise passed over the boat and broke their concentration on Gibraltar. It was neither the winds of the Strait nor a brewing storm. It was a gray British Royal Navy Merlin medium-lift helicopter that thundered overhead, on its habitual surveillance flight over the Bay to see if any Spanish fishing vessels were crossing into British-controlled waters. The forced air of the helicopter blades blew the fez off the taller man, who turned to catch it as it rolled on the floorboards of the ferry. Without the hat, he was now more recognizable as the man often seen in video conferences, as well as the publicity videos of al-Qaeda posted on the Net.

The taller "Moroccan" was in fact Murad the American, who had traveled west from his base in Kandahar. He didn't have his signature flowing beard; years ago, he had shaved it off and instead donned a Hollywood prop, for purposes of disguise. George Clooney dons sunglasses and a baseball cap to escape the tabloid paparazzi; Murad took off the fake beard to avoid detection from the dragnet of international security forces seeking his capture and death.

His partner was Samir Moussab, the deputy commander of the North Africa–based al-Qaeda in the Islamic Maghreb, the AQIM. This group had splintered off in the late 1990s from larger unaffiliated Islamic militant groups in Africa. The name AQIM is explained by the fact that for a mere $40,000 donation of start-up capital from Osama bin Laden, al-Qaeda received naming privileges of the new satellite organization. The AQIM's goal is to topple the government of Algeria as well as to participate in other missions that may be of mutual convenience.

Bin Laden had set up a franchise arrangement for coverage of the North African "market," much in the same way that Mickey D's have sprung up on every other street corner around the world with their golden double arches. Their purpose today on the ferry was to initiate a unified mission that would have lasting implications for all of bin Laden's local terrorist franchises around the globe.

Glancing around to ensure that his cover had not been blown, Murad placed the fez back on his head. The two men returned their gaze to the Rock, at which point Samir said, "This is as good a moment as any." Then, without any sense of oddity about the moment, the two international terrorists turned *turista*. Samir took a camera from his pocket and motioned for Murad to strike a pose with the

Rock in the background, just like those in Michiko's tourist group. As the international spokesman for al-Qaeda, Murad was not camera shy, however, that was when he had his beard disguise. This photo, without his bearded disguise, would be for the "family album" that could only be released after his capture or death, whichever came first.

Murad with his light brown hair safely hidden beneath his fez, turned his blue eyes on his companion and grinned for the camera. Click. *"Insha'allah,"* by the grace of Allah, he said.

"Insha'allah," responded Samir. "Yes, one day soon, we can reclaim for our brothers what is rightfully ours."

Both men felt they were on a path that would forever link their names with the military bravery of General Tariq, and they thanked Allah for the privilege to honor him in this momentous mission. Murad shook his head in wonder. So much time had passed since General Tariq's victory against the Visigoths; it was marvelous to think that he, a modern-day inheritor of Tariq's legacy, had been born in a country, the U.S., that didn't even exist back in 711. A.D. It was both humbling and inspiring.

The men's conversation was interrupted by the thud of the vessel docking at port. The tourists, Michiko and her orderly group, crowded the exit plank with all their booty. Murad and Samir waited out the rush to exit. They held in their hands documents that identified them as two Moroccan businessmen en route to Algeciras for a meeting with Spanish counterparts. The early-morning shift of groggy Spanish customs officers didn't take more than a passing glance at their papers, allowing them through without a problem.

ALGECIRAS'S ARCHITECTURE IS A MIX of charming older buildings with stucco walls and clay-tiled roofs dating from the early 1900s and low-rise, boxlike apartment buildings constructed in the 1970s. The city's port facilities, built on landfill jutting out from the original beach line, are stacked with large mechanical cranes on the docks. If one could ignore and look beyond those large cranes, this would be one of the best vistas of Gibraltar.

Murad and Samir were walking to the old Reina Cristina Hotel, situated in the green oasis of a large park that was a short distance from the docks. Murad turned to Samir and asked, "What should we expect from this Iñaki Heredia today?" His question was about the deputy head of the Euskadi Ta Askatasuna, the ETA, the armed Basque nationalist movement. After several months of tentative approaches and intense negotiations, Samir and Heredia had established an accord for their two organizations to collaborate on select missions in the Iberian Peninsula. The historic, though tenuous, agreement had already resulted in their first joint venture, the bombing in Madrid's airport a few weeks earlier. The volunteer for that mission had been one of Samir's men, Sajid Hossein, a local from Ceuta, Spain's colonial town on the coast of North Africa.

Samir responded thoughtfully. "Iñaki was a good partner for the Madrid mission. One of his men triggered the detonation of the bomb by remote electronic device. We weren't sure if, under the pressure, our operative Sajid would have been able to detonate it alone."

"Wasn't Sajid taking doses of the Cuban serum?"

"He was, but since he was our first test case, we didn't want to take any chances. In the end, he performed perfectly."

"So you recommend the serum?"

"Absolutely. It will enhance the fervor our men."

"Heredia doesn't know about the serum, right?"

"He has no clue. We've had three joint combat training sessions with our men. His only comment was that their fierceness honored the legacy of General Tariq and his men." Samir grinned as he said this.

"So can we trust Heredia and his Basque friends?"

Samir didn't hesitate in his response. "Can we trust anyone, my brother Murad?"

That's not what Murad wanted to hear, but then again, he knew they were in a complex game of cats and mice with deadly booby traps under each tidbit of cheese; one wrong nibble and your head was trapped in a death vise. For the moment, since they held the secret of the Cuban serum, he felt they had the upper hand, but that too could change. Their chosen profession, terrorism, didn't offer many opportunities for long-lasting "friendships." The only thing that they, Islamic and Basque militants alike, could count on were marriages of convenience. And for the moment, they were working in tandem—at least until their respective goals were achieved, or one stabbed the other in the back, whichever came first.

"By the way, were you able to locate the child, Sajid's nephew? Wasn't he with his mother on the day of the bombing?"

"No, no luck. At first, we thought he was caught in the blast, but as it turns out his mother went into the terminal alone. He hasn't surfaced anywhere. We have all our operatives in Madrid on the lookout for him. I met him a few times in Ceuta with his family—a charming young boy. We had plans for him as soon as he was older."

"Keep looking. You know the boy has a special place in the heart of the Supreme Leader."

Samir looked at Murad, not promising any results. Three million people in Madrid. A needle in a haystack.

23

KATE'S HEELS CLICKED LOUDLY as she walked over the iconic seal of the Central Intelligence Agency engraved on their headquarters' lobby floor. Since she never wore a watch, Kate hurriedly glanced at the time on her cell phone: 10:35 A.M. She was always cutting it close and today was no different. She lost track of time at the office trying unsuccessfully to reach Alejandro San Martín in Caracas, and now she was already five minutes late for the interdepartmental briefing upstairs.

She presented her DIA badge to the guard and walked quickly to the elevator. Once on the second floor, she rushed to the conference room. Yep, this is the right one, she said to herself, staring at the two signs on the door: BRIEFING IN SESSION and TOP SECRET. Kate slowly opened the door, hoping to slip in unnoticed, but no such luck. It was a small windowless room with people sitting around a rectangular conference table. All six heads turned as she entered. She recognized most of them, her peers from the CIA, NSA, and State. Her boss, Bill, motioned her to the seat next to him. Given his stern look, she was inclined to find another place at the table, but there were no other empty chairs.

Sorry, she mouthed.

At the head of the table stood Connie Madern, a forty-five-year-old CIA officer. Even though she had twenty years under her belt in D.C.'s tight-knit intelligence community, all her neighbors in suburban northern Virginia, as well as her two teenage daughters, still thought she worked as the marketing manager for an accounting firm. She looked the part, at least: immaculately tailored yellow

Norma Kamali suit, auburn hair in a perfect bob with bangs, and shiny manicured nails.

Kate had never dealt directly with Connie before, but knew she was top-notch when it came to global underground terrorist groups, which is why she looked forward to this briefing. All the more now that her pursuit of the Madrid bombing money trail put her in the middle of a global terrorism plot, something out of the norm for an analyst covering Latin America.

"So, as I was saying," Connie remarked as her eyes peered out over her reading glasses at Kate, "our intelligence indicates that a number of underground cells are increasing activities." She turned to point at the large plasma screen behind her, which displayed a global map with several points flashing in Europe, the Middle East, and Central Asia. She continued in her matter-of-fact tone. "But these locations are only a small fraction of what's probably out there, ready and waiting for the right moment to launch into action."

Kate raised her hand. "Excuse me, Ms. Madern. Kate Molares, DIA. Shouldn't we have more people focused on this?" she asked.

Connie stared, taking further notice of Kate, who reminded Connie of herself at the outset of her career, a little too quick to speak her mind. "That's been my line for the past decade, but in truth, no matter how much money and intelligence assets we throw at it, we'll never know the full extent of these dormant cells. That's the point of 'dormant.' On top of that, they've been making full use of the Internet, increasing their recruitment with disaffected youth, particularly in Europe."

"So if we know their location on the Web, can't we pursue them from there?" Kate interjected.

"Just as quickly as their Web sites spring up, they go off-line, within days, before we even realize what they were up to. They use a wide array of Web sites targeted to different national audiences, even producing music videos and posting them on YouTube." Kate noticed that Connie's face was no longer as stern as before; seemed to her that the senior CIA officer didn't mind her questions.

"We call this initial recruitment stage pre-radicalization. After that, they start reeling them in with increasingly targeted information about the global jihad, including links to sites of past battles.

This month, we're seeing them use a lot of footage of the Madrid airport bombing. While we're spending hundreds of millions on tanks and private contractors in places like Iraq and Afghanistan, these enemies are creating an ideological battlefield on the Internet. Any questions?" Connie didn't look around the rest of the table, just at Kate.

"Okay, but I look at YouTube videos and that doesn't turn me into a suicide bomber?"

"That's good to know, Ms. Molares," Connie quipped, drawing a chuckle from the somber group. "Eventually, they migrate from online chats to in-person training, where they come to accept an ideology of hate and violence. All in all, it's probably an eighteen- to twenty-four-month cycle from first contact to being on the front lines of the global jihad."

"Two years. That's a huge commitment of time *and* money." Kate glanced over at Bill, recalling his mantra—follow the money.

"Indeed it is. That's why your intelligence on those money transfers was key." Connie's lips formed a half smile, indicating to Kate that she had read her briefing and, more important, approved. "Without money, they just don't have the necessary funding to create the next generation of terrorists." Connie looked at her watch and concluded her part of the briefing. "Gentlemen— and lady—I'm afraid I need to leave for a meeting with the Director. Thank you for coming. My colleague Dan will handle the rest of the briefing with you."

As she was leaving, Connie pulled Kate aside. "If you ever want to come over to covert ops, where all the real intelligence gets done, call me. We need more like you here at Langley."

When Kate sat back down next to him, Bill shrugged his shoulders, as if asking what Connie had wanted with her. She leaned over and whispered to him with a smile, "Just some career advice." She then sat back in her chair, now even more certain that money and the movement of it held the key to answers about the Madrid bombing.

24

THE DARK BLUE RANGE ROVER with tinted windows sped down the highway at exactly the posted speed limit of 120 kilometers per hour. The car was traveling south on the Autovía del Mediterráneo, the highway that connected the towns along Andalucía's famous Costa del Sol, Spain's southern coast. The passengers had started their journey last night in Bilbao on the northern coast of Spain, or rather in the Basque Country, as those in the car would argue was the only name for that territory.

The driver was of average height and build, with a cropped military haircut and a distinctive scar that ran across his right eyebrow. He was the able assistant for his important passenger, Iñaki Heredia, the second in command of the Basque armed separatist movement, and the architect of their outreach program with al-Qaeda. The passenger had a full head of short gray hair, and while his face held no scars, it was marked by rugged age lines that made him look older than his fifty years. Decades on the front lines of guerrilla maneuvers, and cigarettes, can do that to a man.

Heredia could see they were passing Marbella, one of the more famous Costa del Sol resorts. It played host to many tourists from Northern Europe, owing to its warm weather and palm trees. It was also a popular stopover for citizens of the Arabian Gulf. What the ancient Moors had not been able to keep through military might was now acquired in massive lots with the power of petrodollars.

But the scenery was of no interest to Heredia. He kept glancing at his watch, trying to estimate when they'd arrive in Algeciras for his important meeting. He reminded the driver, "We need to be there by ten." Their conversation was carried out in the Basque language, which is unintelligible to the common ear because it exists in isolation. It is the longest surviving language in all of Europe with no apparent link to any Indo-European language.

Heredia looked behind them. Another Range Rover, green, was still trailing them. Good, he thought, for inside this second car there were three additional Basque operatives.

Heredia then glanced over at the other passenger sitting beside him in the car, who didn't understand a word of Basque, and knew only rudimentary Spanish. Nonetheless, words in any language flew over his head because like any other nine-year-old boy, his mind was completely focused on the Nintendo DS combat game held in his hands.

The boy's thick dark eyebrows, inherited from his father, dominated his square face, except for his striking deep hazel eyes, reminiscent of his mother. He was a slight boy with olive skin that had not seen much sun. His short life had been largely spent inside his family's small apartment in Ceuta with his mother, who kept him locked up inside like a precious cargo she feared one day would be taken away from her. She had been right.

The boy's native tongue was Arabic, taught to him by his mother, Fadiyah, the young uneducated Berber woman who had met her end at Madrid's airport two weeks earlier, along with her brother Sajid, the suicide bomber with the red backpack. The Basque man with the scar above his right eyebrow, at the wheel of the Range Rover, had been the one who detonated the bomb in the red backpack. Minutes before the blast, he had found the bomber's car and, unexpectedly, the boy inside. In a split second, he decided to take the child with him in the car and leave it to his superiors to figure out what to do with him. This had been the right choice, as the child was indeed precious cargo for al-Qaeda.

The boy was named Mohamed, like his father, Mohamed Atta, the coordinator of the 9/11 attacks. In July 2001, Atta had traveled from the U.S. to Spain to meet with several members of the 9/11 plot to coordinate final arrangements. After a few days of meetings in Tarragona, a town south of Barcelona, Atta had disappeared for eleven days.

In that time, the leaders of al-Qaeda granted him a hundred

niceties befitting his soon-to-be martyr status. Among those niceties was an arranged marriage to a virgin Moroccan woman, whose lowly family understood the honor they had been offered. A child of a jihadist martyr bloodline would bestow on their family special privileges. Their hope was that by offering their fifteen-year-old in marriage, their only son, Sajid, could be saved to support them in their old age. But their plan derailed as their precious only son eventually became a martyr himself. Though not planned, their daughter also perished as a casualty in this international game of terror that, until then, had not touched their simple lives in Ceuta.

The boy, their grandson, was in fact conceived and born in a resort hotel in Marbella. His birth there gave him rights as a Spanish citizen, though these few weeks had been the longest he had ever spent on the Iberian Peninsula. His life until now had been spent in the Spanish enclave of Ceuta on the Moroccan coast in that small one-bedroom apartment occupied by his mother, his uncle, and his two grandparents. Mohamed the boy spent most of his waking hours locked inside, playing his computer games. His lineage had not brought great delight in his short life, and he had learned to shut down the normal glee of a nine-year-old.

No one had explained to him what had happened to his mother or uncle, but he had developed a sixth sense about these things and somehow he didn't expect to ever see them again. Now, all that remained was a shadowy memory of an explosion and a plume of smoke as the car drove away from the airport that morning a few weeks ago. His mother had told him that, one day, important men would come to take him away from her. So he was not surprised to be in this car today with the Basque. However, the day had come sooner than his mother expected and unbeknownst to him, the *wrong* important men now held him.

In the weeks since his mother's death, his young pliable mind focused on his DS game and staying alive. His grandparents assumed that their grandson had perished along with his mother in the bombing. The honor they had sought for their family had instead granted nothing but immeasurable loss.

He's a quiet one, this boy, thought Iñaki Heredia, not at all like my children. Heredia's seven-year-old would be climbing the walls

to get out and play with his friends, but this boy only needed computer games.

The Basque hadn't managed to get even a bit of information out of
him, other than the fact that his mother left him.in the car waiting.
Heredia decided to keep him for the moment, thinking he might be of
value in their dealings with their "friends" in North Africa. The boy,
Mohamed, was simply a commodity to be traded. The mother and
grandparents had controlled the commodity before, and now it was
in the hands of the Basque. Question was—what was the value of
his head?

25

⭢+✦+⭠

MURAD AND SAMIR ENTERED THE LOBBY of the Hotel Reina Cristina, which was decorated with several groupings of burgundy velvet chairs and art deco lamps from another, more glorious, era. The air in the main reception room was dusty, stirred by anyone sitting on one of those ancient chairs. At its height, the lobby would have been filled with early Hollywood stars sipping aperitifs with Europeans who, though polished in appearance, clung to noble titles of very questionable origin. Today, you could hear a pin drop on the lobby's marble floor, since the hotel was only 20 percent occupied. The only other guests were members of a seniors tourist group from England.

At the front desk stood a Spaniard in his mid-twenties. Manuel's dark features and complexion underscored the fact that many centuries before, the Moors had passed through this kingdom and left a legacy of more than just their magnificent palaces and mosques. Young Manuel covered the front desk alone, given that most of the hotel staff was off preparing for Christmas festivities. His frame was too thin for the suit he had borrowed from the regular concierge, a man many years his senior and, judging by the loose fit, someone who had substantially more tapas under his belt.

The two men approached the front desk. Murad took the lead, having a working knowledge of Spanish. "*Buenos dias,* we are here for the meeting of International Bicycle Suppliers. Where should we go?"

"*Muy buenos dias, señores.* Yes, your conference is in Salón Alfonso XII. It's down the hall on the left, facing the bay. Other attendees have already arrived." Since there was no one to replace him at the front desk, Manuel tried his best to direct them without leaving his post. His boss had told him not to mess up today, or it would be his last day on the job.

He eyed the two men with their fezzes as they walked down the hall and thought, What a strange mix of people, this meeting of bicycle suppliers; I shouldn't complain, they're good tippers.

The front desk phone rang and broke his concentration. It was the old British couple from Brighton in Room 209, who were yelling at the top of their lungs about a water leak from the room above them. The young man grabbed a large wrench they kept in the bottom drawer of the front desk console expressly for this purpose. Given the number of times this kind of thing happened here, one could hardly classify this as an emergency. Instead, it was really just another day at a creaky resort situated in a previously charming locale.

MURAD AND SAMIR REACHED THE DOOR at the end of the hall and turned the worn brass knob. It was locked. A few seconds later, the door opened slightly and out peered the stern face of Mahmoud Fakhouri, a British citizen of Jordanian descent. On seeing who it was, he opened the door further and his face took on a smile. "Welcome, brothers."

The men walked in and greeted each of the other "bicycle suppliers" with a traditional kiss on the cheek. In addition to the Jordanian-Brit, there were two other members of the al-Qaeda international franchise, one Egyptian-Italian, who had been recruited personally by Nebibi, and one Lebanese-Dutch man, who in turn had recruited the Dutch "gringo" operative at Yale University.

The manner of dress of the three already in the room was Western: slacks and open-collar shirts, with the exception of the Egyptian-Italian, Ahmir, who could not deny his combined heritage. He wore a dress shirt made of the finest Egyptian cotton, but styled by an Italian shirtmaker with a high Windsor collar, and adorned by a thick silk, British rep tie. These young, Western-looking professional men showed no signs of a harsh life hiding in caves. All three were clean shaven with short crew-cut hair. Equally, their smooth hands contrasted with those who had spent most of their time in Kandahar's underground tunnels.

After the display of camaraderie, the five men sat around a long dark mahogany table. Murad and Samir placed their fezzes in front of them. The ancient Venetian blinds were drawn on all the windows. Judging by the dents and scratches, the wood table had weathered many a heated discussion in its hundred-plus years of service. Some of those discussions had been more heated than others, judging by the sizable nick caused by a stray bullet at one corner of the table.

As the most senior commander present, Murad was given the floor to moderate the discussion. He spoke in Arabic, the language that bound everyone at the table, and the one he was most comfortable with after so many years away from Fresno.

"My brothers, we've reached an important crossroad in our efforts, and only have a few weeks for final preparations. Let's get started because the Basque will arrive shortly. We'll let our new partners know some, though not all, of the details we've discussed here. Trust should be built in stages, not all at once. Ahmir, where do we stand with our recruits and their training?" Murad addressed his question to the young Egyptian-Italian.

"Yes, certainly. We've completed a thorough analysis of our current forces." Thirty-year-old Ahmir spoke with a voice of competency, after which he stood to hand out a PowerPoint presentation book, just like any other recent MBA grad from Harvard with a degree in operational management. In fact, that had been his degree two and a half years prior. The presentation cover read: INTERNATIONAL BICYCLE SUPPLIERS FORUM. Murad looked on with a smile, thinking that the money they allocated in recent years to educate the more talented new recruits had been very well spent indeed and would have a positive impact on their cause for a long time to come.

"As you know, for each successfully identified and deployed front-line military operative, it takes approximately eighteen months of training—"

They heard a noise outside. Murad got up and lifted the blinds; sunlight flooded the room. He looked around and saw a seagull flying away outside. "Nothing," he said, and closed the blinds again.

"Where were we? Oh yes, wait. It takes eighteen months to fully train our best men. And from these, we select only forty percent to execute the most sensitive missions, most of which may require them to sacrifice their lives for the global jihad. Look at the chart on page four." Ahmir looked around the room, making sure his audience was keeping pace before continuing.

"But in order to stay one step ahead of Western intelligence forces, we needed to quicken our pace. This is where our Venezuelan and Cuban contacts have been of great assistance. They've developed a serum that shortens the time required for the final phase, the jihadization of our select special forces." Eyebrows were definitely raised around the room.

The Lebanese-Dutchman whispered to Fakhouri, "Can this be true?" He didn't get a response, because the other man sat with arms crossed, attentive to Ahmir's continued presentation.

Samir stared at the page in front of him and with one hand he unconsciously twirled his fez on the table. He wasn't used to this kind of slick presentation, since his approach was more rudimentary: "how many bombs" and "where is the target" sort of thing.

Ahmir was momentarily distracted by Samir's twirling fez, but he soon focused back on his presentation.

"The serum works very much like steroids that athletes use to speed up muscle-building. Instead of increased muscle tone, though, the Cuban serum allows our special forces to more quickly train their mental state for suicide missions, in half the time." Ahmir pointed to page eight of the presentation.

"Haqqan!" Really! Samir thumped his hand on top of his fez, suddenly stopping its twirling.

"Do the recruits actually understand they're receiving this serum?" asked Fakhouri, who also happened to be a practicing medical doctor in London. He was somewhat skeptical that a so-called courage serum could really be created.

"No, as far as they know, they're receiving vaccines against one or another disease. We performed the first field test of the serum with the detonation of a simple TNT bomb at the Madrid airport last month. Our brother, Samir, tells me that the bomber was amply prepared and willing to lay his life on the line for our cause. And he did, which resulted in one hundred percent mission success."

The hairs on the back of the British-Jordanian doctor's neck sprang to attention. "And so this actually works?"

"Absolutely."

Everyone in the room understood that this would forever alter the playing field for revolutionary movements from here to the mountaintops of Bolivia and the jungles of Southeast Asia. Fighting their oppressors with armies as fierce as General Tariq's men would become the norm. Underground movements would have the strength of fearless armies full of convictions. Correction, that's *convictions on steroids.*

The silence in the room was broken by a knock at the door. Everyone closed their presentation books. Ahmir walked over, immediately concerned that someone was listening to such a critical part of his presentation. He slowly opened the door and saw the smiling face of Manuel, who was barely managing to balance a tray of two large bottled waters and glasses.

"*Permiso*—excuse me, you asked for water? I'm sorry it took me so long. We had a problem with the plumbing that flooded Room 209 and I just finished cleaning that up. *Mil disculpas*—so sorry. May I come in?" Manuel rambled on, while Ahmir rolled his eyes and opened the door wider to let him in.

Manuel was greeted by a room of very stern faces that made him uneasy. He quickly set the tray down in the middle of the table, next to Samir's fez, and started to pour the water. Samir's harsh look dissuaded him from pouring the rest. Manuel excused himself from the room and left wondering if bicycle parts could really be such a serious business.

Ahmir waited a few minutes for Manuel to walk down the hall and then turned his attention back to his colleagues. "Any questions about the serum?" They were still mesmerized by his detailed presentation and couldn't wait to see what would be revealed to them on the next pages. "None? Good. Let's move on to the second part of the presentation, target selection. Next page, please."

Samir was hanging on to every word, his excitement growing with each new page of the PowerPoint. He started fishing through his djellaba in search of cigarettes. He lit one and offered the pack to his colleagues, but they all declined. Samir took a deep puff and returned more calmly to study the numbers and graphs in front of him. Meanwhile, Fakhouri, the Jordanian-Brit, got up and flicked the switch on the wall that turned on the ceiling fan to dissipate some of Samir's smoke.

Ahmir continued above the noise of the rusty fan. "Please turn to the next page."

26

KNOCK, KNOCK.

The men in the room hushed as Samir walked again to the door. He opened it enough to see that it wasn't Manuel, but Iñaki Heredia and one his men. "Welcome, brothers." Samir put on his best smile to put them at ease. The rest of the men in the room rose to greet the new participants.

Introductions were made around the table, after which Murad spoke first. He switched to English to be understood by the Basque. "Welcome, Iñaki."

The other Basque operative stood guard by the door, keeping direct eye contact with Iñaki, who sat on the opposite side of the table. Iñaki spoke in heavily Basque-accented English, "Thank you, Murad. We're very pleased to be here representing our cause and participating in Operation Andalus. For centuries, we've fought all aggressors, particularly those in Madrid, to obtain our right for our own homeland, where we can speak our own language and elect our own leaders. Anything short of that is not true independence." He pounded his fist on the old table to emphasize the importance of his last sentence.

Iñaki took a breath and continued. "Our only option has been armed retaliation to change the will of the Spanish. We have always fought alone, but now we are sure that our joint Operation Andalus will deliver a powerful message to the oppressors in Madrid."

The time was ripe for Iñaki's strong words with this audience. Al-Qaeda and its worldwide franchisees wanted to reinstate the lost glory of an Islamic political empire for a modern world. And the

Basque wanted to end the union of Spain that was first established in the fifteenth century.

"We share your enthusiasm." Murad interrupted what he sensed could be a long discourse on the principles of Basque autonomy by Heredia. "It may be helpful to hear from our colleague, Ahmir, on the logistics for the operation."

"Oh yes, of course. Please proceed." Iñaki straightened himself in his chair, feeling somewhat deflated.

"Just before your arrival, we started to review the targets," Ahmir said.

Iñaki was not necessarily surprised by the fact that they had started the meeting without him, and wondered what else they were planning that they weren't letting him in on.

Murad spoke to Iñaki. "I understand you see a high value in detonating the bombs at a time when there would be fewer civilian casualties. Is that right?"

Iñaki nodded in agreement and responded, "Exactly. Each time civilians are killed, the Spanish government gets more support from its citizens to pursue military tactics against us. The result is a stronger enemy, not a weaker one."

Iñaki's goal in working with Murad and his men was to deliver a multi-pronged threat to the Spanish government. In turn, he felt this could mean the end of the Spanish union, with newly independent nation states with names like the Basque Nation, New Andalus, and New Catalonia. If the Soviet Union could break apart, why not the Kingdom of Spain?

Iñaki knew the moment was right for his next move. He needed to keep his Islamic "colleagues" comfortable with their newfound partnership, and he had a very tangible olive branch to offer. He gave his operative by the door a hand signal. As the man stepped out, Iñaki could see that his departure alarmed some of the men at the table.

"Do not worry, my friends. He will soon be back with a gift from our people. My goal here today is to cement our partnership."

After a couple of tense moments, the bodyguard re-entered the room trailed by his colleague with the scar above his eyebrow. In between the two men was the boy, Mohamed. No longer focused on his DS, his large eyes traveled around the room, taking in these new strange faces around the table. His gaze landed on Samir. "Uncle!" The boy had found a familiar face and rushed over to hug the man, who was not his uncle by blood but had certainly been his benefactor.

Iñaki noted the connection and smiled at the bodyguard with the scar. In that split second at the Madrid airport, it had indeed been a good choice to save the boy, Mohamed, son of Atta, who cemented the success of the Terrorist Concordat of Algeciras.

27

THE ROOM WAS DARK. Pitch dark. Even if there had been a light, Nebibi would not have seen much of it behind the dark cloth covering his face. He was awake, barely. He smelled smoke coming from somewhere close by. He was getting light-headed, no doubt because of the slight incline in which his body lay on the hard surface. His legs were bound and tilted at a 45-degree angle above his head. It was disorienting him and causing waves of darkness to pass through his consciousness. He wasn't sure how long he'd been in this position. He tried to lift himself up, but had no strength left. Even if he'd had the strength, his legs, torso, and arms were firmly bound to a wide, sturdy plank of wood that was propped up at an angle in this dark, smoke-scented room. He tried to stay awake, to figure out where he was and why he was unable to move. It was getting harder.

Suddenly, he felt a drop of water enter his left nostril and then his right one. Because of his incline, they were both exposed, facing skyward. Maybe it's raining wherever this place is, he thought. He was inside, and so if it was raining, drops couldn't much touch him where he was. He was actually further than he imagined from the outside world and any falling rain. The room was underground. Another few drops entered his nose and traveled through his sinuses, causing a searing pain in his face under his eyes and in his upper teeth. Another few drops entered and the pain grew stronger. Now he needed to breathe, but he couldn't. The drops kept flowing in at a steady pace and his brain could only focus on that now—I need to breathe.

He started to panic, thinking, I'm trapped! His access to air was being constricted. He took in a deep breath. Instead, his esophagus took in a flow of water that traveled to his lungs. The feeling of asphyxiation was greater than he could bear. He let out a scream, which only came out as a weak pathetic moan. He was flowing deeper into the darkness to the point of no recovery.

Several men in dark clothes and masks surrounded Nebibi, their prized prisoner. Confessions needed to be obtained or he would be allowed to die. Correction, drown. They raised the plank so that now his head was above his feet and took off the wet cloth covering his face. These swift actions at the very last possible moment brought the prisoner back from the brink. Nebibi started coughing up the water in his lungs and was able to take some quick labored breaths. He had not recovered from the "water cure" by any measure, but he would live to see the next few minutes. At least until the "cure" began again.

Nebibi was no longer the crisp personification of confidence that he'd been in the magnificent boardroom on Fifth Avenue. Instead, he looked like a helpless rodent that had just escaped drowning in a sewer pipe, still desperate for a more lasting escape from death. His skin felt cold. Very cold. He looked down and saw that he was stripped naked on this wooden board. A man sitting just beyond the inner circle of Nebibi's torture was keeping an eye on the proceedings. The man was cloaked in the darkness of this torture chamber. His voice, an icy one lacking any emotion, resonated through the chamber in an unintelligible language. The man was instructing one of his underlings conducting the "water cure" to take action.

Nebibi's mind started racing—What was the language the man was speaking? It wasn't English. Where am I? Have I been captured? How much time has passed? Did Operation Andalus already take place? Who are these people? Nebibi only had questions but no answers.

"¡Confiesate, si no te mueres!" Confess or you will die!

Nebibi tried to decipher the language being spoken by the man. It was Spanish, but a strange dialect he had never heard before.

Nebibi couldn't remember being in Spain. Had the Americans captured him in New York? Was this one of the CIA's black sites? All these thoughts hit Nebibi's brain like a freight train in the split seconds since the last "water cure." He felt the need to regain his footing. He didn't want to crumble and divulge their plans for Operation Andalus.

"*¡Confiesate!*" Confess! The man in the mask was starting to tip the board back to the reclined position to taunt the prisoner. Nebibi walled off the part of his mind that held the details of Operation Andalus. He began to concentrate his remaining energy on different thoughts, building a mental barrier against the next onslaught of torture.

Nebibi thought of the most innocuous set of phrases he could muster. He started reciting, in Italian, the full recipe for Cotoletta alla Milanese. "*Sciogliere il burro in una padella larga e pesante e farvi dorare le costolette da entrambi i lati, su fuoco dolce.*" Melt the butter in a large heavy skillet and brown the ribs on both sides, on a slow fire. . . .

The man was getting ready to place the dark wet cloth back on his head for the next round. Nebibi saw that coming. He stopped his recipe incantation and took a breath to prepare himself for the next onslaught. He just needed to survive this next drowning and everything would be fine. Just look ahead one second at a time, he kept telling himself. This time he'd be prepared.

The cloth was placed back on his face and his body was propped again at a 45-degree angle. Then, the excruciating cycle started all over again. The drops came in through his nose and then down his lungs. The first time had seemed an eternity to him. In fact, it had been only fourteen seconds. Now, if he was lucky, he could hold on again. And he did. His captors took him to that same place of helplessness, and then at the very last moment, snatched him back from the total darkness. This time, he took less time to recover his breath and clear his lungs of water. As soon as the man took the cloth from his face, Nebibi was ready to start his recipe incantation again.

He stopped for a second because he noticed that their leader, who had been hidden in the shadows, had now moved closer into the torture circle. Nebibi couldn't see his face clearly. He wore a robe made from a primitive cloth and a belt made of twine, from which hung a wooden cross. He had a large hood over his head that obscured everything except the faint outline of his face.

"In my ten years conducting this particular torture, I have never seen a prisoner manage to withstand more than two rounds of the 'water cure.'" The person was speaking in an older form of modern Spanish, Castilian, and was none other than Tomás de Torquemada, the Spanish monk, confessor of Queen Isabella and, most notably, the leader of the Spanish Inquisition. Torquemada's reign of terror, which began with the victory of the Spanish Kings in 1492, yielded a rich bounty of tried-and-true barbaric torture techniques, including the "water cure" inflicted on Nebibi. This particular technique had survived more than five hundred years, most infamously as a tool of interrogation, the present day "water boarding." It would have made Torquemada proud to see the lasting effect of his innovative "interviewing" techniques.

Nebibi tried to focus his eyes outside the immediate circle of torturers, but his vision was becoming more clouded. The scene in front of him was becoming a whirlpool of disjointed images. He could make out two other naked prisoners, both held dangling from chains around their bloodied wrists. Suddenly, Nebibi smelled the smoke and realized that it was not smoke from burning wood, but the stench of flesh being subjected to a hot rod. It was the prisoners next to him. Both of them were screaming and writhing, going in and out of a dull consciousness, because of the relentless assault of the red hot rods.

And then, for brief second, he saw them; he knew who they were. That knowledge fell on him like a steel anvil weighing on his chest, forcing all air out of his lungs. One of them was Kate, and the other was his brother Rashidi. Nebibi tried to move to help them but his body was anchored by that heavy weight. He tried to yell out their names but nothing, no air, was coming out. His eyes filled with a rapidly changing kaleidoscope of colors. But it was the stench of their burning flesh and their lancinating screams that finally made Nebibi lose complete consciousness.

Five seconds or five days passed, but this time, through the darkness, there was only a ringing sound in his head. It wasn't going away. *Ringgg, ringgg, ringgg.*

He gasped for air and discovered that his body was entirely wet. The sheets he was lying on were also soaked with his sweat, and his nose was dripping. He was no longer in that dark room. He was in his stark modern apartment. *Ringgg, ringgg, ringgg!* There was that ringing again. It was his cell phone. A call was coming through.

Nebibi had been in a dream, a very real one; the same one for several evenings in a row. Each time he found himself at the receiving end of a different torture by his tormentor, Torquemada, the converter of Muslims and Jews in fifteenth-century Spain. These dreams made Nebibi certain that he could never allow himself to be captured by the enemy. He preferred to die in the cause of the jihad rather than be captured and held in a torture cell to release information he had vowed to keep secret. This evening's visit by Torquemada, however, had brought one change, a troubling addition, the presence of Kate and Rashidi. Their torture was vivid in Nebibi's mind, but he had been helpless to save them.

Ringgg, ringgg, ringgg! He finally reached over to the table next to his bed and picked up his phone. He noticed the time. 6:15 A.M. The ID on his phone read PRIVATE CALLER. "Hello?" Nebibi's voice came out hoarse. Was this part of the dream, he wondered? Then he remembered, he had woken with a head cold yesterday. He reached over for a tissue and blew his nose away from the receiver.

"It's me." It was Murad. In the background, Nebibi could hear the noise of passing ships. The call was being placed from aboard the ferry boat taking Murad back to Morocco across the Strait. Unless he was in the safety of his protected home base, Murad never stayed in one place too long. "I'm calling to remind you that my birthday is on January twenty-fourth. It falls on a Monday this year, and you'll need to buy me a cake."

"Understood. What time do you think I should go to the bakery to pick up the cake?" Nebibi quietly reached over to his night table and yanked out some tissues from an ornate dispenser.

"You should be there by ten a.m. After that time, they might run out of cakes." In less than thirty-five seconds, Murad had communicated the date and time for Operation Andalus and had signed off.

As the call finished, Nebibi took his phone off-line. He needed time to reflect on his dream and the information he had just received from the Bay of Gibraltar. He went to the kitchen and drank down two large glasses of orange juice. He didn't have time for this irritating stupid head cold, but fortunately he was on the tail end of it.

Upon returning to his bed, he stared up at the white ceiling and thought about his fifth visit with the Grand Inquisitor Torquemada.

Did his subconscious doubt his role in all of this or was he simply getting mentally prepared for taking the next and final steps of Operation Andalus? He couldn't make a certain bet on either of those hypotheses. But what he could bet on was that the pieces on the chessboard had been set and the game was in play. His only choice was to move forward. Two images kept flashing though his mind, however: on one side was his brother and on the other, Kate. If Nebibi still had any options that let him come out the other side of this game whole and unscathed, Torquemada had certainly not divulged it in his latest visit.

28

HAVANA, CUBA
DECEMBER 24

INGE JOHANSSEN STARTED THE DAY of Christmas Eve like all her other days in Cuba, jogging before sunrise along the Malecón, the five-kilometer harbor-front drive that stretches along Havana's coastline. She wore shorts and a T-shirt purchased locally so as not to attract attention as a foreigner. Her blond hair was neatly tucked under a royal blue baseball cap with a white embroidered *A* for the Alacranes del Almendares, the famous Cuban baseball team.

She set her watch for her training jog this morning. The time was 6:00 A.M., an hour before the sun would rise fully on the horizon. Later in the day, the Malecón would be bustling with pre-1958 American cars moving along the winding road, and the walking path would be teeming with the vibrancy of the city's culture: Canadian and European tourists, local hawkers competing for tourists' hard currency, and other locals, some fishing, some strolling or sitting back to enjoy the ocean breeze.

She checked her cell phone and noticed a short text message from Kate: Coming for New Year's? She typed a quick reply: Trying to—will call with plans.

She safely tucked it in her hip pack, along with a few euros and her U.N. ID card, and began her jog in front of the Hotel Nacional. She planned on taking a slower pace today, since she'd been overtraining these past few weeks. Last week, her Achilles tendon was feeling a bit tight, a reminder that she wasn't eighteen anymore. Besides, the Malecón was always in need of repair, so even pedestrians had to contend with potholes. She waved to the front-door porter at the hotel, as she did each morning before setting off. It gave her comfort that someone knew where she was at this deserted hour.

As she ran, she felt the cool morning breeze that swept over the ocean. The strong December waves hit the stone wall of the Malecón, splashing mist along her path. Her run took her through the history of Havana, from the newer construction in her neighborhood of Vedado to the art deco of Central Havana and finally to the colonial-era structures of Old Havana.

There was no one ahead of her on the walking path this morning, and in the distance, she spotted a single old American car making its way across the bay front. It'll be a mellow run today, she thought.

The first rays of sunshine were glinting through the horizon, creating subdued lighting for Inge's view of the city on the right. As she did on most of her morning runs, she allowed her mind to clear, and then made mental notes on her to-do list—I haven't heard from Mirella in a few days. Hope she's okay. I need to tell her the good news that her asylum visa to Sweden was approved. She wanted one for her brother, too, but that was going to take more time.

She was nearing her midpoint landmark, the Fortaleza de San Salvador de la Punta, an old fortress built in the sixteenth century by the Spaniards. Inge looked at her watch. 6:12 A.M. A little faster than she intended.

"*Fan!*" Inge let out a curse in Swedish as she tripped over a new-found pothole on her "running track." She managed to barely catch herself, lunging forward and falling hands-first on the rough pavement. Her left knee scraped against the pavement, drawing blood. But that wasn't the real problem. Her right foot had been the one to catch on the pothole, twisting her ankle. The first hint of the severity of her injury came when she tried to stand up. "Ouchhh!" Her right ankle simply sank to the ground, and the pain rapidly spread through her leg. Her first thought was that she wouldn't be able to compete in that marathon back in Göteborg next month! "*Fy fan!*" God damnit!

She sat on the pavement, trying to soothe her ankle. Out of the corner of her eye, she saw an approaching car, the same one from the start of her run. Thank God, she said to herself, I can ask them for a ride back to Vedado. Just in time, because her ankle was beginning to swell.

The car slowed down as it approached her. From her vantage point, she saw two men dressed in polo shirts in the front seat. One of the men looked no more than twenty years old, but the driver was older, about thirty, she figured. Their faces were stern, which was not completely odd for Inge, as some Cubans truly didn't appreciate foreigners in their country. They'd heard the stories about life before Castro, when their country was controlled by the American Mafia.

"¿Me pueden ayudar, por favor?" Can you help me, please? Inge spoke in her heavily accented Spanish.

Her accent was the confirmation the men were looking for. The man on the side of the car closest to Inge rolled down his window. Inge started sitting up when she saw the man reaching his arm out of the car. How odd, she thought. It looks like he is holding a gun. Within seconds, two shots rang out, followed by the sharp shrieks of circling seagulls.

The impact of those shots pushed Inge's body back hard onto the pavement, her head getting the brunt of the impact. The two shots were intended to kill her instantly, but they didn't. One grazed her skull; the other hit her chest. As soon as they were fired, the younger man shouted at the driver to speed off.

Inge lay there motionless with blood oozing from her head; her mind began to race, trying to recover from all the signals of physical danger speeding to her brain. What happened?! She tried to stand up but her body was not cooperating.

Just then, she felt a searing pain in her chest. "Aghhh!" She reached over to touch the source of the pain. She held up her hand and saw that it was now covered in blood. *"Helvete!"* Hell! "Where is all the blood coming from, did he hit me?" she asked herself.

In between the multiple organ-failure messages received by Inge's brain were thoughts of why these men had done this to her. She felt her hip pack still on her waist, so she hadn't been robbed, and there was no sexual assault that she could remember. Nothing in her local duties should have generated such a gangland assassination. There was only one aspect of her recent activities that she knew was sensitive: her contact with Mirella, the Bermudez Institute, and the serum. Who else knows about it!? Kate! She needed to warn her.

She took a labored breath and frantically reached over with her right arm to her hip pack, grabbing her cell phone. Speed dial.

With every last ounce of energy and focus, Inge pressed the number 3 on her cell phone. It was the speed dial for Kate. It was ringing! She hoped she was home. Kate pick up the phone! Inge wanted to yell, but the words weren't coming out of her mouth.

KATE WAS RUSHING AROUND HER APARTMENT in Old Town Alexandria, hoping to get out by 6:30 A.M. She was packing a change of clothes because she was spending Christmas with her father in Connecticut. She quickly threw in the essential items: pj's, change of underwear, a warm sweater, and jeans. Mornings were never calm for Kate. She was opening the door to leave when her cell phone rang. "Great, now I'm definitely going to be late!"

She dug in her purse for her phone to see who was calling. The caller ID started with the number 46–7. She immediately recognized that it was the Swedish country code for calls from a cellular. Has to be Inge, she thought. She immediately answered.

"*Hallå, Inge.*" Kate didn't hear any response. The line wasn't dead; there was just an empty sound, almost like wind blowing. She figured the line got cut off and that Inge was probably calling to wish her a Merry Christmas. Kate ended the call and rushed out the door. She'd call her friend once she got to the office.

KATE WAS SIPPING COFFEE at her desk when a call came through on her cell phone.

"Hello?"

"Hello. This is Jerôme Lemasse. I am the chief U.N. representative in Havana. Who is this?" The man's English was spoken with magnificent French *r*'s.

"This is Kate Molares. . . ." She recognized the name; it was Inge's boss. Kate's heart started beating faster.

"We believe you received a call earlier this morning from a cell phone. . . ."

"Yes, I did. I think it was Inge."

"How do you know Inge?"

"We went to school together. We've been close friends for many years. She tried to call me this morning but the call got cut off. Is she alright?"

"I see. Well, I'm afraid that I have some terrible news. Inge was killed early this morning in Havana. She was shot while jogging along the Malecón. Would you know any reason why she might be the target of such a thing? Had she spoken to you about any strange occurrences?" Lemasse was still at police headquarters—in fact, just outside the room where Inge's bloodied naked body lay on a flat slab of metal ready for inspection by a Cuban forensic doctor.

Lemasse had identified Inge's body, and as he spoke to Kate, the image of the bloodied cadaver on that table kept flashing in front of his eyes. Her body had been found by another jogger, who had pulled out her U.N. ID. The local authorities were trying to keep this quiet for now. Can't have diplomats being gunned down in the streets of Havana; otherwise, Canadians and Europeans would likely cross Havana from their list of favorite destinations. And without their hard currency, this island wouldn't be very sunny for long.

Kate's heart sank. The news cut right through her midsection, making her double over in pain. The cell phone fell on her desk. "Nooooo!" Kate's loud cry made the officer in the next cubicle rush over to see what was wrong. He found Kate gasping for breath, staring at the phone on her desk, which was emitting the hint of a voice yelling from the other end of the line.

LATER THAT MORNING, ANOTHER BODY WASHED ashore a few yards farther down on the Malecón from where Inge had been killed. This body, also female, had suffered severe beatings, as was evident from the massive bruising on the cadaver. But this woman had finally died from a bullet through the head. Thankfully, the Cuban police immediately determined that she was not part of any foreign diplomatic corps. Probably just another lover's spat gone wrong with dire consequences. Therefore, the second corpse found that day was placed a distant second in terms of importance.

It would be days before they would get around to investigating this second killing and determine that it was the body of Dr. Mirella Martínez, medical researcher formerly of the Bermudez Institute. She'd been killed three days prior to Inge's murder. The beatings suffered by Mirella, at the hands of the same two men who had murdered Inge, had resulted in her divulging the identification of Inge as her foreign contact, benefactor, and receiver of the serum samples. However, no one at police headquarters made any brilliant leaps to uncover that the two victims actually knew each other. There was the issue of that outstanding Swedish visa for Mirella, but months would go by before Stockholm would be informed that the intended recipient was now dead.

29

THE INTERCOM'S BUZZ CUT through the Zen-like atmosphere of The Milestones Fund's fortieth-floor offices.

"Yes, Mr. Hasehm." Eunice Jameson answered promptly.

"Eunice, I need fresh tea and a box of tissues." Nebibi sat at his desk, dressed in his habitual business attire, obviously recovered from his earlier morning encounter with Torquemada. His office was the size of an average living room and the carpeting was plush and cream colored to match the walls and leather furniture in the room. It sat along the same side of the building as the large conference room, and so he had an equally impressive view of Central Park. His desktop was devoid of items except for his landline and his iPhone, which was neatly docked to his Mac.

A few minutes later, Eunice entered the room with a gentle stride, balancing a cup of Nebibi's favored mint tea, scalding hot, on a saucer, and a box of tissues decorated with a blue floral print. "Excuse me, Mr. Hasehm, here is your fresh cup of tea." He's a hard one to crack, this Nebibi, Eunice thought, but she'd give it a shot anyways. "Maybe I should go to the drugstore and pick up some cold medicine for you?"

"Not necessary. I'm fine," he answered with no hint of gratitude.

She shrugged her shoulders, sending a signal that she was bothered by being rebuffed. He didn't notice.

"Also, I have a message from Ms. Bretz. She called earlier this morning." Eunice thought she caught him flinching when she mentioned her name to him.

Nebibi looked at the message from Margaux. She was becoming too much of a distraction, and he needed to cut her off.

"Get me Sam Coldsmith on the line," barked Nebibi.

"Certainly." As she left his office, Eunice grumbled under her breath, "Mr. Sorry Ass is certainly in a mood today."

"HELLO, SAM. IT'S NEBIBI."

"Hello, my friend. How are those billions doing in your pocket?" The thought of The Milestones Fund with all those idle billions was never far from Sam's mind.

"They're doing just fine, Sam. Actually, I need to spend them. I understand from the lawyers we can have everything set up in a few weeks."

"Listen, Nebibi. Don't worry about those lawyers. You and I can set the date and I can guarantee you those lawyers will make it happen. All we have to do is wave that fee in front of them and they'll make it happen."

"Yes, I see your point. So let's set a date. I'm looking at my calendar. A January twenty-first closing fits perfectly in my schedule and gives them just under a month to arrange the documentation. Does that work for you, Sam?"

"Hold on, let me check." He was booked solid with meetings in Washington on that date. Sam ignored that. "Yep. That's perfect." Nebibi's idle billions were far more important than meetings with mere government officials, like the Secretary of the Treasury. "Let's carve that in stone. Come hell or high water, we're closing on the twenty-first. Where are we signing? My office? Yours? Or at the lawyers?"

"Actually, I was thinking we should close the documentation in Gibraltar, where our fund is registered. . . ."

"EUNICE. EUNICE!" EUNICE HEARD THE INTERCOM buzz again.

"Yes . . ." She tried to keep her irritation out of her tone, but suspected that Nebibi wouldn't notice, either way.

"I need you to make arrangements for me to be on Gibraltar, first thing next week, and then on January twenty-first."

"Yes, Mr.—" Her voice was interrupted by another bark from Nebibi.

"Also, call Margaux and tell her I had to step out, which is why I haven't called her."

So now I have to do your dirty laundry on top of shining your shoes? she thought to herself. "Sure, I'll call her right away." Eunice held her tongue as she heard him click off on the intercom. She thought again about her excellent salary. "They should double it," she grumbled to herself.

Nebibi's iPhone buzzed in the cradle. UNKNOWN NUMBER. He picked it up. "Hello."

"*Aló.*" Nebibi immediately recognized the voice and accent of Minister Alarcón of Venezuela. "I wanted to alert you that our friends on the island discovered an information leak on the product they sold. They think they've contained it. I don't expect that any of it leaked from here, but we'll start checking as well. Thought your people should know, so that you're not surprised."

"Do we know where it leaked?" asked Nebibi.

"We think at the U.N., but I understand from our island friends that the source has dried up, permanently."

"Thank you for the call." Nebibi cut the call short, but not out of rudeness. People operating in this illicit space knew better than to hang on the line longer than necessary. He couldn't help but think they needed to move quickly before other leaks started surfacing.

30

⊰┼┼┼⊱

KATE SAT IN HER CUBICLE at the DIA, with her chair away from her desk, facing the window and staring blankly out across the Potomac. Her office space was small and not private, but it was still her domain. Her desk was stacked high with newspapers, a sign of the recent turmoil in her life, culminating with the terrible news this morning. Kate's fingers fidgeted nervously with her ponytail as she wrestled with the fact that her dear friend Inge was no longer on this earth.

From the moment of Jerôme Lemasse's call, she was certain that Inge's violent death was somehow related to the serum. So Kate sat there on this gray morning thinking how her friend had been killed, practically by Kate's own hand, because she had brought Inge into this terrorist mess to begin with. She swallowed hard on that thought and it didn't go down easy.

She wanted to pounce into action—any action—but couldn't without Bill's okay, and he was incommunicado, delivering a security briefing on the Hill. His assistant, Samantha, promised to call her as soon as he got back. Until then, all Kate could do was go through scenarios in her mind and try to come up with the best approach to find Inge's killer. And with her dead, who knew how long it would be before they uncovered the link to her. On top of that, whoever was using the serum would get advance warning that the U.S. government was on their tail, making their work all the more difficult.

In the midst of her thoughts about Havana, a picture of Alejandro popped up in her mind. *I was supposed to try to reach him at* home this morning, she reminded herself. She'd been unsuccessful for days, and now the call had even greater urgency.

She dialed the number on her cell phone and waited, getting more anxious with each unanswered ring. *Rinngg. Rinngg. Rinngg. Rinngg.* Finally on the fifth ring, a woman answered. *"Aló, quien llama?"* Hello, who's calling? The person spoke in a numbed tone, devoid of emotion.

Kate replied in Spanish, "This is Kate Molares. Is this Isabel?"

"Oh, it's so good to hear your voice . . . K-kate. . . ." It was Alejandro's wife, Isabel. She was breathing heavily, and then her voice broke off into muted sobs.

"Isabel, what's wrong? Where's Alejandro?"

"He, he . . . ," Isabel stuttered. "He d-d-died last night—"

"What!? What happened?! Was he in an accident?"

There was a long pause, and then Isabel spoke in rapid fire. "We don't know. The doctors couldn't help him. He started throwing up a week ago. He was sick for several days and stayed home, but didn't get any better." She choked, and took a deep breath. "Three days ago, I took him to the hospital. Maybe I w-w-waited too long, because they c-c-couldn't save h-h-him! . . ."

Kate could hear her drop the receiver as someone came into the room, a man, who picked up the line.

"I'm sorry. Isabel needs to lie down for a moment. This has been too much for her, for all of us, really. Were you a friend of Alejandro?"

"Yes, from Georgetown. My name is Kate Molares. I'm calling from Washington."

"Bueno, this is her father, but I must really see to her now. Maybe you can call back another day. I must go now. . . ."

"Of course. Can I just ask one question before you hang up? Which hospital was Alejandro taken to?" Kate's adrenaline was pumping fast now.

"The military hospital in Caracas. Why?"

"No reason. Thank you, *señor.* Please tell Isabel to call me if there's anything I can do for her, she has my number." As soon as Kate hung up the line, she ran to Bill's office.

"Is he back yet?" she asked Samantha.

"Honey, he just walked in the door. He hasn't even taken off his coat yet—"

Before Samantha could finish the sentence, Kate burst into his office, "We have to do something, Bill!"

"Whoa, Kate! What's all this about?"

She quickly filled him in on the two deaths and explained that she was convinced they were related to the serum. Bill slumped into his chair, his coat still on, stunned by the news. "Jeez, I'm sorry, Kate."

"I'll grieve about this later, Bill. Right now, I want to get to the guys who did this." There was intensity in her eyes, just short of a tear.

Bill stood up slowly, taking off his coat and throwing it on an empty chair. He sat back down across from Kate.

"Okay, let's see. Inge's death was definitely foul play, but Alejandro, I'm not so sure about. He could have died from swine flu, for all we know."

"This is just too much of a coincidence. They were both killed within the past twenty-four hours. We have to do something!" Kate pounded her fist on the armchair she was sitting on.

"What the hell do you think I've been doing all morning?! I was up at Congress in back-to-back briefings to the Intelligence Subcommittee *and* the Military Oversight Committee on this goddamned serum!" Bill never reacted well to confrontation, certainly not after the past few days of increased limelight on the serum.

In that time, *T. gondii prime* had become a white-hot issue at Defense. The President had been briefed on it yesterday evening by the National Security Advisor, and it was now top-of-mind throughout the U.S. intelligence community. The order had come directly from the White House to get to the bottom of it. And now there was the death of one of Kate's friends and possibly another.

He paused and sat down at his desk. "Listen, Kate, I'm sorry. I know these were your friends, and yes, chances are they were in the midst of this whole mess."

"I know, Bill, it's just that . . ." Kate was trying to bring it down a notch, but her mind was still racing. "I'm just not good at losing people." She still felt the wounds left by her mother's premature death.

"I know, so let's call a truce and get to the bottom of this. If not, their involvement in all this was for nothing."

"Agreed." Kate relaxed her death grip on the arms of her chair. "So where do we go to from here, then, Bill?" She could only muster a weary, anxious smile.

"Is there anything else that maybe we overlooked? Any more clues on this whole serum thing? Maybe something that can get us on track to find the killers and their plans for *T. gondii*. . . ."

Kate looked pensive for a few moments and then finally spoke out excitedly. "There's Inge's medical research contact! Her name is Mirella Martínez. Can we have our guys down in Havana track her down?"

"Yep, we can certainly get them on the case. Was she working at the Bermudez Institute?" asked Bill.

"Not anymore, as of the last time I spoke with Inge." Kate's voice quivered a bit. She made her brain take back control. "She told me Mirella had been transferred to some field clinic."

"Okay, well, that's good to hear. But if I were on the other end of this serum, meaning the guys planning to use it, I'd make sure that the knowledge of it was secure and preferably contained six feet under. Get the drift of where I'm heading with this? It's time to broaden our approach."

"Like how?" she asked.

"First off, let's feed Mirella's name into the system and get the help of our local staff in Havana to track her down. If necessary, we can bring her to the U.S. until this whole thing blows over. And on Alejandro, let's figure out what killed him. Do you think we can talk to his doctor?"

"He died in the military hospital in Caracas. That's where they treated him for the last three days. . . ."

"Hmmm, that might take a little more work. But I'm sure our guys on the ground in Caracas are creative folks. Send me his details and we'll have a look at his medical records."

"Excellent." That was already a very major relief for Kate.

"Second, we definitely need to get you out of Washington for a while—"

"What? Wait, I need to be here to get to the bottom of this—" The last thing Kate wanted to do was leave this investigation.

"Yes, yes, I know. But here's the deal. If these guys, the killers, figure out your connection to Inge, Alejandro, and the serum, well then, they're gonna come looking for you. So don't worry. We can get you away from your usual D.C. tracks, but you'll still be helping out, just from a different location. As of right now, I'm putting you on temporary loan to the staff of AFRICOM."

Bill could see this plan confused her. The United States Africa Command, AFRICOM, represents the unified military resources of the U.S. government focused on the African continent. This new unit had only been operational for a year, and for the moment it was headquartered in Johannesburg. It sits alongside, and coordinates with, similar military commands in other global regions.

"What the hay? What am I supposed to do in Africa?"

"One of the command centers for AFRICOM is in Morocco. They work very closely with EUCOM on issues related to Spain. The thing on the front burner right now for both AFRICOM and EUCOM is the Gibraltar Sovereignty Summit taking place next month. Given the Madrid airport bombing and the trail of monies we've been tracking, there is great concern that something might be planned for the Summit. Add *T. gondii prime* to the mix, and you've got a lot of people running around trying to figure out what's gonna happen next. If that isn't enough, remember that the President is supposed to attend the March commemorations in Madrid. There will be more than enough to occupy all of our intelligence resources, including you, in the next few months on the Iberian Peninsula."

"Okay, okay. So, just so that I'm clear on this, I'm supposed to work with AFRICOM leading up to at least the Gibraltar Summit at the end of January, right?"

"Yes. After that it will depend on what we find ahead of the President's trip to Madrid. If we don't break up any planned plots before then, this could stretch further. Remember our friends in Venezuela and Cuba had something to do with all of this. Your input on the ground is to make sure that any link with Latin America is not overlooked."

"Okay, so who do I report to and where's my home base?"

"I'll see if we can station you on Gibraltar under General Owens. Actually, he's here in the building today, so I'm going to try to

set up a meeting with him. What time are you here till?" It was
Christmas Eve, after all.

"I was planning to leave at noon to meet my father in New
York. . . ."

"I think you should still go see your father, but just catch a later
flight. Can you do that?" asked Bill.

"Sure, no problem."

"Okay, let me set up that quick meeting with the general. By
the way, he's the commander over there and you would be temporarily assigned to his unit, but I'm still your boss. Got that?"

"Yes, sir." Kate gave him a salute, grateful he'd made that clear.

31

━◄+ +━►

MANHATTAN, NEW YORK
DECEMBER 24

IT WAS CLOSE TO TEN by the time Tomás Molares and his daughter savored their last bite of Soufflés Calvados and stepped out from under the distinctive canopy of La Grenouille, the last of the classic French restaurants in New York. Despite the news about Inge's death, they had both tried to lift their moods with a traditional Christmas dinner.

Kate's father carried her small overnight bag in the chilled December air. Fifth Avenue was packed with wall-to-wall tourists, giving it the feel of a town fair. They strolled slowly in cadence with the crowds, admiring the Christmas windows along the way. Kate smiled at her father. A few hours hidden in this holiday crowd, far away from the worries of the DIA, would be good for her. And for him, too, she thought.

At Saks Fifth Avenue, throngs of children, some held atop their parents' shoulders, were squealing with delight at the sight of characters from Dr. Seuss's *How the Grinch Stole Christmas!* The story, however, was now adapted to a more contemporary global warming message with the Grinch frolicking among palm trees instead of snow-covered evergreens. Evidently, Saks had succumbed to pressure from the United Nations' newly appointed global environmental czar, Albert Gore, to display a story with a "green" message.

NEBIBI HAD STAYED LATE at the office. For many New Yorkers this was an evening of family, last-minute shopping, celebration, and, in some cases, religious observance. But for Nebibi, this was just another Thursday night, a particularly quiet one at the office that allowed him to focus on preparations for the Coldsmith closing in a few weeks.

His cell phone rang. It read CALLER UNKNOWN, but he guessed who it was and picked up immediately. "Yes."

"We have a problem," said Murad. "The handler for our friend this evening didn't make his flight. Can you be there instead? He needs to be watched."

"What time?"

"Ten p.m. at the place."

"I'll be there." Nebibi hung up. The entire call lasted eleven undetectable seconds.

NEBIBI HEADED DOWN FIFTH AVENUE to his apartment building on East Fifty-first Street. He was somewhat taken aback by the throngs of holiday foot traffic on Fifth Avenue, along with the overpriced roasted chestnut stands and hot dog vendors making a brisk business even at this hour. He stopped and bought a bag of roasted sugar-coated almonds from a man tossing them in a large, hot copper pot in his cart; it reminded him of Europe. He popped a couple in his mouth.

Looking at the masses walking up Fifth Avenue, Nebibi thought about their misguided priorities. Consumerism trumped religious observances; clearly, it was more important to these people than honoring the birth of the prophet Isa in prayer. Jesus Christ is "Isa" to Muslims, who look upon him as one of the illustrious prophets that came ahead of Muhammad.

THE "GRINGO" FROM AMSTERDAM RUSHED OUT of the Metro North express train from New Haven, carrying a backpack. He'd left the Yale campus as soon as he'd received word from Murad. He was instructed to meet the contact at the north side entrance of St. Patrick's Cathedral at exactly 10:30 P.M. for final instructions.

The "gringo" sped through the crowds in the great hall of the station, which was filled with the sound of Christmas music accompanied by the traditional laser light show overhead. Most travelers stood mesmerized, gazing up toward the "heavens" of the grand ceiling. The "gringo" ignored the display, weaving his way to Fifth Avenue toward his destination.

He couldn't be late. In the last few weeks of his jihadist training, the "gringo" had become razor-focused on his mission. Nothing seemed impossible; no one could stand in his way. He felt invincible thanks to the "vitamin" shots he'd received from his superiors. His brain was feeling the pressure of time and so he started to bump into some of the people crowding the sidewalk as he made his way up the Avenue.

TOMÁS WAS LOST IN THOUGHT, looking at the children, probably imagining a future time when he might enjoy grandchildren. Kate looked at her watch. "It's ten twenty-five, Dad. I think it's time we stand in line at the Cathedral." She took her father's arm and started pulling him away. In that instant, she felt someone push by her left side, almost knocking her over.

"Hey! Watch it!" Kate regained her footing. She tried to see who had pushed her, but only managed to catch sight of someone's head covered in a gray wool cap weaving through the crowd ahead.

"Are you okay?" Her father looked up ahead of her, to catch a glimpse of the lone man who had pushed through, but he had already disappeared farther into the crowd. "Did he take your purse?"

"Nope, still here." She was hugging it tightly under her arm. "He almost knocked me down." She didn't know that the "gringo" who rammed into her had much bigger issues on his mind than simple purse snatching.

THE "GRINGO" SHOVED A FEW MORE people aside as he cut past the front entrance to the Cathedral till he was finally able to see its north side on Fifty-first Street. The side entrance faced the doorman's post of the Olympic Tower across the street.

The doorman was standing outside, looking at the holiday crowds, when he saw his newest tenant, Mr. Hasehm, come toward him. But then, instead of coming into the building, he crossed the street, toward the north side of the Cathedral. This surprised him, because the gossip of the building staff had informed him that this tenant was a strict Muslim. He'd have to check his info sources next week, because there was Mr. Hasehm in plain view heading to Christmas Eve Midnight Mass at St. Patrick's.

. . .

NEBIBI RECOGNIZED THE "GRINGO" with the backpack from the photo he'd received from Murad, innocently identified as another "bicycle supplier." He approached him and uttered the code words in Arabic: "Isa was a great prophet who came before the greatest of prophets."

The "gringo" responded in kind. "Muhammad is the last great prophet and he will guide us."

"We have only a few minutes and cannot spend too much time together. Your target is this building, where the infidels gather to worship. Are you ready?"

"I will give my life if necessary to complete it," the "gringo" responded rapidly, almost stumbling on his words.

Nebibi looked at the young man's eyes. They were bloodshot and darted back and forth nervously. Is this his religious zeal talking or is it the serum? he wondered. Nebibi noticed that the man's right hand was twitching in a spasm, and so he stood there with his left eyebrow raised in concern, studying the young operative. The "gringo" caught Nebibi's stare and immediately put his right hand in his pocket to control the jittery movement and to hide the bluish color of his nails. "Have you been taking your vitamins?"

"No, I haven't received the shipment yet." Again the "gringo's" speech was rapid, and on top of that, he was lying. He'd started taking the serum three weeks ago, even though the instructions explicitly stated to begin the treatment only two weeks prior to his mission. His curiosity had gotten the better of him, and after that first dose, he experienced an intense feeling of euphoria that combined energy, alertness, confidence, and invincibility. And it was that intense euphoria that caused him to try it again and again. He had become an addict of *T. gondii*.

Now, Nebibi noticed that the young man's skin looked clammy. His concern was elevated because this operative had an important mission, with no room for error. But at this point, Nebibi had no choice but to proceed with the "gringo."

"You must determine the best location inside for the 'package.'" Nebibi relayed his instructions with the stern tone required of his role as a leader in battle.

"I am ready, sir."

"Good. Here's a ticket to enter the Cathedral this evening. Spend your time inside well. I will follow you in, but we must go in separately."

"Yes. *Allahu Akbar.*"

"*Allahu Akbar.*" Nebibi responded in kind, again focusing on the young jihadist's eyes, hoping he wouldn't attract attention once inside.

KATE AND HER FATHER were at the top of the stone stairs leading into the great Cathedral. The people crowding outside were boisterous in their display of holiday spirit. All held tickets obtained months in advance, since this was the equivalent of a rock concert in the ecclesiastical calendar. Once they passed the front portal, the crowd instantly quieted down.

The inside of the Cathedral always took Kate's breath away. The structure could hold 2,400 seated souls and a few hundred more standing. Still holding her father's arm, she took in the vast expanse of white marble. The nave was lined with altars and shrines to individual saints, twinkling with candle offerings lit by believers. Above her was the intricately cut stained-glass window in the Cathedral's façade, with vivid colors lit not by sunlight but by the bright artificial lights coming from Fifth Avenue. The structure had the effect intended by its builders: the faithful felt closer to heaven as they entered this great hall, leaving the earthly bustle outside.

Behind them in line stood the anxious "gringo" clutching his ticket with his trembling hand. He was also looking at the Cathedral's architecture, however from an entirely different frame of mind.

Nebibi stood farther down the line. He wasn't especially looking forward to this evening of Christian ceremony, but he needed to make sure that the "gringo" was following his instructions to the letter. His cold eyes scanned the crowd ahead of him. His eyes stopped at the very front of the line. Kate! What was she doing here!

Nebibi froze. Actually, he panicked. An uncharacteristic reaction for him, except when it came to anything that involved Kate. Adrenaline raced through his body, shortening his breath.

After the first shock of seeing her, he forced himself to regain his composure. He succeeded in controlling everything but the pupils of his eyes, which were now fully dilated. His brain was instinctively preparing his body to gather more information about the situation that had caused the panic.

He quickly turned his head away. Did she see me!? he wondered. He could hide from most people, but Kate would be able to see the nervousness barely hidden under his skin.

Focus, Nebibi! Damn, where's that operative? he asked himself. All of Nebibi's focus had been on Kate, and in the process, he'd lost sight of his operative. On top of it, the agent was acting peculiar, which might attract scrutiny. He looked around but couldn't see him anymore. Nebibi had no choice. He'd have to rely on his slimly held confidence that the "gringo" was focusing on his mission. He looked at his watch. 11:30 P.M. The Mass wouldn't start for another thirty minutes. He convinced himself that she hadn't spotted him.

The voices of the Cathedral's choir echoed in the vast hall, above the hushed shuffling of the faithful finding their place for the midnight service. Kate disappeared with her father into the crowd and found seats in the middle of the Cathedral, too far for her to see Nebibi, who was only now passing through the entrance.

The "gringo" had in the meantime moved cautiously about the Cathedral, staying in the side aisles, hidden by the large stone columns and the standing crowds. He studied the many nooks and crannies of the structure. When that day came, *not today,* but the actual one for his mission, he would be ready to sacrifice his life for *his* religion.

At exactly midnight, the Cathedral's great organ sounded, heralding the emergence of the Cardinal from steps hidden under the High Altar in the front. The congregation stood with prayer books in hand ready to join in the rejoicing of the birth of Jesus Christ, son of God for the Catholic faithful—and prophet, for a certain Egyptian Muslim.

Unknowingly, Nebibi stood next to the statue of Saint Paul, the founder of the Church of Rome, and it was at the feet of this particular saint that he experienced his first and only Christian Mass. In this crowd of thousands, Nebibi's eyes continued to search for one person, the "gringo," while his mind kept thinking about only one faithful Christian in these masses. She would be safe this evening.

Fortunately, thought Nebibi, tonight was only a dry run, and his relief over that was so great that it made his legs momentarily weak. He placed one hand against the base of the statue to steady himself, causing him to finally take notice of the face of Saint Paul. The stone-cut eyes seemed to be looking right through Nebibi, making him feel like all the hidden layers of his life were exposed. As if speaking directly with this Christian saint, Nebibi stared intently, thinking to himself, Do not be quick to judge me, I have many reasons for what I do.

MEANWHILE, KATE LOOKED OVER at her father and smiled. Christmas was not about presents for them. Their tradition of celebrating this holy night here in this great Cathedral together soothed her deep sadness about Inge and Alejandro.

To the far right and one row behind Kate stood two men who were not known to Kate, her father, Nebibi, or the "gringo." They had traveled from Caracas the day before to keep an eye on a young woman, known thus far as a friend of Inge's, who lived in Old Town Alexandria, Virginia. Their task was to find out her link, if any, to a certain secret serum. If one was found, the young woman's cocoon of safety would certainly need to be broken.

32

EFORE THE MASS WAS OVER, Nebibi slipped out of the front portals to beat the exiting crowds and rushed across the street to his building. He dug for his cell phone in his pocket, but instead first pulled out the half-empty bag of nuts. A thought struck him, which made him stop for a second in the middle of the street. There was a particular aspect of the dry run this evening that he would think about changing.

As soon as he had filed away that thought for future reference, Nebibi continued his brisk jaunt to his building across the street. Ignoring the night doorman who held the door open for him, he typed a message on his iPhone as he walked through the lobby. Foot traffic in the lobby was light, since most of the building's mega-rich tenants preferred to winter in warmer climates like Monaco or Punta del Este.

By the time the elevator doors closed, Nebibi had sent off his text message. When he reached his apartment on the forty-ninth floor, he immediately logged on to the Bicycle Suppliers Web site and changed the status of the Yale operative to active. Within seconds, Murad's map refreshed with the new data.

Nebibi then stripped off his clothes and jumped into the glass-enclosed shower. Seeing Kate in the Cathedral had put him on edge, causing those old feelings and desires to bubble up again. Nebibi turned on the strong sprays at the highest temperature setting. He stood under the forced water for several minutes, not moving, with his hands and forearms leaning against the tiled wall. The almost scalding water hit the top of his head and ran down his body, broken by the patches of black hair that started on his chest, as he attempted to wash away his tension.

Standing in the shower, Nebibi allowed his mind to wander down that different path with Kate—Am I doubting my commitment to our cause? Is violence the only way? Can I just walk away at this point? And if I did, would Murad and the others come looking for me . . . and Kate?

The calculating side of Nebibi's brain, the one that understood his commitments to his brother, his parents, Murad, the Supreme Commander, won out. His logic convinced him that relief can come in many forms, not all of them in the embrace of love. For now, his primal urges of vengeance and lust would instead hold sway in this man's soul.

His train of thought was interrupted by a buzz from the lobby. He stepped out of the shower, grabbed a towel, and sprinted to the front foyer. "Hello?"

"Mr. Hasehm, Ms. Bretz is here to see you." The doorman announced the arrival of this perfumed visitor, who sauntered by him wrapped in a full-length sable coat, the edge of which just barely stopped right above the floor. Were it not for her six-inch Blahnik heels, the coat would certainly be sweeping the floor. The doorman caught sight of the back of her head, blond hair tautly gathered in a small bun.

"Send her right up." Nebibi, the Panther, coolly spoke his order into the receiver on the wall.

The sound of Margaux's heels clicking on the marble floor in the direction of the elevator broke the silence of the otherwise empty lobby. Margaux's twenty-dollar tips, both coming and going, always helped her get into the best buildings in town.

And because of that largesse, in less than a minute Margaux stood outside Nebibi's door ringing the bell. As if raising a flag in battle, she released the constriction of her tightly gathered hair and let it cascade over the fur on her shoulders. The door opened, slowly revealing the vision of the still-dripping-wet, chiseled body of the healthy thirty-four-year-old Middle Eastern man wrapped only in a towel around the waist. The lights of the apartment were dark, but his torso was framed by the artificial light coming from the skyline behind him. The apartment's floor-to-ceiling windows framed the spiked tips of the Cathedral's Gothic spires.

A tight smile raised one corner of the Cougar's lips. She was ready for the Christmas present she'd been wishing for all evening and, miraculously, it had come in a simple text message she'd received from Nebibi just twenty minutes ago. It simply read: *Free tonight?* She didn't waste time responding to it; instead she just slipped into something easy to slip out of and rushed out of her apartment on the Upper East Side into a waiting cab. And now she was finally ready to unwrap her present, which was starting to reveal itself from under that wet towel. Margaux slowly closed the door behind her, all the while trying not to take her eyes off of that towel.

She took a step toward him. He took a couple back and she followed him slowly, locked in a tango, each trying to take the lead. Their dance took them to the apartment's kitchen, a barren room for most single New Yorkers, Nebibi included. In a couple of masterful movements, Margaux let her sable fall to the ground, revealing her body, naked save for the Manolo heels, and reached out for Nebibi. Like a cougar, her French-manicured nails seemed to extend farther out from her long fingers, which she used to pull the towel from Nebibi's waist, releasing his full arousal. They both stood there naked, he dripping and aroused and she getting wet at the sight of his arousal. She still held a clutch bag in her left hand, small enough to fit lipstick, some cash, and little else. Margaux's patience this evening had paid off and she thought to herself, *Yes, Margaux, there is a Santa Claus.*

For a brief moment, they both stood there, each taking in the sight of the other's naked skin. Without her coat, the perfumed lotion she had used to lacquer her body earlier now permeated the space between them, rising in Nebibi's face like rare spices delivered from ancient Eastern passages.

He grabbed her naked body and, with a force just crossing criminality, coaxed her to lie on her back on the kitchen's black marble counter, releasing her grip on the clutch bag. The cold stone sent a shiver up her spine, which exited her body through the tips of her nipples. The touch of this man's hands, though, made her warm inside. He lay on top of her, with his arms propped on the

marble surface, and felt an instinct to kiss her, kiss her deeply, but
they, actually he, had an unspoken rule. Lust to the exclusion of
love. No kisses. She arched her back, offering her breasts to his lips
instead. He obliged and took slow turns enveloping each with his
moist mouth. Every lick and nibble caused low moans to rise in her
throat. Her long blond mane now lay unfurled on the black marble,
like a flag blown by strong winds in all directions.

His fingers traveled down her body, touching all the places that
Margaux's trainer concentrated on resurfacing with lean muscle
mass, which she now gladly offered up on this marble altar. His
hand massaged the moist spot between her legs, and like levers, his
exploring fingers made her legs open farther apart. It was an invitation for the next part of their tango.

She reached over for her clutch and quickly pulled out a condom. After she did the honor of placing it on him, he used his hand
to slowly guide himself inside her, and at the first contact there, she
let out a gasp and wrapped herself around him. Her legs also now
rose to embrace his torso, spiny thin heels digging into the surface
of his skin, much like the spiked spires of the Cathedral outside
dug into the evening sky.

He began to move quicker in and out, and with each quicken-
ing, she got closer to that Christmas present she'd been waiting
for. Her breaths were becoming shorter and she was letting go.
Hearing her sounds made him thrust harder and deeper, the sound
of his wet body slapping against hers now competing with her
moans.

They both lost themselves in fulfilling primal desires, blocking
out other desires harder to come by. She, a life with a man who
could both take care of her in the manner she'd grown accustomed
to *and* satisfy her sexual thirst. She wasn't sure Nebibi was willing
to meet the needs of her first goal, but he certainly accomplished
the second better than any man—or woman—had ever done.

He, in turn, looked to escape the grasp of a past that he needed
to forget. It was as if the harder he thrust, the more he could bury
any feelings he had for Kate. And so their lust gave them each an
escape. He thrust harder and she enveloped herself even more.

Nebibi wanted this escape to last, so each time he neared the
edge of climax, he slowed. His change of pace gave her even more

waves of pleasure. And so he did this for what seemed an eternity, till he could control it no further.

"Bismillah ir-Rahman ir-rahim." He let go in one strong spasm, followed by minor tremors that shook his body, all the while still inside her. In this climactic moment, the sublimation of Kate was complete. When he finally pulled out, his eyes half closed in pleasure, he glistened with his sweat and her moistness.

He propped himself on the edge of the kitchen counter beside her, catching his breath. Her moans continued for a few more moments until a full smile came across her face.

"I'M JUMPING IN THE SHOWER?" After round two with Nebibi, in bed this time, Margaux needed to clean off the smell of sex lest she stain the monogrammed silk lining of her sable.

"Please, go ahead, it's straight ahead." Nebibi spoke softly, his head propped against pillows and his naked body partially covered by the tangled bedsheets. He looked over at the time. 2:30 A.M.

In fifteen minutes, Margaux was clean again, perched on her heels, her hair bound in a bun, and wrapped in her fur. She stood at the doorway to the bedroom, looking at Nebibi, now sound asleep.

As she walked past the living room, Margaux spotted Nebibi's laptop displaying a map with flashing dots. She couldn't suppress her curiosity and so she sat down in front of it to get a better view. She pulled out her lipstick, but was distracted by the many colors, with an abundance of dots in places like Cuba and the Middle East.

Margaux instinctively knew this wasn't something she was supposed to know about, so she quickly wrote down the Web address on the notepad on the desk, tore off the top page, and stuffed it in her pocket for future reference. She tried to quietly leave the apartment, but those stilettos were loud no matter how you cut it.

In the elevator ride down, she dug for her lipstick in her clutch bag, but instead only found that piece of paper and an extra condom. She stared at the address and wondered what other deals Nebibi was working on that he wasn't sharing with his investment banker.

AS SOON AS HE HEARD the front door close, Nebibi turned over in his bed and stared at the ceiling in his now quiet, dark apartment. His body was satiated now, but his mind was still racing, trying to un-ravel all the layers of deceit he'd created in these past few hours.

He got up and walked over to the windows looking out at St. Patrick's, remembering the moment he saw Kate standing there with her father. She looked serene, at peace with herself amidst the ceremony of the evening Mass. He came to realize that a much stronger power than Margaux's bedroom performance would be required to combat the passion, no, the obsession he had for Kate.

As Nebibi turned away from the window, his eyes immediately focused on his laptop. He'd been so distracted that he left Murad's blinking map displayed. Did Margaux see it, he wondered? He sat down at the desk to log off and noticed the lipstick case next to the notepad. He pulled out a pencil from the drawer and gently rubbed the surface indentation on the notepad. The rubbing re-vealed the Web address in Margaux's handwriting.

A blast of alarm shot through his heart. And he made a decision that sent his pulse back down. At this stage of the game, no loose ends.

33

⊰◈◈◈⊱

KATE WOKE UP VERY EARLY on Christmas Day. She'd had a restless night; images of Inge and Alejandro passed through her dreams. And now her body felt cold. She looked at the clock on her nightstand. 5:55 A.M. Great, she thought, the only ones up at this hour on Christmas are twelve and under. She certainly knew her father wouldn't be up for hours, not after the champagne and midnight Mass the night before. She fluffed her pillow and grabbed the bedcovers that had fallen on the floor and turned over, trying to get back to sleep. But after five minutes, she still wasn't sleeping, as her mind turned to what might lie ahead for her in Gibraltar.

Finally, she jumped out of bed, turned on her laptop, and started reading her e-mails, but since she wasn't at work, she could only see nonclassified materials. Her eyes scanned the topics: pictures from the DIA holiday party that she'd missed, a reminder from human resources about her annual 401(K) forms, and the itinerary from the travel department for her upcoming trip to Gibraltar. None of these addressed the issue foremost on her mind—the money trail—so, instead, she opted to go for a run on the beach and get her endorphins flowing.

Kate quickly grabbed her black running tights and thermal jacket, which clung to her athletic frame. She tied her hair in a ponytail, reached for her phone, tiptoed downstairs so as not to wake her father, and went out through the kitchen door leading to the back porch.

She stood outside for a moment, taking in the quiet early holiday morning: gray and overcast. The temperature was just above freezing, and a damp fog rose over the wet ground, shading the lower skyline in a muted haze. There were no sounds save the occasional squirrel scurrying up a tree or the distant bark of a dog.

Kate put on her earphones and started at a slow pace to limber up. She started feeling the muscles of her legs come alive, flexible and strong against the pavement. Her body was warm, and a layer of sweat began to flow under her skintight layers.

Within twenty minutes, she reached Greenwich Point Park, a long narrow peninsula that juts out onto Long Island Sound. Hardly a soul in sight. She spotted an older couple walking their golden retriever along the cold sandy waterfront. The concession stand had closed for the season months ago, and the last of the stray ice cream wrappers had been picked up. This desolate scene made her imagine what Inge saw in her early morning run, and all at once, Kate started thinking about her own safety, something she had always taken for granted.

Kate picked up her pace, wanting now to finish her run sooner. She kept jogging along the narrow road that curved on the edge of the peninsula, reaching beyond the point where the people on the beach could see her. There, on a clearer day, one could make out the edge of Manhattan's skyline.

She looked back and spotted a black SUV slowly trailing two hundred feet behind her. It was probably nothing, but still there was a small knot in her stomach she couldn't ignore, so she quickly turned into the woods, finding herself in the midst of dense wild holly berry bushes.

Shutting down her music, Kate paused to listen for the SUV. She peered through the holly bushes and caught a glimpse of the car, which continued driving by. She noticed the light blue color of diplomatic plates, not at all unusual in such proximity to New York and the U.N. She chided herself for thinking more of it. She could see that this whole thing was starting to affect her judgment and knew how important it was for her to stay focused on real leads, not imaginary ones.

She forced herself to relax a bit, taking in the early-morning sounds around her. She heard several seagulls flying overhead and the sound of crashing waves hitting the rocks nearby. Everywhere she looked, there were the spiny green leaves of the season along with bright red berry dots, like a Christmas wreath enveloping her. It reminded her of the many times she'd walked here with her parents. Comforting childhood memories now sprang forth.

Then, the sound of a twig snapping on the ground nearby cut through the seclusion of the tall holly bushes. A prickly sensation rose up in Kate's spine as she turned in the direction of the sound. Her heartbeat increased and a cold bead of sweat traveled down between her breasts. She wasn't quite sure why her base instincts were called into play. Probably just some small animal foraging for food in the middle of winter.

Then, out of the corner of her eye, she thought she saw a tall shadow quickly pass by on the other side of the bushes. *Ohmigod!* Her body didn't wait for her brain to react. She ran in the opposite direction of the shadow. A sharp protruding branch connected to a fallen tree trunk scraped her right ankle. "Aaaahhh!" She wasn't able to suppress her scream. She looked down and saw that the branch had torn through her legging and now blood trickled down to her sneaker. Her scream led to a new round of rustling behind her, closer now. She made a quick sprint forward, despite the pain in her ankle. A shriek from above startled her, making her turn her head skyward. It was only a lone hawk circling above for prey. Was she just imagining things?

She was still feeling uneasy, though, and her breathing was elevated by the rush of adrenaline in her system. Trying not to make a sound, she took a few small steps forward to a pine tree with low branches that could provide her a canopy of temporary cover. There, Kate crouched down, trying to slow her breathing. The pain in her ankle was very real and now her stomach felt queasy. Her mind still raced. She tried to block out all those feelings so she could concentrate on the environment around her and decipher the random sounds coming from the forest. "*¡Qué mierda!*" Shit! she said to herself. Is this just my imagination or is someone following me?

She peered out through the branches. And then she saw the shadow again. This time it was sprinting in her direction. *¡Mierda!* Now she knew it wasn't her imagination! She felt the muscles in her stomach constricting.

She tried to focus her senses to make some quick assessments: Is there just one or more? Stop! Focus, focus! You've been coming

here since you were little . . . you know this park like the back of
your hand. And she hoped whoever was out there didn't have that
same mental map.

And then they came. Two men burst out from behind the bushes,
lunging toward Kate. Her instincts kicked in. She made a swift
turn away from the oncoming men and ran deeper into the forest.
Dead leaves rustled under her long forceful strides. She could hear
them behind her, still pursuing, pushing through the bushes. Her
mind was taking in all the information at breakneck speed: I haven't
lost them. Got to keep running! I couldn't see their faces. Ski masks!?

Kate's legs were tired from her run, but the adrenaline of fear
was still kicking in. She reached a fork and took the smaller less-
clear path on the right. She remembered the older couple walking
their large dog on the open beach. She made the split second decision that if she could get to where they were, *if* they were still
there, then she might just manage to survive this now dangerous,
second part of her run this morning. Or at least not die alone without any witnesses, like Inge.

"Awww!" Her torso hit a large branch. She was knocked back
onto the ground. She tried to get up, but the blow had taken the
wind out of her. She looked down to where the pain was. The
branch had torn her Nike top just above her stomach. In the distance, she could hear the men shouting in Spanish, and they were
getting nearer. She tried to decipher what they were saying, but the
clearer she heard their voices, the closer they were getting.

And then she heard a dog barking, and it gave her the strength
to get up and start her stride toward the beach. She needed to get
to that dog. The men's voices were getting closer.

They heard the rustle in the thicket ahead and were coordinating their approach on either side to block off her escape.

The men could hear the noise of twigs being crushed underfoot
just ahead of them. They could sense they were getting closer to
their prey. From the sounds they heard just on the other side of
the thick bushes, they had managed to surround their target—one
on the left and the other on the right. They slowed in their approach.

At that very moment, the two masked men lunged out from
behind the bushes, fully expecting to grab hold of the woman they'd

been chasing. They both stood there motionless, staring at the prey they had managed to corral between them. A lone young buck stood there, frozen for a second, and then resumed its flight from the hunters, farther into the forest, its hind legs kicking leaves up in its wake.

"*¡Coño de su madre!*" Motherfucker!

"*¡Mierda!*" Shit!

The men had been outwitted by a deer.

One of the men immediately dialed his cell phone and informed a superior. "*La perdimos.*" We lost her.

The voice on the other end responded. "Okay. Leave it be for now. And whatever you do, don't cause any sort of international incident. If you see her alone somewhere, then grab her. Just don't do anything in public. Understood?!"

"*Sí, Señor Ministro.*"

"Did she see you?"

"Just our car . . ."

"*¡Imbéciles!* Get rid of the car before they track it down to the consulate."

KATE SAT IN THE BACKSEAT of Mr. and Mrs. Sheibley's car. Their golden retriever, Hank, was busy licking her hand.

"You must have taken a pretty nasty spill there, young lady." Mrs. Sheibley had looked over at their disheveled passenger and noticed her torn jogging pants and the top and the dried blood-stains on her sneaker.

"I certainly did. I'm really lucky I found the two of you there on the beach. I don't think I would have been able to jog back all the way home." She touched her ankle, and pain shot up her leg. Kate was trying her best to hide her panic. She didn't want to alarm the elderly couple or get them involved in whatever her pursuers were looking for. All she needed to do was get to the safety of her home and then she could figure out her next step. She nervously looked out the back window to see if she spotted them following her. So far, nothing. Maybe she'd managed to lose them back in the woods. But she still wanted Mr. Sheibley to go slightly above the speed limit.

The couple's dog began to lick Kate's hand again. "Yes, thank you, too." Kate patted the golden retriever, who in fact had been her true savior this morning with his unrelenting barking.

"Anytime, young lady. You just need to take it easy on your training or you'll end up hurting yourself. You know, it's not every day that Mr. Sheibley drives Hank and me down to the beach," said Mrs. Sheibley.

"Yep, believe me, I got that message loud and clear. Think I'll lay off jogging for a while." She looked back out the window again, scanning for any sign of a car following them.

"IT'S ME." SHE SAT on the swing on the back porch of her father's house in Old Greenwich, with an ice pack held against her ankle and cell phone next to her ear. She managed to reach her boss, Bill, at his farm in Arkansas, in the middle of cleaning the horse stalls.

"Hey, Kate. Hold on a sec. I'm in a stall right now." Kate could hear the whining of a horse in the background. "Okay, I'm back now. Calling to wish me a Merry Christmas? How sweet . . ."

Kate spared no small talk here. "Somebody knows. I had two guys chase me down today on my morning jog on the beach in Old Greenwich." Bill could sense panic in her voice.

"Are you okay!?" A vision of Kate's friend in Havana flashed in Bill's mind.

"Yeah, I'm okay. A bit shaken. Okay, a *lot* shaken. I just barely managed to outrun those guys. I'm worried that they'll come and find me here now. . . ."

"So where are you now, Kate?"

"I'm at my father's house in Old Greenwich. I don't want to get him in the middle of this. I need to get out of here. . . ." Kate's speech was in quick jabs.

"Did you get a look at them?"

"Not really. I think they were in a black SUV but I didn't catch the number." Her mind wandered back to that first moment in the holly bushes. "Wait, it was a diplomatic plate!" She pictured the official light blue color on the back of the SUV.

"That doesn't narrow it down enough, Kate. There are more than twenty-five hundred diplomatic plates issued in New York alone. Anything else?"

"I only had a second to glance at it." Kate sounded disappointed with herself. She replayed the scenes in her mind, trying to surface even just one clue to go on. Then she remembered. "The men spoke Spanish, with a Venezuelan accent!"

"That does it, Kate. Those guys are after you because of the serum. Call the police right away. Make sure they get a squad car parked in front of your house. I'll call Homeland Security in the meantime and get the FBI over there, too. . . ."

"Okay . . ." She touched her ankle.

"Then you need to get out to Gibraltar." Kate could hear the sound of a horse neighing in the distance. "So when is your flight?"

"I have a flight leaving Dulles on Monday night."

"Okay, you should head out tonight from New York instead. I'm sure you can get a flight. It's definitely better if you 'disappear' over there for a while. And don't worry about your father. I'll make sure my FBI buddies keep tabs on him."

"Thanks, Bill."

"No problem. The least your government can do for you." There was that Bill sarcasm again.

"So, hey, Merry Christmas, Bill."

"Yeah, you, too. Looks like you've had yourself quite a rip-roaring one already, though. Lie low and get going to Mr. Tariq's Rock, pronto."

"Huh?"

"Don't worry, you'll figure it out when you get there."

"Yeah, whatever. Bye."

She hung up the line and started looking at the cut on her ankle. A little swelling, but didn't look like it needed stitches.

The door to the back porch opened. Her father stood there in his pajamas and slippers. "Kate, what are you doing out here? It's freezing. Come inside, I have some fresh grounds ready for your coffee." His eyes then noticed the ice pack lying next to Kate on the swing. "Hey, did you hurt yourself?" Then he noticed that she had her running clothes on. "Were you out jogging already?"

Finally, Kate answered. "Dad, I think I had a little trouble—"

"What!? What happened?!"

"I couldn't sleep this morning, so I went for a jog down at the beach—"

"When?" Tomás was getting more alarmed by the second.

"At six . . . but some guys chased me down by the holly bushes."

"Are you alright?!" Tomás knew exactly the spot she referred to, having been there with her many times.

"I'm okay now. Can we continue talking about this inside?" She motioned for her father to step back in the kitchen. There, she picked up the phone.

"Who are you calling?"

"911. I'm calling the police to come over until the FBI gets here."

That's all Tomás needed to hear. Agreement or no agreement, he was not going to have discretion and patience when it came to his daughter's safety. "What do you mean, the FBI? Is this something related to the DIA?"

Kate relayed basic information about her chase to the 911 operator and then hung up. Meanwhile, Kate's father continued looking at her, waiting for an answer to his questions. She wasn't sure how to respond. Kate knew this had to do with *T. gondii prime,* but that was *way* classified.

"Look, I'm just as happy as anyone that you have this wonderful career in Washington, but I'll be damned if I'm going to sit around and make believe nothing's wrong. So what's it going to be, Kate?"

"I get it, Dad. You're worried. Well, so am I. I spoke with Bill and he's getting the local agents from Homeland Security involved. And then I'm going to Gibraltar as planned, just a few days earlier. I should be there for a few weeks till this blows over and we figure out who these goons were. Homeland Security will stick around here to make sure nothing else happens."

"What the hell is going on?!" Tomás's voice rose with annoyance. "You're acting just like your grandmother, headstrong without thinking things through."

"They'll hang around just for precaution," Kate said.

"What's to say they don't go after you in Gibraltar?"

"Dad, remember I'm going to be working with the commander there, and I'll be surrounded by armed military personnel around the clock. It'll be a lot safer there than most places I can think of. That's why Bill wants me to leave early."

"Look, you can tell that Mr. DuBois of yours that I'm just not happy with any of this. . . . I think you should say *adios* to the DIA and come back to New York to get your old job back at Bear, or whatever it's called these days. At least there, the most you could lose is your shirt on a bad day of trading. . . ."

"Dad, that's just not going to happen. This is my life, this is what I've chosen to do with it. You can either help me, or . . ."

The hint of a threat worked. Her father calmed down long enough to realize that she was just doing her job. "Kate, I'm here to support you, you know that. But you have to understand I just don't want you risking your life."

"I know, I know. But I'm smack in the middle of some important stuff and I can't just get up and leave."

The two struck an uneasy truce for the moment. But Tomás Molares was not going to be sleeping quite well until all this chasing stuff was done and over with and Kate was back to her normal humdrum 7 A.M. to 4 P.M. work life at Bolling AFB.

34

THE IBERIA AIRCRAFT MADE its final descent at Gibraltar's North Front Airport. Kate sat at her window seat, on the left side of the cabin, looking out into the crystal blue sky, while flight attendants made their final cabin check.

As usual, the pilot steered the plane to approach the Rock from the east. Below, Kate could spot the ship traffic heading in and out of the Mediterranean through the Strait of Gibraltar. She began to see the edge of the Iberian Peninsula at Europa Point in the territory of Gibraltar, and then at the very last moment she caught a quick glimpse of the famous Rock as the aircraft sped by. It towered almost straight up into the sky, and Kate could finally understand why this small land mass had been prized for its impenetrable military value for so many centuries.

When the plane hit the short single runway, there was a cheer from the passengers. As it taxied, the aircraft crossed a fully working road, Winston Churchill Avenue. Gibraltar's airport was the only one in the world that had a working road that crossed its runway. And the road was an important one: it was the single artery that connected the British overseas territory with Spain. Construction of a new viaduct was under way, but for the moment, this odd feature remained.

Kate rummaged through her purse for her lipstick. As she applied it, she pondered what lay ahead. Instead of the fear that had been clouding her mind recently, she now felt a simmering anger. Her heart quickened with nervous excitement. She couldn't wait to get back to work, searching for answers to the questions about those money transfers, the involvement of the Basque and al-Qaeda, the coveted *T. gondii prime*, and Inge's killers. Kate was "back in the saddle," so to speak, ready to make sure that she didn't become the next victim of the violence surrounding the *T. gondii* serum.

KATE HELD THE BLACK U.S. diplomatic passport close to her chest. She disembarked from the flight and already, half the passengers were forming lines at the two customs officers' posts. She knew the special status her passport afforded her over normal passengers, but also understood the potential danger of advertising to the world that she held priority status in the U.S. government hierarchy. Only when she was standing right in front of the customs officer did she finally relax her grip and hand her passport to the Gibraltar official. The man opened it, looked at her, and immediately motioned to a British Royal Navy enlisted man who was standing at attention by the exit. Great, now what? thought Kate.

" 'Ello Miss Molares. I'm Lance Corporal Gubbins. I've bin sent by the commander to escort you today." The enlisted man spoke in a heavy cockney accent and looked to have just cracked his twenties.

"Oh, I see." She had gotten word that someone would be here to greet her; she just didn't expect it to be so official in nature. "Well then, please lead the way, Lance Corporal Gubbins. This is my first time in Gibraltar. Or what is it that the locals call it, Gib?"

"Yes indeed, miss, welcome to Gib. Our car is waitin' just ou'side." The young officer escorted her to a gray sedan parked in a spot reserved for official government vehicles.

Here at the entrance to the Mediterranean, the midday sun was warm, even at this time of the year. It felt particularly good on Kate's skin, after the cold dampness of Connecticut the day before. There now, she thought, this isn't a bad place to lie low for a while. The sun was bright, so she fished for her sunglasses at the bottom of her purse. In that instant, just before she put them on, the young lance corporal, now driver, caught a glimpse of her green eyes through the rearview mirror. She noticed his stare. Looking sheepish, like a child caught with his hand in the cookie jar, he immediately diverted his focus back to the road in front of him. The fact that a twenty-something-year-old ogled her was not lost on Kate, and rather than being put off by it, she appreciated the compliment. If this guy only knew what I've been through these past few days, she thought.

The car sped along the two-way Winston Churchill Avenue. Lance Corporal Gubbins headed straight toward the center of Gib. After a traffic circle, the car continued south along the man-made quays on the side facing the Spanish city of Algeciras across the bay.

Gibraltar's land mass is only 6.5 square kilometers, about one tenth the size of Manhattan. A large chunk of it is taken up by the Rock itself, a vast hunk of limestone dating from the Jurassic period, long before humans roamed the earth. The territory's twenty-eight thousand inhabitants were squeezed along the shoreline in buildings dating back a few centuries, as well as some more recently constructed low-level apartments. Gibraltarians' origin is mixed, mostly from Andalusian Spain, Genoa, Malta, Portugal, and of course, England.

As the car wound through the narrow streets, Kate's eyes were glued to the impressive views of the looming Rock. It was a sight that most locals did not think twice about, but that always awed visitors. The car stopped at 3 Europa Road, depositing Kate in front of the Rock Hotel, the territory's oldest and most storied hotel.

Lance Corporal Gubbins handed her bag to the porter and said, "Miss Molares, I'll wait downstairs and escort 'ou to the base for your meetin' with de commodore at 1500 hours." Kate was unaware that Gubbins was in fact assigned to security detail for the remainder of her stay in Gibraltar. Her father would certainly be relieved.

She strained her ear to make sure she could understand most of the lance corporal's English. "Thanks, that'd be great." She looked at her watch; that would give her almost two hours to clean up, unwind from her trip, and get into the cadence of Gib.

SHE CLOSED THE DOOR of her room after the porter dropped off her bag. Well, it wasn't the Four Seasons, from what she could see, but the sheets looked clean. The room was basic travelogue fare, that is until she walked out onto the small terrace. Standing here, she could see across the bay to the Spanish mainland and could make out the Rif Mountains of Morocco on the African continent. "Now, that's impressive," she said out loud.

This was as good a time as any, she thought, so she pulled her phone from her purse and dialed.

"Hey, Dad." Her father answered his cell phone, sitting in his office. She was hoping that he'd calmed down a bit.

"Kate . . ." Tomás's voice seemed laid-back. ". . . are you there already?" He didn't want to identify where she was, in case anyone was eavesdropping.

"Yep, got here about a half hour ago."

"Flights okay?"

"Oh fine, I slept the entire time. I haven't slept that much in weeks."

"Kate, you need to hear me out one last time. Don't you think this thing has gone a little over your head? Why aren't you in some kind of witness protection program, where nobody knows who you are?" As he spoke, Tomás looked out the window to the street below in Greenwich, and spotted the unmarked car across the street that had been trailing him since the beach incident yesterday.

"Everything's *fine* here. I'll be hanging out with a slew of military officers the whole time I'm here, so like I told you, *don't* worry!" Kate was losing patience with her overprotective father.

"Okay . . ." Tomás's *okay* was an uneasy one. But he had no choice. She'd be just as safe hanging around military personnel on another continent as in her everyday surroundings back in D.C. "When are you coming back?"

"No idea at this point, since I haven't even met with my new boss yet." She looked down from her terrace and spotted the pool below. She wondered if it was heated. "I think I'll be here at least until after New Year's, and maybe longer. So we'll have to clink our champagne glasses twice next year. What will you do? Don't stay at home by yourself, Dad. Maybe you can spend it with your old buddies from the U.N.?"

"I'll see. Sam invites me over every year, but I've always had a good excuse to opt out. Maybe this year I'll take him up on it. I'll think about it. How's that?"

"I think that would be good for you. That way I won't worry about *you*."

"*Bueno*—alright."

"Shoot." Kate looked at the old-fashioned clock radio on her night table. "I have to get going here or I'll be late. I'll call you to-morrow, okay?"

"What time?" Tomás's question was left unanswered, as Kate had already hung up the line.

TOMÁS SAT IN HIS OFFICE looking at the photo on his desk. It was a pic-ture of his wife, with Kate as a toddler in her arms. Kate was all he had left of that happy time. His finger gently stroked the picture of his wife's smiling face. "Don't worry, I'll keep her safe," he whis-pered to her.

It occurred to him he might have at least a partial solution to his concern. He dialed a private number in backcountry Green-wich.

"Tomás, what's cookin'? Hey, did you see how Asian markets rallied last night, haywire stuff, huh?" It was Sam Coldsmith, sit-ting in his office suite at home, thinking about the next trade. He liked to say that his doctors were always amazed when they drew his blood: nothing but dollar signs spewed out.

"I saw that our traders in Hong Kong executed a couple of those orders," Tomás replied. "Market's put some good wind in the sails of those trades, but I think we should cash out before their close on Monday. No point in getting greedy, given our negotiation with Milestones."

"Yeah, you're right. Can you send them a message about that?"

"Will do, Sam."

"Are you calling me from the office? It's Saturday, my friend. You need a hobby. Or are you trying to impress the boss?"

"I just needed to catch up on my in-box." Actually, Tomás was feeling cooped up at home with the FBI car outside. "Question for you—didn't you say you were going over to Gibraltar for the Mile-stones closing?"

"Nebibi and I decided to set the date for January twenty-first, and Gibraltar seems as good a place as any. You know, we don't really need to fly over there for a closing, since we could sign the documents via fax. But I wanted to check the place out, never been there myself. Have you ever been?" Sam was never much one for vacations from the market, so trips for business were his way of relaxing and seeing the world.

"No, actually . . ."

"Well, I think you need to come with me. Nebibi was practically your son-in-law, after all. . . ."

"Funny, Sam. Very funny. As far as I can tell, they're not an item anymore. Who can tell, though? I'm not allowed to ask too many personal questions." But at least now I can check on her in person, thought Tomás.

35

━◆◆◆━

KATE TOOK IN THE SCENES of a typical Gib afternoon as her car wound through the narrow streets. Motorcycles weaved in and out of car and pedestrian traffic. The local shops were doing brisk business with the normal overflow of tourists. Kate, however, didn't have shopping on her agenda this afternoon. She was here for the most traditional of all businesses on Gib: military and security. The car was taking her to the military compound to meet the British commander.

Military barracks had been on Gib even before the Muslim general Tariq conquered it, and the current owners, the British, had kept forces there since their conquest in 1704. Now, after three centuries, British control was evident in all aspects of Gibraltarian life, from the use of English as the official language and the Queen's appointment of the governor to the names of local pubs along the narrow streets that could just as easily have been found in London, such as The Pig & Whistle, The Red Lion, and The Angry Friar.

For many locals, it was inconceivable to imagine a Gibraltar the British did not rule. But, in fact, that was exactly what England and Spain were prepared to negotiate in the twenty-first century at their much-heralded upcoming summit. Every day, the newspaper carried stories both opposing and supporting the Sovereignty Summit, which was heatedly discussed every evening at those local pubs.

KATE SAT ALONE IN THE LARGE oak-paneled office of the Commander of British Forces. She knew that was a highly coveted posting within Her Majesty's military ranks. The post was once rich in military significance, but now in the modern age of warfare, its importance was much more ceremonial; it was a prominent place to raise the British Union Jack and one of the few remaining relics of the grand old British Empire.

The incumbent commander, Commodore Horatio Forward IV, was a fifty-two-year-old Eton-educated Royal Navy officer. Both his great-great-grandfather and grandfather had served in the same position in Gibraltar, and so Commodore Forward was following a family tradition of exalted service on Gib. And who knows, if the British did indeed end up sharing control with the Spaniards, he might very well be the *last* Forward military man stationed here.

Kate was admiring the paintings, dating back hundreds of years, of past commanders and scenes of naval battles fought in the waters off the Strait, so she was caught unaware when the commodore finally made his entrance.

"Hello, Miss Molares. Allow me to introduce myself. I'm commodore Forward, Royal Navy. General Owens will soon be here as well." The commodore extended his hand out to Kate.

"It's a pleasure to meet you, commodore. And thank you for arranging for that nice escort at the airport." She remembered to give a firm grip.

He coughed, not because of a cold or dry throat, but rather in the manner of older, proper gentlemen who like to clear the air and announce the coming of speech. "No problem whatsoever. We must help our close friends, of course. Besides, General Owens explained that you may be in need of escorts while you're here. Seems you've attracted—how shall I put it?—the wrong kind of attention." He noted her firm grip and made his assessment of this young American: Backbone, I like that in a woman.

Kate wasn't about to gush information considered highly classified, and certainly not in the first five minutes of her new posting. Not sure what security clearance he had, Kate decided to move the conversation along to less sensitive issues, at least until General Owens arrived.

"I couldn't help but admire the portraits on the wall, Commodore. Such a rich history here."

"Oh, yes." The commodore's face lit up. "These are all my predecessors posted here on Gib. In fact, there are two that I'm related to.

Can you pick them out? No cheating now, you can't look at the inscriptions."

Kate didn't need to stare very long to find one of them, at least. Save for the mid-1800s military garb, full-dress bicorn headdress included, the commodore was the spitting image of his great-great-grandfather. "There, he has to be your relative."

"Yes, indeed. It's hard to miss. The great Commodore Bartholomew Bottomley Forward." The commodore stood next to the portrait, trying to look more stern than he actually was in person. Both men were of similar age, with tall frames, some roundness at the middle, square jaws, and stout noses. Though she couldn't see it in the portrait because of the headdress, Kate imagined that the man in the portrait also had thinning gray hair like the current commodore.

Among all of the paintings of British military glory, Kate noticed one depicting a different type of scene in the corner. It showed a man holding a curved saber leading men to victory on the Rock. By the costume of the man holding the saber, she could tell this battle was fought long before the British arrived on Gib. "And this one, Commodore, is he the Muslim general who conquered the Rock?"

"Indeed. Not much in the way of firsthand historical records to go by, but what is indisputable is that this man, General Tariq ibn Ziyad, accomplished quite a feat of military strategy with courage and pure audacity. The story that has been passed down is that his men were ultimately fiercer than the enemy that outnumbered them, which is why they won out. They were simply hungrier for victory."

"I wonder what drove their fierceness. Was it the promise of riches, something in their culture?" Or maybe somebody invented *T. gondii prime* a long time ago, mused Kate.

"Very simple, it was the smell of death. They bloody beat those Visigoths, eventually all the way to the north of Spain, right next door to the ancient Basques."

"How interesting," said Kate, with sincere attentiveness. "I'll have to read up on the history while I'm here."

"The important thing about our dear Tariq is that his military victory allowed for a tremendous wave of Muslim migration to the Iberian Peninsula. And on that point, we have a wealth of historical record. The rich architectural legacy throughout southern Spain, the centers of learning which became universities, why even the guitar used for flamenco today; all these things came to us from the Muslim civilization, the Caliphate of al-Andalus, as they called it. But by far, the most important contribution made by the Muslims of al-Andalus was translating and safeguarding the largely forgotten knowledge of the ancient Greeks. Astronomy, mathematics, medicine, literature, philosophy. It all flourished in this part of Europe, whereas the rest of the continent plodded along in a dark age. So you see, much is owed to the Muslims of Andalus."

Kate was about to ask another question, but was interrupted by a quick knock. The door opened and in stepped General Theodore Roosevelt Owens II.

"Commodore Forward." The general saluted his peer, who returned the favor. His raised hand gave focus to the "scrambled eggs" of gilt-embroidered oak leaves and acorns on his visor.

General Owens was the highest-ranking African-American in the U.S. military, a true blue four-star general and the son of the first military chaplain to get his wings in combat during WWII. He had started his military career at West Point and had risen quickly through the ranks to make general at the relatively young age of forty-five.

General Owens's most recent assignment was as U.S. Army Commander of all NATO forces in Brussels. Now, at the age of fifty, he was tapped with the sensitive mission of creating an entire U.S. military regional infrastructure from scratch, the newly designated AFRICOM. Assuming this assignment went well, the Joint Chiefs would no doubt consider him for even more important duties going forward. Who knows, maybe even a posting at the White House one day? General Owens was successful because of his laser-sharp focus on accomplishing the mission set before him. And right now, his most important mission was to ensure that the upcoming Gibraltar Sovereignty Summit went off without a hitch.

"Ms. Molares, good to see that you've arrived safely." The general extended his hand to Kate.

"General Owens, good to see you again, and thank you for approving this posting." Kate remembered to firmly shake the general's hand.

"I spoke with Bill DuBois yesterday evening. He briefed me on your most recent encounters in Connecticut and wanted to make sure we keep a sharp eye on you over here. I take it you've met Lance Corporal Gubbins? He's assigned as your round-the-clock security detail."

"Round the clock, sir?" Kate asked with an incredulous look on her face, not too pleased with that arrangement.

"Yes, no choice given recent events. Are we clear?"

"Yes, sir." Kate realized there was no point in arguing with the general, so she resigned herself to having Gubbins trail her, for now.

"Okay, then. Mr. DuBois thinks the world of your capabilities and I'm looking forward to putting your skills to good use while you're stationed here, but we have to keep you safe. You'll be assigned to work as my personal aide and help manage all aspects of the preparations for the Gib Sovereignty Summit. I'll introduce you to the rest of my team shortly. Our goal as moderator is to achieve a workable agreement among the parties, the British, the Spaniards, and the Gibraltar government, to jointly oversee this territory." Owens looked over at the commodore, making sure he was in agreement with that last goal.

The commodore cleared his throat. "We have a golden opportunity to fully normalize relations between Her Majesty's government and our friends in Spain. We've managed some minor successes in the past few years, but now we need a more comprehensive settlement. It's about bloody time to put this question of the Rock behind us. Bloody time indeed."

"And by 'comprehensive,' you mean—?" asked General Owens.

"Joint sovereignty, of course, old chap. For the British and Spanish to share control of Gibraltar." In the modern world of geopolitics, England and Spain were no longer enemies, nor were Germany and France, for that matter. The new real enemies were third parties that cut across all borders, such as underground terrorist organizations.

"I look forward to being part of the team." Kate looked at both high-ranking military leaders and thought this was turning out to be quite a career opportunity.

"Good. Then why don't we get started?" Kate's eyes turned to the general and then glanced over at the commodore. Owens understood and provided her his assurances. "Just so we're all on the same page here, the commodore is cleared for briefings at the top secret level, and of course, he represents our strongest ally here and around the world. So you may speak freely. We're among friends." The general smiled at the commodore.

Kate appreciated his clarification. "Understood, General." He's a sharp fellow, she thought. We're going to get along just fine.

"Alright, then. First order of business is—" The general was interrupted by another knock on the door. A man, a civilian, stood at the door with absolutely no air of apprehension about him. Quite the contrary, he looked like he recognized some of the people in the room already.

"Mr. Galbraith, what are *you* doing here?" The tone of General Owens's question clearly indicated that he didn't appreciate being interrupted.

The man standing at the door was Bernard O'Donnell Galbraith, a lowly deputy assistant secretary at the U.S. Treasury, and former managing director of the now-defunct Lehman Brothers investment bank. He was divorced, his young attractive wife gone to greener pastures the second she saw his Lehman stock sink to five cents. The only asset he was left with was a small Sutton Place apartment that he couldn't sell in this market. He was just over fifty years old, with unkempt, bushy gray eyebrows that didn't match his mostly auburn hair.

Bernard was a holdover from the previous administration, most recently assigned to the Office of Terrorism Financing, where he had allegedly stumbled across the flow of funds from Venezuela to Cuba and Ceuta. In actuality, it was his underling who had uncovered the illicit transfers, and Galbraith had quickly swooped in to bog down any further investigation of this critical piece of financial intelligence. He would still be holding that information close to his breast had it not been for Bill DuBois's constant prodding. And it was that bit of information on Venezuelan and Cuban wire transfers that set Kate on her current path of chasing that money trail.

"Hello, General Owens. Happy to see you, too. The Secretary thought it would be useful to include someone from our office at Treasury for any on-the-ground investigations regarding the money transfers *we* first identified." Bernard was lying through his teeth, as he normally did. He was flying solo on this mission.

General Owens couldn't hide his displeasure. The last thing he needed was this hack scrambling to get credit for things while they were preparing for the Sovereignty Summit. But since he didn't want the commodore to get the wrong idea about how things operate in Washington, he put his professional face forward.

"Certainly, Mr. Galbraith. Welcome and please come join us. Allow me to introduce you to Commodore Forward and Ms. Molares." The general nonetheless made a mental note to himself— call SecDef right after this meeting and get Galbraith on the first flight out of Gib.

Following his perverted sense of professional behavior, Galbraith always judged who was worth knowing based on title and rank, highest to lowest. "Commodore Forward, pleasure." He vigorously shook the commodore's hand like they were old school chums, which, of course, they weren't. "And Ms. Molares, we've met at the interagency meetings in Washington on the funds transfer issue." Following his rule, he merely nodded, no handshake, in the direction of "small fish" Kate, and then quickly turned his attention back to the commodore.

"Yes, good to see you again." Kate, always the consummate professional, nonetheless put her best foot forward, despite the obvious snub. However, she did gauge Owens's tone correctly. He liked Galbraith even less than she did.

"Before we continue Ms. Molares, unfortunately Mr. Galbraith here does *not* have top secret military clearance and so we will need to keep this conversation to those topics cleared at a lower security level." The general put into words the equivalent of the kiss of death to anyone in the intelligence world, where access to information is everything. Kate saw Galbraith wince as if he were just about to be dropped into a vat of piranhas that had been fed nothing but celery for a week.

"Well, please do not allow my presence to hamper the contents of this discussion. I can return at a more appropriate time." Galbraith was forced to say this, but he was hoping against all odds that the general wouldn't take him up on the offer.

But before the general could do just that, the commodore stepped into the fray of this now-tense exchange, using his characteristic cough. "Ahem. Actually, my dear Mr. Galbraith, I would like to request your assistance with the matter of those questionable money transfers. You see, we have someone here from Her Majesty's Treasury who would be most interested in receiving a briefing on this very topic. So opportune that you're here, old fellow." The commodore was no dummy. He saw the underlying tensions and—ever the diplomatic Brit—he came up with an elegant way out of this little interdepartmental imbroglio. "Please, allow me to introduce you." The commodore looked back at Owens and, with a wink, escorted Galbraith out of the room.

Galbraith was not happy to leave the discussion but he had no choice. He'd have to figure out other ways to keep an eye on these matters.

Owens smiled at Kate. He'd noticed that Galbraith had not shaken her hand in a deliberate slight. But she hadn't flinched, making him think that Kate was going to work out just fine. "Now, where were we?"

"We started discussing preparations for the Summit."

"Yes. I'm going to need you on top of all those arrangements. But first, since we're alone, let's cover *T. gondii prime* for a few minutes." Owens had been briefed by others at the DIA and now wanted updates.

"What we know is that it was funded by the Venezuelans and developed by the Cubans. The only other connection seems to be the million that was funneled to Lugano at the same time as the other money went to the Cuban medical research guys. So there may, and I emphasize *may*, be a link with the *T. gondii prime* over here in your region. Maybe not Gibraltar, but possibly in North Africa." Kate didn't go into the stories of how and at what cost she had managed to arrive at this information.

"So how are we getting to the bottom of that million?" asked General Owens.

"The key lies with this Banca di Califfato in Lugano. Most of the money stayed in there except for a small amount, $75,000, which was wired to a money order payment house in Ceuta. After that, all traces go cold. We've been trying to find out more through that bank in Lugano, but no luck yet from the Swiss side."

"That clears it up for me. I was getting mixed messages from Treasury's write-ups. They sat on the info about those transfers for weeks, waiting for Swiss bureaucrats to get back to them. It's a good thing you and Bill picked up the ball on that."

"Thanks, but in any case, General, I think we'll have better luck chasing down the Swiss than following that Ceuta money-order house."

"You're probably right, Kate. Those money-order houses keep poor records on purpose. The other interesting angle here is that our Venezuelan buddies can play the innocent card. They can claim that the money they sent to Cuba was for cancer research."

"Yep, there's nothing we can use to hoist Chávez. It's the Cubans who end up with dirty hands. They have the *T. gondii* research and also sent that million to Lugano, assuming we ever find anything fishy there."

"Touch base with the Swiss. I'll give you the name of our contact in Bern. Let's see what you hear back from them in the next couple of days."

"Yes, sir." Thinking about other loose threads, Kate asked, "What about the Spaniards, are they coming up with anything?"

"They're working around the clock on this. North Africa has always posed a security threat for the Iberian Peninsula. On Friday, we got the CNI forensic report on the airport suicide bomber." The general's staff coordinated closely with CNI, Spain's equivalent of the CIA. "We immediately sent the CNI report to Fort Dix."

"So Lieutenant Khoury is looking at it?" asked Kate.

"In fact, his report came in a few minutes ago. That's why I was late coming over here; I was trying to cut through the medical mumbo jumbo. Long story short, forensics confirmed that the suicide bomber was infected with this *T. gondii* stuff, or more correctly, he'd taken doses of it." The general didn't consider this good news.

"That's huge!" Kate said, fully understanding the ramifications.

"Correct, this is the most alarming part. They're altering the biological makeup of humans to create what they believe will be ultimate warriors. They've opened a real Pandora's box that's never

gonna get shut. Our guys are already trying to copy the Cuban formula, and so there it begins, a new type of arms race. What's the
end game here? A race of superhuman warriors, a perverted form
of Roman Praetorian guards? There's no stopping this now. I just
hope I'm retired before I have to command *T. gondii*–altered
troops."

"But they haven't cracked the code yet, General."

"So what. Mark my words, years from now, they'll look back
at this time and see that we humans started going down a very
slippery slope with this *T. gondii prime*."

"It's the first real-life use of it that we're aware of, right, General?"

"It is." The general's tone indicated how serious this was for future military tactics.

All from a silly story about cats, thought Kate. If only Inge were
around to understand the magnitude of what she'd uncovered. But
Kate also knew that it wasn't going to be worth very much unless
they could figure out where it would be used and by whom—in
time to stop it.

"That points to the Basque and al-Qaeda, who seem to be the
beneficiaries of the Venezuelan-funded Cuban *T. gondii prime*. And
it's now confirmed that they've started using it in their terrorist operations."

The general interjected, "Correction, Kate, by all indications these
are joint Basque and al-Qaeda terrorist operations. And that is
definitely something to worry about." They stared at each other,
each now having arrived at the very same point of analysis of the
T. gondii prime case. Though neither admitted it, the hairs on the
back of their necks were on edge.

"Right." Kate then recalled what Bill had told her in their last
conversation, that she could be the crux to fit all the pieces together because of her knowledge of the case and all the global ac-
tors. "So if they *are* working together and they've already used the
bioterror agent of *T. gondii prime* in the Madrid airport bombing,
then what would they think about our upcoming Gibraltar Sovereignty Summit?"

"This is too close for comfort with our Summit happening so
soon. It's been announced here, in Spain and England, that leaders

from both countries will gather here for this historic Summit. We have senior representatives of the three governments coming, and to add to the pomp and circumstance of this occasion, the crown princes of both England and Spain will also make a ceremonial appearance. If I were looking to make a statement, I'd certainly be attracted to a venue that will have both Prince Charles and Prince Felipe in attendance." The general's face was stern as he spoke.

"So each terrorist group has reasons to disrupt our Summit, then?" asked Kate.

"The Basque aren't concerned with the south of Spain, but rather their homeland in the north. I'm sure, though, they'd be very pleased to create instability for the Spanish government. On the other end, the al-Qaeda splinter group in North Africa has been talking about reclaiming the lands of the ancient Muslim Caliphate of al-Andalus. That's the territory that extends across the southern half of the Iberian Peninsula. And guess what? Gibraltar, like it was for General Tariq in 711, is the symbolic gateway to that territory. It would change the whole security and military dynamic in this part of the world—a Muslim invasion of Europe; correction, a Muslim military reinvasion of Europe. And no telling where such a movement from within Europe would stop." The general sounded like he was practicing his briefing for the SecDef on this.

"Are you saying that we should count on terrorist action during the negotiations?"

"I wouldn't be at all surprised, Kate. Given the latest news about *T. gondii prime,* we need to rethink every aspect of the Summit. I'll be damned if a suicide bomber's gonna create a royal bloodbath under my watch." The general would be certain to lose out on any assignments near the Oval Office with that kind of "red" mark on his record.

"What's the next step, sir?"

"I need to take you around to meet everyone. Our command headquarters is in South Africa, but for the moment, due to this Summit, we've set up temporary quarters for my immediate staff here on Gib. I'd like for you to stay here until at least after the date of the Summit, primarily working with Lieutenant Melzi to coordinate arrangements with the Gibraltar authorities."

"Sir, I'd be honored to work on the Summit. I take it you also want me to research a couple of angles on the financial transfers and terrorist threats, is that right?" Kate was hoping the answer was yes.

The general nodded thoughtfully. "I know you have personal reasons for wanting to track the *T. gondii* case. Bill told me that this temporary move to Gib was meant to keep you out of the limelight, but I'm afraid that based on our most current assessment, it seems you're right back smack in the thick of it again. We're probably sitting on ground zero for the next use of *T. gondii prime*. So yes, follow up with Berne, but keep me informed."

"Thank you, General. Given my history with this case, I think I have a lot to contribute. . . ."

"I have no doubt about that, Kate. Just remember that this Summit is my top priority. If we go through with it, that is."

Kate's eyebrows shot up.

"We need to keep people thinking that this Summit will take place. But I plan to go up my chain of command and recommend that it be postponed or at minimum, moved to a new undisclosed location."

"What do you think the chances of that are?" Kate asked.

"I'm not counting on it getting canceled. Spain has been waiting since 1713 to move this topic forward and I can't really see how even the threat of multipronged bio-induced terrorism is going to stop it from taking advantage of this window that the British have opened. If we're lucky, we can get them to move it at the last minute. So for now, we need to act as if nothing's happened and plan that the Summit will take place on Gib as originally scheduled on January twenty-fourth. Any questions?"

"What about Galbraith?"

"The last thing I need around here is some low-level bureaucrat getting in the way of what is now a covert military intelligence operation. I'll take care of him in my call with the SecDef."

"Perfect," said Kate. "Meanwhile, I have a couple more leads I'd like to pursue." Not the least of which in her mind was to find out what the hell Galbraith was doing here in Gibraltar. She made a mental note to check in with friendly counterparts at Treasury.

"Just remember," the general cautioned. "We are now in the middle of a full-blown military intelligence mission and I just can't have anyone flying solo, you included. I need teamwork here, not single highfliers. All your actions must be cleared through me. Understood?"

"Yes, sir, understood." Kate squelched her desire to salute the general. She'd never worked under such a strong leader before. Not to say she didn't appreciate Bill's laissez-faire management style, it's just that she knew that at this particular instance, strong leadership, like the general's, was essential to succeed in the mission at hand, which had gone from the simple task of making sure there were enough chairs at the Summit negotiating table to maintaining the geopolitical status quo of this part of the world.

"Good. Now let's go get these guys."

It crossed Kate's mind that this general was definitely going places.

"Ahem." The commander had returned. "Apologies for my delay. Your Mr. Galbraith insisted I hear his full debriefing. Dare I say, both of you owe Her Majesty's government a pound of gratitude for taking him off your hands. Any progress here?"

The general looked over at Kate and said, "Why don't you provide the commander the same briefing you provided me. That'll give me time to get on the horn with the Pentagon."

36

NEW YORK CITY
DECEMBER 27

"WHY DID YOU CALL ME, MARGAUX?" Nebibi asked with a detached tone.

"I was wondering if you wanted some company?" replied Margaux, trying to take on an equally nonchalant tone, but that second martini in her hand wasn't helping. It was early Monday evening, and the driven Margaux was feeling vulnerable for not having a man around to cuddle with. It happened every holiday season, without fail.

"It can't happen again, Margaux. It was a mistake."

Ouch, that cut deep. It was no mistake, she thought; that one time with Nebibi had been the best sex she had had since college. She soothed the pain of his brush-off with another gulp of her drink. Rein it in, Margaux said to herself, bring it back to business.

"I'm curious about your interest in bicycle supplies. Is that your next deal? If so, I want in. Besides, I'm the one that built your reputation in New York and I should be getting a piece of the next pie, actually all the next pies." If Margaux couldn't get him into bed, the least she could do was realize some cash for her trouble.

Nebibi's face turned stone cold. He didn't know what else she knew, but it didn't matter. He'd already set in motion what needed to be done. There wasn't any room for error.

"There may be some future deals, Margaux. Why don't we talk about it tomorrow?"

"Sure, I'll be in the office in the morning. . . ." Her tone softened again.

"I need to go, Margaux. I'll have Eunice call you."

"Are you sure you don't want me to—" Margaux gave it another shot, but Nebibi hung up before she managed to finish. "—come over now?"

At least she'd get some more business out of her romp with Nebibi, she thought. Besides, she never let them see her cry when these things ended. Like other times before, she planned on dulling the longing for companionship with several more martinis. But when she reached for the gin bottle, there wasn't a drop left. Time for Plan B, she decided.

MARGAUX MADE HER WAY UP the wide staircase, and as soon as she saw the artwork of hundreds of bronze rods suspended from the ceiling, she smiled and threw her shoulders up. She wanted to make her proper entrance into the Grill Room of the Four Seasons Restaurant. This was her favorite haunt since those first days when her paycheck allowed her to pay for their sixteen-dollar martinis.

By the time she reached the top of the stairs, her mood was already lifted. She headed straight for her favorite stool at the southwest corner of the square-shaped bar. Margaux placed her black Hermès Kelly Crocodile bag on the stool next to her, which besides being conveniently within reach, also served to advertise the size of her bank account. With the floor-to-ceiling windows framing Fifty-second Street and Park Avenue behind her, she had a clear view of anyone entering the room. She looked up every few minutes to see if anything caught her eye.

She scanned the faces of those dining in the banquettes next to the bar, noting several captains of industry and finance she knew. A few waved from across the room, but this evening, she wasn't interested in talking business with fifty-something gray-suited executives, so she stayed put in her perch, sucking on the olive of her dry martini, scrolling through e-mails on her BlackBerry. She was about to order another one when a male voice interrupted her train of thought.

"Miss, is this seat taken?" A man with short blond hair and in his early thirties held her Hermès bag in one hand and pointed to the stool next to her with the other.

Margaux could see that more than half of the twenty-seven stools around the square bar were empty, which underscored his interest in sitting next to her. She sized him up. By his accent, open demeanor, and broad-shouldered physique, she figured him for an oil man from Texas. Perfect timing, thought Margaux. Now she wouldn't have to drink alone and would have something pretty to stare at.

"No, feel free," she said, placing the bag on the bar.

"Thanks, can I offer you a drink?" His arm brushed up against hers as he reached for the nuts in the small bowl in front of her, a message not lost on her.

"Sure. Dry martini. Ben here knows exactly how I like them." Margaux smiled at the Four Seasons' long-tenured bartender.

"Make that two, then," nodding his head at the bartender. He turned to Margaux and introduced himself. "Name's Jim Fowlmer. Been stuck in New York since before Christmas trying to close a damn deal. High-priced lawyers here lookin' to suck every last dime of my company . . ." To Margaux he was coming off as somewhat naïve, a trait she welcomed following her recent dealings with the all-too-cunning Nebibi.

"Nice to meet you, Jim. Margaux. Margaux Bretz." She extended her hand out to him, and instead of shaking it, he raised it in his rough-hewn hand and kissed it. Her cheeks flushed; it was either that kiss or the gin finally taking effect. Either way, she decided to enjoy herself this evening in the company of this young Texan. It would help clear her mind of Nebibi's rejection and allow her to concentrate on business in the days ahead. Plan B was working out better than expected, she concluded.

Margaux didn't have an extraordinarily active libido—hers was no different from that of any of her middle-aged male counterparts. She just wasn't shy about it, like most women.

Therefore, Margaux spent the next hour downing a couple more martinis, telling the young Texan the ins and outs of dealing with Manhattan corporate lawyers. At 9:15 P.M., the bartender started closing out the open tabs, and Margaux quickly grabbed the Texan's arm and reached for the check instead. She dug out a couple of hundred-dollar bills and left them on the bar.

Still holding Jim's arm, she started to ask him if he wanted to escort her to her apartment, "How about—?" But before she could finish, he beat her to the punch.

"I know a great place downtown where we can continue our

party. . . ." His free hand reached and touched her leg just above her knee.

Pleased by his interest and initiative, Margaux quickly responded, "Let's go."

THE NEXT DAY, COMMUTERS ON their way home plopped down their two quarters for the evening edition of the *New York Post*. The editors knew their juicy cover would sell a lot of newspapers today, particularly at the corner of Wall Street and Broadway. The large headline "Wall Streeter's Fatal Attraction" was blazoned above a photo of a woman's head covered by a tight-fitting black latex mask.

The front-page story went on to describe how the body of a well-known Wall Street investment banker, a certain Margaux Bretz, was discovered in the early morning hours at an underground TriBeCa S&M club. She was found naked except for a black latex mask, a leather mouth harness gag, and her Manolo Blahnik heels, hanging in the dungeon room of the upscale S&M club on Walker Street. The cause of death was asphyxiation, of the erotic play kind, often practiced in these exclusive clubs. Police called to the scene were able to immediately identify the dead woman by her business card—stuffed in her mouth under the gag. The NYPD classified this as a simple case of the high and mighty digging too deeply into the city's rough underbelly, with an unfortunate but expected outcome.

The article made no mention of either an Hermès Kelly Crocodile bag or a tall young Texas oil man. Seems Margaux had not adequately sized up her company at the bar. By the time police were able to trace Margaux's steps to the Four Seasons, the young Texan was far gone, in Laredo, Texas, crossing the Mexican border with only a small valise holding $100,000 in cash.

37

IT WAS LATE AFTERNOON ON GIB and Kate was in a conference room in the U.S. command's temporary headquarters, pacing with a pad of paper in hand and a pencil stuck behind her ear. She was reviewing her to-do list, most of which involved security checks on officials slated to attend the Summit next month. However, she had drawn a box around several items on that list, which she considered her real priorities, all relating to the money trail. She decided she needed to deal with the box around the name *Galbraith* first.

Kate looked at the clock on the wall, 5 P.M., which would make it 11 A.M. back in D.C. Perfect time to reach Bill on his secure line back at the DIA.

"Hey, Bill. How goes it?"

"Kate. Still in one piece, I see."

"Yep, I haven't managed to blow up the place or, more likely, haven't been the target of a bombing, yet. But I'm working on it."

"Well, I ran into Connie Madern over at the CIA yesterday and *she* certainly doesn't think you could do *any* wrong," Bill said with heavy sarcasm.

"I guess she liked my briefing on the money trail, huh?"

"I'm sure she did, Kate, but I also know she tries this shtick with each and every up-and-coming intel officer. Look, if she's looking to recruit you for the CIA, you need to let me know first. And then we'll have a sit-down to go through the pros and cons of a full-time covert ops assignment. You do realize you would literally hand over your life to them, don't you?"

"What do you mean 'hand over my life'?"

"Connie couldn't tell her husband she was in intelligence until five years after they were married. Her daughters still don't know, and probably never will. That's what I mean."

"Well, she's not trying to recruit me . . . ," Kate lied. "Besides, I'm already having too much fun at the good ole DIA and have no plans to start commuting to Langley. Anyways, that's not why I'm calling you. I wanted to get your thoughts on Bernard Galbraith."

"What about him?"

"He turned up here yesterday?"

"What—in Gibraltar?"

"Yeah. I was sitting down with General Owens and the commodore and in walks Bernie, all smiley-face. I felt like he was tagging me or something. Any idea who sent him over here?"

"No idea, but I can ask a couple of my buddies over at Treasury." Bill started to go through his mental Rolodex of who he knew there.

"The general certainly wasn't happy to see him here. He practically kicked him out of Gib."

"Yeah, well, we know that Galbraith sat on the info about those wire transfers for a good week before he let us know, and then, only after the Madrid bombing actually occurred. Would have been a helluva lot better if we'd had that intelligence beforehand. Who knows, maybe we could've done something? And I'm sure General Owens is not forgetting that anytime soon. If I were Galbraith, I'd stay clear of that part of the world."

"But that's just the thing. I called his office to see when he was expected. I made an excuse like I wanted to meet with him. His secretary said he's not getting back for a few days. She said he had an urgent trip to Switzerland. I tried to get his cell number, but she just made excuses."

"Nothing strange about that. Those Treasury guys always find a reason for a trip to Switzerland. If they're not busy reining in UBS, they can always find an excuse to drop in on the Bank for International Settlements in Basel."

"Okay, maybe you're right."

"Maybe the guy's got a little Swiss miss he's bangin'. That's what I call really fostering international cooperation." He chuckled as he said this.

"Bill . . . really," Kate replied with a mock chiding tone.

"Sorry . . ." Bill mindlessly started clicking into the IntelWiki, looking for any recent postings by Galbraith.

"So anyways, where were we?" Kate asked as she started pacing the room again.

"From the looks of it, Galbraith had nothing to report about his last trip to Switzerland. You said he went there about a week ago, right? There's nothing here on IntelWiki. He's got a lower level security clearance, so we should be able to see whatever he posts there." Bill kept staring at the screen.

"That does it. I need to get a handle on what he's doing on this whole money trail investigation. What if he's sitting on something else?" Kate added.

"Agreed. At minimum, the two of you should be coordinating on your respective investigations."

"I haven't had much luck getting ahold of him, Bill, but I'll keep trying. In the meantime, I'm contacting the Swiss authorities about that Califfato bank. It's definitely one of our missing links and I'm not going to wait around for Galbraith. And yes—before you even go there—I've already cleared all of this with the general."

"Sounds good." Bill was pleased to hear confidence back in her voice. I made the right move in sending her over there, he thought. "Listen, I've got to go. A call's coming in from Buenos Aires—"

"Okay, okay. One more quick thing. Any word from the hospital in Caracas about Alejandro's records?" Kate still wanted to know what had actually killed her friend.

"If you can believe it, the military hospital's records are digitized; it's one of Chávez's pet projects for the military. I talked to our cyber guys to see if they can quietly hack themselves into their server and get a copy of his records. That'd be a helluva lot better than walking in the front door and asking for them. I'll let you know what they come up with. Listen, I really have to jump. Bye." Bill hung up the line, his mind already concentrating on the next intelligence mini-crisis.

Kate kept thinking about Alejandro as she hung up the line. "I hope they find that his death had nothing to do with the serum," she said to herself. It would go far to alleviate her sense of guilt for involving him. Deep down, however, she had a hunch that Alejandro died in pursuit of the truth behind those money transfers, which meant they led somewhere that someone powerful wanted to keep hidden.

38

NEBIBI STEPPED OUT OF THE CAR into the bright Gibraltar sun, dressed in his well-tailored suit and crisp white shirt. Nothing in his attire indicated that he had just gotten off an overnight flight from New York.

He carried a small black Bally briefcase with yesterday's *Wall Street Journal* tucked into the side pocket. The bottom half of the front page carried an item about the bizarre death of Margaux Bretz, along with an etched picture of her in better times. That was all the confirmation Nebibi needed.

Before him was the Gibraltar Government House, a white-columned building dating to the early 1800s. At the bottom of the building's marble steps stood Hilliard Humphries, Nebibi's London solicitor, and his junior partner, Fredric Tarlock, anxiously waiting for their client.

"Good to see you again, Mr. Nebibi. I trust you had an uneventful trip?" Mr. Humphries gave his client a wide smile and firm handshake.

"Indeed, the trip was smooth and thankfully without interruptions."

"Good to meet you in person at last, Mr. Hasehm." Tarlock shook Nebibi's hand vigorously. If Humphries was solicitous of Nebibi, Tarlock was tenfold that.

"Happy to hear you had a smooth trip, since we've booked your most important meeting for first thing this morning. This was the only time available on the governor's schedule, and given the short time frame for the closing with Royal Lane, we thought it best to take it." Governor Colin Trippet, who was the senior representative of Her Majesty's government on Gibraltar, was directly appointed by the Queen and, most important for today's meeting, Humphries's old classmate from Eton.

Gibraltarians were British citizens and they had a voice on all local governing issues, except with respect to defense and foreign policy, where the UK government remained in control. In his ceremonial duties as the representative for the British Crown, the governor held considerable sway behind the scenes on most issues in Gibraltar, much like the Queen does in British society.

"I would never complain about your sense of urgency on these matters. Please lead the way, Mr. Humphries."

"Perfect." Humphries was adding up the juicy fees for his invoice in his head. "Well, this shouldn't take very long; it's a formality, really. The governor just needs to meet you in person to finalize that highly beneficial tax exemption that we were able to obtain for your fund." The team of Humphries and Tarlock was delighted about securing this tax break for its client, unaware that Nebibi wasn't at all anxious about that. He just wanted the cover of legitimacy provided by Gibraltar, far from U.S. authorities. And then, of course, there was the historical significance to consider. Humphries's rich legal fees were a cheap entry ticket to this land of legitimacy.

The trio quickly stepped into the white government building. The governor's office on the third floor was situated between two small adjoining conference rooms, which was an especially convenient feature in the case of competing bidders for government contracts.

The governor's secretary, a broad woman in her late fifties who was originally from London, greeted them with a cheeky smile and escorted them to the conference room on the right, seating them at a round wooden table. "The governor will be with you shortly. He's just finishing off with another meeting, if you don't mind waiting here. May I get you something to drink in the meantime, luvs?"

"No, thank you, not for me. Mr. Hasehm, maybe you'd like to have a coffee?" Tarlock was thinking about his client's overnight travel.

"A mint tea would be appreciated."

"Of course, I'll bring it straightaway, dearie."

"Thank you." Nebibi's right eyebrow turned in a slight peak in reaction to the secretary's manner of address. Meanwhile, the two solicitors gave each other a knowing grin; this secretary was probably the first and last person ever to refer to their client as *dearie*. She was in her own busy world and took no notice of any raised eyebrows.

"Is this our last step for the fund to be a fully accredited entity here?" Nebibi directed his question to Humphries.

"Yes. A formality, but nonetheless a required one. You're still planning on closing the Royal Lane transaction next month?"

"We have the agreement in principle with Sam Coldsmith, just waiting for this formality to be concluded and then you can work with the New York lawyers to buy a portion of Royal Lane's assets. We've locked in January twenty-first as the closing date. Presumably, that will work out well from your end."

"Absolutely." The sooner the better, thought Humphries. "It will be forty-nine percent, right?" He looked forward to adding to his invoice of legal services.

"That's the deal."

The door opened and the secretary returned with Nebibi's tea, steaming hot as he liked it. "Here you go, luv. I just checked in with the governor and he's just saying his good-byes at his other meeting. He'll be with you gentlemen in a few moments."

IN HIS OTHER CONFERENCE ROOM, Governor Trippet and Commander Forward were in a heated debate with the small delegation from the U.S. led by General Owens.

"How credible is this intelligence, General?" Governor Trippet wanted a straight answer as to why the U.S. wanted to postpone the Sovereignty Summit.

Kate looked over at General Owens, who flinched at the question.

"Well, uh, yes, I understand your concern. The scenario we've laid out may seem to be incredible, but the point of the matter is that there is sufficient intelligence traffic to suggest concern about the Summit. The best possible course is to cancel it. . . ."

The governor took a strong tone that he wasn't used to exercising. "General Owens, with all due respect, I am simply not sure you understand the long road we've traveled to arrive at this particular point in our two countries' histories. The issue of Gibraltar has been blocking full normalized relations between Spain and England for centuries. This is our moment to finally find the framework that will allow our two nations to put this behind us and govern the Rock jointly as the closest of allies. Bloody hell, even our Royal Families are related, both the princes' great-great-great-grandmother was Queen Victoria! We *must* continue with the Summit as planned; otherwise, who knows when all the parties will again be ready to sit at the table to discuss this."

"Understood, Governor. Rest assured the U.S. government is clear about the historical significance of this Summit. Our concern is all the more acute given that the Princes will be here as well. I'm sure you agree that they are attractive targets for any terrorist group."

The governor's secretary poked her head in, leather desk agenda in hand. "Governor, your next meeting is waiting in the other conference room. Would you like them to keep waiting, luv? You were scheduled to see them twenty minutes ago."

"Who is it again?" asked the governor.

She looked down at her agenda with bifocals perched on the tip of her button nose. "It's Mr. Humphries with his client. I have it on our calendar simply as 'Milestones.'"

Kate's back immediately stiffened. Could Nebibi really be here? It was strange, he seemed to be wherever she was. She recalled her father mentioning something about his fund having an office in Europe. She just hadn't realized it was here in Gib. But now wasn't the time to focus on him; she tried to get back to thinking about the topic at hand, the Sovereignty Summit . . . and *T. gondii*.

"Oh, bollocks. That's right, I did agree to Humphries's request for that meeting." Obviously, his current meeting had made the governor forgot all other appointments today. He turned to the Americans. "General, I think we should continue our discussion. I just need to step out for a few minutes. It won't take long. Just a formality."

"Certainly, Governor. We can wait."

As he left, Kate stood up and followed him out. She looked back at the general. "I'll be right back." She asked the secretary, "Could you please direct me to the ladies' room?"

Kate's head was pounding. As the governor opened the door to the conference room, she caught sight of Nebibi's profile standing up. He *is* here! Kate reminded herself that now was not the right time for him to see her, not with the general here. She saw him turning around and so she made a quick dash out of the office toward the ladies' room.

There she caught her breath. She stood in front of the sink and stared at herself in the mirror. Without thinking, she was checking to see how she looked in case she ran into Nebibi in the hall. Not great, but okay, she decided. The thought of running into Nebibi made her headache come back stronger. She rushed back down the hall to return to the meeting, all the while fishing through her purse for a Tylenol.

NEBIBI HAD FINISHED HIS MINT TEA and was looking at his watch. He was not pleased to be kept waiting; this was not the way meetings with him normally went. He usually kept others cooling their heels.

Tarlock looked over at Humphries nervously, seeing that their client was reaching a point of annoyance. "Maybe I should go check and see what the holdup is—"

At that moment, the secretary opened the door for the governor. His face looked a little flushed. He was already gearing up to call London and alert them of the supposed terrorist threat; he would make this meeting, a formality really, short and sweet.

"Governor, pleasure to see you again." Humphries was up on his feet to greet his old classmate from Eton.

"Humphries, good to see you, old chap." The two shook hands and patted each other's backs with enthusiasm. They were British school chums after all.

"Governor, may I present my client, Mr. Nebibi Hasehm, founder and senior partner of The Milestones Fund."

"Mr. Hasehm, good to meet you."

"Governor. A pleasure." Nebibi extended his arm and gave him his firm handshake, in the process revealing his silver saber cuff links.

"Mr. Hasehm, I understand from Humphries here that you have amassed quite a large-sized investment pool. We are certainly pleased that you chose Gibraltar as the home base for your operations."

"Yes, we're fortunate that our Islamic finance approach has been so well received by the market."

"Governor, Mr. Hasehm's Milestones Fund has tapped into vast pools of money that can only be available to financial institutions willing to abide by *Shari'ah* principles. We expect that his $120 billion fund will be the start of much more to come."

For a moment, the governor forgot all about the upcoming Summit and terrorist threats. *$120 billion!* The number caught him off guard. Immediately, the governor pictured a very profitable future roadmap for himself in this conversation, leading to a very fat early retirement account. First order of business was becoming a "senior advisor" to The Milestones Fund, once he retired from his current post. What's an advisory fee of a few million here and there when you're dealing with billions? The governor held the power to make sure that Milestones got every possible green light from the Gibraltar government before he had to hand over the reins of this little rock to someone else, British *or* Spanish.

"Mr. Hasehm, we certainly wish to encourage the development of new capital sources for the international market, and all the more if it is concentrated right here in our territory."

"So good to hear that, Governor," said Humphries, eager to wrap up the deal. "There is still the question of the fund's tax status here on Gibraltar. I believe you felt we could qualify for certain benefits given the additive aspect of the fund, is that correct?"

The governor continued looking at Nebibi as he responded to Humphries's question. "Absolutely. Mr. Hasehm, as of this moment, you can consider your fund fully qualified to operate here on Gibraltar, *with* the incentive of reduced capital gains tax. We look forward to the success of your fund and a close relationship with our government."

He then looked at Humphries. "The paperwork will be directed by my office through the appropriate channels. You should expect to have everything in order before New Year's." This brought broad smiles to the faces of both solicitors. Mission accomplished. Break out the bubbly.

Given his new retirement prospects, the governor wanted to get to know the Territory's newest partner better. "We should continue our dialogue, Mr. Hasehm. We're hosting a reception tomorrow at Mount Barbary, I trust you can join us?"

"It would be a pleasure, Governor," Nebibi said.

"Please, call me Colin." The governor had found a new best friend.

The governor then looked over at the rest of Nebibi's entourage. "Humphries, I expect you can join us as well, old chap?" He had been the source of this newfound friend, after all. "You as well, Mr. Tarlock." Happy to see that their mission was accomplished better than they could have hoped for, the two men nodded their heads in agreement.

"Well then, gentlemen, my secretary will provide you further details, but now I'm afraid I must rejoin my other meeting. I look forward to seeing you tomorrow evening."

THE GOVERNOR STEPPED BACK into the meeting with the American general in a jovial mood. He quickly tempered the grin on his face to suit the serious subject at hand. General Owens wasted no time in repeating his firm plea to the governor and the commander to cancel the Summit. "If not canceled, your government should at least consider changing the venue for the meeting. And so you know, we are delivering the same message to representatives of the Spanish government."

"General, if I may?" Kate interjected. Seeing the general's affirmative nod, she continued. "Governor Trippet, I've been front and center on this investigation since the day of the bombing. I know that some of what we've told you sounds quite incredible, but I can assure you that based on my firsthand knowledge and the death of two contacts already, the stakes are very high here. These people will stop at nothing."

Kate then paused and leaned forward on the table for emphasis. She stared directly at the governor and asked, "My question to you in the meantime, sir, is: Do you want to take a chance with the Princes' lives? I can tell you that, in my case, I wish I hadn't taken that chance with my two contacts." She leaned back in the chair, the sting of her friends' deaths now evident on her pained face.

The general wanted to overlay Kate's impulsive yet heartfelt words with his own firm assurances. "Governor Trippet, we are working around the clock to provide your government with irrefutable evidence that indeed the Summit has been targeted by extremists. Our primary objective is to protect the lives of the men and women who seek to make this Summit a success, the Royal Princes included."

Kate's question had in fact given the governor pause. Though still not convinced to cancel the Summit, he was at least swayed by her to further consider the consequences. He still had serious doubts about the American theory regarding possible terrorist attacks. Even if they were right, he thought that bringing in another Royal warship to sit in the bay should dissuade anyone from trying to interfere with the Summit. Nonetheless, Kate's words succeeded in forestalling a final decision.

"Very well. We will take your report under advisement and relay it to Whitehall," said the governor.

"We will equally relay your position to Her Majesty's Defence," the commodore chimed in.

"Pleasure to meet you, Miss Molares." The governor shook Kate's hand and then looked over at General Owens. "I'm happy to see that you have attracted such capable resources here to assist with the Summit. We would be most pleased to invite you to our reception at Mount Barbary. . . ."

39

◄━┿━┿━►

"CEUTA, PER FAVORE." NEBIBI RESORTED to using his fluent Italian to make up for his lack of Spanish at the ferry ticket window in Algeciras. He was buying a round-trip to Ceuta, one of Spain's enclave territories across the Strait on the North African coast.

"*Setenta euros, por favor, señor.*" Seventy euros, please, sir. Nebibi handed him cash to avoid any traces of his ferry crossing.

"*Grazie.*" Thank you. Nebibi took the ticket and headed to the boarding dock.

He was dressed more simply now than he was earlier today for his meetings with the Governor of Gibraltar and his solicitors. He wore charcoal slacks, a black turtleneck, and a dark suede jacket. The colors of this more relaxed attire allowed him to blend in with the crowds boarding the ferry, most of which fell in the category of either shipyard workers heading home for the day or tourists seeking new adventures in North Africa.

Nebibi's face was a little flushed. He'd rushed from his meeting with the governor, making excuses of his jet lag to avoid additional appointments with his solicitors. His driver dropped him off at the Rock Hotel, where he quickly changed to his less noticeable garb. He preferred to bury any tracks of his Algeciras venture, so he opted for a cab rather than calling back his driver. The thirty-minute drive took him out of Gib into the Spanish territory across the bay.

His phone rang. PRIVATE CALLER. He thought it might be his next appointment, so he answered immediately. "Hello?"

"Mr. Hasehm? . . ." Nebibi recognized the voice, and it wasn't who he had been expecting. It was Minister Alarcón of Venezuela.

"Yes. How are you?" Nebibi purposely didn't refer to him by name so as not to alert anyone listening into cell phone traffic, either over his shoulder or through the satellites overhead.

"Are you in New York?"

"No, not at the moment." In the type of business they were both in, no one really let anyone else know the whole story.

"I only have a few moments before meeting with my boss. . . ." The minister was of course referring to President Chávez.

"Yes. Understood. Is there something wrong?" Nebibi wondered why he was calling him. Damn, I'm going to miss the ferry, he thought.

"We have information that the security cordon around our Havana research project has been breached. . . ." The minister's tone was hushed and belied his concern about being found out.

"We have reason to believe that a person in the United States has knowledge of the serum."

"But how could that be!?"

"There was a security compromise with one of the researchers in Cuba. The researcher and her contact have been quieted, permanently, but we have reason to suspect that another person outside of Cuba was also contacted. Our men have been tracking this person in Washington, New York, and Connecticut since last week."

Nebibi stopped in his tracks—Could it be!? Washington, New York, and Connecticut. Too much of a coincidence. Without thinking, he asked, "Do you know the woman's identity?"

"It is a woman. How did you know?"

"A lucky guess . . ." How could I let that slip?! he thought to himself.

"Well, yes, so you are very lucky in your guesses. We have her name, and pictures taken by the Cuban secret police while she was in Havana speaking to her local contact. I understand two agents almost apprehended her, but she managed to elude them." The minister was alarmed by these latest events. His country was not supposed to be involved in murder and kidnapping. But if this mysterious woman knew about Venezuela's involvement in the serum, then there was no choice but to find and silence her.

"So what is her name?" Nebibi asked guardedly, deep down hoping his intuition was off the mark.

"Katerina Molares."

The color drained from Nebibi's face, like he'd seen a ghost. No, like he'd seen an apparition of Allah himself. He swallowed hard before asking, "So where is she now?"

"We lost track of her a couple of days ago and have not been able to find her. She hasn't showed up in any of those locations."

"Do you have any of the surveillance photos of her? I need to know what she looks like, so that I can alert our people." Nebibi wanted to make sure it was Kate in the photo.

"Probably a good idea." The minister was not happy having to explain this mess to his president. "I will have someone send you an e-mail with the photograph."

"That's fine, but don't worry, I'll deal with this. All will go according to plan, and that's exactly what you should tell your boss."

"Let's hope you're right." The minister would be relieved only when his entanglement was finally over. Then he could get back to just running the country's finances as opposed to colluding with international terrorists. The latter had not been what he had signed up for. "Hasta luego."

"Good-bye, and send me that photo." Nebibi began to board the ferry, which was set to leave in a couple of minutes.

"Boleto, por favor." Ticket, please.

Nebibi handed the ferry agent his return ticket.

"No, señor. I need the one for Algeciras to Ceuta."

Nebibi had allowed this latest development to fluster him. He quickly handed over the proper ticket and boarded the ferry.

Unless there was another Kate Molares floating around Washington, his Kate *was* involved in this, or at least that's what the Venezuelans and Cubans thought, he told himself. But maybe she knows nothing, which is what he hoped, so that he could protect her. Nebibi was drawing on an attribute he'd long ago buried— compassion. And so he wondered, what hold did she have on him that he could risk so much to keep her safe?

No need to make any conclusions yet, since the Venezuelans didn't know of his link to her. Wait for that picture, he told himself. Having resolved to compartmentalize that bit of information from the minister, Nebibi occupied himself by studying the crowd on the ferry. He made an effort to relax his shoulders and his face.

His eyes fixed on a tall American tourist with light brown hair who was engrossed in taking pictures of Gibraltar; his khakis and button-down blue cotton shirt clinched it. The sun was low on the horizon, making it a mixture of rose, orange, and azure hues. The colors framed the famous Rock magnificently for the pictures this American tourist was presumably taking for the folks back stateside. *Presumably.*

Nebibi joined the tall man on the bow of the ferry boat. The tourist acted like he didn't notice the person standing next to him, and just kept taking his pictures.

"Would you like me to take one of you with the Rock?" Nebibi asked the tourist in a somewhat sardonic tone.

"No, thanks. I already have some of those for the scrapbook." The tourist, Ted Morton, looked over at Nebibi.

"*Asalaamu alaykum*—peace be upon you." Nebibi greeted his comrade-in-arms, Murad the American, whom he had not seen in person in three years.

"*Wa alaykumu asalaam*—and upon you peace, my brother."

In an uncharacteristic move for both men, they hugged vigorously. They were part of a small elite brotherhood in a guerrilla struggle that did not allow for long-lasting friendships. The distance and isolation of their duties rarely provided such opportunities. And even then, they both knew they faced the daily possibility of discovery by their enemy, which would lead to death, or even worse: torture and betrayal.

This moment was a brief respite from such concerns as they traveled in these waters where the Mediterranean met the Atlantic, a borderline where the ancient Greeks imagined the world ended, and crossing over would mean falling off the flat world.

As the crowded commuter ferry picked up speed and the sun continued to set on the horizon, the brisk winds of the Strait forced most of the passengers inside. Murad and Nebibi remained outside, far from the earshot of other passengers.

"So are you all set for the twenty-fourth?"

"Milestones will be completely up and running within the next forty-eight hours."

"I saw the press on the capital raise. Congratulations. All is going according to plan. *Insha'allah*—by the grace of Allah."

"Yes, *insha'allah,* my brother." Nebibi knew he should mention to Murad the minister's phone call, but something held him back. He would take care of it himself, as he couldn't put Kate in danger. Everything else was going according to plan, except for one remaining area of concern. Nebibi was thinking of his recent encounter at St. Patrick's Cathedral. "Are all the operatives ready and in place?"

"The Basque helped several of them settle into temporary quarters in Andalus."

"Ah, our 'friends' the Basque. How is that going? On the financial end, they've been good partners in the fund. Just wondering if they are cooperative in other, more delicate matters?" Nebibi asked.

"Good question. I keep reminding myself that lasting allegiances take time to flourish. I think this partnership will be good for us in the long run, but we need to be cautious. One thing is certain, though, their good faith was certainly demonstrated when they rescued the child from the airport bombing. Thanks to them, we have the child back safely in our care . . . and training."

"Speaking of training, how is the serum performing? I saw the operative in New York. I sensed he could be overusing the serum." Nebibi recalled the young man's wild eyes and blue nails that evening at St. Patrick's.

"I got a message from him last week that he needed more since, according to him, he didn't receive the first shipment. Could that be possible?"

"I doubt it; he looked like an addict. Do we know what happens if our agents start taking too much of it?" Nebibi asked.

"We've performed tests, and yes, eventually the serum wears down the immune system. On low dosages, they achieve a sense of euphoria that does lead to addiction. It's lethal, though, if they ingest it in a single dose."

"If he's abusing it, that's not good, but I think by the time January twenty-fourth rolls around he'll have been on the serum for just under three months. It's too late to install someone else for that mission, so we'll have to make do with him. If there's a problem, I'll send you a message through our normal channel." Murad looked at his watch, noting that they had another few minutes before reaching Ceuta. "Is there anything else we need to cover?"

"No, nothing else." Nebibi answered unwaveringly, hiding his

knowledge about the woman that was being tracked by the Cubans and Venezuelans. By *not* relaying this bit of quite important
information to his comrade-in-arms, Nebibi quite knowingly had
crossed a line. And the question that even Nebibi couldn't answer
for himself was, would he be able to cross back, or had he just
fallen off the edge of the world?

40

"SIR. MR. HASEHM. WE'VE ARRIVED." The driver held open the door for Nebibi. His sedan was parked in front of the elegant entrance of the Mount Barbary mansion, located on an exclusive bluff of Gibraltar. Other guests, the more luminary residents of Gib, dressed in their cocktail-hour finery, walked past Nebibi's car, wondering who was keeping this driver waiting with the open door.

If they had peeked in, they would have seen Nebibi, dressed in his crisp suit and his usual saber cuff links, sitting motionless, frozen actually, in the backseat. He stared at the e-mail that had just appeared on his iPhone, sent from an anonymous Yahoo account. The e-mail said nothing, but the attachment said plenty.

It was the picture promised to him by Minister Alarcón. Had it been anyone else in the picture, Nebibi would have claimed that it was too blurry to really identify anyone. But the person in the photograph was clearly and unmistakably Kate. There she was, sitting alongside another woman, in a tropical location, engaged in what seemed to be an animated discussion. The picture was taken by the Cuban secret police at the bar of the Hotel Nacional in Havana, on that evening of one too many *mojitos* with Inge. It was a picture that bore no hint of the future tragedy.

So now that Kate had been identified as the leak by both the Venezuelans and Cubans, *now what*? Nebibi was doing his best to come up with options in the ten seconds since he had opened the e-mail.

Meanwhile, his driver once again tried to break through Nebibi's concentration. "Uh, Mr. Hasehm, would you like me to take you back to the hotel?"

The driver's voice finally broke through. "Yes? Oh, no. That won't be necessary. . . ." Nebibi spoke haltingly, his mind now trying to multitask, both deal with the driver and the photo in his hand. He closed the e-mail and the attachment. He tried to work through his mind how to assess this new bit of important data. He needed to consider all his options, and those for Kate. He also wondered if she knew that he was involved in this.

"Sir, should I move the car?"

Nebibi knew that he had to get inside, shake the governor's hand for a few minutes, and leave to figure this thing out. He stepped out of the car, preoccupied with the problem the photo presented, not focused on his surroundings.

Bang! Bang!

There was a sudden loud thud on the roof of the car. Nebibi's mind raced, and because of his military training in Afghanistan, he instinctually crouched down, ready for the worst.

Have he been targeted!? An aerial attack maybe? A grenade? Crouched down beside the car, Nebibi listened for any more fire falling down around him, but there wasn't any. He looked for debris next to the car. None. He looked at the driver, standing next to him, who was waving his arms at something on top of the car. Nebibi slowly stood up. If that wasn't an armed attack, what was it?

As Nebibi's head reached the height of the car, he found himself staring eye to eye with a monkey. Correction, it was a Barbary macaque, one of more than two hundred that make the Upper Rock their home. The monkey measured no more than twenty-five inches and its short fur was tan with a hint of dark brown. The pink skin under its fur was more prominent around its mouth, nose, and ears. The monkey crooked its head at an angle, directing its pale green eyes inquisitively at Nebibi, as if to ask, "Where is my food, human?"

The Barbary monkeys had lived here in the wild since before the British conquered the territory. In fact, scientists believe that the Moors originally brought these monkeys over from North Africa. As the only apes to live in the wild in all of Europe, they were a major tourist draw on Gibraltar. These wild monkeys had come to rely on the feeding kindness of humans, so sometimes they left their usual habitats high up on the Rock in their search for food, just like the one now staring down at Nebibi.

The driver noticed that his passenger was not charmed by this little monkey. In fact, Nebibi looked quite frazzled by the whole episode; "nature" was obviously not his thing. "Don't worry, sir. He's just come down looking for food. Just step back a little and he'll soon realize we don't have any bananas to hand over."

"I see." Nebibi was certainly not in the mood for a nature lesson today.

"Now at least, you can say you've had a good look at our famous Barbary macaques. You know, there's an old legend about these monkeys that says that when they leave Gibraltar, the British will leave as well."

"Yes, how fortunate that I saw one then . . . while they're *still* here." Nebibi's sarcasm either was ignored or went over the head of the driver.

Such was the strength of this legend that in 1942, when the local population dwindled to a mere seven monkeys, the British Prime Minister, Winston Churchill, had ordered the immediate importation of more monkeys from Algiers and Morocco to repopulate the territory. Clearly, Churchill was not ready for the British to relinquish this important military outpost in the midst of World War II. And most certainly not because of a few wild animals.

The driver waved his arms again at the monkey, chasing him off the top of the car. The little creature scampered into the trees of the adjoining garden. "You see there? He's going back home. So, Mr. Hasehm, what time would you like me to come back to pick you up."

Nebibi watched to make sure the monkey jumped over the wall and was safely at a distance, and then turned to his driver. "I suggest you park down the street and wait. I'll call you when I'm ready, but when I do, I'll need the car right away." Nebibi wasn't certain what plan, if any, he'd devise for later.

"Very well, sir. I'll be parked just down the street."

"Good." Nebibi turned to climb the stairs and enter the mansion. He glanced over his shoulder to make sure that the little monkey had not returned. The last thing he needed right now was a monkey on his back.

41

THE MOUNT WAS BUILT as the official residence for the highest-ranking officer in the British Navy in eighteenth-century Gibraltar. Now, it was mostly used for official receptions, like the one being hosted by the governor this evening.

Nebibi could see that most of the guests were already gathered in the main hall of the mansion. The crystals hanging from the chandelier reflected the rays of afternoon sun that poured through the large windows facing the Mediterranean. Waiters in starched white bolero jackets darted between the guests, balancing trays of champagne flutes. The air had a festive quality, befitting the day before New Year's Eve.

There was much talk in the lively crowd about the upcoming Sovereignty Summit. Many thought Gib should remain in the hands of the British. A smaller group argued that it was time to include the Spaniards in some power-sharing arrangement. Still others, usually the multigenerational Gibraltarians, thought they should have more autonomy from the British, without oversight by the Spaniards. The governor had not intended to invite anyone of a fourth persuasion, that is, anyone who felt that Gib should be returned to its ancient Muslim owners. But with the arrival of Nebibi, that point of view, though not disclosed to anyone, was also now represented at this gathering.

"Mr. Hasehm, Mr. Hasehm." It was his ever-solicitous solicitor, Tarlock, stalking Nebibi from across the room. His tie was slightly askew, showing that he was his firm's workhorse, not show horse.

"Mr. Tarlock." Nebibi gave him a quick nod and kept his hands clasped together behind his back, lest he be subjected to another vigorous hand-rattling. "And your colleague, Mr. Humphries, is he here already?"

"Oh yes." Tarlock nodded enthusiastically. "We arrived about forty-five minutes ago. Isn't this such a lovely gathering?" Tarlock was certainly most impressed by the Mount and delighted to finally be included in such a luminary crowd. But he also knew which side his toasted English white bread was buttered on. His presence at this auspicious event was due entirely to the financial sway of his firm's newest client, Nebibi Hasehm. So, Tarlock would do his very best to keep an eye on his prized client and make the evening as enjoyable for Nebibi as it already was for him.

A waiter passed by with a tray of freshly filled flutes. "Here you go. . . ." Tarlock placed his empty glass on the tray and grabbed two new ones with fresh bubbles rising to the surface. He took a sip and turned to Nebibi, offering the other glass to him. Nebibi glared at him without saying a word. In his giddiness, Tarlock had broken a cardinal rule of dealing with the manager of an Islamic fund: no liquor.

Nervously, Tarlock put both glasses down on a table, wiped his hands on his suit jacket, and said, "Would you like me to take you to where Mr. Humphries is? He's in a tête-à-tête with the governor."

"Of course. Please lead the way."

"Brilliant." He convinced himself that his client Nebibi had already forgotten his faux pas. But judging by his rosy cheeks and glassy eyes, Mr. Tarlock was also feeling the effect of his fourth glass of champagne.

"They're right over here, outside on the terrace." Tarlock walked in short fast steps, leading Nebibi through French doors that opened onto a landing outside. Originally, the early British military commanders stood at this admirable vantage point, which offered a round-the-clock window into potential threats from maritime invasions during their centuries-long control of their prized Gibraltar. By the twenty-first century, however, it was used to impress the many visitors that stood in this same spot.

In another time, such a vista could have made a Muslim warrior cry, seeing the land where they came from, North Africa, from atop a land they had only recently conquered, Andalus. Nebibi stood for a moment in that spot, mesmerized by the same panorama that had once inspired General Tariq.

He started thinking about his brother Rashidi—If only he could see how we're taking Islamist motivations far beyond his planned bombing. Maybe after this mission, I can disappear, leave this violence behind, and start another life, the one *I* was destined to have before all of this.

As Nebibi's mind wandered over ethereal issues of destiny and chance, his eyes stared blankly ahead at the small group gathered around the governor, but he wasn't really looking at them. He was staring without really focusing on anything in particular.

Something, or rather someone, moved in that small group, which made his pupils refocus. It was his other solicitor, Mr. Humphries, coming straight at him. His movement away from the group cleared the line of vision to other persons standing next to the governor. An African-American man in a U.S. military uniform, with many medals and stripes, and next to him, a woman. She's here! Nebibi felt the blood rising to his head.

Did she know of his plans? Nebibi was filled with apprehension and he needed answers fast. They were too close to their target date. Should he call the minister and tell him he's found the mysterious contact his men were looking for? At the same time however, Nebibi wondered if this was just another chance meeting like at the Coldsmith estate. Were they caught up in a destiny that neither one could avoid? Was Allah showing his sense of humor?

Before Nebibi could conclude the intense dialogue going on his head, Humphries stepped forward and extended his hand, relieved to see that his client had finally arrived.

"Hello, Mr. Hasehm. I'm just so pleased you could change your plans to stay here another day for this event." Humphries turned to Tarlock. "Would you be a good fellow and track down one of those waiters for me? I need a refill." He handed his junior partner his empty flute glass, marking a sorry pause in Tarlock's hobnobbing.

Humphries turned to Nebibi. "Come, do join our discussion."

As they walked across the room, Nebibi kept his eyes on Kate, trying to gauge her reaction.

The governor was pleased to see his retirement meal ticket, Nebibi Hasehm, approaching. He quickly turned his attention to him.

"My dear fellow, so good to see you here. I trust your visit with us on Gib has been enjoyable. Please allow me to introduce you to some new friends of mine."

"General Owens, may I introduce Nebibi Hasehm. He's the latest businessman to understand the value of our little territory. He's just completed raising billions for a new Islamic fund and decided to register it here. It's quite a coup for us, you know. Bermuda and Guernsey were quite keen on getting his business, and we're glad Mr. Hasehm finally decided upon our little protected territory here, instead."

"My pleasure." Nebibi acknowledged the governor's praise.

The governor continued his velvet accolades. "In fact, we are reviewing our criteria for financial advisory business here, in the hopes of making Gib an important center for Islamic finance in the world. . . ."

General Owens gave Nebibi a firm handshake and looked him square in the eye. "Good to meet you, Mr. Hasehm. I'm looking forward to hearing about this famous fund of yours."

Nebibi studied the general's face in return and tried to decipher any hint that this representative of the U.S. military knew about his other nonfinancial dealings. He saw no such sign.

"And this is his very capable assistant, Kate Molares. . . ."

Nebibi studied every nuance of Kate's facial expression. She didn't seem surprised to see him here, which concerned him.

Before Nebibi could say a word, Kate spoke up. "Actually Governor, we've met before. . . ." Kate extended her hand out to Nebibi. "I believe Mr. Hasehm is doing business with the firm my father works for back in the U.S." As their hands touched, a tingle of recognition hit each of them.

This was delicate terrain for Kate. As a person in the U.S. intelligence community, she was required to report ongoing current contact with foreigners deemed to be "close" ties. Given their last lunch in Greenwich, she had kept Nebibi under the heading of "not close" acquaintance. So as she stood there, next to her commanding officer, she felt comfortable to acknowledge that she knew Nebibi, but only in a distant manner. That's the way Kate framed it in her mind, at least.

Suddenly, Nebibi realized he was holding Kate's hand longer

than a mere acquaintance would have called for. He quickly re-laxed his grip, hoping no one had noticed. Nebibi tried to stay fo-cused on the conversation, but her smile was disarming him at the same time. He was left with the question of why Kate had not mentioned that they knew each other from a long time ago. Was she being discreet, or was she hiding something from her general?

"Yes, that's true. We saw each other at a reception in Greenwich hosted by Sam Coldsmith, do you know him?" Nebibi's question was met with knowing nods. Anyone who read the *Financial Times* and *The Wall Street Journal* knew who he was. "Our fund is work-ing on a transaction with his fund."

"Oh really? In what sector, Mr. Hasehm?" Mr. Tarlock had re-surfaced with the fresh champagne for his senior partner, just in time to join the conversation.

"If I told you, Mr. Tarlock, I'd have to kill you. That type of market intelligence needs to be kept close to the breast." The group all chuckled at the expense of poor Mr. Tarlock, who was now wishing that he'd stayed in the other room for a few more minutes.

"In that case, maybe you can enlighten us about Islamic fi-nance?" asked General Owens. Rightly or wrongly, these days, the professional curiosity of anyone in the U.S. military was always raised whenever a topic started with the word *Islamic*.

"Of course," Nebibi replied, pushing his feelings for Kate and his true purpose with the fund into safe little compartments. "While some like to make it *sound* like an intricate science, it's really quite simple. We follow the principles of the Qur'an. The most basic te-nets we follow are: One, we cannot 'lend' money, because the col-lection of interest is forbidden in the Qur'an. So instead, we create systems of ownership. But since we're an equity fund, we end up owning the underlying instruments like stock anyways, which is permissible. Second, our investments can only be in sectors that abide by the Qur'an. This gets back to Mr. Tarlock's question. We would find it impossible, for example to invest in a company like Disney—"

"What's wrong with good ole Mickey Mouse?" The general was a defender not only of the U.S.'s military interests but also its cultural icons.

"It's not Mickey Mouse per se, but rather some of the films

produced by their subsidiaries. One of those is Miramax, and from time to time, they'll release films that are rated PG-13 and above. The depiction of sexual content in those films is completely forbidden in the Qur'an."

"So what is acceptable, Mr. Hasehm? Seems your choices are limited."

"To an extent, yes, General. But there are also large segments of economic activity that do qualify. Manufacturing is a good sector. Infrastructure's another one. Real estate also works, as long as no one's looking to dump sub-prime mortgages. Our fund likes defense-related industries, for example."

"I can't argue there. The world we live in has a big need for increased spending on defense systems. . . ." The general's mind wandered to Venezuela's investment in a certain serum.

Kate spoke up. "So who invests in your fund, Mr. Hasehm? Is it mostly large institutions?"

"Not necessarily. We just harness the wealth of millions of individuals all across the global Islamic world through larger institutions and place that wealth in investments allowed by the Qur'an." Nebibi didn't mention that there could be slight but important distinctions in interpretations of the Qur'an, some more radically militant than others. Nor did he mention that certain allies of the U.S. in the Gulf were in fact investors in his fund.

"That's quite impressive. . . ." The general decided that this was another area of finance that Galbraith at Treasury had no idea about. On top of that, he'd heard that Milestones was now the most important financial vehicle registered in Gib, making Nebibi a valuable financial connection that might be a good resource in the money trail investigation. He made a mental note to get Kate to follow up with Hasehm for a more in-depth briefing.

"Now that I've bored everyone with the workings on Islamic finance. I'm wondering, General, about your work here. It sounds more diplomatic than real military issues, is that right?" Nebibi asked.

The general's voice took a low tone. "If I told you the answer to that, Mr. Hasehm, I'd have to kill you." Everyone was quiet for a second, until Nebibi grinned first. Then, they all laughed at the general's retort, which for this crowd was much more convincing coming from a man dressed in a uniform than from an Armani-clad fund manager. If they only knew that the opposite was so much closer to the truth. "Only joking, Mr. Hasehm. But, yes, in fact our work here is of the diplomatic kind."

Their conversation was interrupted by the horn siren of a passing ship. They all turned to look at the Libyan oil tanker crossing the Strait below on its way to a refinery in Algeciras. About a tenth of the world's maritime traffic passed through this Strait, including up to fifteen oil tankers each and every day. It was a critical link in the logistics supply chain between the Mideast and Western economies. Without it, there'd be significantly less oil at the local pump, and it would be priced at a steep premium.

Meanwhile, Nebibi couldn't help glancing over at Kate. He asked, "So, Ms. Molares, have you been on Gibraltar long?"

"Actually, I've only been here all of forty-eight hours—still getting to know my way around."

So this is where she ran off to, thought Nebibi. No wonder the Venezuelans and the Cubans couldn't find her. In the company of the general, she was well protected; in fact, Nebibi pitied anyone having to tangle with him and his troops. What does she know and what is she doing here? he wondered.

Owens wanted to turn the conversation back to business. "Mr. Hasehm, can we consider your voice to be an independent one when it comes to the issue of local sovereignty? We're moderating this Summit, so I'm not really allowed to give my opinion, but I'm curious to hear from someone in the local business community."

"Good question, General, especially since I have the senior representative of Her Majesty's government standing here right next to me. . . ."

The general smiled. "Didn't mean to put you on the spot there, Mr. Hasehm. I'm sure the governor won't hold your answer against you."

"How does the old legend go? 'British dominion over Gibraltar will end only when the Barbary macaque departs' . . . and as far as I can tell, they're still thriving here." The vision of the macaque that had stared down at him kept flashing through his mind.

"Kudos to you, Mr. Hasehm, you've managed to answer the question *and* save face in front of our host. We'll have to keep an eye on that monkey population."

Kate looked over at Nebibi and smiled. She was impressed by his aptitude for putting everyone at ease. In this small glimpse of his humanity, a slender corridor opened to her heart.

Nebibi's voice interrupted her musing. "So have you seen those monkeys yet?"

"No, I've been too busy for any sightseeing." Kate moved her eyes slightly in the direction of the general, as if to signal that she didn't expect to take any vacation for the duration of her assignment here.

"I bet you haven't seen our famous Barbary macaques, Mr. Hasehm." Obviously the governor had missed the earlier episode in front of the mansion.

"No, as a matter of fact, I uhm—" He paused, staring over at Kate. "—But yes, I'd like to." He wondered if she would take the bait. He wanted to see her in a more relaxed setting to find out what she knew. . . .

"I think we can manage a day without you, Kate, so go ahead. I can't say that will be the case after New Year's, though." The general was basically ordering Kate to take a vacation day, which she found completely odd, given where they were with the *T. gondii* investigation.

"Yes, sir."

"It's not an order, more like good advice from your commanding officer." He could see that Kate was perplexed, but intended to explain later that his goal was to expand contact with Nebibi, as he might prove helpful on the financial side of their investigation. The general knew he had security assigned to her, so safety wouldn't be an issue.

"Sounds like good advice, Ms. Molares," Nebibi chimed in.

Against what she thought was better judgment, Kate took the bait. "Well, then maybe we could both see those famous monkeys?"

"As our British hosts say, that's a 'brilliant' idea. How about tomorrow morning?"

"Great. Let's meet at eight thirty a.m. at the Cable Car station in town?"

"It's a date." Nebibi caught her knowing smile as he said that.

Just then there was an elevation in the conversation of the guests in the main hall. The Spanish consul had made his entrance with a retinue of four assistants, and the crowd parted like the Red Sea as they walked through the main hall.

"I'm afraid that I have to leave the festivities despite the coming fireworks." He looked over at the main hall as he said that. "It's noon in New York and I have a couple of deals that need tending to. If you would all excuse me. Governor. General. Ms. Molares. Mr. Humphries, Tarlock. A pleasure."

"Certainly, Mr. Hasehm. You must make sure those billions are well tended to, as you are now under our regulatory supervision." The governor made this oversight sound like a straitjacket, but Gib supervision was about as strictly policed as the flow of hot money into places like the warm Caribbean.

One of the Spanish consul's assistants was towering over a much shorter Gibraltarian official who had consumed too many flutes of champagne, and heated words were being exchanged. "Oh dear, I had better go and smooth things over." The governor was beginning to regret his invitation to the Spanish delegation. Of course, it had been the diplomatically correct thing to do, but he also needed to be careful that canapés didn't start flying across the room.

Nebibi called his driver as he walked through the main hall, avoiding the crowd standing around the Spaniards. "Please come pick me up in front. Also, make sure there are no monkeys this time." By tomorrow, I will have had my fill of them.

42

ESPITE LEAVING THE PARTY LATE, Kate was still wired. She sat on her hotel room bed making a diagram on a notepad. She wrote various names on the page: Inge, Alejandro, and Mirella—surrounded by several connected boxes that read *Serum, Madrid, Havana, Caracas,* and *Ceuta.* She stared at the sheet for several minutes, studying the known connections. She added GIBRALTAR in capital letters with a question mark next to it, which she kept tracing over. She knew the vital link that could tie Gibraltar to the rest of the diagram was still missing. Kate circled *Califfato* and wrote *call Galbraith* next to it.

She then remembered she had to meet up with Nebibi in the morning to see those monkeys. She mindlessly wrote his name in one corner of the page with her other notes, and pondered their chance reencounter at the Coldsmith party. And now, he was here. Was it really chance? she wondered. She stared at his name on the page and asked herself if the window on their past could be reopened.

Suddenly, a feeling of embarrassment came over Kate, realizing she was pining for a lost love like a schoolgirl. She closed the notepad, deciding there were far more sensible ways for her to spend her time.

Kate looked at the time, late afternoon in D.C. She called Bernard Galbraith's office in the Treasury Department. The phone rang several times until Bernard finally picked it up, when he saw it came through as CALLER UNKNOWN. Given his recent dealings with Nebibi, these kind of calls were usually the important ones.

"Hello?" His voice was perfunctory, angry that his secretary had not picked up the call. How the mighty have fallen, he said to himself. In his Lehman heyday, he had *two* personal secretaries.

"Is this Bernard Galbraith?" Kate asked.

"Yes . . . Who is this?" replied Bernard, hesitant because he didn't recognize the voice.

"Hello. This is Kate. Kate Molares."

"Oh, yes. I was just about to step into a meeting. . . ." He had no meeting to go to, but he also had no interest in speaking to someone he thought of as an underling.

"I'm calling from Gib. . . ." Kate's mention of Gibraltar made Bernard flinch, recalling how he had been summarily banished by General Owens. "I wanted to see if you had any further news about Banca di Califfato? Bill DuBois told me you were making inquiries with your Swiss contacts. . . ."

Bernard's back straightened up in his chair at the mention of Califfato. The picture of the account statement he received from Nebibi in Zurich flashed before his eyes. If someone were to dig a little deeper, he could be linked directly to that same bank that was now top-of-mind for this eager DIA analyst. Remain calm, he told himself as a bead of sweat started inching down his forehead.

"I don't believe I've heard back from the Swiss bank regulator in Berne. Allow me to follow up with him again and see what I can surface. Would that work for you, Kate?" His tone had changed to just short of pure honey in an attempt to redirect her interest elsewhere, at least for a few days.

Kate hesitated for a moment because her instinct was to follow up on this herself, but she had no choice, since banking regulators were normally the domain of Treasury, not Defense. "Sure, that'll work. When do you think I can hear back from you?"

"Well, let's see, today is New Year's Eve. The earliest I can probably get ahold of somebody over there will be next Tuesday or Wednesday."

"Okay, let me give you my number—"

"I have it from your e-mail," he said.

That told her that he had read her e-mail, but had chosen to ignore it. "Till next week, then. Oh, and Happy New Year."

Bernard had no time for celebrations; he had an urgent call to make. He ended the call with a perfunctory "Bye."

He's a real jolly type, that Galbraith, thought Kate.

KATE WORE A BATHROBE TO HIDE her one-piece Speedo as she closed the door to her hotel room. She tried to tiptoe by her security detail, Lance Corporal Gubbins, who was asleep on a chair near the elevator. The noise of the elevator doors opening startled him, however. He immediately straightened up, smoothing down his uniform shirt, and said, " 'Ello, miss. Going for a midnight swim?"

"Yes indeed, Lance Corporal. It's a perfect time to head down there. Peace and quiet and no one else there."

"Yes, miss. Allow me to accompany you."

As she was entering the elevator first, Kate rolled her eyes, thinking this level of security was just too excessive for her. Gubbins had not gotten the hint that she was looking for some alone time.

The lights in the pool made the water glow in the darkness and created eerie shadows off the surrounding palm trees. Save for Gubbins, who sat just inside the doors that led to the pool, there was no one else there. Kate dipped her toe in the water. The air was cool, but the water still retained the warmth of the day's sun. Kate took off her robe, placed it on the chaise, and dived into the deep end of the pool.

She started her ritual of counting laps, but thoughts about tomorrow seeped in between her count. 10. 11. 12. 13. One step at a time. I know it seems like he wants to see me, like there's a thaw. Remember, don't run and dive in the shallow end of the pool. 14. 15. 16. . . . Take it slow . . . 17. 18. 19. . . . Check in with Bill and Dad when you get back to the room. 20. 21. 22. . . . .

NEBIBI STOOD ON THE TERRACE of his suite looking out onto the grounds of the hotel below. He was feeling the effects of his trip from New York and the hectic schedule of the past few weeks. His body was bone tired but his mind was working overtime. Operation Andalus, Coldsmith, the Kate complication, and now possibly the U.S. military on the trail of the serum.

He looked down and noticed a figure walking toward the pool. The person took off a bathrobe, revealing a female figure. She turned around and he could see that it was Kate. Can't seem to escape her these days, can I? he thought.

He watched as she dived into the pool. Flawless, hardly broke the surface. He remembered she had been a good swimmer, had even beaten him. The strength of her stroke was not in showy splashes above the water, but in sinewy muscled strokes pushing water hard and deep below the surface. He imagined she was powerful enough to save just about anyone from drowning in the deep end.

Nebibi remembered that she had told him, "Swimming is my yoga." He figured she must be trying to relax. But we're sitting on opposite sides of some issues now, he thought. If she's chasing the serum, wonder what she would think about me, in the middle of it. Could she understand my reasons for what I'm doing? Do *I* still believe in those reasons? Maybe if she had met my brother, she'd understand. Despite their long separation, he hated the notion of Kate thinking the worst of him. He much preferred that she hung on to that earlier memory of him, the idealistic grad student that fell in love with her.

His thoughts were interrupted by his buzzing cell phone.

"Hello?"

"Can you talk?" It was Murad.

"Yes." Is there a problem? Did he find out about Kate through the Venezuelans? Nebibi wondered.

"Good seeing you again, my brother. Your observations about our operative in New York concerned me. Since you're in Gibraltar, you should also meet our 'friend' in Granada, to check up on him. Can you?"

Nebibi pondered the question, knowing he had to respond quickly and without hesitation. He looked down at Kate turning her laps. He didn't want to break his date in the morning. He knew that he needed to get closer to her, to uncover her role. But he didn't want Murad to know that he'd already crossed that line. He had to deal with her in his own way, in his own time. Besides, he had a reputation in this tight-knit network for being obsessive about every detail of any mission, including the suitability of operatives on the front lines. "Yes."

"Good, I'll arrange things on the other end."

"Okay. E-mail me when and where."

"Will do." They both hung up.

He'd made up his mind. If she was involved with the serum, there was no better way of finding out than by sticking close to her. For Nebibi, however, getting close to Kate again was like swimming in the strong currents of the Strait of Gibraltar and being dragged to the edge of his world.

NO SOONER HAD HE HUNG UP the line with Murad than another call came in. A Washington number that he recognized. But after Nebibi deposited that last hefty payment at the Vereinten Kantonalbank, he didn't expect to hear from his D.C. contact again.

"Yes," Nebibi answered curtly.

"Do you have any loose ends at Califfato?" It was Bernard O'Donnell Galbraith, fidgeting in his seat at the Treasury Department. As he spoke, he kept his eyes on the door to his office, afraid someone would barge in. His ill-begotten millions sitting in Zurich were making him increasingly nervous, making him think that someone was on to him at every turn.

"Why do you ask?"

"Someone is snooping and I don't want any fucking trouble. The funds you deposited in my account in Zurich originally came from that bank, didn't they?" Galbraith added in hushed decibels.

"And so what if they did? That bank is closed. If anyone goes looking there, they'll hit a Swiss roadblock. So who is asking questions?" Nebibi countered.

"It doesn't matter; when one person asks, they all start asking." Galbraith was embarrassed to admit that the inquiries of a young, relatively inexperienced woman were making him nervous.

"So what is it that you want me to do? You're on the inside with official authority. Go and clean up any loose ends with the Swiss—the sooner, the better," Nebibi admonished.

Click.

Galbraith had hung up, but Nebibi wasn't concerned. He knew their interests were aligned and that Galbraith wouldn't rest easy with his ill-begotten millions until all ties back to him were erased, which would equally protect him and the mission.

43

GIBRALTAR
DECEMBER 31

THE RAIN WAS COMING DOWN in a constant sheet and the air was on the cool side. Wearing a light raincoat, Kate stood under the canopy next to the ticket booth for the cable car and, happily for her, with no guard in sight. She had managed to convince Gubbins that she would be well accompanied by Mr. Hasehm and that General Owens knew about it.

A small group of early-rising tourists were lining up to buy their tickets for the ride up to the top of the Rock. She glanced at her watch. 8:45 A.M. Where is he? she wondered. Nebibi should have been there fifteen minutes ago, and he was never late. I'll give him another ten minutes. She looked around again, but still no sign of him.

Kate made use of this idle time by tapping a quick e-mail to her father. It was better to send him one before he started calling.

Hey Dad, Everything okay on this end.
Nothing new to report.
Love, Kate.

Just then, a car pulled up and honked its horn. Kate turned around and saw a silver BMW with European Union plates. The license had a solitary *I* on the left side, signaling that the car was registered in Italy. The driver's-side window began to lower.

"Kate! Over here." It was Nebibi. His driver from Milan, Hasani, had brought the car down to Gibraltar for him overnight.

Finally! What's he doing in a car, she wondered? Eager to get out of the rain, Kate hurried over and sat down in the seat next to

Nebibi. "Hi." Her hand touched the soft cream-colored leather of the seat.

"Good morning. Sorry about the delay. It took forever to get my car from valet parking this morning."

"No problem. I was beginning to think that you'd chickened out. . . ."

"No, not at all. Should I be worried?"

Nebibi asked his question with such seriousness, Kate paused to meet his gaze before answering. "Definitely, very much so, especially if I don't get to see those monkeys as promised." She could see that he wasn't getting her humor. "It's a joke, Nebibi. Lighten up. So why the car? Are we driving up to the Rock, instead?"

"We could do that, sure . . . but a much better idea came to me this morning. How about we take a little detour to Granada instead? It's only two and a half hours from here and I guarantee you'll see far more interesting things there than a few monkeys. Besides, with this rain, the monkeys are huddled in their trees staying dry."

Kate wished she could read his mind. Was his interest in her personal or professional? And should she really trust him again, after all she'd been through? "Can we make it there and back in a day?"

"Sure, if that's what you want. If we leave right now, we can get to Granada in time for lunch and then take a stroll through the Alhambra. It's one of the wonders of ancient architecture, not to be missed." Nebibi looked at Kate for a reaction, but she was hard to read.

Kate glanced back at the cable car, irritated but also excited that Nebibi was throwing her this curveball.

"Up to you, Kate. Why don't we play it by ear. Let's spend the day in Granada and then see how tired we are. I'm sure there are hotel rooms to be found at the last minute, if need be."

Kate thought about that last statement for a second. Maybe if I just look at this as a tourist excursion with an old friend and nothing more, then maybe it's a go. Besides, the general wants me to use him as a contact for our investigation.

"Okay, Nebibi, let's go. But I'm not taking anything other than my purse with me, so we'll definitely have to get back tonight." For a brief second, she thought about e-mailing the general about the change of plan, but thought it was ridiculous to bother him with such minor details. Besides, he'd asked her to develop this contact. So she was just following orders—and her own strong will.

"Sure, that's fine. Seat belts, Kate." He looked over at her with a grin more reminiscent of his youth rather than the cool controlled emotions of the Panther.

Kate strapped herself in immediately—she remembered how Nebibi drove. He kicked the V-12 engine into gear and they were soon speeding through the dry earthy terrain of southern Spain. At this rate, they were only going to need an hour to get there.

For the first few moments of their drive, they both sat in the car listening to the music and taking in the scenery around them. A memory surfaced in Kate's mind that took her to another time, a time when they would escape the confines of business school and take drives in the French countryside to discover the medieval villages and castles of the Dordogne. There they would find small inns to spend the night and block out all the bigger issues and responsibilities of the world that lay ahead of them. It had been an idyllic time, for both of them. It had been her first great love, and it had been his last.

Kate pressed a button on the armrest on her side by mistake. Immediately, two small flat screens lowered in front of each passenger seat in the back. Boys will have their toys, she thought. What she didn't realize was that Nebibi used this as his roving command center and the conversations related to Operation Andalus alone that occurred in this car would occupy all the staff at Defense Intelligence and U.S. Treasury for weeks.

"Sorry about that. Do I just press it again to bring them up?" Kate asked Nebibi as she looked back at the screens.

"Don't worry. I can close them from here." Nebibi pressed a button console on his armrest.

Kate looked over at Nebibi, trying to figure him out. I think the weight of the world has caught up with him. He's not carefree like those days we spent in the Dordogne. He's too serious most of the time and he seems preoccupied by something . . . or someone . . . or both.

As Gibraltar faded in the distance, so did the rains. They passed the frontier between Gib and Spain in full sunshine and now traveled on the A-7 Autovía del Mediterráneo—Mediterranean Highway—which hugged Spain's southern coast. They entered the region of Spain known as Andalucía or al-Andalus, so named by its ancient conquerors, the Moors.

Kate scanned radio stations for some local music. She recognized a song she found and said to Nebibi, "It's called 'Way to Alhambra.' How appropriate . . ."

"Perfect." He glanced over at her with a smile that reflected their reemerging warmth on one side, and on the other, his need to uncover more about what she and American intelligence knew about Operation Andalus.

"It's a group called Chambao. They're originally from this part of Spain—Málaga, I think. They're famous for fusing flamenco with electronica."

"And flamenco itself is a fusion of several cultures, the heaviest being the Muslim influence."

"So there, Nebibi, you see, it's always about fusion, yesterday and today. One culture can make another stronger and more vibrant. Look at me: parents from different countries, carrying a U.S. government passport. Look at you. Italian attached to your Qur'an."

"I get it, Kate. Fusion, the way to go . . ."

Somehow in passing the border from Gib to Andalucía in Spain, they broke with the past and headed toward a new beginning of hunter and prey, and though neither one of them knew it, they were both hunter and prey to each other.

44

✦✦✦

GRANADA, SPAIN
DECEMBER 31

THE SUN WAS SOAKING UP the early-morning rain by the time they reached the outskirts of Granada. On the right, they saw the outline of the snowcapped Sierra Nevada less than an hour away. Nebibi pulled off onto a smaller secondary road, which ended at a crest overlooking the city. He parked the car and motioned for Kate to get out with him. He grabbed his iPhone from its cradle and tucked it into his pocket.

"Come on, this is one of the best views of the city." He led her a few yards ahead to a clearing. "Look! All of Granada at your feet." The city lay at a distance underneath a canopy of clouds that were clearing away to reveal streaks of sunshine. On the next hill were rows of wind turbines, a modern nod to energy needs in this ancient land of Andalus. No Don Quixote in sight.

"It's beautiful. Is that the Alhambra I see over there?"

"Yes. You know the story of how the Muslims lost that jewel, right?"

"I know that it was part of the *Reconquista*—Reconquest by the Catholic Monarchs, Isabella of Castille and Ferdinand of Aragon, wasn't it?"

"Right. In 1489, the Catholic Monarchs set up their position in Santa Fe over there, a few miles way toward the northwest. They wanted to take the city, which by then was the last vestige of the vast Western Caliphate of Islam that had ruled over most of the Iberian Peninsula, save for a few minor kingdoms to the north and, of course, the Basque Country."

"So the Basque had their independence streak even then. . . ."

"And well they should. They're the oldest surviving indigenous

people in all of Europe. They had more independence under the
Islamic Caliphate than they now have under Spanish rule."

"That's all fine and good, Nebibi, but I'm referring to their terrorist acts. It's hard to justify that . . . ," she clarified.

Nebibi's expression hardened. "It's all a matter of perspective.
One man's terrorist is another man's freedom fighter." His mind
wandered to thoughts of his brother. He couldn't get into this type
of discussion with her right now, because when it came to questions of his brother, he found it difficult to contain his emotions.
The depth of what his brother meant to him, and the private truth
of how his brother's absence had caused him to become engulfed
in a life not of his own choosing, were simply off-limits. So why
did he feel that old urge to pour his heart out to this woman?
Nebibi turned his steely gaze toward the city of Granada. He reminded himself that he was here to find out what the U.S. government knew about Operation Andalus. Nothing more.

Kate looked at Nebibi. His stare was fixed on Granada and
there was tightness around his jaw. What was he trying *not* to say?
His eyes looked intense, focused, and yet she thought she saw
moisture forming at the edges.

"So tell me, Nebibi, what happened after the Catholic Monarchs set up camp?"

Kate's question was a welcome distraction for Nebibi. "After
several years of constant attacks, the city finally surrendered in
January 1492. Correction, the last Islamic ruler of Granada, Abu
'abd-Allah Muhammad XII, or 'Boabdil the Unfortunate' as he's
better known, surrendered the city and the Alhambra. That palace
took a generation to build and it was the jewel of the Western Caliphate in Europe. With that loss, the Islamic Empire was finally
pushed out of Europe and back to the borders of the Eastern Caliphate, whose capital was then Baghdad. Now, there's a place the
U.S. is still unwilling to leave. What do you think, Kate? Will the
Americans ever leave Iraq?"

"It hasn't been as easy as everyone promised to get our troops
out of there. All the same, I can't wait to see the ancient capital of
the *Western* Caliphate up close." Kate knew better than to get into
a discussion about official U.S. policy. She knew too much to debate that with Nebibi.

"When you see it, think of this very spot we're standing on and you'll understand why it remains a symbol of a glorious past for Islamic people all these centuries later. It's funny how the course of history can be altered at every turn."

"What do you mean?"

"When Boabdil surrendered the keys to the city to the Catholic Monarchs it was in a ceremony filled with pomp, circumstance, and retinues of armies and emissaries of the Pope. Even Christopher Columbus was there and wrote about it."

"Columbus was there?"

"Yes, but not because he wanted a tour of the Alhambra. He was asking Queen Isabella for venture capital for his voyage to discover new maritime spice routes. He waited patiently while the Queen was preoccupied with defeating the last stronghold of the European Islamic Empire. Had that struggle with Granada and Boabdil continued a few months longer, who knows what would've happened instead?"

"Okay . . . go on."

"Imagine for a second that Boabdil *had* managed to hang on and not surrender when he did. Columbus certainly wouldn't have waited forever for Queen Isabella to make up her mind about his proposal. In all likelihood, he would have gone to the other super-power of the day, Portugal, for his funding, and today quite possibly Brazil would be as large as the entire South American continent."

"Wow! That certainly would be something: Chávez and Castro speaking Portuguese . . ."

"Well, don't stop there, Kate. Picture what would've happened if the Muslims had managed to hold on to this territory, and maybe even expanded it farther into Europe. All the wars that would have been avoided, all the lives saved, all the resources used for the good of man, for knowledge, libraries, hospitals. Maybe, just maybe, Europe today would be a truly pluralistic society, with all religions coexisting in true harmony side by side like they did back then in al-Andalus."

"Could they really coexist, Nebibi? Sounds a bit idyllic, doesn't it?"

"Today, I can't really picture it, you're right. But back then, with a slight turn of history, who knows? In any event, Boabdil did surrender that January, which cleared the way for Isabella to consider Columbus's venture. On the same day of his surrender, Boabdil left the grand palace of the Alhambra through one of the many gates. As he fled south, he stopped at this very bluff to stare back at his beloved Alhambra and what he had lost, what Islam had lost. The sight of it from here made him weep. Standing beside him, his mother famously said with disdain, 'You do well to weep like a woman for what you could not defend like a man.' This spot is known to all in the Islamic world as 'The Moor's Last Sigh.' And many think that what Boabdil surrendered will one day be reclaimed."

Was Nebibi weeping for the lost grandeur of Granada? Kate wondered. "Look at the bright side of the story, Nebibi, and there always is one. Now the Alhambra belongs not just to Spain or Muslims, but to the world."

"True . . ." Nebibi had said more than he'd intended. Besides, he thought, she can't truly understand what the Islamic culture and the world lost here so many centuries ago. "Why don't we get going. It's eleven thirty, we'll arrive just in time to find a spot for a quick bite."

"Sure."

Just then, Nebibi's phone rang. He looked to see who was calling, and knew that he had to take the call. "Give me a second, Kate, I think I'd better take this call." He walked a few paces away to be out of Kate's earshot. Kate motioned for him to go ahead, and meanwhile, she grabbed her phone and checked for messages.

"HELLO." NEBIBI SPOKE IN a hushed tone.

"It's me. I've made arrangements with our operative in Granada. He will meet you outside the Gate of Andalus at six a.m. tomorrow morning. Will that work?"

Nebibi thought about that for a second. "I thought he was meeting me today?"

"He's traveling down from Madrid, where he picked up his last shipment of the serum. So that's the earliest he can be there. . . ."

Nebibi wondered how he could get Kate to stay the evening. He'd just have to figure something out. "Okay. How will I know him?"

"He's seen your picture. He'll approach you and say 'Andalus.' Got that?"

"Yes, I'll be there," replied Nebibi.

"Okay. Any problems, call me."

"Fine."

MEANWHILE, KATE STOOD A FEW YARDS away speaking to General Owens. ". . . I'm sightseeing with Mr. Hasehm."

"Did you let your security detail know your change of plans?"

"Uh, no, not yet . . ." In their quick change of plans, Kate forgot to call Gubbins.

"They need to know where you are at all times. Even though you're there with someone you know, who also happens to be a trusted friend of the governor, we still need to run a tight ship in terms of security. It's important for the conference. Make sure you fix that as soon as we hang up."

"Yes, sir. Any developments on the cats?" Kate made a mental note to text Lance Corporal Gubbins when she was back in the car.

"Only that we've been monitoring the cellular traffic of the usual suspects and have surfaced some threads of conversations talking about an upcoming strike of some sort."

"Any more detail on that, sir?"

"None yet. Analysts are working around the clock manually scanning the data."

"Should I head back to the base?"

"No point yet, Kate. Bolling and Langley are working on it. Not much we can do from here until they sift through the intelligence traffic. I'm heading down to Johannesburg for the day. The next thing on the roster is a prep meeting with the Spaniards and Brits on Sunday in Gib. You need to be back and ready by 1100 hours. By the way, have you gotten through on the Lugano angle?"

"No word yet from Treasury. I'll follow up again."

"Look, Kate, I have another call from the Pentagon coming in. I need to go. See you Sunday morning."

"Sure . . ." The general hung up before Kate could sign off.

"READY?" NEBIBI STOOD NEXT TO KATE, motioning to get back into the car.

As Nebibi headed back on the highway, neither of them noticed the dark blue Range Rover with tinted windows that had been hiding beside the highway entrance. The car had been following their path since Gibraltar.

Alone in the car, the driver was finishing off a quick call. "I have the car in my sight. I'll report in later."

45

NEBIBI DROVE THROUGH WINDING STREETS on the outer edges of Granada. The sun was warming up this winter day to the low 60s, so people on the street were dressed in sweaters and light jackets.

"In the mood for lunch?" Nebibi was trying to make sure his tone sounded more relaxed, on the surface at least.

"Sure, where can we grab something quick?" Kate didn't want to waste time on a leisurely Spanish lunch, preferring to preserve more time to roam the Alhambra.

"I know the perfect place. You're going to feel like you've left this continent."

He was sounding more relaxed. It almost felt like old times again to her, except she needed to remember that things were different now.

Nebibi's route took them through the city's traditional center. Built on a several hills, Granada was settled before the time of the Romans; its name derived from the Iberian word for the pomegranate fruit abundant in this area. By the eighth century, a large Jewish community was already thriving here, and it had sided with General Tariq and his Berber Muslim armies to conquer Granada. That was the beginning of mutual cordiality between Muslims and Jews that would last most of the seven centuries of the Islamic Caliphate of al-Andalus, a fact now unfortunately overlooked amid the deep-seated antagonism of modern geo-politics.

With political stability, Granada became a center for art, design, science, and literature. The Moors, as the Muslims of Andalus came to be known, brought with them the culture of Islam and strengthened it with the knowledge of the ancient Greeks. While the rest of Europe fell under the oppressive darkness of the Middle Ages, al-Andalus flourished and became the continent's most advanced civilization.

One reason for the success of Andalusian society was the Muslims' purposeful policy of religious *convivencia*—coexistence. Because of this, the cultures of Islam, Judaism, and Christianity thrived side by side in the Caliphate. Furthermore, the common language of Arabic bound this civilization and allowed both commerce and scientific discovery to flourish. And it was here in Granada that the Moors, with all their refined tools of aesthetics, built their most magnificent architectural masterpiece, their gift to the modern world, the Palace of the Alhambra.

Part of Boabdil's surrender pact with the Catholic Monarchs was that all three religions would continue to be respected after the departure of the Muslim rulers. This was a promise the conquering Catholic Monarchs did not keep; soon after following their reconquest, Jews and Muslims were forced to convert to Christianity or be expelled. The golden age of Islamic *convivencia,* and the relative harmony under which these religions had coexisted and prospered in the centuries of the enlightened al-Andalus, was over.

Another, more hidden treasure of Granada is the ancient Muslim district of the Albayzín, situated on a hill over the Darro River directly across the valley from the Alhambra. This is what Nebibi wanted to show Kate today.

Nebibi parked the car on a wide street bordering the Albayzín and handed a street guard a twenty-euro note to watch his car. As soon as Kate closed the car door, she looked across the hill and saw the Alhambra. She stood there trying to take in this complex of structures, awed by its sheer size. The plateau on which the various palaces were built stretched across thirty-five acres of prime Granada real estate. The red hue of the buildings was more vivid with the midday sun hitting its walls.

"Amazing, isn't it? The name comes from the Arabic, *Al Hamra,* which means 'the red,' because of the red clay it was built from." Though he didn't do it often in her presence, she enjoyed listening to his voice forming the different sounds of his mother tongue.

"Don't worry, Kate, we'll have plenty of time to take a stroll there. Now come with me." He extended his hand out to her, some-what forgetting himself. It seemed natural to him, like old times, but he soon remembered that much water had passed under that bridge. He knew it was too late for him to pull that hand back.

Without thinking and caught up in this moment of new discoveries, Kate grabbed hold of his arm and walked alongside him.

"Now we're in the section inhabited by my ancient cousins, the Moors of many centuries ago. This is where the artisans that built the Alhambra lived. I think there are still some old buildings around here dating back to that time." This area was known for white-washed houses and inner courtyard gardens hidden by high walls, all connected by a system of narrow winding streets. Kate tried to imagine what this area would have been like six centuries ago with the Moors, Jews, and Christians living here in adjoining neighborhoods.

"What's that tall tower over there?" Kate pointed to a white tower, capped by red tiles, farther up the hill.

"The Mosque of Granada. It was built less than ten years ago, and it's the first new mosque here since the time of Boabdil."

"How do you know so much? Have you spent a lot of time here?"

Nebibi shrugged. "Some." He felt the need for more caution. "But it's a major destination for anyone interested in Islamic history. The Islamic community here is thriving. It's getting even bigger because of immigrants from North Africa."

"Sounds like what Boabdil lost will be reclaimed by the wave of modern-day immigrants."

"Wouldn't that be just the right ironic outcome?" Nebibi smiled at Kate, seeing that she seemed genuinely interested in all of this.

They turned onto Calle Calderería Nueva, and this simple turn was akin to taking a ferry across the Strait to North Africa. The street was lined with Moroccan shops and teahouses. The heavy waft of cardamom and other Middle Eastern spices told Kate that they had reached a very non-Spanish part of the Iberian Peninsula. Shop sellers displayed their North African wares. The buildings stood close together and were no more than four stories high, with terraced windows overlooking the narrow street below.

"Way better than those monkeys, right?" Nebibi inhaled the

rich fragrance of the neighborhood, allowing his shoulders to relax.

"Definitely." Kate beamed.

"Let's stop here." Nebibi pointed to a tiled arched entrance in the Moorish style, over which read, TETERÍA AL-ANDALUS—Teahouse of Andalus.

Inside, several low-level seating areas surrounded small octagonal wooden inlaid tables. In one corner, two men sat at a table that held a *shishe,* a Moroccan water-cooled smoking pipe that is essentially a colored-glass urn topped by a brass cylinder ending with a clay pipe bowl. One of the men held the smoking tube in his mouth and was taking a puff. The aromatic tobacco smoke he exhaled permeated the room. The other man spoke in a hushed tone, not in Spanish, but Arabic. Obviously, these were two of the more recent *remigrating* North African Berber Muslims.

Kate and Nebibi sat in another corner, amidst scattered woven carpets. "I'll order us some tea to properly welcome you to this ancient capital of the Caliphate of al-Andalus."

The server came by, and Nebibi spoke to him in Arabic. "Two mint teas for us if you would be so kind. Also, do you have any *bastilla?*"

"Certainly we do, freshly baked this morning, Mr. Hasehm." Kate noted that the man responded to him by name, evidence Nebibi was something of a regular at the Albayzín. The waiter returned with the hot fragrant mint tea and a dish of Moroccan *bastilla,* a traditional Moroccan pastry made of layers of eggs, crushed almonds, and pigeon encased in phyllo pastry, all topped with cinnamon and powdered sugar.

"The tea will soothe your soul, the *bastilla* will satisfy your hunger, and then you'll be in the right frame of mind to enjoy the rest of your day in Granada."

"Honestly, Nebibi, my soul is already soothed. I'm glad we're here." She paused to take a sip of her tea and then, feeling relaxed, tried to strike on another topic. "So tell me how you and your fund ended up in Gibraltar?"

"That's very funny, Kate. I was just about to ask you the same question."

"Okay, so me first, then. I take it that you're registered in Gib because of favorable tax status, right?"

"Zero taxes will do the trick each and every time. Better returns for our investors." Nebibi smiled.

"Do you work at all with North Africa? I'm trying to get a handle on how financial intermediaries operate in Morocco. . . ." Kate was of course trying to further her understanding of regional finance, namely payment remittance houses in Ceuta.

Nebibi looked at her quizzically. "I thought you worked on Defense issues? . . ."

"Never hurts to expand one's knowledge base, Nebibi." She took another sip of her mint tea.

"Well, I'm not an expert on that but I can pass you some contacts that could give you a bit more background."

"That'd be great. Thanks," replied Kate as she reached over for a slice of the *bastilla*.

"So tell me again exactly what your job is? . . ." Having agreed to trade some contacts, Nebibi felt he could pry a little further—but his prying made Kate clam up.

Instead of answering his question, she mumbled with a mouth half full of *bastilla*, "This is delicious! What's in it?"

DOWN THE STREET FROM the Tetería Al-Andalus, a man with a scar above his right eyebrow leaned against a dark blue Ranger Rover, speaking into his cell phone. He was the same man that Fadiyah had noticed at the Madrid airport a few weeks ago. He was also the one who had "saved" the boy Mohamed at the airport and had driven him to the Algeciras conference.

The man wasn't speaking in either Arabic or Spanish. His language, Euskara, otherwise known as Basque, has no historical link to the other two languages more prevalent in this section of modern-day Granada.

"He just went into a small café." The man spoke in a whispered tone.

Iñaki Heredia, sitting in his hideout in Bilbao, had been receiving periodic reports from his trusted aide. "Is he still with that woman?"

"Yes, Commander. They both went in together."

"Have you been able to get close enough to see who she is? Is she British or some Gibraltarian whore he picked up last night?"

"No, I haven't been able to get close enough."

"You need to keep a close eye on him. He's pivotal and, at this late stage, we can't have surprises. He's supposed to be on Gibraltar making arrangements for his fund. Find out what he's doing in Granada and the identity of that woman."

"Yes, Commander."

"Okay. Report back. I don't want him or any of his Muslim thugs showing up at my office one day. They can have their stab at reclaiming their precious Andalus, but our homeland is not part of the bargain. We cannot trust anyone with the safety of our territory."

"Understood."

KATE'S SENSES WERE OVERWHELMED. They had entered the Alhambra and were walking through one of the inner palaces completed in the fourteenth-century Nasrid Dynasty. The rooms and courtyards of the Alhambra were designed to balance Granada's hot summers and cooler winters. The structures' high ceilings and thick walls keep the rooms at a balanced temperature, while the courtyards' fountains and pools convey the aesthetics of life-giving oases in the middle of arid deserts.

Because of the late hour and the fact that today was New Year's Eve, the last tour group had tramped through fifteen minutes ago, so they practically had the place to themselves.

Kate thought about what Nebibi told her at the restaurant. He was vague about his family as well as his career. Was he just being self-deprecating? She found herself giving excuses about why she was still single, and mentioned the fact that she wanted children. How did he get her to talk about such personal things? At least when Nebibi pressed her about her job, she managed to remain vague. It was exhausting talking to him so carefully, so she was glad of this break to enjoy the Alhambra.

Kate stood at one end of the long marble corridor that encircled the rectangular pool in the Court of the Myrtles. The oil from the leaves of the lush myrtle bushes in the courtyard gave off a spicy aromatic scent. All around, the courtyard was framed by white columns supporting half-circle arches, each carved in decorative Moorish style and inscribed in the soft undulating patterns of Arabic that flowed rivers of praise to Allah.

The entire layout of the rooms and courtyards was meant to lead visiting dignitaries ever closer to areas where the Sultan presided. They walked to the other end of the courtyard and stepped through an elaborate archway that led into the Hall of Ambassadors, the throne room for official receptions. The room thrust upward to a height of sixty feet. Every niche, arch, and wall of this tall, square room was intricately decorated with etched poems exalting Allah. This was the room where visitors would finally see the Sultan, and the ornate decoration conveyed the immense wealth and power of the Caliphate. Kate stood in the middle of the square room, peering up at the decorative patterns on the ceiling.

Nebibi joined her. "It's a depiction of the seven levels of Heaven. In Islam, there is not one Heaven, but seven."

"So is that where the phrase 'seventh Heaven' comes from?"

"Exactly. The seventh level of Heaven is the highest, leading to the eighth level, which is the throne of Allah. See there, the cupola right in the middle, that represents the eighth level." Nebibi pointed to the small indentation in the center of a ceiling decorated with seven successive bands of interwoven star polygon designs. "When the Sultan sat on his throne here in this room protected by the canopy of Heavens and Allah above him, it signaled to all where his power came from—not from man, but delegated to him by Allah."

As they concentrated on mapping out the seven Heavens above, Kate and Nebibi didn't notice the man walking outside in the Court of the Myrtles. The Basque man was pacing on both sides of the courtyard, looking for Nebibi and his female companion.

Nebibi thought he heard someone outside, turned his gaze for a moment away from the ceiling, and then looked back through the grand portal of the Hall of Ambassadors.

"Magnificent." Kate was still admiring the seven Heavens above. She took out her camera and started to take more pictures.

Nebibi stepped near the entrance to the room and peered outside. He saw a man pacing down the corridor looking in each entrance leading to the Court of the Myrtles. Was he lost or was he looking for someone? Nebibi wondered.

"Come on, we only have another hour before they close for the evening." Nebibi now moved with a watchful eye to see if that man was still about. He was feeling protective of her as they walked back through the Court of the Myrtles.

As they walked past a row of columns, their pursuer ducked into an alcove. They entered the most treasured of the Alhambra's rooms, *el Patio de los Leones*—the Court of the Lions. This rectangular open-air courtyard owed its name to the twelve lions that sprayed water into an alabaster basin that in turn irrigated the four sections of the courtyard, each representing a different part of Paradise.

The courtyard was bordered by a second-story gallery supported by 124 white marble columns connected by half-circle arches. Kate imagined the Sultan's harem, in all their finery, looking down upon visiting dignitaries who admired the lions and Paradise below.

Nebibi checked the time. 5:30 P.M. "Kate, we'd better get going. We only have a half hour before they close. Let's go out through the Upper Alhambra. You don't want to miss that."

The Upper Alhambra was an unirrigated section with many ruins from both the Muslim and early Christian times, and this is where Kate and Nebibi's stroll ended.

They stood facing the high thick wooden doors called the *Torre de los Siete Suelos*—the Tower of the Seven Floors. The wooden gate was framed in stone by a three-quarter circle in the Moorish style. On either side of the heavy doors were two imposing towers.

"Over the centuries, locals have passed down stories of Muslim apparitions at this spot, because this is the gate from which Boabdil departed his beloved Alhambra after his defeat." Nebibi looked up at the locked door as he spoke.

"Really? I've seen a painting of that. All of them dressed in splendid costumes, banners waving and Catholic bishops in tow. Must have been quite a scene."

"Yes, and it took place right here on this spot more than five hundred years ago. Knowing this was a heavy loss for the Islamic Empire, Boabdil asked the conquerors to seal the gate. Queen Isabella felt pity for him and complied with his wish so that no one else could pass through it after his departure."

"When this gate closed behind Boabdil, it closed the history books on the Caliphate of al-Andalus for all Muslims. And symbolically, only through this gate can the Muslim people regain the glory of their kingdom in Iberia. The Spanish call it the Gate of the Tower of the Seven Floors, but I think a better name for it is the Gate of Andalus."

Kate could see the intensity in his eyes when he said "Andalus" and now understood the importance of this place in the hearts and minds of Muslims around the world.

Maybe it was the fact that it was New Year's Eve, or that she felt far removed from her world back in D.C., that prompted her to take a first step. Kate reached over and caressed his face and drew closer to kiss him. This is where you reciprocate, Kate wanted to say, but she didn't need to.

All the concerns about the commitments he'd made and still had to fulfill were swept away in this single kiss in front of this ancient gate. It was as if the modern-day Moor, Nebibi, surrendered his heart into the hands of this Catholic woman, like Boabdil's surrender of the keys to his beloved Alhambra to the Catholic Queen Isabella.

Nebibi let out a sigh, not of regret but of relief that a weight was now lifted. He held her close to him. He whispered in her ear, "Even when I'm with you, I can't stop thinking about you. I want to spend the night in Granada. With you." This had not been his plan, but that didn't matter anymore. The old Nebibi was coming out to reclaim a path from his earlier years.

She had wanted to hear this from him ever since they'd seen each other at the party in Greenwich a few weeks ago. She replied in a soft hushed tone, "So do I."

The moment was broken by the sound of footsteps approaching on the pebble path. They unlocked from their embrace. Nebibi looked up. It was the man from the Court of the Myrtles. Why is he here? Nebibi asked himself, knowing that the gate wasn't part of the regular tour.

Kate also looked, but was not apprehensive, seeing this stranger for the first time.

The man approached them. "*¿Cómo se sale de aqui?*" How does one get out from here? He spoke in perfect Madrid Spanish.

Kate responded in her Venezuelan-accented Spanish, "This is not the exit, you need to return over that way."

Nebibi looked at his watch again. 6:00 P.M. on the dot. They only had a few minutes before the main gate closed.

"Are you leaving? Maybe I can follow you out of here. I'm afraid I lost my map," said the tourist.

"Sure, no problem. My friend here knows this place like the back of his hand. Right, Nebibi?" said Kate in a friendly tone.

Nebibi smiled back, but thought, This is a funny kind of tourist, without a map or a camera.

46

A S THE "TOURIST" STARTED WALKING DOWN the road back to the center of Granada, Kate and Nebibi sat down on a nearby bench waiting for a response on a hotel reservation. Kate busied herself with her camera and started looking through her many digital photos.

A cell phone rang. They both pulled out their identical iPhones and looked to see if a call was coming in. Nebibi smiled at Kate; it was his ringing. CALLER UNKNOWN. "Hello?"

"Good morning, Nebibi." It was Clifford Cheswick of White Weld & Co., calling to check on his favorite client. The Milestones account was proving to be a gold mine for him and his firm. "Have I caught you at a good time?"

"Hello, Clifford. Yes, I have a few minutes. Everything on track? . . ." He glanced over at Kate, immersed in her photos.

"Absolutely. I'm back in London and we've been assisting your New York team with the investments you selected. Our brokers have been buying discrete blocks of shares in those defense industry stocks."

"Good. How far along are we?"

"We should be completed in two weeks, assuming, of course, that your transaction with Sam Coldsmith is still on track. If not, we'll need to look for other investment opportunities."

"Good news, Clifford. And don't worry, we're right on schedule with Sam. We may need to start thinking about a second capital raise. How does $30 billion sound to you? There's more from where our first tranche came from, you know. . . ."

"Absolutely. We certainly look forward to a second Milestones Fund. . . ."

"I trust the fee arrangement is still satisfactory?" Nebibi knew full well that the White Weld & Co. bankers had lost half their net worth and were hungry for any new, non-mortgage-related, business.

"I'm sure I can convince my management to continue on the same basis, Nebibi."

"Excellent, Clifford. I'll be back after New Year's. Let's touch base then."

"Okay. Have a good New Year's. Any special plans?"

"Possibly . . ." As he said that, Nebibi glanced over at Kate. "Speak to you next week."

"Alright. Cheers, then."

Possibly, thought Nebibi, just possibly. He still tasted that kiss from a few minutes ago on his lips. He wanted more.

CLIFFORD HUNG UP THE PHONE CALL and looked out his office window at the gray London skyline. St. Paul's Cathedral loomed on the horizon and the London Eye was farther beyond, across the Thames. One more year with Nebibi, and Clifford would be set for retirement, and with this latest news, he was in a position to consider upgrading his dream house from Provence to the Côte d'Azur. That house he'd had his eye on in Saint-Jean-Cap-Ferrat was now in his price range.

Clifford picked up the phone again and dialed his real estate agent in Cap-Ferrat to see if that house on the Avenue Jean Cocteau was still on the market. He could already see himself sitting on a terrace amidst the bougainvillea, sipping his Earl Grey tea and feeling the warm breezes of the French Riviera touch his pale British skin. Yes, thanks to his Nebibi Hasehm, Clifford was ready to say . . . *Bonjour, Cap-Ferrat!*

KATE AND NEBIBI DIDN'T NOTICE the Basque man pointing the lens of his cell phone in their direction.

Click. The man immediately e-mailed the photo to Iñaki Heredia in Bilbao and then called him. "Hello."

"What news do you have for me?"

"I just left them at the Alhambra. I got a closer look at the woman and also sent you a picture of her. She speaks Spanish, but with a South American accent, and English. American accent, I would say."

"Interesting. So she's not from Gibraltar, then. What's her name?" asked Iñaki.

"He called her 'Kate.' Don't know her last name."

"When I get the picture, I'll ask around with some of our 'colleagues.' Maybe the Venezuelans or Cubans know who she is? If our Mr. Hasehm is spending time with her, we'd better find out who she is and how she fits in with the Andalus plans."

"Understood, Commander. Should I keep following them?" He was hoping the answer was no, so he could rush back to spend some time with his family in Bilbao, at least on New Year's Day.

"You should stay close to them and report in with me tomorrow again."

"Yes, sir." He hung up the phone and, for a second, bemoaned this fight for the Basque cause. Another holiday with his family— missed. As usual, though, it was only a passing feeling. This was a war and he was entrusted by his people to be one of its capable and committed field lieutenants.

KATE CONTINUED THUMBING THROUGH HER PICTURES. She vaguely overheard Nebibi's conversation about his fund, but wasn't focusing on any of those details. Then, she stumbled over something on her camera's small LCD screen that attracted her attention. There. In that one. Behind the column. Again, in this one, too!

The man they'd met at Nebibi's Gate of Andalus had been following them for most of their trek through the Alhambra. He appeared in several pictures, caught stepping behind alcoves and columns in several scenes. Coincidence? Kate pictured the men that had chased her in Greenwich less than a week ago and her heart started beating faster.

"So how did your photos turn out?" Nebibi's question interrupted her train of thought.

"Oh, really well." She decided not to mention the man to Nebibi.

"Let me see. . . ." He reached over and grabbed the camera before she could react.

Nebibi scrolled through the photos and quickly arrived at a similar conclusion. The man was either tracking him or Kate. Or maybe both of them. He made a note to call his bodyguards to be on the look out for a man with a scar.

Kate saw the reaction in his face, his left eyebrow raised. Does that mean he also saw what I saw in those photos? she wondered.

His thoughts were sidetracked by his vibrating cell phone, signaling that the e-mail he'd sent himself had finally arrived. He made believe he was reading it for the first time. "My secretary just sent word. We have a room for the night and it's very close by. So close, in fact, we don't even need to move my car."

Kate was confused. "What are we doing, setting up a tent inside the Alhambra?"

"In a manner of speaking, yes. We've got a room in the Parador de Granada San Francisco, which is inside the Alhambra."

The hotel, originally the house of a Moorish nobleman, was converted into a monastery soon after the Catholic Monarchs conquered Granada. Given its unique location, it was Spain's most popular *parador*. While the regular rooms always had a waiting list, there was a room that was not always booked, mainly due to its price, the Torre del Alba, Room 304. And for tonight, it was booked under the name of the modern-day Muslim noble, Señor Hasehm.

Kate's eyes lit up. For a moment, she put aside theories about the tourist without the camera. She wanted to take this moment for herself, New Year's Eve inside the Alhambra. "Your secretary really is resourceful. Isn't she?"

"Yes, she is. But nothing is impossible when you put your mind to it."

For a second, ever so brief, Kate thought about the fact that she didn't have a stitch of clothing to change into. That issue, however, was secondary to her desire to continue where that kiss left off.

"So let's go check out this famous hotel your secretary booked."

"Sure, give me a second. I just need to grab my bag from the car."

"You had a bag packed already? . . ."

"Uh, well . . ." He fumbled with words, rare as it was. "I always have a bag packed in the trunk in case of emergency. . . ."

"Yeah, right. Always prepared, eh?" Kate wasn't fooled, and

she couldn't help letting him know that she saw through his ruse. He'd planned this from the beginning. Equally, though, a smile crossed her face, knowing that Mr. Hasehm was pursuing her.

AFTER CHECKING IN AT THE FRONT desk, the porter led them through the ancient structure.

"Here we are. Room 304. The best room in the entire *parador*. You were very lucky. The guests that had reserved this room missed their flight from Australia and had to cancel yesterday."

"Yes, very lucky indeed, right?" Kate looked over at Nebibi with a smile as she said this. He looked back with a sheepish grin that reminded her of their days in Caracas, before everything had fallen apart.

The porter held the door open for what he thought was a newly married couple. It wasn't what Kate had necessarily expected. She thought the room would be in the same motif as the rest of the *parador*, with heavy wooden furniture and old walls reeking of the five centuries gone by. Instead, the room was furnished in sleek Scandinavian furniture, with a simple unadorned writing desk in blond wood. The fully stocked minibar was in a recessed alcove in the wall.

The porter placed Nebibi's bag on the rack near the entrance. "I hope you enjoy your stay here." He stood by patiently, while Nebibi handed him the tip.

Nebibi spotted the simple flat screen sitting atop the desk. He took out a power adapter from his bag and plugged it into the wall next to the desk. He then connected his iPhone and placed it on top of the desk to recharge.

Meanwhile, Kate climbed the stairs to the second-floor bedroom; the first thing her eyes landed on was the high-pitched ceiling, which was supported by neat wooden beams that were matched in color to the highly polished floors.

The walls were equally stark white in the bedroom, but here, the monotone canvas was broken up by large windows on each of the four walls of the room. There were no curtains. Instead, each frame had a double set of wooden shutters. She stood in one corner of the room looking out. Before her were unparalleled views of the gardens of the Alhambra illuminated for the evening and of the city of Granada beyond. This is why this was the best room in the house. She opened one of the windows facing the gardens, allowing a fresh breeze to waft into the room.

Her focus on the views was broken by the sound of a door closing downstairs. She turned around to head back down to look for Nebibi, but saw that he was already upstairs staring at her.

He searched for any hesitation in her face. There was none. He slowly stepped forward, bridging the few steps that separated them, all the while keeping contact with her eyes.

At this moment, in this room, he was neither the richly paid Argonaut conquering new strata of international finance nor the central catalyst of terrorist plots taking up the sword of General Tariq's ancient triumphs. He was simply a man looking for refuge from the conflicts in his life, in the arms of a woman whose very scent excited him.

They now stood only inches apart. He could smell the remnant of her favorite fragrance, Chloé, which was blending with the faint aroma of myrtle from the gardens outside. His hand reached out to caress her cheek. She let her head lull into that caress, a gesture that drew him even closer. He wrapped his arm around the side of her waist, bringing her body to brush against his. His hand moved down to rest at the nape of her neck, and there, his fingers grasped her thick hair, releasing it from her ponytail.

There was slowness in their movements, but this was not to be confused with hesitation. It was just enough breathing room for either one of them to halt any of this. Neither did.

She wanted to touch him and her hand settled on his chest. Through his clothing, she could feel deep breaths of excitement expand and tighten his upper body. She touched his face and her skin tingled at the feel of the short stubble of his beard. She reached under his jacket, touching the soft cashmere covering his muscled torso, trying to wrap her arm around his frame. His broad back was larger than the length of her arm, so instead, she let her hand travel under his sweater, and there her fingers felt the rising warmth of his skin. Kate nestled closer to him, tightening her arms around his body. She rested her head against his broad shoulders, exposing her slender neck.

His lips moved down her cheek and then touched that spot on

her neck just below her ear. Once there, he remembered it from before. His mouth wanted to stay there, in that soft spot that held the essence of her scent. He breathed in deeply and it intoxicated him. The gentle rub of his stubble on her soft skin sent a wave of pleasure. She tipped her head back, her green eyes trusting, her mouth starting to curve into a smile.

"It's been a long time . . . ," Kate said in a hushed tone, searching in his dark eyes for answers as to why he'd disappeared without warning, so many years before.

"Too long," he said in a deep voice, and with that response, his mouth came down on hers, kissing her deeply and letting go of his self-control and doubts.

Kate pulled closer, ravenous for the feel of him everywhere. She held on to his shoulders to keep her balance, to feel his warmth against her body and the passion rising in his groin.

Their body language now unleashed the full story of their desire in this moment, in this room. No longer was she the strong-willed intelligence officer uncovering plots of international terrorism. She was simply a woman in search of this man in front of her. And this realization made her want to embrace him fully, to satisfy her desires and passions, if only for one last time.

His lips traveled from her mouth to her neck and down to the top of her blouse where her breasts pressed tightly against the silk material. She moaned lightly, feeling the roughness of his chin against her breasts and the eager kisses on her skin, gentle at first, and then more demanding.

Then his hands were in her hair, pulling her head back so that he could have her mouth once again. He paused for a second, looking down upon her face, her eyes closed and her mouth slightly parted. In that moment, he had a choice. He could either kiss her again or reject entanglement with a U.S. intelligence officer. He choose to let pure desire guide him forward. His mouth moved closer, touching her lips lightly, until his mouth encompassed hers once again.

She separated from him just long enough to fumble with her buttons. No hesitation. No questions. They took off the rest of their clothes and now stood naked facing each other, their bodies framed by the illuminated backdrop of the ancient palace of the Alhambra around them.

At that moment, two distinct sounds from Granada swept into the room through that small open window. There was the distant *adhan*—the call to prayer—at the mosque in the Albayzín. The voice was melodious and strong, providing a compelling invitation for the faithful to gather:

"Allahu Akbar. Allahu Akbar." Allah is Most Great.

In a layer beneath the song from the mosque were the distant bells of the *Capilla Real*—the Royal Chapel of Granada—ringing their own call to prayer. The tintinnabulations were deep and slow, owing to the size of the bells at the cathedral.

But all of this, the sound of two cultures fused in their competing calls and the red clay monument around them, didn't matter. They knew this moment belonged only to them. No culture, no religion, no politics, no civilizations. In their ears, the soundtrack coming from outside was drowned out by their murmured breathing, which filled the room with powerful waves of anticipation. And in their eyes, the magnificence of the views around them was overshadowed by the beauty of their young bodies moving in tandem with each deep intake of air into their lungs.

Before the calls to prayer of Muslims and Catholics ended, the two bodies in this room locked together to write the second chapter of their story. The Catholic reaching out to the Muslim. The terrorist touching his pursuer. The woman embracing the man, and for this single moment, rescuing each other from the conflicted world outside.

47

EEEEP.

Beeeep.

Kate was roused from her deep sleep. Her eyes didn't want to open, but the low periodic beeping sound would not let her fall back to sleep. She slowly lifted her head from the pillow and opened her eyes. She brushed the hair away from her face to get a better look at the outline of Nebibi's body lying next to her, framed by the faint light coming from downstairs. All she could see was his dark hair and broad shoulders, halfway covered by the rumpled sheets.

She smiled, remembering the hours they had spent in bed, interrupted only by the sound of fireworks over the Granada skyline at midnight, marking the passage of another year. And then, finally, they'd fallen asleep in each other's arms.

Beeeep.

Beeeep.

There it was again. What is it? she wondered. It's coming from downstairs. I'd better go check. I can get a drink of water while I'm at it. She slowly eased out of bed, quietly so as to not rouse Nebibi. The room was cold and so she grabbed the first thing she saw, Nebibi's sweater on the floor, and slipped it on. Better. She walked over to close the open window. They didn't need church bells and calls to prayer waking them up later.

She walked down the stairs, which were illuminated by the lights from the first floor.

Beeeep.

Beeeep.

It was coming from her purse, sitting on the desk. It was her iPhone: low battery. Kate needed to recharge it because she couldn't be incommunicado. She saw that Nebibi had plugged his phone in, which was now fully charged. She unplugged his phone, placed it on the desk, and then replaced her phone on the charger. The beeping stopped. She looked at the time. 3:00 A.M. Back to bed, she thought. She grabbed a bottle of Perrier from the fridge and drank it as she walked back up the stairs.

He's still asleep, should I wake him? Kate wondered. No, too early. She decided to join him instead, grabbing the duvet that had been kicked off the bed and gently pulling it up over Nebibi. She took off the sweater and then slipped back into bed naked again, thinking about what had happened here this evening. She didn't have expectations about where all of this was headed. All she knew was that their closeness had fed a need in both of them. Question would be, how much of an appetite would they still have in the light of day? She was hoping they'd both still be famished. With thoughts of that breakfast buffet swimming in her head, Kate snuggled up to Nebibi under the duvet, where his warm body and musky scent lulled her back into a deep slumber.

NEBIBI'S EYELIDS OPENED. HE REMEMBERED his appointment. The one set up by Murad. His night with Kate had made him forget himself for a few hours. He looked at his watch. 5:55 A.M. Damn, I'm late!

He moved slowly, looking over at Kate, her head peeking out from under the duvet and one leg exposed over the bed. She's beautiful, he thought, and it made him want to roll over and get close to her again. But he needed to go, right now. He quietly got out of bed and walked downstairs. He grabbed running shorts, a T-shirt, and sneakers from his bag. If anyone else was about at this early hour, they'd think he was on a morning jog around the Alhambra.

His hand was on the doorknob, and then he remembered—My phone! He needed it in case something went wrong with his appointment. He rummaged through the side pocket of his bag and found his saber cuff links, but no phone. He looked around the room, and finally noticed it on the desk connected to the charger. With the iPhone in his pocket, he slowly closed the door behind him and walked quickly through the hotel lobby toward the exit.

. . .

NEBIBI EXITED THROUGH THE ARCHED STONE portal entrance of the Alhambra. He started jogging along the surrounding wall to quickly get around to the other end of the Alhambra, to the Gate of Andalus. His legs took a few moments to find their pace, but soon his body was awake in the motion of a short fast sprint. I hope I haven't missed this guy. I can't believe I overslept. Damn! I was weak last night. My personal needs above the mission; can't let that happen again!

Nebibi managed to make it to the Gate in less than six minutes. His body had a gleam of sweat as he stopped in front of the Tower of the Seven Floors. He looked at his watch. 6:10 A.M. Seeing no one there, he walked in front of the locked massive Gate of Andalus and stood for a few moments, looking around somewhat anxiously, feeling angry with himself for missing the appointed time. The sweat on his body was starting to feel cold on his skin in the brisk winter morning air.

A man in his early twenties was lurking behind some trees a few yards away. He nervously eyed any movements near and around the Gate. He pulled out the photo he had in his pocket and tried to compare it to the man standing by the Gate. He was too far away to see the man's face clearly. He stepped forward from behind the trees and, as he approached Nebibi, recognized him as his contact. The young operative was excited to meet this man; he'd heard that he was very high up in the leadership of their global organization.

Now certain that this was the man in the photo, he stepped closer and uttered, "Andalus."

Nebibi noticed the serious expression and the purposeful stride of the young Moroccan approaching him, and on hearing the code word, extended his hand out to him. *"Asalaamu alaykum."* Peace be upon you. Nebibi sized up this recruit. Dressed in worn jeans and a rough leather jacket, he looked like any other recently arrived immigrant worker from North Africa. Good, Nebibi thought, he blends right in.

"Wa alaykumu asalaam." And upon you peace. The Moroccan responded in kind.

"Where were you?" Nebibi couldn't find a good reason to admit any tardiness on his part.

"My apologies, I got here a few minutes after six. I wasn't

familiar with the bus system in Granada and took the wrong bus. It won't happen again, sir," said the young Moroccan with concern.

"See that it doesn't," Nebibi said sternly. "So where are you with your preparations?"

"I've been in Granada for two weeks. I smuggled the necessary nuclear materials from Morocco. But the explosives were easy to obtain here."

"And you are trained in how to construct the device?"

"Yes, we practiced that aspect many times in our camp in Algiers. As instructed, though, I won't build the device until the day of operation. . . . Will there be other target locations at the same time?" The young man had been isolated in an information silo.

Nebibi didn't respond immediately. That information was only available on a need-to-know basis. And this boy didn't need to know the answer to his question in order to carry out his mission. "You must only concentrate on carrying out your mission to perfection. Understood?"

"Yes, sir." The young man quickly backed down.

Nebibi looked into the young man's dark eyes. He was searching for any signs of overdosing. He seemed balanced: no rapid movements, clear eyes, not bloodshot. "Have you been taking doses of the vitamins?"

"Yes, for the last week, since I received the shipment."

"Good." Seems like Murad is tightening his control on the formula. "And how are you feeling?"

"Sir, I am honored, and my family is honored for me to be selected to carry forward the triumphs of our ancestors. I'm very ready for the mission and prepared to sacrifice whatever is necessary to accomplish it."

Nebibi could see that the serum was working perfectly with this recruit. When they expanded their serum program to more troops, in more countries, they would be unstoppable, and the world would be a very different place, spinning on a very different axis of power than today.

RRIINNNG!

Kate was enjoying her second round of REM sleep. The sound

of a phone ringing started seeping into her dream state. Not again, was her first reaction to the ringing sound.

Rriinnng!

She lay on the bed, her head half buried in the soft down pillow. Do I have to get up? she asked herself. What if it's important? Maybe it's the general with some news. She raised her head, expecting to see Nebibi still sound asleep next to her. He's not here. Maybe he's downstairs. Doesn't he hear that phone ringing?

Rriinnng!

"Alright already, I'm coming!" She quickly glanced at the clock on the side table. 6:35 A.M. "Ughh!"

She got up, naked. *Mierda,* it's still chilly in here. Before rushing downstairs, she grabbed the duvet and wrapped it around herself. "Nebibi, are you down there?"

Rriinnng!

She picked up the cell phone on the fourth ring, but it was already too late. The caller hung up and didn't leave a message. A New York area code? Who's calling me from there? She didn't recognize that number.

She looked around for Nebibi, expecting to find him downstairs. But he wasn't in the living room, and the bathroom was empty. Maybe he's having coffee in the lobby, she ventured. His stuff was still here, so no disappearing act this time, at least.

She sat on the couch for a second, the iPhone in her hand, trying to regain the calm spirit she started out with before the call. She remembered a date that she had filed away in the back of her mind for the past few years. His birthday's coming up. By the looks of it, this year I can think about buying him a present. Who knows? Maybe we can have another visit like this one? Maybe, just maybe. I wonder what day of the week it is this year? She clicked the iPhone to go to the calendar function. Let's see, January twenty-fourth. On the same day as the Sovereignty Summit. She wondered why *Andalus* was written in for that day? She knew she hadn't entered that.

Just as she pondered this calendar entry, another call came in, from that same New York number.

"Yes," Kate answered.

"Hello? This is Eunice Jameson from Milestones. I'm trying to reach Mr. Hasehm." It was Nebibi's secretary.

Kate looked at her cell phone, confused by a call for Nebibi coming in on her number. Whatever the case, she wasn't about to let someone from his office know that she'd spent the night with Nebibi, so she replied, "I'm sorry but you have the wrong number."

"Oh, sorry. Good-bye." Eunice hung up the line.

Kate looked at the cell phone again and started putting two and two together. She realized that Nebibi had taken her phone and that the one in her hands was his!

"Well, that was interesting," Kate said out loud to herself.

"What? What was interesting?" Nebibi had returned and stood at the door, sweat dripping from his brow, shirt wet and tight against his body.

"So you were jogging?" Any immediate thoughts about that entry in Nebibi's calendar were filed away for future reference. There were more pressing matters at hand. All she could think of was that it was time for breakfast now and *she* was famished. Kate let the duvet wrapped around her fall to the floor.

KATE LOOKED OUT THE WINDOW at her last views of the Alhambra, seen through the soft rain that had started just when they left at 11 A.M. They were both heading back to Gibraltar, each lost in their own thoughts.

Suddenly, Kate remembered their switch of iPhones. "Nebibi, you have my phone and I have yours. You must have grabbed mine this morning when you went out for your jog."

Nebibi sounded concerned. "How do you know it's mine?"

"That's the funny thing. A call on your phone woke me up this morning. Thinking it was mine, I took the call. It was someone from your office, a woman, Jameson."

Nebibi's hands tightened around the steering wheel, blood draining from his knuckles. The discomfort of Kate speaking to his assistant made him uneasy. However, more discomforting would have been if Murad had called instead. He knew he needed to get control of himself again. Making mistakes because of my personal distractions. "I can call her back tomorrow. Any other calls?"

"No. At least, not that I'm aware of. Here, this one's yours." She handed him his iPhone. He, in turn, handed the iPhone in his jacket pocket to her. "Thanks. Did I get any calls?"

"No, none that I'm aware of. . . ."

"So, Nebibi, what is your schedule like this week?"

Without hesitation, his voice was all business now. "I head back to New York this evening."

"Oh, okay. So I guess I won't be seeing you in the near future. . . ." Is he pulling another disappearing act on me? she wondered. "I assume you need to come back, though? Don't you have your closing coming up?"

"Sure." Nebibi's mind was elsewhere.

"So when is that supposed to be?"

"If all goes well, it should be on the twenty-first." Nebibi kept his eyes focused on the highway.

"How long are you going to stay?" Kate kept pressing forward.

"Not sure yet. Are you going to be here?"

"Hard to imagine that I won't still be here."

Nebibi was getting more interested in the conversation, since it was dealing with Kate's duties. "Why? Has something changed? Something come up that requires you to be here?"

"No, nothing's changed. The Gibraltar Sovereignty Summit takes place on the twenty-fourth, so unless something comes up elsewhere, I need to be here through that date, at least."

"I see. . . ." Nebibi pondered what that meant for him and his mission. She's still going to be here through the twenty-fourth, and he still wasn't sure how much she knew about Operation Andalus.

"So where are you going to be for your birthday?"

Nebibi had completely forgotten about that date, and it sank in to him that this was why she was asking him about dates. We're in the clear, he thought; if she knew anything about Andalus, she wouldn't be asking about my birthday.

"Not sure where I'll be that day. I may have other business to take care of after our closing on Gib. I'm going to play it by ear," Nebibi replied.

"If you're in town for your birthday, then let me treat you to dinner to celebrate, okay?"

"Sure. It's a date, Kate," he said, relieved she was focused on his birthday. In his mind, however, he knew other things would happen on that day that were going to take up all of his time. And hers.

THEY CLEARED PASSPORT CONTROL at the entrance to Gibraltar. The last half hour on the road had been relatively quiet between them, each thinking about their time at the Alhambra as well as what lay ahead in their professional lives.

"How about catching up on some news of the world?" Nebibi said as he turned on the radio to break the silence. Kate just looked and smiled, knowing that they only had a few more minutes before arriving at her hotel.

"Here, let me find the local English station." Kate started scanning FM signals.

". . . this is a special report from the BBC World Service . . ." A mellifluous female voice with an educated British accent poured out from the speakers.

"Perfect," said Kate as she relaxed back into her seat.

The announcer continued, ". . . a few moments ago, the U.S. Secretary of Homeland Security announced the arrest of three Afghani men in Petaluma, California, suspected of planning to detonate a bomb on the Golden Gate Bridge."

Kate immediately straightened up in her seat.

The news reader continued, "Government agents searched their motel room near the Redwood Highway and found thousand-pound bags of urea, a legal substance used in fertilizer that is also known to be used for explosives, along with four small black boxes containing timers. In his prepared statement, the Secretary did not indicate how long they had been tracking these three men, or if others are involved. This has been a special report from the BBC World Service. We now return you to our regular programming." The car filled with the sound of a U.K. soccer match.

Kate reached over to shut off the radio, asking herself—Why didn't I know anything about this investigation? Was this the terrorist plan they'd all been chasing? Her phone buzzed and it startled her. She looked down and read an instant message from Bill: *call me*. She wanted to call him right away, but couldn't, not with Nebibi in the car. She stared out the window and subconsciously tapped her fingers on the armrest, feeling a rising anger because she'd been kept out of the loop.

Nebibi stared straight ahead, oblivious to Kate's nervous finger-tapping, because he, too, was going through his own set of questions. Why didn't he know about this operation? Did Murad know? Was he being tracked by the Americans?

Nebibi then glanced at Kate and noticed she was preoccupied, maybe even anxious. The news seemed a surprise to her as well. But yet, he couldn't help wonder if she was an agent sent to get close to him. If that was the case, she had certainly succeeded in her mission. But now he knew better. He trusted no one. He started second-guessing everything.

48

ROCK HOTEL, GIBRALTAR
JANUARY 1

WHAT HAPPENED?!" KATE WAS TRYING to keep her voice low as she spoke on her cell phone, but she couldn't hide the frustration swirling inside her. She turned on the TV to drown out her voice for anyone passing in the hallway outside her hotel room. CNN International was blaring the latest news about the Golden Gate plot.

On the other end of the line in D.C., Bill pulled the receiver away from his ear. "Cool it, Kate. I didn't know anything about this either!"

"What do you mean? How can that be . . . on something this big? Bill, we just had that briefing from Connie Madern a week ago. She must've known about it." Kate's eyes closed slightly, recalling that CIA meeting.

"Yeah, I know. I tried to reach her but haven't gotten through yet. I'm sure there's a story behind this."

"Yeah, I'm sure." Kate's voice sounded resigned as she questioned whether Bill had the political clout to get to the bottom of this. "So what does this mean for the money trail and the Sovereignty Summit?" she asked while pacing around her hotel room with the phone held up to her ear.

"Whatever these guys in Petaluma were planning has been stopped, and that's good. Homeland Security is bringing the suspects back East for 'interviews' and a helluva lot of resources are being redirected to dig out what these Afghanis were planning and who their contacts were."

"So the heat is off our investigation, then?" Kate asked.

"It just won't have the same level of attention as before. Most of the flies are swarming around this new carcass now, right-fully so."

"What about the money angle?" she asked.

"That's the thing, the one piece I managed to scrape up out of the San Francisco team this morning was that one of the Golden Gate plotters received some money into his local bank account from—"

"Let me guess, Banca di Califfato—"

"Bingo! You were definitely on the right track. You should stick with the general through the Summit and continue trailing that money. Hopefully, it'll build a more complete picture of the Golden Gate plot. We'll see where we go after that, okay?"

"Sure, whatever you say, boss." As Kate hung up the line, she wasn't entirely convinced that the Califfato trail ended so simply and elegantly on the Golden Gate Bridge.

IN HER OFFICE AT LANGLEY HEADQUARTERS, Connie Madern was on the phone with her boss, the Director of the CIA, briefing him on the failed Golden Gate plot. "We had no prior signals on this, sir. First word came through an anonymous e-mail sent two days ago, to the Commerce Department official attached to our embassy in Kabul. It was encrypted and went through five different remailers. Whoever sent it wanted to make sure they wouldn't be found."

"Is the Commerce guy one of ours?" asked the director.

"Yes, he's been on our payroll since last year." Connie referred to the Commerce official's covert status as a CIA operative on top of his day job.

"Let's keep him under wraps. What are you telling our friends at Homeland Security?"

"Nothing. As far as they know, we had been tracking these Peta-luma characters for months." Connie stared out of her office win-dow as the Presidential helicopter hovered over their headquarters preparing to land.

"Perfect. Just keep them thinking that for the moment. Does me no good for people to know that this whole thing just fell into our laps through some anonymous tipster. Better they think we're at the top of our game keeping these jackasses from blowing up our fucking bridges. I need that PR angle on this to get our new budget approved up on the Hill." The CIA director played this through like the consummate Washington insider that he was.

An instant message from his secretary reading POTUS appeared on the director's screen. "Listen, Connie, I have to go," he said hurriedly.

"Yes, sir," Connie responded as she furiously took down notes of their conversation. She had also been around the block a few times and always took such precautions in case some future Congressional oversight panel came knocking on her door. She knew better than to trust anyone.

49

N EBIBI WAS DRIVING ON Spain's Carretera 145, heading to the Principality of Andorra, the small landlocked country in the Pyrénées Mountains bordered by Spain and France. He had quickly said his good-byes to Kate and then departed Gibraltar, driving the 780-mile trip through the night.

The news about the Golden Gate plot had shaken him up and this solitary drive gave him time to think through his options, maybe even including his mission. He had already made one decision. He would make a certain delicate matter a priority—the still-active account of the defunct Banca di Califfato.

Thirty minutes outside of Andorra, he pulled in at a gas station to dial up a usual correspondent. He knew that much hung in the balance on how this call would go. The phone rang on the other end only once when the line was picked up.

"Hello."

"It's me," Nebibi responded.

Nebibi had reached Murad, but he strained to make out his voice. There was a lot of background noise, like he was riding in an open truck, quite the opposite of Nebibi's airtight cocoon of his BMW. Murad was constantly hunted by the Americans and he and his men were only as safe as their hefty payoffs to the corrupt Pakistani and Afghan military allowed.

But money was tight for those hiding in Kandahar, because their liquidity was tied up in The Milestones Fund, and that couldn't be released until after Operation Andalus was completed. So the very survival of Murad and his men, hiding in the rocky no-man's-land between Pakistan and Afghanistan, hinged on the success of this operation.

"Is everything set?" Murad's question was barely audible.

"What do you mean, is everything set!? What about California? Why didn't I know about that? What else are you keeping from me?" Nebibi wasn't his cool self. His anger, brewing since yesterday, rose immediately to the surface.

There was a long pause on the other end of the line. Finally Murad spoke. "We needed to make that sacrifice. Your mission is much too important for us. We led them to that solitary cell to confuse our enemies—"

"*You* did this?!" Nebibi asked, wondering if he, too, would be sacrificed when it proved expeditious for other goals.

"It was a sacrifice we needed to make. Our brothers will give their lives differently. You need to understand that." Murad *had* made a sacrifice. He'd personally recruited the leader of the Golden Gate plot, but knew that the eventual impact of that bombing would be dwarfed by the results of a successful Operation Andalus. So he sacrificed them in order to send intelligence forces sniffing on a different trail, far from Nebibi's Andalus.

"Are we agreed?" Murad asked, not hearing any reaction from Nebibi.

"Don't keep anything like that from me again or I'll disappear."

"Understood, my brother," Murad said with certain relief. "Everything in place?" Murad knew they only had a few more seconds to speak.

"Yes, I've met with each of the operatives. Everything's in place. Only thing left is confirming the date. We can keep to the original schedule." Nebibi was careful not to mention the date, known to both of them, over the open phone line.

"I agree. We can't put this off for much longer. Too much depends on it." Murad was looking forward to having cash flow again after the mission was completed.

"When will you communicate with the operatives?"

"Forty-eight hours before the event they will find a message posted in the usual spot." Murad's usual spot being the bicycle parts suppliers' Web site.

"Okay. I recommend that we cut off communication between us until after the mission is completed. We must avoid leakages."

"I agree." Murad thought about all the American spy satellites that kept trying, without much success, to crack their web of cells around the globe. They couldn't rely on the continued incompetence of U.S. intelligence at this final stage of Operation Andalus. "Alright, my brother. *Salallahu alayhi wasalaam*." Peace be upon him. Murad hung up the line.

Nebibi sat in the car, parked along the road, thinking about what Murad said. One thing was certain in his mind now: there was no one to trust. He started the engine, watched as a blue SUV passed by, and then continued on the highway.

Within minutes, Nebibi saw a sign on the highway in the official Catalan language of this part of Spain confirming that he had arrived in the Principat d'Andorra. He just needed an hour there and his business would be done. It was 11:15 A.M. He calculated he could make it to nearby Barcelona Airport by 3:45 P.M. to catch the late afternoon Air France flight, connecting at Charles de Gaulle this evening, back to JFK. He'd be back in his New York apartment by midnight.

Nebibi parked across the street from the Banca Seguretat d'Andorra, but before heading into the building he placed a call to his driver, Hasani.

"You need to pick up the car at Barcelona Airport in Terminal A parking lot. Drive it back to the Rock Hotel on Gibraltar. I'll pick it up there when I return in a couple of weeks."

"Yes, sir."

Nebibi didn't waste time on either hellos or good-byes. Just orders to be followed to the T. After his next, and very possibly last, visit to Gib, he didn't expect to have use for this car again.

ON HIS DRIVE OUT OF ANDORRA to the airport, Nebibi recalled Kate's reaction to the Golden Gate news. She had been surprised by it as much as he was. Maybe her focus wasn't on terrorism activities after all. In two days of close proximity, her conversation didn't hint at anything more than just helping organize a summit between two friendly nations.

Nebibi made another call, this time to Caracas. He'd thought through what he needed to do about that picture of Kate he received via Venezuela's minister a few days ago. It was the only way to keep her safe from whoever was chasing her down. He managed to immediately reach Minister Alarcón on his cell.

"Good morning, Minister."

"Mr. Hasehm, I wondered if I'd be hearing from you again. Did you receive the photo?"

"Yes, I did. And we're handling the situation. We're trying to get close to her and find out what she knows or doesn't know about the serum. In the meantime, you need to control our Cuban colleagues so that we can do our work without interference. Remember, the less interference from the Cubans, the less links there are to your government. That should be in your interest, correct?"

"Without a doubt. I'll take care of the Cubans as long as you're taking care of that woman."

"Yes, don't worry. Just leave it in my hands." Good, thought Nebibi, Kate's pursuers were now held back. He didn't want to sacrifice her in all of this mess, certainly not after their time in the Alhambra.

50

A RINGING PHONE BROKE THE SILENCE outside the inner sanctum of the Prince of Wales's private office. The Prince's Deputy Private Secretary for Foreign Affairs slowly opened the door to His Royal Highness's office, the Garden Room, on the ground floor of his official residence in London, Clarence House. Prince Charles sat at his favorite desk, first acquired by his great-grandfather, King George V. Ignoring his usual stack of briefing papers for the moment, he had been gazing out the window at the rose garden, which was bleak and bare at this time of year.

Near the end of his working day, the Prince was reviewing his calendar of upcoming benefits, trips, and ribbon-cutting ceremonies on behalf of the Queen. He had spent almost five decades of his adulthood as first in line to the throne. In the last five years alone, the Prince had presided over almost three thousand events and written more than ten thousand pieces of personal correspondence in support of his Sovereign while biding his time.

Every day that he sat waiting to become king brought more events—benefits, ribbon-cuttings, and so on. This is why he had highlighted the day of the Gibraltar Sovereignty Summit in bright yellow on his calendar. It had been years since something of this substance in foreign affairs had landed on his desk and so, for the past couple of months, Prince Charles had devoted an hour of each working day poring over briefings from the U.K.'s Foreign Secretary. Truly historic, he thought, developing the mechanism for peaceful power-sharing of that historic Rock. And he would be in the thick of it, something of real significance and not a single ribbon to cut!

"Sir?" James, the deputy private secretary, impeccably dressed in his Savile Row finery entered the room and saw that the Prince was lost in thought.

"Oh, yes, James, who's on the telephone?"

"It's your cousin, Prince Felipe." It was his counterpart, the Crown Prince of Spain, twenty years younger than Charles. "He's on the line from the Zarzuela Palace."

"Please patch the call through. Let's not have him waiting on the line forever; you know how my Spanish relatives are. . . ."

Charles's signet ring on his little finger caught the light of the lamp beside the telephone as he reached to pick up the line. "Felipe, Happy New Year. How are you, cousin?"

"*Feliz Año* to you also. I'm very well. How's the weather there?"

"As to be expected in December: cold, rainy, and gray. Are you trying to rub it in about the warmer breezes of Madrid?" Prince Charles stared out the window at the gray late-afternoon sky.

"Certainly not. Though now that you mention it, I'm calling you sitting outside in the garden. . . ." He *was* rubbing in it. They were related, their countries were strong allies, but there would always be that little thing about Elizabeth I defeating the mighty Spanish Armada in 1588. . . .

"Well, by the looks of it, Felipe, I will have the pleasure of enjoying your warmer climates very soon."

"Exactly, the Gibraltar Sovereignty Summit. Just what I was ringing you about."

"Is your Prime Minister still on course? He's not wavering, is he?" In the case of Gibraltar, both Spain and England had strong factions of nationalism to deal with when it came to any power-sharing solutions for the Rock.

"Did you see the intelligence reports from the Americans? Seems like they think there's a terrorist threat looming there."

"Yes, I read through it quite carefully, as did our advisors at Whitehall. But I have my doubts, you know."

"You as well then, cousin?"

"Well, how shall we say this? . . . It is true that both our governments have fallen for that type of intelligence before, haven't they? Her Majesty's Defence ended up having eighteen thousand

British troops stationed in Iraq and Afghanistan. All because of that so-called intelligence."

"Most certainly, but don't quote me on that. We ended up with thirteen hundred of our own troops there as well. All because of those damned U.S. intelligence reports."

"So, Felipe, are your government ministers getting weak knees about the Summit?"

"Some of them are always weak-kneed. I'm afraid that the Americans' intelligence reports have given our nationalist factions a reason to delay the talks. In my view, however, given the difficult economic times, we need as many open borders in our European homelands as possible." Principe Felipe was not forgetting that Spain still had the highest unemployment in the European Union. "Besides, from the looks of it, the plot the Americans were chasing was in San Francisco, not Gibraltar."

"Well, why don't we, the two sovereigns in this game, present a united front? I know that we both have democracies to contend with, but certainly, we each have some power to sway the tone of conversations of our two governments, don't we? So, my dear Principe Felipe de Borbón, what do you say, shall we gently prod our governments forward with the negotiations?"

"Cousin, Your Royal Highness, I quite agree. I am throwing that American intelligence report into the rubbish."

"As a sign of the goodwill between our countries, will the Prince honor me with his presence on the Her Majesty's Yacht *Britannia III*? Camilla and I will be docked in the Bay of Gibraltar and Algeciras for the duration of the Summit." The British Royal family had finally managed to get approval from Parliament for a new royal yacht, on certain conditions that had involved the sale of the previous one, HMY *Britannia II*.

"The newest Royal Yacht? How could I decline? Cousin, I look forward to it. *Adios.*"

"Cheers, cousin."

51

BAY OF GIBRALTAR
JANUARY 5

THREE MEN IN UNIFORM and one woman in civilian clothes gathered in the cramped conference room aboard the USS *Winston S. Churchill,* which had arrived at the Bay of Gibraltar from its home base of Norfolk, Virginia, a few days earlier.

The ship was a modern guided-missile destroyer, one of the largest and most powerful destroyers that the U.S. Navy had in its Atlantic theater of operations. The destroyer's missiles could hit precise targets more than sixty nautical miles away, and it housed hangars that accommodated two Seahawk helicopters armed with air-to-surface missiles. The vessel's radar systems incorporated the latest innovations in electronic detection capabilities. More important, it was the first class of U.S. warships designed with an air-filtration system to guard against nuclear, biological, and chemical warfare. The warship was here in this bay for an express purpose: to detect, deter, and defend against any possible terrorist threat.

By the luck of the draw, it also happened to be the first U.S. destroyer named after an Englishman, and because of it, the only one flying the British Royal Navy's white ensign alongside the Stars and Stripes. The sight of the USS *Churchill's* 509 feet of steel anchored in the bay this morning was a very clear message of U.S. support for the upcoming Sovereignty Summit to anyone contemplating overt *or* covert threats.

"Okay, let's get started." General Owens got the meeting under way and then looked over at Kate. "Welcome back, Ms. Molares. I'd like a debrief later about Islamic finance."

"Certainly, General." Kate's back stiffened.

"Good. Okay, now. Lieutenant, please get Bolling AFB on the screen."

The seaman in charge of secure communications operations tapped a series of codes on the laptop. The LCD screen they faced was black except for the 3-D rotating image of the USS *Churchill*'s seal and its motto scrolling below: In war: Resolution; In peace: Good Will.

Within seconds, the screen lit up with the image of a room that Kate recognized immediately. It was the televideo conference room down the hall from her cubicle at the DIA. There were several familiar faces, including Bill and Lieutenant Khoury.

"Good morning, I mean, afternoon, General Owens." Bill was just beginning his day back in D.C.

"Good morning, Mr. DuBois. I see you've assembled your team there on your end. Allow me to introduce Commander Robert Svensk of the USS *Churchill*. He's been cleared for this mission. Commander, Mr. DuBois has been designated by the SecDef to spearhead the DIA's investigation on the matters related to *T. gondii prime*. Mr. DuBois, of course you know our other participant here."

"Hello, Kate." Bill was putting on his formal tone for the transatlantic secure satellite video feed.

"Good morning, Bill." Kate followed suit, but caught the smile at the edge of Bill's lips.

The general continued speaking. "The purpose of this meeting has changed. I just received final word from the Governor of Gibraltar that the Spanish and British governments insist on going ahead with the Summit on Gibraltar on the twenty-fourth. We weren't able to sway them with our findings. The plot uncovered in San Francisco has them convinced that our intelligence traffic was related to the Golden Gate plot. So, unfortunately, our work here is no longer focused on postponing this tripartite get-together, but rather on preventing any potential terrorist action. So on that note, please proceed, Mr. DuBois."

Kate interjected. "Excuse me, General, but didn't the Golden Gate plot worry them? When will we get better intelligence from those actual plotters?"

"Intelligence analysis is in the eye of the beholder, Kate. They're thinking that the capture of those three Afghanis was the end game on all the noise we've been tracking, your money trail included."

Bill piped in. "Also, most of our resources have turned their attention to San Francisco. It seems like our whole national intelligence apparatus has a new focus as of yesterday."

"But for those of us on the ground here, we still need to keep our focus on the Summit and anything that might endanger a smooth execution. Understood?" The general looked sternly around the assembled table and into the televideo monitor. "Please proceed, Mr. DuBois."

"Certainly, General. We've tracked communications in and out of southern Spain, Andalucía, and below, as well as the usual spots in North Africa and Afghanistan. There's the usual banter among terrorists: noise about al-Qaeda, bragging rights on 9/11, et cetera. In the past forty-eight hours, traffic has died down to a standstill. There haven't been any new real leads, except for one item kicked back by our computers a few days ago. It's a reference to a particular place, one that doesn't exist anymore. We performed a manual scan, which unfortunately delayed our search, but we needed to be sure we could pinpoint what we were hearing."

"And, so what was that reference?" the general asked.

"One word surfaced in at least five separate cell phone conversations in the last month: *Andalus*."

As soon as Bill spoke that word, Kate's leg twitched under the table. *Andalus!* Did he really say that? she wondered.

"Sorry, Bill. Could you repeat that?" Kate wanted to be sure what she heard.

"Andalus. It's spelled, *A-n-d-a-l-u-s*. Our colleagues on the Europe desk here immediately knew that it was the name given to the ancient Islamic Caliphate that ruled over the Iberian Peninsula from the eighth till about the fifteenth century. Needless to say, that sparked our interest to investigate further."

Kate's leg continued to twitch under the table, though her face didn't relay any hint of undue concern. Is it a coincidence? Wasn't that the word Nebibi had in his calendar for his birthday? Maybe he was just being a good Muslim and referring to Gibraltar as Andalus. Or maybe she was a fool, ignoring the obvious.

"So, is there any link between that intelligence and our Sovereignty Summit on the twenty-fourth?" asked Commander Svensk.

"We want to make sure this is airtight before we reach any 'definitive' conclusions. It's possible that this intelligence 'noise' might involve the Sovereignty Summit by simple virtue that Gibraltar was the gateway that the ancient Muslims took to conquer Iberia. But we're not ready to say that definitively. . . ." Bill was speaking the language of couched statements that was the norm for intelligence officers—at least for those, like Bill, who wanted to survive into early retirement.

"So what other avenues are you pursuing?" The general could smell safe doublespeak even across the Atlantic.

"We have our parallel investigation going on with respect to the serum uncovered by Kate last month." She was being hailed as a hero within high military circles at the Pentagon for her sleuthing in Caracas and Havana. This compliment didn't really sink in with Kate, though. Her mind was still sifting through how to assess the intelligence on *Andalus* and if it had something to do with Nebibi.

"Lieutenant Khoury can give us an update on that front."

"Thank you, Mr. DuBois. General. Commander. We've continued analyzing the sample brought in by Ms. Molares. We're getting closer to copying it and are confident we'll be able to accomplish this in the next few weeks. Based on our tests on various animals, we're certain that *T. gondii prime* amplifies focused aggression that would otherwise lie dormant or be overpowered by all normal countervailing reactions, such as fear or emotional attachments. The test subjects demonstrate unwavering aggressive behavior. If this were used on humans, let's say terrorists, they would definitely be a challenging corps of soldiers to fight in normal combat."

What Lieutenant Khoury was completely unaware of was that there was already a second, more secret U.S. laboratory at CIA headquarters that had not only unlocked the secret to the formula, but was already testing it on human agents, successfully. Whatever the outcome of the Sovereignty Summit or the impact of this word *Andalus,* the genie of bio-medically manipulated troop warfare was now out of the bottle forever, and the more radical factions of the U.S. intelligence apparatus intended to deploy it.

. . .

BACK IN HER HOTEL ROOM, Kate stared at the Web page on her laptop. On a whim, she had Googled Nebibi, surfacing a healthy number of hits, all related exclusively to the launch of The Milestones Fund, nary a mention before that. As far as the World Wide Web was concerned, Nebibi didn't exist until his fund was formed. That was odd, she thought. He really had disappeared those years after graduate school.

She further pondered the issue of Andalus and Nebibi, trying to convince herself that it was a coincidence. The Google hits certainly indicated there couldn't be any links. If he was such a successful fund manager, why would he need to be involved in anything illegal or worse, something to do with terrorists? The only reasonable conclusion she could draw was that he was being forced into something that he didn't really want to be a part of. That could explain a certain distance she noticed in his posture at times.

But she knew she couldn't clear him without knowing more about that entry in his calendar. She couldn't ask Nebibi directly, because that would compromise the general's mission on Gib. And if she approached the general with her questions, she was sure he'd waste no time in taking Nebibi into custody. So she dialed up the one person she could trust with this.

"Hello, Bill DuBois here."

"Hi, Bill. You looked good on-screen."

"So did you. I expected more of a tan, though," Bill joked.

"Yeah, right! We're all just lying around the pool here, catching rays, drinking sangria."

"You're not?" Bill couldn't pass up the opportunity pull her leg.

"Listen, I've got a bit of an issue. Remember how I started with the *T. gondii* thing, a little bit on a hunch?" she asked.

"Yeah? . . ."

"I've got another case like that, but I just need to track it on a low-key basis for now. I'm trying to avoid the mega-galactic forces of intelligence swooping down on this right away. It would blow the whole thing. . . ."

"Okay, I'm listening. . . ." Bill's tone was no longer jocular.

"I need you to listen in on someone's phone calls."

There was a pause on the other end of the line. Bill pondered what she was asking for. His retirement horse farm in Arkansas with that horse trainer flashed across his mind. But he also knew Kate. He was certain she'd thought this through and probably had more than just a hunch. Besides, he could slip in one more number to track into the whole surveillance operation they already had and nobody would even bat an eyelash.

"Okay, Kate. What's the name?"

"Nebibi Hasehm." She spelled the name out for him.

"Okay. I'll handle it personally. Give me a couple of days."

"Thanks, Bill."

"You owe me one, kiddo."

52

◄┼┼┼►

MINISTER FERNANDO ALARCÓN STOOD by the window of Venezuela's Ministry of Finance in downtown Caracas, looking out onto Avenida Urdaneta. Demonstrators, mostly university students, were waving anti-Chávez banners. A growing number of Venezuelans were tiring of the President's attempts to extend his tenure, particularly now that lower oil prices were curtailing Chávez's social welfare promises. And each dollar drop per barrel created greater economic disarray, which only expanded those legions of dissenters.

When will all of this finally settle? the minister asked himself. He wasn't thinking about the protests below, but rather the sordid plot his government was embroiled in. The deaths of those innocent people in the Madrid airport still hung heavy on his mind. And now the Americans had broken up a plot in San Francisco, parading the three terrorists in front of the TV cameras. It all made him uneasy. More than anything, the minister wanted to get back to the true work of government and be rid of entanglements with terrorists.

Minister Alarcón opened the door to the safe hidden in the wall behind the portrait of President Chávez. He grabbed the sole content, a folder, which contained various reports. There were the wire transfer orders to pay off the Cubans for their serum, as well as the equity investment they made in The Milestones Fund. Finally, he found what he was looking for: a photo.

It was the picture of that mysterious woman, Molares, who supposedly knew about the serum. It troubled him that there might be a loose end, but he had no choice. He had to leave it in the hands of Mr. Hasehm, because he certainly didn't want to get any closer to these messy issues. He placed the folder back in the safe, putting off for another day telling his President about the breach of confidentiality.

Just as he sat down at his desk, a call came through on the minister's cell phone.

"Good morning, *Señor Ministro*. I have some further news that will be of interest." Normally, Iñaki Heredia, the deputy head of ETA, would go through intermediaries to get messages through to the minister, but today speed was of utmost importance.

"Why are you calling me directly?" asked the minister, concerned about any traces leading back to him.

"This couldn't wait for normal channels."

The minister sat down at his desk, bracing himself for more complications. Good news never traveled as quickly as bad news. *"¡Madre de Dios!"* Mother of God! "Yes, so what is it? . . ."

"We finally found that woman, Molares."

The minister had not told his Basque contacts that he had spoken to Nebibi about her.

"How?"

"My agent has been tracking her movements in Gibraltar. My agent sent me a photo, and it seems she spent the weekend with our Mr. Hasehm. . . ."

"Send me that picture, through the usual Yahoo account." The minister was anxious to see evidence of Nebibi's entanglement.

"There's no mistaking the photo, you'll see. But that's not the only thing. We've been watching her going in and out of the Gibraltar Government House, so we thought she was part of the local government. But this morning, she boarded a U.S. warship that arrived in the bay yesterday, and she walked out accompanied by a U.S. general!" Heredia was still alarmed by this news he'd received only a few hours ago.

"¡Puta!" Fuck! "So you're telling me that this woman is dealing with Hasehm and works for the Americans!" Should I have trusted Nebibi when he told me he'd take care of this? the minister asked himself.

"Yes . . . ," Heredia answered unequivocally. "Did you get the photo yet?"

From his personal laptop, the minister logged on to a wireless network outside the confines of the Ministry and, masking his IP address, he opened the e-mail. The photo came up on his screen. There was Nebibi, sitting on a bench, talking on the phone. And next to him, there was no mistaking it—that woman. Nebibi said he would handle her. The minister just didn't imagine that he'd planned to get this close to her, and that made the minister nervous. The photo confirmed that the plot had gotten far more complicated than his President had originally estimated.

The minister wondered how he could manage to keep this news from his President. The minute he found out that the Americans were involved, who knew how he'd react. He'll probably want to declare war, just to divert attention away from their involvement.

Heredia had more news to deliver. It was something that he had known for a few days, but it hadn't struck him as significant at first. Now, however, with the news of the American woman, he'd started putting several pieces together and was drawing more troublesome conclusions.

"There's something else. We followed Nebibi a few days ago, after he spent the weekend with the American woman. He drove all night alone and made a short side trip to Andorra before returning to New York."

"So he likes sunny climates. So what?" said the minister.

"Well, he couldn't have enjoyed it very much since he only spent sixty minutes in the country, and it was entirely inside the Banca Seguretat d'Andorra. So what business does he have there, that he had to do all alone, without his usual bodyguards?"

"You must be concluding something Heredia . . . so what is it?"

"We think he's struck a deal with the Americans and he was busy in Andorra setting up accounts for his eventual payoff."

"That's crazy, Heredia, and I'll tell you why. First of all, I spoke to our Mr. Hasehm about that woman several days ago and he assured me that he was taking care of it. I didn't think he'd be personally getting this close to her, but that is the plan he described to me in order to find out what she knows or doesn't know, without tipping anybody off to our plan and, most important, our involvement."

Heredia took in what the minister was saying, but he wasn't entirely convinced that Nebibi's actions were quite that innocent.

The minister continued. "Besides, if Hasehm was working with them, don't you think the Americans would be making accusations by now, or even bombing us? Trust me, if they knew our plans, the American government would have blanketed the airwaves with publicity about another failed terrorist plot, besides the one in San Francisco. Yes, our friend Nebibi may be up to funny business, and even sleeping around with U.S. officials. But it doesn't involve the mission. That part is safe. The money and our ownership in that fund of his is another question altogether. And that's what we should be keeping a close eye on."

"So what do you suggest, Minister?"

"I'll call him and see what he's found out about that American woman. Either way, we let him finish this closing. It's only a couple of weeks away. After that, we have no use for him. Then you can send in your man to do what you feel is best. But don't involve us in any way. I will tell you this, I'd sleep a lot better at night if Nebibi's knowledge about our involvement was erased and forgotten. So we wait till after the closing, agreed?"

"Agreed." Heredia said this begrudgingly, because he was convinced Nebibi's motives couldn't be trusted. It wouldn't be the first time that a man thought with his sex organ instead of his brain. The Venezuelans could wait this out if they wanted, but he knew that they needed to take care of the woman, and also the man she was sleeping with, sooner rather than later.

53

BERN, SWITZERLAND
JANUARY 10

ERR BOEGLIN, THE FORTY-SEVEN-YEAR-OLD assistant director of
the Swiss Federal Banking Commission, was busy reading the morning edition of the *Zürcher Zeitung* in his
office, glasses perched at the tip of his nose, taking occasional sips from his cup of Nescafé. A phone call interrupted the
peace of his daily ritual, causing a slight frown of displeasure to
come over his face.

"*Hallo,* Boeglin here." He answered on the second ring, the receiver tickling a bit as it brushed against his full mustache.

"Good morning, Herr Boeglin. This is Kate Molares of the U.S.
Defense Department. I'm currently on assignment in Gibraltar. Do
you have a moment to speak with me about Banca di Califfato? I
believe Ambassador Lacey alerted you to my call." Kate was fed
up with Galbraith dragging his heels and decided to take matters
into her own hands. So what if she was trampling on his turf; she
had an investigation to run.

His face softened a bit and his tone fell into the singsong cadence of his Zurich-dialect German even when he spoke his accented English. "Oh yes, the U.S. Embassy did alert me. How may
I be of assistance, Miss Molares?"

"Thank you. We've been working with our Treasury Department on finding out about some fund transfers that we believe
may provide further insights on the Madrid bombing last month."

"*Ja, natürlich*—yes, of course. Actually, we received a visit from
one of your Treasury colleagues last week. A gentleman by the name
of Bernard . . ."

"Galbraith. Yes, he mentioned that he might see you, I just

wasn't sure if he'd have the time before heading back to Washington," Kate lied. Last thing Galbraith told her was that he was going to "call" his contacts, and not a word about taking an actual trip to visit with Herr Boeglin in Berne. Obviously, teamwork wasn't Galbraith's forte. With the receiver cradled in her neck, she quickly signed on to the secure military server and looked up Banca di Califfato on the IntelWiki to see if Bernard had filed a report from his visit. None. Typical, she thought, he just wasn't the sharing type.

"We gave him open access to our file on the bank, its owners and history. You know, the usual sort of thing. Unfortunately, not much more than that I'm afraid, you see, it was closed by its owners just last month. All on the up and up, nothing extraordinary there. Banks open and close here every day."

"I see. Since I'm on the continent, would you mind if I stop by and take a look at that file? I could be there tomorrow." She stared at the empty Califfato thread on her screen, making the split-second decision that working with the Swiss would be far easier than negotiating an exchange of information with her peer at Treasury.

"*Ein moment, bitte*—hold on a second, please. Let me see. Tomorrow, Tuesday. *Ja*, that would be fine. Would you be able to meet me in my office at say eleven o'clock?"

"That works for me. Thank you, Herr Boeglin."

"Look forward to meeting you, Miss Molares."

THE NEXT MORNING, KATE LOOKED AROUND Herr Boeglin's compact office in the Banking Commission's Headquarters. A picture of his wife with their two young sons was propped on one end. The other end was reserved for his other passion, the foot-high volume of Swiss banking regulations. The door swung open and Herr Boeglin returned with a folder in his hand.

"Here it is, Miss Molares, our full background on Banca di Califfato. It seems rather slim, probably because the bank was established more than twenty-five years ago. I can assure you our investigation of banking applications is far more exhaustive these days." Herr Boeglin pointed to a large stack of significantly thicker applications for new banking licenses on his shelf.

"May I?" Kate extended her hand out to receive the folder.

As she scanned the papers, Herr Boeglin asked, "So, Mr. Galbraith seemed to indicate that this bank has something to with the Golden Gate plot? . . ." The question was one of great concern for the Swiss. The last thing they needed was for the Americans to once again criticize their less-than-tight supervision of their bankers, particularly if they were involved in anything that smacked of terrorism.

"Yes, but nothing definitive yet. Hopefully your records can uncover further clues for our investigation." Kate was flipping through the papers in the folder and was staring at Abdul Rahman's 1965 banking application and a deposit slip for the one million Swiss francs of founding capital.

"I guess back then, that was quite a king's ransom." Kate raised the deposit slip for Herr Boeglin to see.

"Indeed. I'm sure he was quite well received with that money, back then in Lugano."

"Do you know this Abdul Rahman? Is he still in Lugano?"

"The last record we have of him is a private residence on the other side of Lake Lugano. There should be another slip in there. But since the bank closed last month, we haven't had any contact with him or his lawyers."

"What else should be in here?" she asked as she sifted through the folder's contents.

"You should see a list of all the shareholders and directors. Normally we wouldn't provide such information, due to bank secrecy, but given your government's involvement and the fact that the bank is now officially closed, the Banking Commission Director felt that we should provide it to you. Do you see it in there? It should be on an old carbon copy."

Kate flipped through various papers, but couldn't recognize anything that revealed shareholders. "Nothing like that as far as I can tell."

"That's odd. It was a point of much discussion before Mr. Galbraith's visit last week, and having decided to provide it, we made sure that the information was in this file. May I?" Herr Boeglin reached out for the folder.

He quickly flipped through the papers with expert eyes. "You're right. Nothing here. That is quite odd. I'm sure it was here last week."

It wasn't odd to Kate. She knew that her dear "collegial" colleague Bernard had found a way to take that information and keep it to himself. The U.S. government can put in place all kinds of mechanisms to support interagency intelligence sharing, but it still couldn't guarantee basic teamwork skills.

"Is this the only copy?"

"No, the originals are in our main vault. Secret location. Getting a copy out of there may take weeks. Would you like me to request it?"

"Yes, please. Here's my card."

"I'll put a rush on it, but I can't promise anything."

"Thank you, Herr Boeglin." Kate just kept thinking that the mysteriously slim volume was thicker before Bernard's visit last week. In typical fashion, he would sit on the information before he shared it with anyone, and only deal with it when he was good and ready. So much for an effective intelligence apparatus. Galbraith is either being incompetent or criminal, thought Kate. She'd find out which and throw him to the wolves in either case.

LATER THAT AFTERNOON, KATE RANG BILL up at DIA to talk about her Bern findings, or more correctly, the lack thereof.

"Hey, Bill."

"Hiya. Where are you?"

"I just finished a meeting in Bern with the Swiss banking regulators." Kate stood outside the Bern train station.

"So how was Bern? Hey, isn't that where they make Toblerone—did you buy me some?"

"No chocolates, and not much else either. Seems my good friend Bernard has already been here."

"Then he should have filed a report on IntelWiki."

"Wishful thinking, Bill. I already checked. Zippo."

"Hmmm. Maybe I should give Bernie a call," Bill suggested.

"You'd probably get further with him than I would. I'm just a peon to him." Kate recalled their last rushed phone call. "Should we be hitting him harder for withholding info? Maybe he's up to something more than just holding back. . . ."

"Kate, we don't have any evidence of either withholding info or otherwise, so be careful what you say."

"Yeah, yeah, I know the drill—no shooting from the hip. But there's something about him that rubs me the wrong way."

"The fact that he doesn't give you the time of day doesn't mean he's some criminal . . . ," Bill said.

"It's not like that at all, Bill. I'm not looking for friends or admirers here. It's just that I look at him and there's nothing behind those eyes. He gives off this vibe like he's working really hard to hide what's going on in that little head of his. And so it comes down to the fact that I just don't trust him, plain and simple."

"So now we're going on women's intuition?" Bill quipped.

"Bill . . ."

"Okay, okay. We'll call it a trained analyst's instinct, then."

"That's better."

"Let me give it a shot with him. Ten to one, he's just sitting on the information, not knowing what to do with it. What should I focus on?" he asked.

"Check if he has any info on the shareholders or other officers of the bank. That might lead somewhere. Anywhere would be better than where we are now, which is not any closer to uncovering Califfato's role in all of this. By the way, any news on that wiretap we talked about last week?"

"It's in the hopper. Give it another few days to see what comes back in the transcripts."

"Okay, okay. I've got to catch my train to Lugano. Going to see if I can find the bank's founder, a certain Abdul Rahman."

"Are you going alone?" Bill the protector surfaced.

"I'm going with the Swiss regulator, Herr Boeglin. He's meeting me here at the station. Like you said, the Swiss don't want any mess on their hands when it comes to this sort of stuff. He's taking this very seriously. Listen, Bill, I only have a few minutes before he gets here, and I need to call General Owens to update him."

"Sure thing. Remember, Toblerone . . ."

"YES, I THINK THIS IS IT coming up here." Herr Boeglin looked at the address he had written down for Abdhul Rahman from his Califfato file. "Please stop here."

Kate and Herr Boeglin stepped out of the taxi, which now sat idle in front of the gated entrance on Via Belvedere. They rang the security buzzer several times, but there wasn't any answer. No-body home.

Kate looked down the street, noting this wasn't the only secured entrance. She commented to her companion, "Seems like quite a ritzy part of town; I guess Califfato had a very generous bonus structure." Herr Boeglin returned the comment with a somewhat nervous smile, the implication being that whoever was part of this bank was making more than just your average community banker.

As they rang the buzzer again, a pickup truck pulled up on the road and stopped at the same address. It was piled high with gardening equipment. A man wearing stained jeans stepped out of the driver's side; weathered skin made him look older than his actual thirty years. He took a last puff of the cigarette in his mouth and then dropped the butt on the ground, grinding it with his worn dirty boots. He looked over at Kate and Herr Boeglin and, judging them to be outside his line of business, thought they might have answers for him.

"*Signore, signora . . .*" The man spoke rudimentary English and was evidently from the Italian side of Lake Lugano. "De gentle-man here not-a hom-a. I come here forrr my job-be, to keep-de gardens, but nobody hom-a forrr many week-se. Maybe you know when-ne they come back, no?"

Herr Boeglin replied, "I'm sorry, but we are also looking for Mr. Rahman."

"*Ah sì, Signor Rahman. Sì, no?*"

"No, we don't know where he is, I'm afraid." Herr Boeglin then looked over at Kate, shrugging his shoulders. "I'll keep trying through local sources to find out his whereabouts." Given the taint of Kate's question, however, Herr Boeglin hoped that any further attempts to get to the bottom of Califfato's link with Madrid would lead to the same conclusion as today's visit. *Nobody home.*

54
⊸╋╋╋⊷

THE MASSIVE METAL GATES SLOWLY OPENED at the only numbered address on Royal Lane in Greenwich. The two security guards posted at the entrance tipped their hats as the black SUV with tinted windows sped through on its way to Westchester County Airport. The wind chill had dropped the temperature down to 20 degrees Fahrenheit at this early evening hour, and any remaining patches of snow on the sides of the road were now blocks of ice. Inside the car, the sole passenger, Sam Coldsmith, was busy working the phones.

"Hey, Hannah, did I catch you at a good time?" Sam had dialed the private home number of Hannah Merton, the CEO of WR Shipley & Co. She was the only member of the select group of CEOs of major world financial institutions that used the ladies' room. And because of that, she had finally reached the number one position on *Fortune* magazine's annual ranking of the "50 Most Powerful Women in Business." In her ten-year rise to the top of that list, she had hit as high as number three, and then stalled for a few years. This made her current number-one position that much sweeter. And she didn't plan to be off that list until she retired, in her own time, on her own terms, or until she got a call from the President asking her to fill the top spot at Treasury. And yes, that would be as the first woman Treasury Secretary of the United States.

"Oh hi, Sam. This is fine." She looked at her watch. Seven P.M. She had just sat down to dinner with her husband, an event that had become increasingly rare since assuming the reins of the bank six months ago. But Sam was her personal client, dating back to her first days on the trading floor, and now his fund was one of the bank's more profitable accounts. She mouthed *sorry* to her ever-patient husband, once again seated alone at the dinner table, and took the phone to her home office.

"Good. I'm traveling to Europe this evening for our closing with Milestones tomorrow. I wanted to make sure that my positions are all in the black." That was a mouthful. Sam was betting his fund's future on a $2 trillion derivatives position, 133 times the value of his equity in the hedge fund portfolio. And that kind of bet didn't have middle ground—he could either make or lose a boatload of money—nothing in between.

"As a matter of fact, the head of Capital Markets gave me a full rundown on your positions this morning, Sam. Everything's in order and all your positions are way in the money. The Dow is up, the dollar is holding steady, and I hear whispers that next week's jobless report is finally going to stop bleeding. The only thing that could disrupt that would be if markets took dives like they did in '08. But we're both old hands at this, right Sam? It's all about market cycles. We've just had the longest downturn since the Great Depression and it'll be another hundred years before we get that kind of volatility again. So don't worry, my old friend. Your fund is safe."

"Good to hear that, Hannah. It's way time I got out of this shell game. Regulators are starting to breathe down my back to start sending them reports. The minute I do that, it's gonna take all the juice out of this racket. Time to move on to greener pastures."

"Can't agree with you more. So just concentrate on your closing and then let's sit down when you get back to talk about those 'greener pastures.'" Hannah hung up the phone, her face sullen because her one moment of peace in the daily grind of her responsibilities had been interrupted. Let's just hope his fund *is* safe, she thought. As a risk taker, Sam felt comfortable with his risk exposure. However, his banker was increasingly less so, and for good reasons.

First of all, the U.S. government had finally zeroed in on exactly those derivatives exposure concentrations, but she managed to side-step the most onerous of the soon-to-be-enacted financial reforms by shifting that portfolio to their subsidiaries in more friendly

Asian jurisdictions. However, the mergers forced on her bank by the government during the crisis had actually increased their risk-concentration problem.

Secondly, Sam was the bank's single largest derivatives counter-party. If anything went wrong with his positions, it was liable to shake her bank's house of cards. And since Hannah had succeeded in keeping her bank intact while others dropped like flies around her, she'd be damned if, in her first trailblazing year as the only woman CEO of a money center bank, she would let that house of cards tumble, let alone even wobble.

So each morning, Hannah checked on Sam's derivatives portfolio. While the U.S. President had a daily national security briefing at the start of each day, Hannah demanded a daily institutional risk report for her bank be delivered to her desk each morning by 7 A.M. Their models told them that the bank's credit exposure on their derivatives exposure was equal to more than three times the bank's capital. Not a pretty picture, but manageable, they told her; assuming the models created by her MIT economists were reliable.

She'd built a profitable derivatives business over twenty long years on the trading floor. In fact, it was the very reason that she was CEO today. Hannah was the only senior executive at the bank with the smarts *and* stomach to see their derivatives exposure through each and every day without suffering a massive coronary. And since derivatives and trading represented a quarter of the bank's income, their bottom line and stock price depended on keeping that business alive and running. Each business day that ended *without* a major market calamity was another day on that derivatives risk tightrope for her career and the bank's capital.

She took two reports out of her briefcase. The first was the Comptroller of the Currency's most recent quarterly report, which showed in plain black-and-white numbers the derivatives exposure of the top twenty-five commercial banks in the country. She faced this report with a combination of pride and trepidation. Her bank continued to be number one on the list, with about $100 trillion of derivatives. The "problem" she needed to grapple with, is that they were number one by a hell of a lot; they had 50 percent of the market, more than twice as much as the next bank on the list. No wonder the New York Fed keeps harping on this, she thought. We have excessive concentration risk, and because of our sheer size, if things swing against us, it'll touch everybody in the market. And by everybody, she meant every man, woman, and child. It would make 2008 look like a kiddie Ferris wheel ride. *Shit!*

Then there was the second report, and because it was presented to her in a black folder, she called it the "Stealth Report." It was only seen by a handful of her most trusted lieutenants at the bank. It was the "what if" scenario, as in, what if a major derivatives counterparty goes under? The Stealth Report answered the question, and every day since becoming CEO it had never been good news. Today was no different. Her underlings used Sam's Royal Lane fund as the base case example for their analysis. She scanned the columns of the stress model output.

On $2 trillion of credit derivatives, if there were swings in credit spreads for prime corporates as in the recent crisis, potential losses would be in the $50 billion range, which was several times more than the value of Sam's equity after the sale to Milestones. One brisk wind and Sam's cherished Royal Lane fund was essentially bankrupt. *Fuck!* Hannah opened the drawer and took out her prescription pills, which she'd started taking just after the last financial crisis—one for her high blood pressure and another one for her ulcer. Time to get back to dinner, if she could stomach it.

55

⊸+✦+⊷

OMÁS MOLARES PARKED HIS OLD JAGUAR in front of Sam Cold-smith's Westchester County Airport hangar. It was 7:15 P.M., and "wheels up" departure was in fifteen minutes. He rushed toward the gate, where a steward accompanied him on the short walk to the waiting aircraft. Sam had been the first, very lucky, private business customer to receive delivery of Boeing's latest aircraft, the 787-8 Dreamliner.

As he stepped on the tarmac, Tomás saw Sam's newest toy, with its state-of-the-art Rolls-Royce engines humming at low decibels and all 186 feet of its aluminum, carbon, and titanium composite fuselage painted in a shiny gold. While the tail emblem identified its owner, the nose of the plane had been painted to resemble the face of a shark, a golden shark.

Sam had paid a rich premium to have the famous British modern artist, Damien Hirst, conceptualize this moniker, which was now registered at Sotheby's as the only piece of modern art that flew. Hirst called this piece, *Gold Shark Swimming in Air*. Always a sucker for a good deal, Sam happily paid the artist his usual exorbitant fees, as the notoriety added far greater value to his flying mansion, increasing its worth way beyond that of any other simple flying machine.

As Tomás boarded the aircraft, a stewardess greeted him. "Welcome aboard the *Gold Shark,* Mr. Molares. My name is Ana. Here, let me take that luggage for you." They both now stood in what looked like the foyer of an exclusive Greenwich home, an oval-shaped room with curved ceilings framed in highly lacquered chestnut wood and a marble floor with patterned gold inlays. Unlike the stark lighting of commercial aircraft, the small pockets of recessed lights throughout this plane's cabin gave off a warm glow.

"Thank you, Ana."

"Please follow me. Mr. Coldsmith wanted me to bring you to his private office as soon as you boarded." She smiled broadly, part of the job.

Tomás knew that Sam found interesting ways to spend his money, and by the looks of it, the *Gold Shark* was no exception to that rule. In a normal commercial configuration, the interior space can hold up to 210 passengers in three classes of service. In the Sam Coldsmith world, however, it held room for only ten very privileged guests.

Ana led him down the hallway to the main cabin. The first room on the right was a conference room with a long table, currently occupied by four lawyers engrossed in closing documents.

The next section of the cabin spanned its width, with nine seats arranged with more than ample space between them. Each of those seats reflected the latest in airline comfort, capable of reclining a full 90 degrees into a comfortable bed. He noticed a few faces that he recognized from the office: Royal Lanes' corporate counsel and their head trader.

The second-to-last room in this long corridor was Sam's office. The last room was the state room, where a stewardess was busy providing turndown service and fluffing the pillows on the king-sized bed. That would explain why there were only nine sleep recliners on the *Gold Shark*. The tenth passenger, Sam, had his own private suite, bathtub included.

Tomás stepped into Sam's office, which had a long desk on one end facing a half-circular leather sofa. Sam was standing at the far end, holding a golf club and practicing a shot. Before acknowledging his latest guest, he made his shot.

"Tomás. Come in. You're the last to board, so we're all set to go. Ana, please tell the pilot that my crew is all here now." Sam was in an ebullient mood, due in large part to the fact that his favorite derivatives trader had just told him that his trades were "way in the money" and also because he was jetting off on his new toy to close the deal of his career. Life was definitely good for Sam Coldsmith this evening. Nothing could go wrong now.

"You know Clifford Cheswick, of course." He'd managed to thumb a ride on this flight as part of Nebibi's investment banking team.

Tomás had not immediately noticed him sitting on the couch. "Oh, hello, Clifford. Good to see you again."

"My dear fellow Tomás, all set for our closing tomorrow?" Clifford extended his hand.

"Looking forward to it. Our friend here loves this deal." As an insider, Tomás knew the exact numbers; Sam stood to personally make about $15 billion on this deal. So while he wasn't getting the IPO he'd originally wanted, Sam was getting a not-too-shabby consolation prize in the form of some hefty "pocket change" with which he could easily afford a few more shark tanks and Boeings.

Finished with his golf club, Sam sat down on the couch, his Cheshire cat grin expanding. "So, Clifford, tell me about our mysterious Mr. Hasehm. What have you learned about him?"

"We've been looking at a lot of deals with him over the past few weeks. After your deal tomorrow, his Milestones Fund will be almost fully invested. He has another $17 billion lying around for future opportunities. Not bad for a little over a month's work, I'd say. I've learned far more about Islamic finance than I ever expected to." And Clifford was more than happy to, considering that he had just made a down payment on that house in Saint-Jean-Cap-Ferrat.

"He's been able to find investment opportunities despite the Islamic restrictions?"

Tomás interjected, "Most opportunities in industries like alcohol, entertainment, banking, weapons, and tobacco are off-limits. But his mullah gave him a bit of leeway. As long as he invests no more than 5 percent of his fund in all of these combined, then he's okay. It ends up being the difference between dipping your toe in those sectors as opposed to your whole leg."

"So he's got a conservatively managed fund. He's just not gonna make a lot of return, that's all," Sam interjected.

"That's one aspect, Sam. But then Islamic law doesn't allow the charging of interest, as I'm sure Clifford knows." Tomás looked over at the investment banker, who was nodding his head, like he knew everything Tomás was about to say. He continued, "And because of that, Nebibi has very little exposure to bank and insurance stocks, making his fund perform differently than most of the market."

Sam listened with great interest, but also wondered why his bankers hadn't managed to get this far into the numbers. "Okay, so go on. . . ."

"Islamic finance is all about interpretation. There is no one rule book on this stuff. Mullahs who advise on the implementation of *Shari'ah* law all differ; some are more liberal than others. Nebibi's more-liberal mullah does impose restrictions that are worth noting. His fund excludes any company that relies too much on leverage to fund its operations."

"Where did you pick up all of this?" Sam wondered why he'd never heard this plain explanation from his investment bankers.

"Just the due diligence you wanted us to perform."

Clifford felt somewhat uncomfortable at being shown up by Tomás, but then again, he always had his British charm to fall back on.

Tomás continued. "So Mr. Hasehm's fund would have performed beautifully during the 2008 mess. Companies that weren't tied to the availability of easy debt survived far better than those that bet the farm on leverage. The question is, what happens when the market fully recovers—can Mr. Hasehm keep up in terms of yield?"

"And what's the answer there? . . ."

"We'll have to see how it pans out for him, Sam. But what I do know is that he has an advantage that most don't. The thing about Islamic finance investors is that they're willing to give up some profit potential as long as their investment principles hold up. Just to be clear, though, the investment criteria for Islamic investors is of a much higher social consciousness than tax evaders and dictators."

"So what could happen then?" Sam asked further.

"If the proverbial 'shit hit the fan' again, then our mysterious Mr. Hasehm would be sitting on a veritable fortress of solid investment worth much more than he paid, and the rest of the market would be licking its wounds. But what are the chances of that happening again?"

"Well done, Tomás, well done." Having heard a good financial bedtime story, Sam was finally ready to retire to his king-sized mattress.

56

KATE SAT FACING HER LAPTOP in the temporary office assigned to her at the Gib Government House. Her cell phone rang. "Hello?"

"Hello, Kate."

"Dad, what are you doing up at this hour?" She looked at her watch. "It's nine thirty a.m. here, so it's the middle of the night for you. Is everything okay?"

"Everything's fine. I landed on Gibraltar a few minutes ago—"

"Gibraltar! What are you doing here? You didn't tell me you wanted to visit." The last thing she needed right now was her father trailing her on Gib.

"Actually, I'm here on business for the closing of the Milestones deal. And yes, I also wanted to surprise you. Is that okay?"

"Of course. So when can I see you?"

"I'm busy most of the day with lawyers and documents. But there will be a closing dinner tonight and I want you to come with me. Interested?"

"Sure. I feel like I haven't seen you in months, but it's only been three weeks. I assume Nebibi's going to be there tonight, right?" She asked this gingerly, since she hadn't heard from him since their good-byes after the Alhambra.

"Of course he'll be there. His fund is the guest of honor. Sam's footing the bill for this shindig, since after today he'll have a great deal more of it on hand. Actually, so will I!" Tomás said this with a certain glee, like a guy who found a winning lottery ticket.

Just as she hung up the call on her cell phone, the landline on her desk rang. Very few outside of base had her number here. She picked up the call.

"Hello?"

"Kate, it's me." *Me* was Bill, and his voice was the only identification Kate needed. "I've got some transcripts for you."

"Great. Anything?"

"Nothing jumps out at me. The analysts sifted through the Hasehm conversations as part of a few other phone taps, but they didn't pick up anything noteworthy. There's the usual Wall Street garbage—a lot of stuff about deals closing and due diligence, calls with lawyers and investment bankers. Who is this guy—does he know what he's doing? Maybe I should be taking notes for my own portfolio."

"He's just someone I reconnected with while I've been over here." Officially, none of what Kate said was a lie. Okay, white lie, in terms of what she left out, maybe.

This wasn't easy for Kate. She knew she had crossed the line in submitting Nebibi's name for electronic eavesdropping in the first place, and in addition not disclosing how close she was to the subject. She liked things to be in black-and-white, and right now she was definitely in a light gray zone regarding the rules of intelligence gathering. She convinced herself that she would cross this line, but not far over it. If the transcripts revealed that Nebibi knew something about this mysterious Andalus that was being picked up in other conversations, then, and only then, would she fess up to the full extent of *her* involvement with him.

"In any event, the conversations are all pretty innocuous. I'll send it to you on secure e-mail. It will be part of a larger transcript of other conversations we've been tracking. Okay?"

Kate understood that Bill was masking the transcript of Nebibi's conversation by including it as part of a larger package of transcripts.

"Okay."

"Look through it. If you find something we didn't pick up, you know who to call."

"Will do. Thanks again."

. . .

BILL'S E-MAIL ARRIVED IN a few seconds, all 140 pages of it. Ugh, I'd better get crackin', she thought. I've got that dinner tonight.

She found the spot with where Nebibi's calls began, page thirty-five, and started reading— Hmmm. Okay. Calls to lawyers in London. No big deal. Call to his secretary because there was no car to pick him up at JFK. He doesn't seem to be too pleased about that, now, does he? Who would be, after traveling overnight? Okay, more talk about deals with guys at White Weld & Co. Seems like they just follow his orders. Not too many bright lights there. Not a single mention of Andalus here. Bill was right. Pretty boring stuff, really.

She kept reading, though her mind was now more focused on peeking into Nebibi's day-to-day life. It was like she had found his personal diary and was rummaging through the pages. This is not what intelligence was supposed to be about, but she'd already crossed that line a couple of times already.

The phone rang again and it startled her.

"Yep!" Kate answered curtly, bothered by the interruption.

"Kate?"

"Oh, hi, Bill. I thought it might be another wrong number. I got your e-mail. Thanks. The analysts were right. Nothing there of interest."

"That's what I'm calling about. Seems we overlooked something. Not in the actual phone transcripts, but it's about this guy's name. There's somebody else with that same last name. A person of interest, of great interest to the U.S. government, in fact. So much so, that he's one of the last guys they have sitting at Gitmo. The guy's name is Rashidi Hasehm."

"Does this really have anything to do with Nebibi, though?"

"Well, it looks like they may be brothers. We have to look at the interrogation logs at Gitmo, but that's like pulling teeth from the guys at CIA. They're still running scared on the whole prisoner-camp thing. They're trying their best to claim they had nothing to do with the mess of secret prisons and torture."

"Is this confirmed?" Kate recalled Nebibi mentioning that he had a brother who died in the war, but she didn't know any more details. Nebibi always clammed up whenever she asked questions about his family, and so she never got to the bottom of which war he meant.

"We won't know for sure until someone at Gitmo is willing to cooperate and confirm this," said Bill.

"But even if they're brothers, it still doesn't mean that Nebibi is involved in anything that would be 'of special interest' to our government. We both looked at those transcripts and there's nothing there."

"You're probably right. Listen, if I hear anything I'll let you know. In the meantime, if you see him, I wouldn't mention anything about this person in Gitmo, 'cause it may be nothing in the end."

"Okay, but keep me posted, okay?" Mega-billions to manage and potentially a brother being held in Gitmo. Kate had to face the fact that this Nebibi was certainly more complicated than the one she knew in grad school. The question she hadn't answered for herself yet was whether or not that complication was worth more than just one night in the Alhambra.

57

GIBRALTAR
JANUARY 21

SAM COLDSMITH AND HIS TEAM of advisors, including Tomás Molares, arrived at the Gibraltar offices of The Milestones Fund's solicitors, Finchley, Emerson, Eggleston & Saunders, at exactly 2:00 P.M. Messrs. Humphries and Tarlock were on hand to direct the traffic of legal documents that needed to be signed. Clifford Cheswick and his team from White Weld & Co. were also present to make sure the deal was concluded, and most important, that their relevant fees were paid today, as is customary, off the top of all cash proceeds.

The solicitors had spent the morning making last-minute changes. By noon, they had a final document agreed upon by all. Nothing glamorous here, just the nuts and bolts of finance.

Nebibi had already signed these documents in this same office an hour ago. In truth, Sam could have signed these documents in the comfort of his office in Greenwich or even given power of attorney to a trusted subordinate, but he decided instead to sign them in person. After all, this was the most momentous day in his career, since that day he'd made his first trade at his first job at that third-tier Wall Street firm, almost three decades before. And in that time, he'd built an empire worth billions. Now he was about to sign away a significant portion of it and move into the less stressful role of senior statesman in financial circles, sitting on his billions and watching as his remaining portfolio was protected with the "insurance" of derivatives.

After twenty minutes, Tarlock announced to Sam, "Only one signature left, Mr. Coldsmith, and then we're all finished." Sam sat patiently, firmly holding on to his Mont Blanc Meisterstück fountain pen, waiting for that last signature page. It's not that he wasn't looking forward to realizing his billions; it's just that he was going to miss being at the center of market action.

Tarlock opened the last document to the signature page. This is it, thought Sam, no turning back. He moved his hand to the signature line, which read "Royal Lane Advisors LLC as Seller," next to that of "Milestones Capital Partners Fund I, L.P. as Buyer." As the tip of his pen touched the page, Sam's hand quivered. He took a deep breath, concentrated on holding his hand steady, and made the strokes of his name, but nothing appeared on the page. Maybe it's a sign, he thought for a split second.

"No ink." Sam shrugged his shoulders, looking at the entourage around him, all of whom stood to benefit tremendously by the simple act of him fixing his signature on that last page. Before Sam could take this as a sign *against* the deal, six arms were quickly extended, offering an array of working pens, mostly made of quoted commodities of either gold or silver. He selected the only one that wasn't: Tarlock's simple BIC classic ballpoint pen. That was the sign he needed. It was the same kind of pen he had used to sign the trade ticket on his first deal all those years ago, and so it was the only way to close his final big trade today. As soon as he had signed, the small number of men in the room broke out in a festive mood of congratulatory handshakes all around.

Humphries and Tarlock then got on the phone with bankers in New York to confirm the execution of the documents and to complete the final step—the transfer of the cold hard cash. Within the hour, the final step was done. The Milestones Fund had acquired 49 percent of Royal Lane Advisors' assets in return for a cash price of $103 billion. The lawyers and investment banks got their ton of flesh in those transfers as well, leaving a net profit to Sam of just under $15 billion. In their next ranking of the world's billionaires, *Forbes* would be moving Sam from his previous position of number 302 all the way up to number 62.

Sam Coldsmith emerged from the building into the afternoon sunlight, lighter on his feet, fatter in his checking account, and with a newly acquired BIC pen in his breast pocket. His hand was very steady now and he was ready for a celebration.

·   ·   ·

"CONGRATULATIONS, SAM, YOU MUST BE PLEASED." Tomás was alone with Sam driving to their next destination.

"Yeah, I guess I am, or should be, at least. But I can't help thinking that I'm going to miss the good ole days, sitting on the trading desk and pushing my way into deals. . . ."

"You just pushed yourself into the biggest deal of your career."

"Yep, point taken. I've got to focus on thinking about it like that and move on to this next stage of my life. Hey, don't forget, you're getting a nice payout here. So, how about we have ourselves a real celebration, like they've never seen here on Gib?"

The car stopped and the driver jumped out to open the door. Both men stepped out onto Queensway Quay Marina on the western side of Gibraltar.

"There it is, our home away from home, starting tonight." Sam pointed to the middle of the Bay. Anchored there was his latest acquisition, Her Majesty's Yacht *Britannia II*. It was a result of another trade masterfully executed by Sam.

Ten years ago, HMY *Britannia II* was in need of a serious retrofitting at a price far more than either the Queen or Her Government had been willing to spend. So this ship, with its historic pedigree, was relegated to sit in dry dock as a tourist attraction in Edinburgh, Scotland, a fact that had brought a public tear to even the usually stoic British Queen.

Twelve months earlier, the British Royal Family had received Parliament's approval for the construction of a new royal yacht, the HMY *Britannia III*, but only on the condition that they unload the previous royal yacht for a profit. Luckily, they found a willing buyer in a hedge fund king who was set to come into some serious cash. As with his aircraft, Sam made the purchase by borrowing on credit against the value of his holdings in the fund. And through that line of credit, the pushy Bronx-born trader was now the proud owner of the Royal Yacht *Britannia II*.

After spending a king's ransom to refit the yacht to modern standards, Sam had rechristened the yacht with a new moniker, the *Royal Britannia*. There was talk in certain corridors of Her Majesty's Government that the good deed of giving the Queen a hefty gain on the sale of *Britannia II*, and thereby funding the cost of the *Britannia III*, would result in a new knight at Her Majesty's next investiture ceremony. Sam was now not only the sixty second wealthiest person in the world, the owner of two Boeing aircraft *and* the *Britannia II,* but also in line to be a Knight Commander of the Most Excellent Order of the British Empire, that is "Sir" Samuel Coldsmith.

A STEWARD HELPED KATE TO CLIMB the last step aboard the ship. It was 6 P.M., and cocktails would be served in a half hour to coincide with the sunset over the Bay of Gibraltar.

Speaking with the proper kind of British accent, the steward welcomed Kate to the former floating residence of the Queen of England. "We are so pleased to have you on board the *Royal Britannia* this evening, Ms. Molares.

For most, being on the Royal Yacht was a unique treat. But for Kate, a boat, any boat, large or small, dinghy or royal yacht, was absolute torture. For starters, there was that thing about motion sickness. And then, there was the feeling of being trapped on board without an option to just get up and leave, unless doing the Australian crawl in heels was considered a viable exit strategy. Only one reason was strong enough to persuade her to leave terra firma—her father. Correction, two reasons. There was also that opportunity to "run into" Nebibi.

"Your father is expecting you. Please follow me." The steward led her through a long corridor of cream-colored walls with raised paneling. Overhead, she glimpsed a detailed coffered ceiling. As she walked, Kate counted ten double doors leading to the vessel's comfortably large staterooms. The steward opened one set of these doors, leading straight to where her father was. She stepped in and the steward closed the doors behind her, stepping backward, as if the Queen were still on board. Old habits were hard to break.

In the stateroom were French doors leading to a private balcony. The waters of the bay looked calm, but Kate could still feel the bobbing motion of the vessel. She turned around to find her father asleep on a sofa in front of the TV.

She tapped her father's shoulder gently to rouse him from his nap. Noticing who had woken him, he got up and gave her a big hug. They had certainly had their arguments over the past few weeks about her foreign assignment and its potential dangers, but had arrived at a truce of sorts because deep down she knew that his concern for her was something he would always struggle to keep in check. Better that he meddles—at least it shows he cares, thought Kate.

"Let me look at you, *hija*. You're looking good, much better than when you left."

"Yeah, yeah. So did everything go okay with the closing?"

"Yup. All of it signed, sealed, and delivered. Sam is trying to get used to a future with a less hectic workday, and I, in the meantime, should be feeling pretty good about myself. Come Monday, I'll be getting a $20 million gain on the sale. Pennies compared to our friend Sam, but I certainly can't complain."

"Are you kidding me? Of course, you should be pleased! When was the U.N. going to give you that kind of payout?"

"It's too bad she's not here to enjoy this with us," Tomás commented.

Kate looked at her father with an inquiring glance. It was very rare for him to speak of her dead mother, because when he did, he would usually shed a tear. Even now. "Mom would have gone out and bought the most expensive bottle of champagne possible and toasted your accomplishment. She would be real proud." Kate reached and gave him a big hug.

"She certainly would have, Kate. . . ." It comforted him to speak of her without getting sad.

"By the way, did you see Nebibi at the closing?"

"Kate, you keep asking about him. Is there something between the two of you that I should know about?" He'd traveled thousands of miles in order to ask the questions any father would, correction, *should* ask.

"Could be, not sure. I spent some time with him a couple of weeks ago."

"He's on board already, arrived earlier to talk shop with Sam. Hey look, it's six thirty p.m. We'd better get up to the deck for cocktails. We'll drink our toast there. Also, you can see your famous Nebibi. I tell you, I've never seen a couple have so much trouble getting on the same page. Do I need to go and nudge him to take you out on a date?"

"Oh jeez, no, don't you do that, Dad!" Her father didn't even know the half of it.

THEY REACHED THE AFT DECK, which had sofas arranged for optimal viewing of the sunset across the bay. There were no more than ten people outside, all gathered around Sam, who was holding court. Kate immediately recognized one of the men, the Governor of Gibraltar, Colin Trippet, who turned to greet her.

"Ms. Molares. What an absolute pleasure to see you here. You do travel in diverse circles, don't you? I'm beginning to think you're running for the post of deputy governor." The governor entertained the notion of hiring her after he left the government and started advising Nebibi's fund and his investors.

"So nice to see you again, Governor. Don't worry, I'm just here as a guest of my father. This is Tomás Molares."

"Immense pleasure, Mr. Molares. Your daughter certainly is making her mark around here. We had a lively discussion on Gibraltar sovereignty at our last reception."

Sam spotted Kate with her father. He walked over and gave her a big hug, worthy of a rich "uncle."

"Good to see you in one piece, Kate. Your father was worried about you over here. I told him to lay off. And you see, Tomás? I was right. She's all in one piece. So are you still managing to keep the world safe for big fat capitalists like me and, now, your father?" Sam's jolly mood indicated he was getting used to those extra billions.

"Always, Sam. Congratulations on your transaction today." Kate raised her glass of champagne and clinked it with Sam and her father.

The group that had previously stood around Sam was now dispersed, though some of them kept drifting closer to Sam, eager to bask in his success. One person whose back was to Kate turned and stared at the commotion around her. He noticed the glow in her face and it made him smile. She looked up and caught Nebibi's gaze and noticed the small smile that was imperceptible to anyone else there. It was the same look he gave her as they lay in that bed in the Alhambra just before they had finally dozed off in the early-morning hours. She smiled back at him and felt exhilarated. The Alhambra meant something to him, too, she thought.

The transcripts didn't surface anything unusual. But there was still that bit about Andalus in his calendar, and Bill's call to her an hour ago, confirming that the man in Gitmo was in fact Nebibi's brother. Why hadn't Nebibi ever said anything more about him to her? Did he really not know that his brother was caught up in terrorism? Kate knew that no phone call could show her what Nebibi was really thinking behind those vibrant brown eyes of his. The only way was by getting closer to him.

58

✦✦✦

NEBIBI STARED OUT AT THE EVENING sky, facing the African continent from his suite's balcony on the second floor of the Rock Hotel. His mind reviewed his to-do list and he smiled, satisfied that all was proceeding on track. His fund was almost fully invested, leaving $17 billion of excess liquidity. He'd decided to keep that liquidity untethered for now. Untethered and undisclosed, at the Banca Seguretat d'Andorra, that is.

The evening was clear, allowing the moon to bathe the grounds of the hotel in a blue hue. As if on cue, a lone figure appeared below by the pool. It was Kate, nodding to the hotel guard, who was making his evening rounds. This time, she'd managed to tiptoe by Lance Corporal Gubbins, who was still asleep at his station upstairs by the elevator.

As he watched her slip out of her bathrobe, exposing the contours of her athletic body, all thoughts about Milestones that had been swimming in Nebibi's mind were pushed down below the surface. She put on her goggles and the moonlight touched the slope of her long neck and the roundness of her breasts under the Speedo. His eyes focused on those exact spots on her body that he knew so well and that, now, he wanted to touch again. The sound of her body splashing into the water broke his train of thought.

He wished they could have spoken on the yacht. But what else would he say to her that he hadn't already said before in Greenwich. There was no future for them, because where he was headed was no place for a U.S. government intelligence analyst. And by getting involved with him again, he'd gotten her mixed up in a complicated situation, actually a dangerous one. She was in way over her head, much more than she could handle. I need to keep her safe, he thought. I owe her that, at least, he said to himself as he walked back inside his suite.

THERE WAS A MOVEMENT behind a grouping of large ferns, near where the guard was strolling. Hearing the rustling of vegetation, the guard turned his head, but not seeing anything or anyone, figured it was a Barbary ape scrounging for food. As he turned around to continue on his appointed path, something hit his right temple. The muffled sound only woke up a few birds in the trees. The guard fell to his knees first, by which point he lost consciousness. His body then slumped, falling hard to the ground. Before anyone appeared on the scene, the body was dragged by unseen hands behind the ferns.

NEBIBI HEARD A MUFFLED SOUND coming from just outside his window. To his trained ear, it sounded like a muffled gunshot, so he rushed out onto his terrace. He saw Kate still swimming her laps, with no other commotion around the pool area. Still perplexed by the sound, Nebibi remained on the terrace, scanning the grounds for any movement.

KATE'S HEAD EMERGED THROUGH THE SURFACE of the water. She took in a deep breath. It felt a bit colder this evening, but invigorating. The mindless counting of laps had done its trick. It was her meditation time, blocking any other noise or distraction from her mind. She felt completely refreshed.

Kate jumped out of the pool into the cool evening air and rushed to put on her robe. She started to dry her hair with a towel, bending down slightly. As she straightened up, she felt a sharp, sudden pain around her neck and a strong jab at her side.

Her mind raced to capture information. Ugh! What is it?! Who is it!? I've got to run! Her arm muscles were taut from the swim and now she used that strength to try to free herself. With both hands, she tried to tear away the arm that was choking her throat. She tried to yell for help. "Ughm . . ." The strong arm around her neck was stifling her voice. I can't yell! I can't breathe!

She continued her struggle to free herself using her legs and elbows. Her breath only came in short spasms and her strength was giving way to panic. Not working! I can't breathe! Then she heard the threatening whisper of a man's voice next to her ear, spoken in Spanish. "My finger is ready to pull the trigger right here." At the same time, she felt the barrel of a gun jabbed farther into her side. "As long as you keep quiet and follow me, you'll live to have another swim."

His grip was choking her. She needed to breathe, but was feeling dizzy. The more she tried to break free from him, the tighter he held her. She had no choice and stopped resisting. He loosened his grip just enough for her to breathe. She took in a deep breath and, straining her injured vocal muscle, she managed to mutter a hoarse "Okay."

Kate felt a sharp stab as the gun's barrel pressed even farther into her lower back. Her arm was yanked and twisted behind her in a lock hold. The man pushed her forcibly toward the hotel's service entrance. That's where his car was parked, away from the traffic of the main lobby.

But then, Kate felt a strong weight push her. The vise-hold on her arm was released, causing her to lose her balance. Her body propelled forward onto the concrete.

"Ugghhh!" Kate cried out as her hands and knees bore the brunt of the fall. She quickly got herself on her feet. "Ooww!" Her knees were now bloodied. No time! Run! She sprinted in her bare feet toward the hotel's service entrance.

Something, or someone, had hit the man from behind, knocking him down. The force pummeled him to the ground, making him lose his grip not only on Kate, but also on the gun, which landed a couple of feet in front of him. The man lunged for the gun, and in one swift move, grabbed it and turned over on his back, pointing it at whoever had attacked him from behind. Sweat streaked down his forehead. He expected to see a guard from the hotel, or worse, another one of this woman's colleagues from the U.S. military. Instead, his barrel was now aimed directly at Nebibi Hasehm!

Nebibi had no idea who was on the other end of that barrel, but he recognized the face. It was the "tourist without a camera"! Nebibi wondered if this was one of the Cubans or Venezuelans still on the loose hunting down Kate.

As she ran, Kate looked back and now also recognized her attacker. He was after her! She did a double-take. Nebibi! She saw that he was staring down at the man with the gun, his arms raised to show that he was defenseless. She also realized that it was Nebibi who had delivered the blow that knocked the man down. I have to do something! Her instincts took over. She stopped. The thought of losing Nebibi this way was not something she could allow. That man was looking for me, not him!

She shouted to get the man's attention. "I'm the one you're looking for!"

Nebibi turned in panic, knowing the danger she was putting herself in, "No, Kate! Stay back! He's got a gun!"

The man kept his gun locked on Nebibi, but glanced over at Kate. He faced a choice of possible victims. His boss had told him to concentrate on the woman, and then wait until after Operation Andalus to find Nebibi. And now he had them both. He knew he couldn't manage to get both of them in the car by himself. So he had to make a choice.

In that instant of indecision, Nebibi's mind clicked on a clue. If he's chasing Kate, why is he hesitating? Why is the gun still pointed at me? Is he looking for me, too? Nebibi asked himself.

As the "tourist" slowly stood up from the ground, he saw out of the corner of his eye that Kate was moving toward him. He turned and pointed the gun at her, his free hand motioning Nebibi to stay put.

And Nebibi did, because he could tell by the man's gaze that he'd welcome any excuse to pull the trigger. Nebibi looked at Kate. She was standing still about six feet ahead of the man. She caught Nebibi's eyes, his left eyebrow raised. He was giving her a signal. A signal for what, though?

Nebibi blinked his eyes at her and made a slight nod of his head toward the right. She moved slightly in the same direction. Her movement alarmed the "tourist," but he kept his gaze on her, pointing the gun at her heart. Nebibi made his move and, with all his strength, lunged toward the man from behind. The "tourist" pulled the trigger as his body slammed against the pavement. The gun fell out of his hand, landing a few inches away from Kate.

Nebibi heard the shot and immediately looked over at Kate in panic. Oh no! She's on the ground! She's hit!

The "tourist" scrambled to retrieve his gun. Both he and Nebibi spotted it at the exact same moment. Nebibi sprang to his feet first, but the "tourist" managed to get hold of his ankle, knocking him back to the ground, facedown. The sudden forceful impact against his chest left Nebibi momentarily breathless, giving the "tourist" just enough time to stand up. But as both men looked up, they saw Kate was also now standing—slightly crouched over because of the pain—yet standing.

She was concentrating every ounce of will left in her body to hold her right arm steady. It was stretched out in front of her, her hand wrapped tightly around the gun. The whole scene was now distilled down to Kate's index finger held taut against that trigger. Nebibi saw intensity in her eyes, jaws clenched and sweat rolling down her face. He'd never seen her in this light—playing the role of fierce fighter and protector. That it suited her is what took him aback.

Even as her outstretched arm began to tremble, Kate had locked her sights on the "tourist." She wouldn't hesitate to pull the trigger if he made any sudden movements.

Options for the "tourist" were dwindling. He had already lost the chance to capture both of them. And now, all he was hoping for was to escape to fight another battle, another day. He made eye contact with Kate and slowly raised his hands up in the air. Despite the man's sign of surrender, however, she continued pointing the gun directly at him.

Nebibi walked toward Kate, watching as she struggled to keep her arm steady, the other hand grasping her shoulder. When she saw Nebibi finally standing next to her, it was her signal to release. She let out a low moan, and then her legs gave out from under her. He managed to hold on to her as she fell to the ground. He saw that she was unconscious, yet still breathing. He needed to get help for her, and quickly.

Nebibi quickly grabbed the gun from her hand and turned around to point it back at the "tourist." But he was no longer in the same spot. Where was the "tourist"? he asked himself as he turned around still raising the gun defensively. Then he heard an engine start—a dark blue Ranger Rover sped down the driveway. He was getting away! Nebibi immediately hid the gun in his pocket. I need to dispose of this before anybody does a trace for fingerprints, he thought.

He looked at Kate's wound. The bullet had only managed to graze her shoulder, but the shock of being shot had made her faint. He held her hand in his and felt her stirring. "You're going to be alright, Kate. I'll keep you safe, I promise you."

Kate looked at Nebibi, thankful they had both managed to survive this. She had questions about who the "tourist" was and what he was after, but right now she wanted to tell Nebibi some critical information.

Kate tried to speak, but her voice came out in a slightly husky quiver. "Nebibi, I want to tell you something that you need to know. It's classified and I shouldn't be talking to you about it . . . but I can't keep this from you. . . . I know about your brother. . . ."

Nebibi's face turned ashen. "Rashidi? What do you know about him?"

"I know where he is. . . ."

"He's alive!?"

". . . He's at Gitmo. I know that you have nothing to do with what he was involved with, but I thought you should know that."

Nebibi's mind raced with questions for Kate, but before he could ask them, he heard the rush of footsteps behind him. He looked up to see two hotel guards rushing over.

"HOW ARE YOU DOING, KATE?" General Owens stood next to the gurney in the infirmary aboard the USS *Churchill*.

"I'm fine, General. The bullet just grazed me. The doctor says I can be out and about tomorrow morning."

"That was a close call, Kate. They don't give purple hearts to civilians, you know."

"Yep, close call."

"Too close for comfort, I'd say. I want you stationed on this ship until after the Sovereignty Summit. Necessary precaution. Understood?"

"Yes, sir." The thought of being aboard the ship's cramped

quarters for more than an hour at a time was already making her queasy.

"So, Kate, any ideas about the assailant? Do you think he's part of the group that tried to get you back in the States?"

"Not sure, General. The men in Old Greenwich spoke with a Venezuelan accent. This one was definitely a Spaniard."

"By the way, we tried to find Mr. Hasehm, but it seems he's no longer at the hotel. He left after you were picked up by the ambulance. Any idea where we can reach him? Our military police need to get a statement from him for their report on the incident."

"I think he said he needed to get back to New York. He just closed a big deal here with Sam Coldsmith. You know how those financial types are; he's probably working on the next deal." Or at least, I hope he is, thought Kate.

In fact, Nebibi was not very far away. He was just on the other side of the Bay in Algeciras, and yes, he was working on the final details of his next deal, Operation Andalus.

59

MUSTAFA MOUSSAB CAREFULLY COILED THE WIRE around his twenty-five-pound bundle of TNT. He took a deep breath before picking up the explosives and carefully passing the wire underneath. He exhaled with great relief when the bundle remained intact, rather than blowing up in his hands. He clearly remembered all the instructions from his weeks of training, but now, alone on the morning of his mission, he felt the weight of the moment. Other than the sound of his rapid breathing, there was no other noise in his small apartment. It was 3 A.M. in the Muslim working-class neighborhood of Ceuta, the North African city across the Strait from Gibraltar.

Mustafa had a few hours before boarding the first ferry to Algeciras along with all the other cheap laborers who lived in Ceuta. As he picked up his precious bundle, he noticed that his hands were trembling. A purple hue framed the edges of his nails, like someone had slammed a door on his fingers. His heartbeat was elevated, his eyes were darting back and forth, and the walls of his capillaries were beginning to weaken. The serum was taking hold.

"Good, finished the first step." Mustafa admired the bundle of explosives. "Two more steps to go." He opened a small lead box sitting on his worktable. Inside were eight three-inch lead cylinders with screw tops. Each one of these contained an ounce of radioactive material, cobalt-60 in a fine powder form that is normally used in cancer radiation therapy. Mustafa's allotment of cobalt-60 had been "conveniently misplaced" by the hospital in Casablanca. While the twenty-five pounds of TNT would be more than ample to kill a dozen or more innocent bystanders later today, it would be the broadly dispersed cloud of powdered cobalt-60 that would result in widespread havoc, affecting a far greater number of people.

Mustafa was a young man. He had just turned twenty-four. Reed thin with olive skin tanned by the strong African sun, he had cropped black hair, and eyes the color of the Mediterranean Sea on a sunny day. He was a modern-day Berber, a descendant of the fearless North African Muslims who had accompanied General Tariq on his voyage across the Strait all those centuries ago.

Mustafa understood the importance of this mission, and it was an immense honor that he was eager to fulfill. Young Mustafa, his name meaning "the chosen," was the nephew of Samir Moussab, the deputy commander of the North Africa–based al-Qaeda in the Islamic Maghreb. Even in the terrorist world, it seemed that connections made all the difference when applying for that first position. If all went according to plan, Mustafa's name would be remembered for generations to come, alongside that of General Tariq's. And he, with the blessing of his family, was ready to make the ultimate sacrifice for that honor.

Mustafa rehearsed his simple checklist for today. Arrive in Algeciras, take the bus from there to the center of Gibraltar, go to the restaurant in front of the Gibraltar Government House at exactly 9:30 A.M. and order a late breakfast. At exactly 9:57 A.M., leave the restaurant, walk toward the stairs of the Government House, and wait. At exactly 10:00 A.M., he would sacrifice his life for the honor of following in General Tariq's footsteps.

Mustafa didn't waver in his conviction, thanks to the serum. As a mere foot soldier, he was not aware that his actions were being matched by other such soldiers in different time zones, all pursuing a different leg of the mission known as Operation Andalus.

60

GIBRALTAR
JANUARY 24

"Hello?" KATE ANSWERED HER IPHONE.

"*Guëte morgë*—Good morning, Miss Molares," said Herr Boeglin from his office in Bern. "Some good news. I've just received another copy of Banca di Califfato's shareholders and directors, the most recent one we had on file before they closed. Where can I send it to you?"

Talk about bad timing, thought Kate. She was in the Gibraltar Government House in the midst of final preparations for the conference, which was set to start within the hour. "Can you e-mail it to me?"

"I'll ask my secretary to scan it; you should have it shortly. Would that be alright?"

"That'd be great, thanks!" Kate spoke quickly, preoccupied because the Spanish delegation had included an extra representative they hadn't planned for, which meant he wasn't pre-cleared from a security point of view. She quickly ended the conversation with the only words of Schweizerdeutsch she knew, *"Merci villmool."* She looked at the time. Got to rush! The Crown Princes should be arriving in twenty minutes.

KATE STOOD AT THE TOP of the stairs of the Government House waiting for the British and Spanish Royals. Her iPhone vibrated and she saw that a new e-mail from Herr Boeglin had arrived. She quickly perused its contents. List of Banca di Califfato shareholders, Abdhul Rahman, several Middle Eastern government entities and Muslim charitable organizations. No news there, thought Kate.

She scrolled further for the bank's directors. Rahman again, okay, she thought. Her hand trembled when she read the next name. Nebibi Hasehm. That can't be! How could I have been so blind!? Her mind raced back to various conversations these past few weeks. Did he know that the bank was somehow involved with *T. gondii* and the Madrid bombing? Or did he stumble into plots created by others? But then there was the issue of his brother, a prisoner at Gitmo, to consider. But he saved my life the other night, for God's sake.

She tried to analyze what this all meant and what her next step should be, but her mind fogged over with a mixture of rage and concern for Nebibi's safety. Should she tell the general or find Nebibi and confront him alone? Was there any time to do that?

Her thoughts were interrupted when she caught a glimpse of highly polished, handmade black Oxfords making their way quickly up the marble steps. She raised her head and found herself staring up at the smiling face of the immaculately dressed Prince of Wales, surrounded by his entourage. She stuffed her iPhone back in her pocket, cleared her mind, and with no need for any greater protocol, stuck out her hand and said, "Your Royal Highness, I'm Kate Molares with the U.S. government, please allow me to escort you inside."

"VOICE MAIL, AGAIN," FUMED KATE under her breath. That was her third attempt to reach Nebibi in the last few minutes. There could be a thousand explanations for his involvement with Califfato, all of which were swimming in her head right now. But for her to accept any single one of them, she needed to hear it directly from his lips. Nothing else would suffice. Not now.

She looked up at the large clock on the wall: 8:55 A.M. She scanned the large room where the thirty-odd persons involved in the Sovereignty Summit were seated. The more senior reps sat at a large square table, which was covered in a deep burgundy cloth, with junior staff behind them.

In front of each person at the table was a white tent name card. The American delegation, led by General Owens, sat on one end, next to the Governor of Gibraltar and his staff. On the opposite side sat the Spanish and British delegations, and in between and across from the general were the Crown Princes of Spain and England, the two representatives of their titular monarchies; their white tent cards had no formal titles attached to their names. Merely royal.

Kate sat directly behind the general, staring at the back of his closely cropped head. She couldn't hold back on this information any longer, particularly since she hadn't been able to get a hold of Nebibi. She knew that whatever Nebibi's true role turned out to be, the fact that she hid their relationship would kill her career. No intelligence officer in their right mind would have kept such information from the chain of command. And now she had no choice but to fess up. It was, she decided, her only choice.

So Kate took a deep breath and reached out to tap the general's shoulder. "Excuse me, sir. I need to speak with you. Alone."

"Now?" The general's voice sounded tense, due to the hectic preparations leading to this very moment. "Can it wait till later?"

Kate would gladly have delayed the conversation, but having made her difficult choice, she could no longer hold off, lest she change her mind again. She needed to inform her superior about the critical information from Herr Boeglin. She knew it would point a finger at Nebibi, making him a person of high interest in the investigation. Like it or not, it was her duty, in spite of that night in the Alhambra.

"No," she said, "it can't."

61

NEBIBI TOOK PURPOSEFUL STRIDES through the empty lobby of the Hotel Reina Cristina in Algeciras. Young Manuel was manning the front desk night shift, not quite awake. His head was slumped over his arms. The sound of loud footsteps on the marble floor coming down the hallway woke him. He immediately straightened up.

"*Buenos dias, señor. . . .*" Manuel's voice trailed off but he hadn't been quick enough in his greeting. Nebibi was already out the front door. The young man wondered where this guest was headed at this hour, since all the tourist places were still closed.

If someone were to ask Manuel to describe the man who just walked through the lobby, he wouldn't be able to recall one single feature, only that it was a man. Such was the attention span of the front desk clerk at this rustic locale on the southernmost region of Spain. A perfect place for someone looking to go unnoticed. Like Nebibi.

Nebibi got into his parked car. His overnight bag was already packed and in the trunk, as usual. He wasn't going far, just a few blocks to the Algeciras ferry station. Once there, he parked nearby and then sat at a café facing the bay. Around him was the early Monday-morning bustle of people having their coffee before heading to work at the docks or waiting to take the ferries across the Strait.

Nebibi noted that there was still time before the arrival of the first ferry from North Africa. From this vantage point, he could see and hear all the ship traffic coming in and out of the bay. In the distance, he saw Coldsmith's yacht anchored alongside another yacht, the HMY *Britannia III* waving the royal standard. The Princes had arrived. The plan was perfect, he thought.

He noticed a jet taking off, banking around the bay to give its passengers a postcard view of the Rock. The morning sun brought out the glimmer of its golden fuselage. The flying artwork known as the *Gold Shark Swimming in Air* was taking off.

Nebibi turned his attention back to the crowded café, looking around cautiously to see if he recognized anyone, or if anyone recognized him. He couldn't be too careful this morning.

He turned on his cell phone and it immediately flashed a message—three missed calls, unknown caller. He didn't have time for conversations now and instead tapped the address for the bicycle suppliers' Web site. At the log-in prompt, he entered his ID and security code. His screen displayed a global map with marker dots on all continents. Several of these were flashing in red, indicating that "bicycle suppliers" were now in motion as of this hour. *The final signal; there's no stopping this now. . . .*

Nebibi blended right in with the rest of the café's customers this morning. He was wearing a pair of worn jeans and a beat-up leather jacket that he'd picked up at a secondhand stall in Algeciras yesterday. He still had the gun from his encounter with the "tourist," neatly tucked in his right jacket pocket, and a small vial in the other.

His manner of dress wasn't the only thing that was out of character. The thoughts swimming inside his head were no longer just focused on accomplishing the mission at hand. Over the last two days, something else, or rather someone, had seeped into his brain—first a few drops, then a trickle, and finally a full-fledged stream of opposing needs and emotions.

The last thing that Kate said to him certainly put the entire matter in a different context. *Your brother is alive.* And if his brother was still alive, then what exactly was his fight about? Her simple words had unlocked a door, a gate, that he thought had been sealed forever.

As Nebibi sat in that crowded café, not a single human on earth knew that he was here at this very spot, at this very moment. He was alone, a panther tired of hunting, knowing that he would likely travel like this, like a ghost, far from all who had known him, till his last breath.

Nebibi's thoughts came back into focus, jarred by the horn blast of an incoming ferry. He looked up and saw the ferry from Ceuta turning slowly to dock. Nebibi was searching for one particular passenger, and though he didn't know the passenger's face, he did know what to look for. He dropped a couple of euros on the table and left the café to walk over to the arrival platform.

After the first passengers disembarked, Nebibi saw what he was searching for: a young man tightly grasping the straps of his backpack, not about to let go of it at any cost. Nebibi could also see a fiery determination in his eyes and the quick movement of his eyeballs from side to side. *The serum.* While his fingernails would confirm it, Nebibi already knew it was him.

Nebibi walked up to him from behind and whispered one word in a very low voice: "Andalus."

Mustafa's back stiffened in shock and he immediately turned around. He worried that he'd been discovered and that his precious mission would slip through his hands. He saw only one man standing still while all others continued in their march toward the bus station.

"I'm here to help you." Nebibi immediately noticed the blue hue around his fingernails.

Mustafa instantly recognized Nebibi, remembering him from a visit he had made to his uncle, Samir, a few years back. Nebibi was known as a senior member of the command structure and one who would rise further in the future. Mustafa was immediately at ease, seeing that a high-ranking resource had been sent to assist him on the mission.

"*Asalaamu alaykum*—peace be upon you. You know my uncle, Samir Moussab. My name is Mustafa."

"*Wa alaykumu asalaam*—and upon you peace, Mustafa." Nebibi now placed the face. "I know that you have several hours before your 'final destination' this morning. I'm here to make sure there are no disruptions on your path. Better that you are isolated until that last possible moment."

Nebibi directed the young recruit to his car. As they started their short journey to the Gibraltar border, Nebibi spoke to him with the voice of a new mentor. "Do you have any doubts about your mission today?"

"No, I'm ready, sir. We must all fight for what Boabdil lost."

"Good." The serum had enhanced the young man's singular focus on his mission, as intended.

They approached the border checkpoint; Nebibi presented his Italian European Union passport and Mustafa presented his Spanish one. Without delay, they were waved through by the border guard.

Nebibi had his own particular mission to accomplish today, and he knew where he could do that with a little less attention. "Have you actually seen with your own eyes what your mission will gain for our people?"

"What do you mean?" asked the younger man.

"Have you seen the Rock of Tariq?"

"Only from a distance, when I crossed the Strait on the ferry-boat."

"Okay, we'll go up there and wait till it's time for you to go to the Government House. It will be quieter there than in the center of Gibraltar." There was more than enough time before this operative needed to get back down, thought Nebibi.

Nebibi pulled out the vial from his pocket and handed it to Mustafa. "Here, take this. It's the last dose of the vitamins. It will help you complete your mission."

The young Mustafa held up the vial containing that now-familiar liquid. The taste of exhilaration and invincibility it gave him was still fresh on his palate. Of course, he would take the dose—it had become his all-consuming desire since that first exposure weeks earlier. He uncapped the vial and downed the entire contents in one gulp, flinching as the concentrated potion stung the lining of his esophagus. Then, leaned his head back, his eyes closed, waiting for his system to absorb the strong dose. Within seconds, he felt that courage and constancy once again swell in his chest. His eyes opened with intensity, ready to take on General Tariq's mission and retake his Rock. Nebibi glanced at Mustafa and noticed a sudden tremor traveling from the tips of his fingers up to his wrist.

That was the clue he was looking for; this young recruit would not live to complete his mission on Gib today.

Nebibi drove along Rock Gun Road, a winding street without guardrails that reached one of the highest elevations. He parked the car overlooking the cliff on the eastern face of the Rock, a side shown in the famous logo of Prudential insurance, a sheer cliff ending at empty sand dunes far below.

Nebibi opened the windows and turned off the engine. A cool breeze passed into the car. The easterly Levanter winds had brought moisture this morning that hit against the tall cliffs, pushing the air upward where it condensed to a gray mist at the top of the Rock. At this hour, the Rock was peaceful; it was too early for most vacationing sightseers, just rousing from sleep in their hotel rooms.

Mustafa took in the view while Nebibi got straight to business. "Are the radioactive materials safe? Do you have them properly encased?"

"Yes, I taped the cylinders to the explosives and then attached the detonation device."

"Good. Let me double-check it."

"Yes, sir." Mustafa unzipped the backpack, revealing a plastic bag that he had tied with a small wire. Inside the plastic was a simple box. Mustafa began to take the box out, but his hands were trembling too much.

The serum again, thought Nebibi, and in another few minutes his whole nervous system would collapse.

"Here, let me take that out." Nebibi reached in and carefully extracted the box from the plastic bag. He held it up. "Take the bag away." Nebibi then gently placed it on the armrest between them and lifted the top to reveal the core of the crude explosive device. Alarm was rising in Mustafa. He tried to hold his arms together in a vain attempt to hide his body's increased trembling from Nebibi.

Meanwhile, Nebibi was instead concentrated on the backpack device. He hoped that Mustafa had made this stable enough. The movement of the package in the backpack these past few hours alone could have loosened the connections.

"It looks like you did a good job." In truth, Nebibi could see that the jostling had loosened the tape holding the lead cylinders in place next to the bundle of TNT. He was about to carefully reattach the tape, but then he heard a small thud. He looked up and saw that Mustafa's body was slumped against the car door. Nebibi firmly grabbed Mustafa's head between his hands.

"Mustafa, wake up!" He slapped his cheeks, but there was no light in the young man's eyes. Nebibi grabbed his wrist and found no pulse either. Dead within only minutes of taking that concentrated dose, he thought. For a second, Nebibi felt sadness for the recruit's short unfulfilled life, but then remembered that the loss of this one life also meant saving many more, the most important of which was Kate.

A postmortem examination of Mustafa's body would immediately show the toxic levels of *T. gondii prime* in his system, so Nebibi knew he had to prevent any such autopsy from ever occurring. He sprang out of the car. When he opened the passenger side door, Mustafa's body fell out onto the pavement. He locked his arms around Mustafa's upper torso and started quickly dragging the body to the other side of the car.

Just when he was almost on the other side of the car, Nebibi's ears perked. He heard a sound coming from the passenger side of the car. He quickly crouched down and released his hold on the torso. He pulled out his gun and steadied it with two hands, ready for any possible threat. Still crouching, he inched toward the other side, his back sliding against the car. *There was that noise again.* Now he pinpointed it coming from the passenger side. He was just inches away from that open door, ready if someone jumped out from the front seat. But instead, he came upon four Barbary apes scrounging for food. They smelled a human and looked up at Nebibi, each of them with metal cylinders in their paws.

"Damn monkeys!" Nebibi shot a warning shot in the air. They jumped out of the car and scurried out with the cylinders in their paws to the nature preserve on the west side of the Rock. Only when they needed both their front limbs to escape through the trees did the Barbary apes release the cylinders. They fell into a steep ravine. Nebibi looked down to see if he could spot the metal casings, but he knew they would be impossible for anyone to find. He pitied the person that one day would stumble on them on a nature hike and would, out of curiosity, unscrew the tops, revealing their toxic content.

He saw the backpack on the front seat, its explosives still armed and ready. Nebibi turned back to look at Mustafa's body lying on the pavement; the first casualty of Operation Andalus.

The mist was still thick, obscuring the death high atop the Rock. Nebibi needed to clear this scene quickly before sightseers arrived with their cameras. He dragged the body onto the driver's seat and closed the windows. He took out Mustafa's wallet from his jacket. Let's make sure they don't keep looking for me, he thought. Nebibi placed his own wallet in Mustafa's pocket.

He also placed the gun he held in his hand, with his fingerprints, on the front seat. He left his overnight bag in the trunk and Mustafa's backpack of explosives on the front seat. And then with the scene of the "crash" set, Nebibi put the car in neutral gear and gave it a push forward toward the cliff.

The car's wheels turned only one rotation before gravity took over. The drop was sharp and steep. The back of the car hit a cliff about halfway down the thousand foot elevation, causing the gasoline tank to ignite. For the remaining distance, flames engulfed the tumbling car like a fireball. At an elevation of two hundred feet, Mustafa's TNT ignited, causing a second, far greater explosion, which hurled shards of metal over the empty sand dunes.

Along with the metal, the explosion sprayed the beach with pieces of human tissue, incinerated beyond any recognition. All that investigators would be able to gather and reconstruct in the days to come were the pieces of the car's Italian EU license plate. They would determine that the shards of metal had once been a BMW registered in the name of a certain up-and-coming international financier, presumed to have been the driver, whose remains were pulverized in the explosion of his car.

Nebibi stood on the cliff high above, watching. The Panther was dead now. Right after the second explosion, he walked away on the road leading back down, disappearing like a ghost into the thick mist of the Upper Rock. She will be safe today.

62

⊰✦✦✦⊱

KATE AND GENERAL OWENS STOOD against the wall, out of earshot of the other participants at the conference table.
She was about to show him Herr Boeglin's e-mail when
they both heard the muted boom of an explosion coming from somewhere outside the building. "Did you hear that!?"
she asked him.

"Yes. Sergeant, call Commander Svensk on the secure line right
away," barked the general to the officer at the door.

"It couldn't have been part of the opening ceremonies. We already had that welcome. . . ." Kate looked at her watch. 8:59 A.M.
The meeting was just about to start and already something unexpected had happened.

They looked around the room and could tell that others had
heard the explosion by the alarmed looks on their faces. As for the
Princes, despite their lifetime of training, neither was able to hide
their alarm. Even a century later, visions of the assassination of
Archduke Franz Ferdinand of Austria still danced in the minds of
European royalty.

The sergeant returned and leaned over to whisper in the general's ear. His face didn't let on what he was hearing. It could have
been notice of an impending nuclear attack or just news about a
parking ticket, but the look on the general's face would be the
same. Such was his training.

He motioned for Kate. "I need you to go with the sergeant here
and investigate the explosion. Our ship's radars picked up an explosion at 8:58 A.M., on the other side of the Rock. As soon as you
know anything, call me here. If there's any danger, we need to act

quickly. In the meantime, I've given instructions for our men to be on high alert. I'll advise the governor that his forces should do the same."

"Yes, sir." She looked at the clock on the wall as she left the room. 9:03 A.M. For now, questions about Nebibi would have to wait.

THE SERGEANT DROVE ON Devil's Tower Road, which swung around to the other side of the Rock. When they crossed over to the eastern façade, Kate noticed that several Gib police cars and an idle fire truck, with its lights flashing, were already on hand. A police vehicle blocked the road off from traffic. An officer waved his arms and shouted, "You need to move along! Nothing for you to see, gents—" The Gib police officer stopped in midsentence when he saw the sergeant's U.S. military uniform.

Kate got out of the car and extended her hand to the officer. "Kate Molares, sir. We're here with the U.S. delegation at the Sovereignty Summit." She flashed her government ID at him. "We picked up the explosion on our radar systems." As she said that, she pointed to the USS *Churchill* sitting in the bay. *If my badge won't convince him, maybe the destroyer-class ship will,* thought Kate.

"Oh, yes, of course. I think you may want to speak with that gentleman over there." The officer waved the sergeant through to park his car alongside the other official vehicles.

Kate walked over to the man giving out orders. "Hello, Detective, we meet again. . . ." Kate recognized Detective Sebastian Wright of the Gib police force. She'd met him as part of her duties ahead of today's Summit, and he had been on hand to take her statement regarding the shooting at the hotel the other evening.

"Pleasure, Miss Molares."

"Your men certainly arrived here quickly, Detective. . . ."

"We were right on the other side, there by the airport, when we heard the blast."

"So what was it?" Kate looked around them. Several officers were combing the remnants of the blast. "Looks like a missile hit a target and blew it to smithereens. . . ."

"Not as fantastic as all that, I'm afraid. From what we can tell, this was probably nothing more than an unfortunate accident.

Some unlucky tourist probably took a wrong turn up there on the Rock. We're figuring that the morning mist blocked their vision and the driver ended up taking a wrong turn and boom. Next thing you know, they're taking the quickest route down, like a missile straight down a thousand feet. There's metal everywhere down here."

"So there's nothing to ID here?" Kate wanted to get a slightly more complete picture before getting back to the general.

"We found a small piece of a license plate, looks like an EU one, and also the *B* and *W* of the car's emblem. No bodies to speak of, though. The explosion made the inside of the car an incinerator before it crashed down here at the beach. Whoever was inside burned into ashes in seconds. We'll have to continue scrounging around for other fragments. That'll be our best course."

"Nothing out of the ordinary to report, then, Detective?"

"No, unfortunately this seems to happen more than once a decade around here. The roads up on the Rock don't all have barriers and there are some hairpin curves that are challenging for the novice Gib driver, particularly if they just got back from the bar. . . ."

An ambulance siren approached at breakneck speed. "We won't have much use for these gentlemen this morning, I'm afraid."

"Excuse me for a second, in that case. I need to report back to my general so that the Summit participants can rest at ease."

"Yes, certainly."

Kate stepped a few paces away and rang up the general. He picked up the call immediately. "Hello, General Owens?"

"Yes. Shoot."

"I'm on the other side of Gib. Nothing peculiar here, so far. Local police arrived a few minutes ahead of us. Looks like it was just an unfortunate tourist driving the winding roads of the Rock. They figure the guy took a wrong turn off a cliff, a very large one, as you know. They're sifting through debris now. They're trying to find something to ID the driver and any passengers."

"How many were there?"

"We have no way of telling. The remains are completely incinerated."

"How could one gas tank accomplish that? I think something more powerful may have caused that explosion. Dig deeper. Our onboard systems didn't record any missile activity, so whatever caused that car to explode was *in* the car. . . ."

"Yes, sir. . . ." Kate's eyes traveled to what one of the officers was carrying over to the detective. Something familiar about it, even from her vantage point a few paces away. She signed off the call with the general. "Detective, Detective! What's that?"

"Officer Devlin found it over there by the cliff." The detective held an overnight bag in his hand. "Not sure if it has anything to do with this crash, though. We had our bomb expert scan it first."

Kate stared at the bag. Deep burgundy leather, soft. The kind used by skilled workmen in leather craft. Italian leather. *Is it?!* She remembered seeing one like this recently. . . . "May I?" She looked over at the detective.

"Certainly."

She opened the zipper and looked inside. . . . Some running shorts and shoes, a starched white shirt, shaving kit, an embellished Qur'an—Wahhabi edition. An inside pocket with a zipper. She opened it and dug her hand in to fish out the contents. There she found something she didn't want to find. She held them in her fist and slowly opened her fingers. Two cuff links, silver sabers. A picture of Nebibi at the Coldsmith party wearing his cuff links flashed through her mind. He told her that he always kept an extra pair of these on hand.

"No!" Kate cried out in a low murmur.

"What is it, miss?" Detective Wright stared at Kate as the color completely drained from her face. "Are you alright? Miss?"

All sorts of thoughts passed through Kate's head. She couldn't accept that he was dead, and certainly not like this, in a freakish accident. Maybe this is just a coincidence or maybe he wasn't even in the car. But if he wasn't, why was his overnight bag here? He wouldn't have left it. So what was he still doing here? Was he really involved in all of this? Maybe this was his end, here on this cliff. Suddenly, Herr Boeglin's revelation about Nebibi's link to Califfato seemed of marginal importance.

None of her thoughts led to any definitive conclusions, except for one. *Something happened here today; something very bad.*

63

NEW YORK CITY
JANUARY 24

N EW YORK CITY WAS BUILT on the sturdy backs and rough hands of immigrants. A previous century saw huge waves of Italians, Irish, and Germans washing up on the shores of Manhattan, coming with all their energy to stake their claims on the American dream. In this new millennium, new waves come through every day with equal energy. Because of that, in addition to pizzerias, Chinese takeout, and Irish pubs, most Manhattan neighborhoods will boast the likes of Korean vegetable grocers, Indian newspaper kiosks, Middle Eastern falafel stands, and Colombian flower merchants.

One of the more recent additions to New York's vendor landscape are the roasted nut carts positioned at the most heavily foot-trafficked corners of the city. These small canopied carts specialize in roasting peanuts and almonds, caramelized with sugar, over hot copper pots, in the traditional Swiss-German way. These carts, however, are not operated by Swiss-Germans, but rather by immigrants from another country, one south of the U.S. border, that boasts one of the world's largest deposits of copper, Chile.

At night, these nut carts are kept in a desolate warehouse on Manhattan's West Side. They are wheeled out by their owners before the morning rush hour to prized busy intersections. This morning, however, four of these carts were wheeled out at the extraordinarily early hour of 3 A.M. The streets were still dark, and almost quiet save for occasional taxis, the sound of a distant police siren, and the squeaky wheels of these nut carts.

The second odd thing about these four carts was that the men pushing them were not Chilean. This morning, they were manned by Europeans of Middle Eastern origin, all in this country on legitimate student visas, one of them down to only one course at Yale University. Each man was dressed in a heavy winter parka, their gloved hands wrapped around cold steel handles, pushing their carts forward. A closer inspection underneath those gloves would have revealed the blue edges of their fingernails.

They'd broken into the warehouse facility at midnight and selected these carts for their work today, which had nothing to do with roasting nuts. Instead, under each shiny copper pot, the men had lodged fifty pounds of dynamite along with twenty ounces of cobalt-60.

Before they parted ways, they extended their wishes for the blessings of Allah upon each other. Two of them rolled their carts in the direction of Wall Street, while the other two pushed up to Midtown.

By 3:30 A.M., the two men heading south reached their downtown destinations. One settled into position on Liberty Street, between Nassau and William Streets. He looked up at the tall empty buildings around him. For a brief moment, his thoughts traveled back to his poor neighborhood in Milan, where he could hear his mother shouting for him from the kitchen while she cooked the family meal in the traditional Egyptian way. But he had long ago said his good-byes to his family and made a martyr videotape that would be premiered across Islamist extremist Web sites later today. That would be his family's last picture of him, the one they would cry over in the days and years to come. Their only solace would be that their son had given his life in a worthy mission for Allah. Paradise awaited him.

The "gringo" locked the brake on his cart and looked around to see if anyone was walking in the streets. *No one.* The tall buildings on either side of him had round-the-clock guards.

On the south side of the street was the postmodern sixty-story glass tower housing the back-office processing facility of the largest bank in the country. More significantly, this was also the bank that was tangled up in more than half of all derivative transactions contracted by U.S. banks, equal to the country's money supply and seven times its GDP. Such market leadership numbers were not easily swallowed by the bank's internal risk managers, at least not without a hard gulp. Any way you measured it, WR Shipley & Co. was like a meatball of limited capital proportions drowning in the immense bowl of very tangled spaghetti of derivative contracts that overflowed and touched every facet of the world economy.

On the north side of the street stood the Federal Reserve Bank of New York, an imposing stone structure in the style of a Florentine Renaissance palace. It was the most important arm of the U.S.'s central banking system. Buying and selling more than $2 trillion of U.S. Treasury Securities on a daily basis and supervising the New York banking market, the Federal Reserve ensured the "safety, soundness and vitality of our economic and financial systems." At least, that was its goal on paper.

In the global economic crisis, the New York Fed had played a key role in emergency measures geared to restoring market confidence. That crisis had left it with expanded authority to oversee its district, but also woefully stretched when it came time to deal with that troubled landscape of banks addicted to the profits of dangerous concentrations of derivatives portfolios. Despite the passing of Washington's financial regulatory reform, there was still much to do to make those reforms a reality in the day-to-day marketplace.

It was precisely the derivatives exposure of WR Shipley & Co., a powder keg of $100 trillion, that kept the Fed's President awake at night. In fact, it had been the much smaller derivatives exposure of AIG, a mere $3 trillion in comparison, that had prompted the New York Fed to intervene to prevent a market hemorrhage. Simply put, the plotters of Operation Andalus saw eye to eye with the Fed on this. The massive portfolio of WR Shipley & Co. was an explosion waiting to happen.

So a detonation dispersing a radioactive cloud here in this spot today would not only unleash the destructive power of interwoven counterparty risk in the country's largest derivatives portfolio, but also cripple the entity best equipped to contain that destructive power, namely, the New York Fed.

Two guards stood just inside the ornate iron-gated entrance to the Federal Reserve Bank building waiting for the end of their night shift. There was a skeleton crew of evening personnel monitoring markets around the world, but they were in seclusion somewhere in the bowels of the building. The guards saw the cart rolling by and deemed it nothing unusual in the context of Manhattan streets, particularly at this corner. During any given week, everything from a coffee cart, a falafel stand, a fresh fruit vendor, and even a mobile U.S. Postal Service van would appear at this very spot.

One of the guards, a tall, wide man from Staten Island, noticed the cart from afar. He commented to the other guard, "Hey, Jack. Look at that poor slob. He don't know people around here ain't gonna eat no damn peanuts for breakfast. . . ."

His partner laughed in response. "Yeah, probably whatever country he comes from, that's what they do there. Jeez, peanuts for breakfast?! He'll figure it out when he ain't selling any of these before lunchtime. Watch, tomorrow he won't show up till eleven. Live and loin, right?"

JUST AROUND THE CORNER, the other cart had stopped at the intersection of Wall and Broad Streets. On one side of the intersection was the Federal Hall Building, best known as the location of George Washington's inaugural. The other side was far more important. It was the neoclassic building that housed the New York Stock Exchange, the largest stock exchange in the world in terms of dollars changing hands, making it the most important symbol of global capitalism. A detonation here today would further amplify the market psychosis caused by the failure of the single largest counterparty in the global derivatives market. And today, after more than two centuries of operations, the NYSE would be the target of a plot to hobble the U.S. economy executed by simple street vendors armed with shiny copper pots.

IN MIDTOWN, A THIRD OPERATIVE PUSHED his cart into position on Forty-sixth Street, midway between Park and Madison Avenues. He looked up at the imposing dark tower that was the global headquarters of WR Shipley & Co. Decades earlier, this had been the Union Carbide Building, but that company's deadly chemical disaster in Bhopal, India, had forced them to sell this prized location to this bank. And if all went as planned today for this little nut vendor, chemicals would again have a deadly impact on this building's tenant. *What goes around, comes around.*

A few blocks farther uptown, the Yale student, the "gringo" from Amsterdam, pushed his cart heading east. The streets in Midtown at this hour were equally desolate, the squeaky wheels of his cart reverberating between Midtown's postmodernist skyscrapers. He was careful about the time and stopped for a moment to look at his watch. 3:30 A.M. Only thirty minutes left before the end of this mission, he thought.

He struggled to push but his fingers were numb, a direct result of taking double the required dose of the vitamins. Addicted for weeks, he was barely managing to hold on to his sanity. Since last week, he'd suffered cluster headaches and had gone with no sleep for four days. Two weeks ago, his nails started turning blue around the edges and yesterday, the symptoms had progressed further to the point that his hands were stiff. Every step he took pushing the cart was excruciatingly painful.

He had only two blocks to go, but the joints in his legs were numb. He wondered if paralysis came next. Either from the lack of sleep or his elevated heartbeat, the young man's eyes twitched every few seconds. In the rarefied ambiance of a Yale lecture hall, he would definitely stand out, but on the streets of Manhattan, he could easily be mistaken for just another soul that had slipped through the holes of Medicaid and was in serious need of stronger meds.

As the "gringo" gritted his teeth against the pain, he welcomed finishing his life along with his mission. He finally saw the southern edge of St. Patrick's Cathedral. *Almost there.* He looked down the avenue. The traffic lights were turning from red to green in their timed choreography. His mind was mesmerized by their timed dance stretching down the avenue, and he stood there motionless in the middle of the intersection of Fifty-first Street and Fifth Avenue. His concentration on the lights took his mind off the aches and tremors of his weakening body.

Suddenly a car honked its horn; a speeding yellow taxi broke his trancelike state. The mission almost ended right there and then. Before he could move away, a police car slowed down as it passed by him. The officer made a short beep of his siren and spoke through the loudspeaker. "Move along now." *This one's not going* to be selling any coffee unless he gets out of the road, thought the officer as he saw the man push the cart slowly to the other side.

The Yale student gave a final push to the opposite side of the street. There he stopped and took a deep breath, trying to remember exactly where he was supposed to place the cart for the final detonation. Though his mind was cloudy, he knew there wasn't much time left.

AT THAT VERY MOMENT, a young operative with a full backpack hid behind trees and underbrush about a hundred yards away from the Gate of Andalus at the Alhambra in Granada. The local time was 9:30 A.M. and the city was up and alive everywhere with the bustle of a Monday morning. The Alhambra had opened its doors to visitors a half hour ago, but the tour groups focused their time on the main palaces as opposed to this nondescript tower on the south side of the complex. The young operative was neither nervous nor apprehensive. He was ready for his people to take back this magnificent structure that Boabdil, the last Caliph, had so long ago given up. The serum was doing its trick beautifully, in this case.

THE TWENTY-FIVE-YEAR-OLD CHEF, AN INDONESIAN MUSLIM, rolled a cart out of the galley of the *Hellespont Alhambra* laden with breakfast for the crew on the bridge. The Panamanian-registered, VLCC class, crude oil supertanker was making a routine run from the Gulf of Sidra to Europe, fully loaded with 300,000 deadweight tons of crude.

"Good morning, sirs," said the chef with a hint of deference to his superior officers. "I have all your favorites today." The chef was taking special care of the cloth-covered cart, not because of the bounty of breakfast items displayed but because of the backpack he had stuffed under it.

The chef stood on the bridge for a moment, looking beyond the 1,100-foot length of the massive tanker, out to the sea ahead. In the distance, he could make out the tip of the Mediterranean, ending at the Strait of Gibraltar. The promised land of Andalus, he thought. The end of his mission was at hand.

The captain broke the Indonesian's concentration by asking, "Hey, what happened to your fingernails?"

64

GIBRALTAR
JANUARY 24

A T EXACTLY 9:57 A.M. IN GRANADA and Gibraltar, and 3:57
A.M. in New York, seven flying insects, dragonflies,
began to hover overhead at specific locations: Liberty
and Wall Streets, St. Patrick's Cathedral, the Gate of
Andalus, the Gibraltar Government House, and the supertanker
Alhambra two miles offshore from Gibraltar. The relatively large
dragonflies fluttered approximately thirty feet off the ground, right
over the heads of the operatives. The seventh dragonfly hovered over
the square facing the Government House, but there was no operative there. It whirled around a few times, but did not find what it
was looking for today, the operative named Mustafa Moussab.
The dragonfly could not have processed the fact that the incinerated pieces of Mustafa already lay scattered across the sand dunes
on the other side of the Rock.

The dragonflies simultaneously dropped down ten feet, at
which point the operative at the Gate of Andalus spotted it. As he
got a closer look, he realized it wasn't a living insect. Instead, it
was a mechanical creation measuring about ten inches long with
small beady eyes. Probably somebody's toy, he thought. But why
here and why now? he wondered. Unbeknownst to the operative,
the mechanical dragonfly had a small camera lens in its belly that
was transmitting still images to a computer server, images that instantly made their way to the desktop of Murad the American in a
cave somewhere in that no-man's-land that spanned the border
between Pakistan and Afghanistan.

These mechanical dragonflies were in fact micro air vehicles,
MAVs, purchased on the black market from the Chinese military.

Murad and his men had been using these unmanned drones for surveillance purposes around their hideouts. Today, they were modified
for use as Murad's backup insurance policy; backup in case any
operative lost his nerve today, serum or no serum, and hesitated in
pressing the final detonation required for their missions.

The dragonfly MAVs' capabilities were limited to two important functions. First, they provided Murad with a bird's-eye view
of each of the target sites, and second, they could detonate explosives by remote radio signal. They were programmed to circle the
target locations overhead until their batteries ran out. Right now,
they had another twenty minutes of charge left.

As the dragonfly MAV made a perfect circle above, the Granada
operative looked around to see if anyone was controlling it nearby.
He checked his watch again. 9:58 A.M. He looked up. That toy is still
up there. Who's controlling it? he wondered with growing concern.

He stared up at it again. It was as if the MAVs beady eyes were
staring directly at him. And then the "toy" blinked. The eyes
turned into bright red lights and began to emit the MAV's short-
range radio signal in the same frequency as the detonation device
of the bomb below. Simultaneously, the eyes of each of the other
six dragonfly MAVs were also now lit. At exactly 9:59:01 A.M.
Granada and Gibraltar time, and 3:59:01 A.M. New York time, six
powerful bombs ripped through their enclosures and released lethal clouds of radioactive cobalt-60 into the morning air.

The operatives didn't have that last minute to think about pressing their own detonation buttons; Murad had done it for them a full
minute earlier than planned and the blasts immediately obliterated
each of the unsuspecting suicide bombers. Their lives on earth were
cut short by one more minute than had been agreed upon, but also
their rise to Seventh Heaven was hastened by that same minute.

IN GRANADA, THE SOUND of the explosion was heard from as far away
as the top of the Albayzín section across the valley from the Alhambra. Much closer, Michiko, the young, able, but harried tour guide
was leading her group of thirty Japanese senior citizens through
the Court of the Myrtles at the other end of the Alhambra. When
they heard the loud noise, they immediately ducked down and
screamed.

Michiko was the first to raise her head, and after a few moments, the rest followed suit. They slowly stood up in unison, realizing that whatever had made that sound was thankfully not in close proximity. They looked around and realized they had all survived intact. Then, they smelled smoke from the blast that now blew over the main part of the Alhambra. The sky was no longer a bright clear blue; instead a haze dulled the sheen of the morning. In their fashion, these thirty Japanese tourists, survivors of a nuclear attack on their own nation, whipped out their digital cameras and began to take pictures of each other with the backdrop of the haze covering the sky. Had their cameras been able to take pictures at a microscopic level, they would have seen that the real danger was far from over. The particles of cobalt-60 that traveled in that haze were settling in the ancient stones of the magnificent Alhambra Palace as well as the lungs of these thirty senior citizens.

At the other end of the compound, the Gate of Andalus was now a pile of rubble, over which was a clear path to enter the grounds of the Alhambra. What had remained purposely locked all those centuries since Boabdil's exit had been blown apart. Symbolically, the floodgates of renewed Muslim migration to the European continent were now open. And the southern Iberian Peninsula was destabilized, leaving further room for the Basques to reclaim their independence in the north from a soon-to-be-weakened central government in Madrid. *Finally.*

IN THE BAY OF GIBRALTAR, the staff aboard the HMY *Britannia III* was arranging china place settings for the dinner the Prince of Wales was hosting this evening for his cousin, Principe Felipe. One of those crew members happened to be looking up, staring mindlessly at the supertanker that was crossing the Strait. His daydreaming was interrupted by the massive explosion that first ignited at the bridge of that vessel and then lit the contents of its berth, which was followed by the sound of several plates crashing in the State dining room.

AT 10:04:01 A.M., A GIB military officer standing guard at the Government House was startled by something that hit his helmet. He ducked and put his rifle in an offensive position, ready to shoot.

He and his colleagues were already on edge because of the heightened security concerns drummed into them by the American forces. Then there was that false alarm caused by the car crash over the cliff earlier and now, just minutes ago, the sound of an explosion off the coast. His eyes quickly scanned around for anything signaling imminent danger. *Nothing.*

"What the bloody hell was that?" He looked at his colleague, who was also now crouched with his rifle pointed outward. Then he noticed it: lying on the ground in front of him was a toy in the shape of a dragonfly. One of its wings was broken, the part that had nipped his helmet. He picked it up, noticing that its eyes were just barely lit in red and then dimmed out completely. The batteries had run out. He held in his hands the most complete remaining evidence of Operation Andalus. He thought to himself, I'll take it home and see if I can fix it for my little boy.

At that moment, a rush of people stormed down the Government House steps. It was the American general followed by his staff. Then a corps of U.S. Naval officers followed in unison, forming a cocoon around the two Crown Princes and the Governor of Gibraltar. They were all headed to the safety of the USS *Churchill.*

Besides the flaming supertanker lighting up the Strait, General Owens received news from the Pentagon of several bombs in New York and one nearby in Granada. Without hesitation he gave immediate orders to evacuate the Sovereignty Summit. As he rushed from the building, the general devised his next steps of action. There wasn't time to analyze the data coming in right now. He just needed to get the delegations out of here. He shouted at his lieutenant, "Call Molares and get her back on the ship! *Now!*"

IN MIDTOWN MANHATTAN, THE SOUND of sirens came from every direction in search of the blast that had interrupted the early morning desolation. Two levels of windows of WR Shipley & Co.'s headquarters facing Forty-sixth Street were blown out. Building security sprinted over from the other side of the building and now stood at the site of the explosion, taking in deep breaths of cobalt-60-infused air. While on the surface the damage looked manageable, it was quite unlikely that Hannah Merton would be making any calls from her corner office on the ninth floor today.

A few blocks farther north, St. Patrick's Cathedral lay intact except for the front left spire, which lay broken across Fifth Avenue blocking the police cars that were racing to the scene. The explosion had blown open one the Cathedral's front doors and particle dust floated in, permeating the stone structure from the inside. In short minutes, the contaminated air would travel through the front of the Cathedral to the attached Cardinal's residence.

Guests from the New York Palace Hotel, one block away, were milling about in front of the Cathedral. They had left the relative safety of their rooms, worried that staying inside the hotel presented further danger, when in fact the air they were breathing into their lungs would put every one of them on the list of eventual fatalities from Operation Andalus.

ON WALL STREET, THE BRASS DOORS of the New York Stock Exchange were part of the rubble now. A dust cloud filled the air above the bloodied, lifeless bodies of the two guards. Cobalt-60 particles attached themselves to the microscopic holes and crevices of the building's stonework, which soaked in the radioactive content like a damp sponge.

Around the corner, the ornate gated entrance of the New York Fed lay in ruins. The Federal guards who had noticed the nut cart just before it exploded would no longer be on guard, anywhere. Across the street, the bank building's structure was relatively unscathed, except for the shattered windows of the bottom three floors. The street below was strewn with glass shards, along with the shredded body parts of the man who had rolled the nut cart here this morning.

It was through those gaping wounds of the bank building's windows that the cobalt-60 particles traveled, blown in by the strong downtown breezes, and there the dust seeped into the breathing apparatus of the building. The air-conditioning system of the building became a highly efficient delivery system for the radioactive particles. Within thirty minutes from the time of the explosion, the entire building was contaminated. The back-office operations center of WR Shipley & Co. would be inaccessible for the 5.26 years of cobalt-60's half life. That is, unless CEO Hannah Merton instituted a new dress code for her bankers consisting of corporate-blue hazmat suits with, of course, the bank's distinctive logo embroidered on the upper right-hand breast pocket.

65

⊸┽╋┾⊷

TODAY, THE PRESIDENT OF the United States got a break. The wake-up call in the darkness didn't arrive until 4:30 A.M.

"What is it?" The President's voice was groggy and the First Lady was drowsing next to him.

The National Security Advisor spoke in rapid-fire, his voice tinged with a foreign accent. The advisor's car had left his home in Vienna, Virginia, ten minutes ago and was now crossing the Arlington Memorial Bridge at 75 mph. He could see the illuminated Lincoln Memorial approaching quickly ahead of them and the Jefferson Memorial passing on his right.

"Mr. President, we have reports of four explosions that hit New York City twenty minutes ago. We've also heard from General Owens about two explosions in Spain, plus they're investigating another one that may have occurred in Gibraltar earlier this morning. The Sovereignty Summit wasn't hit, but in any event, General Owens took the precaution of escorting Prince Charles, Prince Felipe, and the Governor of Gibraltar to the safety of the USS *Churchill*."

"Damn! You people were supposed to keep a lid on this stuff. You managed to do that in San Francisco! So what the hell happened here?!" The President had wanted above all else to keep a pristine record of zero security breaches on U.S. soil. Now that goal was out the window. The best that his Administration could hope for was to contain the fallout.

By now, the National Security Advisor was used to the President's outbursts when the cameras weren't on him. "I called a meeting of

the National Security Council at the White House at four forty-
five a.m. My driver tells me we should be there in five minutes."

"Good. Make sure you get General Owens up on the screen, too."

"Yes, will do. Thank you, Mr. President." He made a mental
note to keep an eye on the political rise of this General Owens.

THE EIGHT REGULAR MEMBERS of the National Security Council crowded
around the relatively small conference table that was the epicenter
of the White House Situation Room, the "Sit Room," as the regu-
lars referred to it. On the right sat the Vice President and the Secretaries of State, Treasury, and Defense. Facing them on the left
were the National Security Advisor, the Chairman of the Joint
Chiefs of Staff, the Director of National Intelligence, and the President's Chief of Staff. For security purposes, they had each deposited their cell phones and BlackBerries at the lead-lined cabinet in
the reception area. The head of the table was reserved for the
President, who was at that moment kissing his wife and children
good-bye before they were whisked away to the safety of an undisclosed location. While there were no reports of imminent attacks
in D.C., this was standard operating procedure adopted after 9/11.

The walls of the relatively small conference room were covered
in a muted fabric to absorb noise, and adorned simply with six
flat-screen monitors, the largest opposite the wall where the President sat. Two small screens indicated the type of meeting being
held. Today, it read simply in white letters on a dark background,
TOP SECRET.

Everyone stood as the President walked in. "Gentlemen, ladies,
let's get down to business." The President looked stern, knowing
this would be a defining moment for his Administration and would
also shift that inevitable Presidential aging process into high gear.

The National Security Advisor spoke first. "Four explosions
went off in Manhattan at exactly 3:59:01 A.M. this morning: two
in downtown Wall Street, one outside the New York Stock Exchange, and the other outside the New York Fed, which also caused
damage to a WR Shipley & Co. building across the street. A third
bomb exploded in front of St. Patrick's Cathedral, causing some
damage to the structure, and the fourth, at the bottom of WR Ship-

ley's headquarters on Forty-sixth and Park. Two bombs also went off in Spain: one in Granada and the other off the coast of Gibraltar. They all went off at the same time. They are definitely related."

"Who's claiming credit?"

"No one's surfaced yet, sir, but we're scanning the usual sites."

"Give me the casualties."

"So far, we know of the four guards at the NYSE and the New York Fed and, of course, the six suicide bombers."

"Fortunately, the New York bombs went off in the middle of the night and the one in Spain was in a desolate part of the city. The one off the coast was on a crude oil supertanker. We're not sure of the environmental impact yet."

"What are the financial implications?" The President looked at the Treasury Secretary, his third since taking office. The Administration had spent most of its time in office trying to get the economy back on track. Like a patient after successful major surgery, the economy was in early recovery, but still weak and wobbly on its feet. The prognosis was good, but the patient needed more time to fully recover and these bombings were like a second coronary, this time potentially fatal.

"Uhm, well. Too early to tell the full impact. Tokyo was closed just before this happened, but in after-hours trading we're seeing weakness in the dollar and a rise in commodities. Oil is breaking one hundred dollars a barrel. Again. If it was terrorism on a grand scale, I'd expect that to continue going up. Markets in Europe opened down this morning. They're digesting the news. As soon as we're done here, I'll be getting on the phone with my G-7 counterparts. I'm worried about their economic nationalism springing up again. If this story is isolated to what we know now, I think we can manage the spin. However, we should not be surprised to see big swings again when our markets open in a few hours."

"Mr. Secretary, with all due respect, what the hell do you mean 'when our markets open'? How the hell are 'markets going to open' when they fucking bombed the damn entrance to it!!" The screen on the left showed the live feed from CNN in front of the New York Stock Exchange.

"Yes, I understand that, Mr. President, but the NYSE has

contingency plans for a backup trading floor in New Jersey. It's something they put in place after 9/11. It's never been tested live before, so we expect that there will be some hiccups. The best thing we can do to alleviate market concerns is to deliver information to people as soon as possible. Dribs and drabs of rumors will create more panic in the market." The Treasury Secretary was trying to deflect some of the focus of the discussion toward the Defense and Intelligence side of the table.

"Okay, but what about the Fed? Have you spoken to them?"

"I managed to get a hold of the New York Fed President just before this meeting. Skeleton staff was on hand and they're all safe. The street's blocked off, and there's a heavy police presence down there trying to assess the full damage. I understand there's a military unit down there as well. From the looks of it, the entrance was the focal point of damage, though."

"What do we have up in the air right now?"

All eyes turned to the Chairwoman of the Joint Chiefs of Staff, General Andrea Schwarz, the ultimate military authority in the country just below the Commander-in-Chief.

"Air patrol didn't witness any unusual air traffic activity before, during, or after the attacks. Satellites are telling us the same thing. We're definitely not facing a 9/11 case here; no flying bombs, these were pure land-based attacks. Still, we've grounded non-military flights, and our ground and air resources are on high alert, as per your orders. Given the time of night, it was easier to do than last time." For the second time in recent history, the air space above the continental U.S. was empty of any civilian air traffic.

"I just spent an entire week hitting every news channel morning, noon, and night, bragging about our crack intelligence that broke up the San Francisco plot. So now, how is it in God's name that all this slipped through our so-called new and improved intelligence apparatus? I'm sitting in this chair because I campaigned on criticizing the previous administration's slipshod intelligence. What the hell do you propose I tell the American people now!?"

The President looked around the room, but there weren't any takers. The leaders of the highest echelons of the U.S. government just averted their eyes downward and shuffled their papers.

"Don't everybody jump in all at once now! What the hell are we paying you for?!"

Finally, the Director of National Intelligence spoke up. Since his title actually had the word *intelligence* in it, he had no choice. "There are several important points. First of all, we need time to assess who was responsible for this. Right now, all we have are the mangled body parts of the suicide bombers, and as we speak, these are being transported back here for autopsies and analysis. We'll get the Spaniards to cooperate and send us that body in Granada, or whatever is left of it—"

"If I may, Director?" It was General Owens on-screen with the backdrop of the small conference room of the USS *Churchill*.

"Certainly, General."

"We've been tracking two threats from our end—"

"Sorry to interrupt, General. . . ." The President's tone seemingly indicated more respect for Owens than for most of the other subordinates gathered in the room. "How are the Princes doing on board?"

"Actually, we've already flown them out. They're both on their way home to Madrid and London. With all our U.S. flags flying and all, I thought it best to take them off this ship in case these bombings were being directed at American installations. If anything happens to them at this point, it'll be in the hands of their countries' respective intelligence arms and governments."

"Excellent tactical thinking, General Owens." The President was pleased to see that *someone* was finally doing what they were paid to do: think. "So, now tell me about those threats, General."

"Mr. President, there may have been another bombing intended for Gibraltar. . . ."

"What do you mean?" The President squinted his eyes, bracing for news of yet another bombing.

"I have Ms. Molares here from the DIA who went over to the site earlier to investigate. Ms. Molares, please relay your findings to the President."

Kate took one very deep breath and focused her thoughts. Just a few years ago, she was selling derivative contracts to corporate clients and now she was about to brief the most powerful person in the world. She swallowed hard to clear her throat, and thought, Stay away from that Nebibi angle for the moment.

"One hour before all the other bombings, there was a car crash on the other side of Gibraltar. The local police are classifying this as an unfortunate, but normal, car crash off the cliff of the Rock. However, we have our doubts given the extent of the damage to the vehicle. Even with a full tank of gas, the car could not have sustained that level of damage. We plan on investigating this car crash as a possible related, seventh bombing."

"No survivors, I take it?"

"No, sir." She gulped, thinking of those cuff links hidden in her pocket. "We're collecting fragments of a license plate to see if we can trace the owner of the car."

General Owens interjected, "If that seventh bombing had detonated successfully, who knows what kind of damage we would have sustained given the senior representatives attending the Summit. Today, we'd potentially be explaining the deaths of the Crown Princes of two strong allies."

The President's wiry Chief of Staff, ever the politico hound and master spinner, grabbed on to a little nugget for today's news cycle. He pictured the headline: "Bombing Averted. Princes Saved." He quickly wrote that down on the legal pad in front of him, his writing captured for historical posterity by the Sit Room's overhead cameras, recording this meeting from above.

Kate's thoughts turned to Nebibi's bag, which had been found on the beach. It looked like he saved the day, again. This time, though, he may have sacrificed himself in the process. No answer on his cell phone, and given what was happening in Manhattan, she didn't think she'd be able to get ahold of anyone at his office today.

The general moved on to the second threat. "The other aspect that we think is related to all of this, and which will have significant future ramifications, is something called *T. gondii prime*."

Under the safety net of the general's briefing, the National Security Advisor quickly interjected his two cents. "It was part of my daily intelligence assessment a few weeks ago. . . ." He looked over at the President for some nod of approval. He didn't receive any, which made him think, Is this general gunning for my job?

"Yes, I remember, the story about those crazy cats." The President's first reaction when he was briefed about the cats was laughter, but now no one was laughing. Kate straightened up in her chair.

Her story about crazy cats heard over *mojitos* in Havana was now top-of-mind for the President of the United States.

The general continued. "If biopsies turn up traces of *T. gondii,* then these bombings are part of a larger plot and will be the tipping point for unprecedented terrorist attacks in the future." He stopped there, but he pictured the U.S. starting to resemble places like Bagdad, outside the Green Zone, and Islamabad.

"You don't paint a pretty picture, General. So what do you suggest I tell the American people?"

"In my opinion, the best approach is a direct and frank one. Unfortunately, while our country's resources remained focused on Afghanistan and bolstering our economy, our true foes, those looking for opportunities to perpetrate subversive acts against our government and our way of life, have been working on new and creative ways in which to attack us. Sir, with all due respect, it's time to give the American people the truth."

A soon as the general finished his eloquent advice to the President, the cameras above recorded the Vice President writing down the name General Owens. The Vice President, who never furrowed his Botoxed brow but always looked behind his back, saw potentially stiff competition for the ear of the young President coming from a certain general, an Eisenhower in the making. Below the general's name, the Vice President wrote a reminder note, now also recorded for history: Get *Dossier*. It seemed that, with rare exception, all the President's men, and women, were mostly focused on saving their hides.

A military analyst, who had been in the communications booth right outside the Sit Room, walked in and slipped General Schwarz a note with a time stamp of 5:18 A.M. "We have a new development. They're putting Lieutenant Colonel Favata onscreen for us now." All eyes in the room turned to the screen on the left. The lieutenant colonel was transmitting via his laptop in a military vehicle, wearing a white hazmat suit. Outside his van, there was the sound of heavy commotion, as would be expected at a bomb site.

"You have all our attention, proceed."

Because of the news he had to deliver, Lieutenant Colonel Favata had no room to be intimated by the audience listening to his briefing. "We have a situation down here. Our van is parked outside the

New York Fed." Favata spoke in short breaths, having just jumped into the van to escape the growing panic on the street. "We just finished our air analysis of the area and found strong traces of cobalt-60. We wanted to be sure, so we performed the analysis twice. We also checked down by the Wall Street bomb and found the exact same thing. I sent a team to look at St. Patrick's Cathedral. We're dealing with fallout from a radioactive dispersion device. We need to evacuate this area right away and quarantine everybody down here." No one in the Sit Room needed any explanation about cobalt-60 or what the implications were.

On the right-hand screen, CNN was broadcasting the scene outside the NYSE. Armed military personnel in hazmat suits were directing civilians into large transport trucks, including CNBC's Dylan Ratigan, who by now had complete panic in his eyes as he reported the news about the dirty bombs that had detonated in Manhattan. He was no longer just reporting a story. He was the story.

"Shit! So much for containing the goddamn fallout on this!" The President's voice was way past its normal cool demeanor.

66

⟨+♦+⟩

GREENWICH, CONNECTICUT
JANUARY 24

ANNAH MERTON RUSHED OUT of her house into the black car
waiting in the driveway of her Greenwich McMansion
on Lake Avenue. She had her briefcase in one hand and
her cell phone held up to her ear in the other. "Hold on,
I'm getting in the car right now. Call me right back on the car
phone." Hannah slammed the door and barked at the driver. "Go!"
She'd been woken up at 4:30 A.M. by the head of bank security
about explosions at their Manhattan locations. And from then on,
the news just got progressively worse.

When the phone rang in the backseat, she took the call on speakerphone and raised the partition for privacy. "Hello, hello! Okay
run through that again." She was speaking with Suresh Narayan,
head of the bank's European operations. She pulled out the black
folder from her briefcase. Stealth Report from last Friday, too
early for today's version, she noted.

"I'm standing in the London trading room." There was a lot of
background noise on Suresh's end. "The markets are going haywire
here and the traders can't keep up with the volatility. The dollar's
being dumped all across Europe. I haven't seen it this low since . . .
I can't even remember, Hannah. Not even with the great recession
was it this low. It's at $1.90 to the Euro right now. No, make that
$2.00! Commodities are going through the roof. People are look-
ing for something, anything, real to hold on to. Gold is hitting the
$1,500 mark. Oil's up to $115 already and nothing is standing in
the way of it going higher. On top of that, there's this biased senti-
ment going around in the equities markets. Everybody's looking at
which European corporates have business exposures in the States.

It's like anything that even smells of U.S. exposure is bloody nuclear. It's far worse than 2008! Like somebody yelled 'fire' and everybody's headed to the exit doors as fast as possible, trampling over bodies. Our portfolios here and in Frankfurt are crapping down the toilet." This time, European markets weren't going to wait excruciating weeks for bad news to trickle out from the U.S. The mass exodus would be swift and, therefore, much more damaging.

"Fuck, fuck, fuck!!" *The fucking shit is hitting the fucking fan. What the hell are we supposed to do now!?* Hannah stared at the last page of the Stealth Report. It was causing a searing pain in her temples and her blood pressure to spike with every passing minute, and no amount of medicine was going to get it down now. Her cell phone rang. "Hold the line, Suresh. I need to take this call." She put him on mute and took the incoming call. "Hello . . ."

"Hannah?" It was Damion James, her old boss, the former CEO of her bank, her mentor, and now the Treasury Secretary.

"Damion, I'm here. I'm on my way to check out the damage at our offices. Europe's going crazy with this news of the bombs—"

"You can't go there, Hannah."

"What do you mean? You know I have to go check on things. Got to make sure we can open those facilities today. You know, it's where we moved our trading floor back-office after you left. It was meant to be temporary but with the merger task force and all, we've had a lot of front-office issues to deal with—"

"Damn," the Treasury Secretary muttered, *not* comforted in knowing that the bank's processing capability was crippled. As the bank's former CEO, three-quarters of his net worth was tied up in WR Shipley & Co. stock, and since joining the Administration, those holdings were held in a blind trust that he couldn't access. Given the news, he wasn't sure he wanted to look at his next financial statement without a stiff drink in his belly and another one in his hand.

"What? What's wrong? As far as I've heard, a couple of windows were blown out on our side of the street. We should be up and running by nine o'clock." She looked at her watch. 5:25 A.M. Yeah, more than enough time, three and a half hours to get ourselves back online, she calculated.

"Hannah, I just got out of a briefing with the President. It wasn't a simple bomb down there. It was an RDD—"

"A what?!?"

"An RDD, a radiological dispersion device. A dirty bomb. Everything south of 125th Street has been cordoned off by the military. It's gonna be years before anybody does any business there again. . . ."

Hannah's left hand tightened in a spasm, crumbling up the last page of the Stealth Report. In that instant, Hannah Merton, the rough and tumble woman who had built the market's tallest derivatives house of cards, finally broke the ultimate glass ceiling. The years of stress and lack of exercise on her way to the top had accumulated on her just like any other one of her *male* colleagues. This latest piece of news, which would no doubt cause that house of cards to burn to a crisp and then tumble, was the last straw. Her body tensed one last time in the spasm of a hemorrhagic stroke. Within a minute, all life left the body of Hannah Merton, making the top spot on *Fortune*'s list of the "50 Most Powerful Women in Business" once again available for contention.

The Treasury Secretary kept talking for another few moments, not realizing that Hannah had moved on, so to speak. He was on a tight schedule, calling his counterparts around the world. The Finance Minister of Spain was on line one, the Head of the European Central Bank was on line two, and the Chancellor of the Exchequer had already called twice. He finally hung up the line with Hannah, deciding to try to calm waters elsewhere.

The speakerphone was still engaged in mute, but the noise of Suresh shouting at his traders could still be heard through the loudspeaker in the backseat.

"Hannah! Hannah! Are you still there? Pick up! Bloomberg's reporting that the bomb on Wall Street was radioactive! All downtown is off-limits to anyone but the military. Reuters is calling it a state of siege in Manhattan." Suresh's voice was now pleading. "Hannah! Listen, we've got to do something. The dollar is continuing to slide, it's in a free fall. Japan, Germany, and China. They're all dumping it and moving into euros. Spreads on credit default swaps are widening like crazy and quotes for our bank's risk are the ones going up the fastest. The market knows that two of those bombs hit us. Rumors are flying around that you were caught in the blast. We're up to one thousand basis points already. Listen, we need to figure out how to calm our counterparties down. This is getting way out of hand. Hannah, say something!!"

If Hannah were still alive, none of what Suresh was describing in his increasingly panicked tone would have come as a surprise. Her trusted lieutenants, the brain trust, had already modeled this scenario for her. They called it the "Doomsday Scenario," one that could never happen because it required too many independent variables to converge. Now, last Friday's Doomsday Scenario, which lay crumbled on the backseat next to Hannah's contorted body, foretold the impossible events of today in stark black Arial font, 10 point, on white bond paper:

1.   Terrorist attack on the bank's premises
2.   Unprecedented fall of the dollar
3.   A crippling of equity markets
4.   Failure of one of the market's primary derivatives dealers

The bottom of the page of the Doomsday Scenario always showed a loss of the bank's entire capital base. But as Hannah's brain trust always told her, that was okay because it simply could *never* happen. It was just statistically impossible. That's what their models said. And many a night until her death, she had lulled herself to sleep with that thought; that it could never happen.

The Doomsday Scenario had become so real in European markets that by the time traders, investment bankers, and deposit holders in New York awoke, Hannah's bank, the country's largest institution just a few years shy of its second century of successful operations, was well on its way to becoming essentially broke with nowhere to turn. And yes, it was "too big to fail," but unfortunately, it was also *too big to save.*

The bank had nowhere to turn because the U.S. government's reserve of capital, political or otherwise, wasn't enough to go around to save everybody. And ever since, Administration officials had warned those institutions that had managed to remain on their feet that they needed to get their risky houses in financial order. The next default couldn't be treated with such kid gloves because the bailout fund just wasn't big enough to make everybody whole. Protectionism and populism were the dominant themes in Washington and Main Street, and officials would find it politically unfeasible to use taxpayer money to prop up irresponsible banking houses, not to mention safeguard the personal portfolio of the highest-ranking Treasury official.

As the sun rose later that morning in Manhattan to the eerie scenes of military vehicles rolling down Wall Street, financial markets began to digest the fact that the "impossible" had indeed happened. With lightning speed, every risk model on Wall Street adjusted itself, prompting further hemorrhaging from the sores first opened by WR Shipley & Co. The market had already been trained by the previous crisis. This time nobody waited around for things to get better or for governments to intervene. They all knew that things could get worse, much worse, very quickly. It was every man for himself; the corrosive power of capitalism at work in hyper-speed.

Every passing minute of market turmoil caused those "perfect" Wall Street computer models to automatically escalate their firm's counterparty margin requirements. Virtual walls of escalated capital requirements were going up at each institution, trying to block further trading with other firms. And those capital requirements rose at an exponentially faster rate when it came to the banks that held the largest derivatives portfolios, led by Hannah's bank.

As rumors bounced from BlackBerries onto cable news networks, it was impossible for traders to decipher fact from fiction, causing a market stampede of withdrawals and redemptions. Everyone scrambled for the last drops of liquidity.

It no longer mattered whether or not WR Shipley & Co. had a backup operations center in New Jersey or could access limited special assistance. The market's perceptions of counterparty risk had moved very quickly beyond that, and the loss of that bank's very vital CEO in those early hours of the crisis had the bank's brain trust on Park Avenue scurrying to contain the ultimate financial public relations disaster.

And it didn't stop there; over the next twenty-four hours, banks inflicted further wounds on each other through their interbank lending, which became a deadly efficient contagion channel that spread the liquidity problems of derivatives-dealing banks to the broader financial system. And before long, every citizen would feel the impact of markets playing out the financial equivalent of something much feared in the world of nuclear weaponry: *mutually assured destruction.*

"YOU'VE GOT TO LOOK AT the deal more seriously. If WR Shipley goes under, we all go under." Treasury Secretary James was trying to force a bargain-basement sale of the nation's largest bank to Matthew Kelly, the CEO of National City Bank, the nation's *second*-largest bank.

"Damion, I just don't think this is a good deal for my shareholders. I'm focused on holding on to our own bank and the last thing I need is the headache of a merger right now." As he said this, Matthew's eyes focused on the split screen in front of him. One side showed the second-by-second assaults by short sellers on his bank's share price, and the other showed their dwindling cash levels.

"Listen, Matt, I understand, we both barely got through the last crisis in one piece. We saw a lot of things we never expected, but that was all an unfortunate confluence of market events. This time, someone is trying to make this happen on purpose. They're trying to kill our economy and we can't let them get away with it." Damion James also looked on-screen at the second-by-second fall in *his* share price, the U.S. dollar.

"Okay, okay, I just don't want to be painted like the enemy when all of this is over. I'll have my guys start looking at Hannah's books. Given their size, though, it'll take a few days. . . ." Matthew Kelly said this, knowing full well that in a few days, his bank might be the next one needing a white knight to save *them* from bankruptcy.

"We don't have weeks or even days. We've got to get a deal together before markets close today." Damion was seeing privileged data from the Fed that told him things could deteriorate even further than what those market rumors were touting. And yes, they had an agreed system for the orderly bankruptcy of large institutions, but not the majority of them all at once.

"There's no fucking way I can go along with that!" Matthew was getting suspicious that the Treasury Secretary was going to extraordinary measures to preferentially save the hide of his former bank.

"Besides, Hannah made her bed and it cost her her life *and* legacy. Now, I'm not about to go tell *The Wall Street Journal* this, but we both know full well that she thought she could get away with ignoring regs by shifting their derivatives portfolio to Asia. And that's where she had the freedom to keep betting the bank in that casino. Well, her luck finally ran out, didn't it? And now who knows what other toxic shit is hiding in that balance sheet of theirs? Are *you, Mr. Secretary,* gonna cover any potential losses for my shareholders?"

Damion James mulled that last question in silence on the other end of the line. He knew he didn't have the political capital to guarantee the transaction.

Hearing no response, Matthew said, "Just like I thought. You want me to be left holding the bag. Well that is just fuckin' not going to work! You'll have to find another stooge for that transaction. I suggest you ring up your friends in Asia." Matthew didn't wait for a response this time. He just slammed the phone down.

Despite the Treasury Secretary's best efforts, there was no time for shotgun weddings for failing institutions. Potential grooms were falling right and left, while anxious brides were left waiting at the altar with their withering bouquets of toxic balance sheets.

67

SOMEWHERE OVER NOVA SCOTIA
JANUARY 24

SAM COLDSMITH FELT REFRESHED after his deep slumber in the master cabin of the *Gold Shark Swimming in Air*. On these transatlantic flights, the captain tended to take longer routes in an effort to avoid turbulent winds. On Sam's aircraft, speed was never as important as a smooth ride to allow for uninterrupted sleep. He grabbed the remote from the nightstand and opened the shades, revealing the crystal blue skies. As usual, the flight attendant had left a glass of fresh juice for Sam's refreshment when he woke up. He held it up, studying its color. Evidently, in Gibraltar, the staff had picked up a crate of Spanish blood oranges, his favorite. He sat up in his king-sized bed, in his extra large silk pajamas, and sipped his freshly squeezed blood orange juice.

"Uhmm." As he savored the juice's natural sugars, Sam remembered that as of last Friday, his fund was now 49 percent smaller, but far, far richer in cash holdings. Before the week was out, when there was more time, he'd arrange for the fund to formally buy him out of his full personal stake. But for now, he was happy to see the cash sitting on the fund's balance sheet.

Sam was looking forward to an interview with *The Wall Street Journal* later this morning and to showing up at CNBC this afternoon to chat with his old friend Maria Bartiromo about the deal. With or without the jolt of extra sugar in his veins, Sam felt like he was on top of the world and riding a strong wave of good luck and good timing. At that very moment, he felt safe, secure, and satisfied. For now, all he wondered about was what the chef was preparing him for breakfast.

Sam looked at the time. 6:30 A.M. It was time for him to get dressed and join the rest of the passengers for a full-fledged breakfast before landing back home. He got out of bed and headed to the shower. His left foot was about to step into the shower when a voice came over the intercom in the bathroom. "Mr. Coldsmith, I think you'd better come out here." It was the captain speaking.

Sam yelled back, "I can't right now, I'm in the shower!" He was irritated to be interrupted in his peaceful process of awakening.

"Sir, we think you really need to come out here. I'm afraid it can't wait."

Sam dried off his foot and slipped into his thick Egyptian cotton robe. In his bath slippers, he walked into the main cabin, picking up a fresh glass of juice along the way. The rest of the passengers were sitting in the boardroom of the plane, their eyes glued to a flat-panel TV showing the mayhem of military vehicles invading Wall Street. Sam glanced at it for a second and thought it was some TV show.

"What's this all about?" he grumbled.

Tomás pointed at the screen. "Sam, that's happening right now on Wall Street."

"What!? What happened? Did they fly planes down there again?"

"No, Sam. Two radioactive bombs exploded there earlier this morning, plus two in Midtown. Manhattan is under military quarantine now. Nobody can get in or out of the island. Plus, there were bombs in Gibraltar and Granada, too." Inside, Tomás was frantic about Kate but had no way to get in touch with her.

"Are you fucking kidding me? What happened in Europe? What are markets doing?"

Tomás turned and said, "They reacted in the worst possible way, Sam. WR Shipley & Co. was the first to go, followed by Citi and Goldman. I'm sure our friends at Treasury and the Fed are scrambling to try to patch some deal together to salvage things, but I don't think there'll be any banks left in the top ten to negotiate with."

Sam didn't need to ask any more questions. He didn't need a Stealth Report or a Doomsday Scenario to explain it to him. He knew full well what this all meant for him, for his fund, for his estate, and for his sharks, both the ones that swam and the one that flew. If WR Shipley was tanking, his remaining 51 percent of Royal Lane Advisors was worthless many times over when it was tallied against what he would have to pay out on all those derivative bets he'd made. He threw his glass, smashing it against the screen, and dropped to his knees, pounding his fists on the floor of his prized flying shark.

Bartiromo would have a thousand stories like this one in the coming days, weeks, and months. The individuals and institutions would change, but the byline blazoned across the TV screen would become a permanent addition: "The Death of Capitalism."

AT 8:30 A.M., VIDEOS BEGAN to surface on the Internet claiming credit for the bombings. What dumbfounded U.S. and European intelligence analysts was the fact that these videos indicated collusion between the likes of al-Qaeda and the Basque Nationalists. And what worried them going forward were the further linkages that could be made between the other forty-two groups that the U.S. designated as Foreign Terrorist Organizations, and most critically, which one of those had supplies of *T. gondii prime*.

AT 9:00 A.M. EST, the President of the United States stopped making phone calls to foreign leaders for just enough time to make an address to the nation regarding the radioactive explosions in Manhattan. There was no way of putting a positive spin on the news from Air Force One.

"My fellow Americans, early this morning, New York City suffered a series of radiological terrorist attacks of unprecedented proportions. Effective six a.m. this morning, I authorized the declaration of a state of military emergency in the borough of Manhattan. U.S. Army forces have established a blockade at 125th Street and the navy has cordoned water access around the island. Until further notice, there will be no incoming or outgoing traffic to Manhattan unless authorized by me. The National Guard will perform an orderly transition with civilian police forces until we can safely assess the extent of radioactive fallout."

The President continued, and the news wasn't getting any rosier or definitive. "Our economy is now suffering a very significant fallout from these terrorist actions and our economic national interests are being compromised with each sale of the U.S. dollar in foreign markets. The Treasury Secretary, the Chairman of the Federal Reserve Bank, the Secretary of State, and I are speaking with global leaders to stem the tide of the current economic free fall. I have ordered that U.S. financial markets remain closed until we are able to safely assess the damage to our economy. My Administration will not rest until we find and hold accountable those who are behind these evil acts. Thank you and God bless America."

The President didn't manage to answer the pressing question on the minds of Americans and countries around the world: Could the U.S. survive this second blow? The reason it wasn't answered was that every economic model being run at Treasury and the IMF right now was coming up heavy on the red ink. Average citizens on Main Street didn't need those models. They knew enough of economics and finance at this point to understand that what they were facing was far worse than 2008. This was 2008 *plus* 9/11, a real-life apocalyptic horror movie, all wrapped up in a single day.

And so, despite all the good intentions on Inauguration Day, this President's time in office, just like the last, would be consumed by reacting to a terrorist event. Except now, the arsenal available to the Administration's policy makers would not include the power of the mighty dollar to help get its citizens through this dark new age.

WHILE THE U.S. TREASURY SECRETARY nervously watched the reserve currency figures in those first days and weeks following the attacks, most others in the market were instead focused on the immediate loss of the final vestiges of a consumer society. Everyone except for one lone economist-cum-novelist and financial journalist, sitting on his ranch in Northern California, who had presaged the profound damage that the U.S. economy would suffer in what he called The Great Crash.

ERDMAN'S WORLD
THE GREAT CRASH
Commentary: The Last Days of the All-Powerful Dollar

By Paul Erdman, MarketWatch
Last update: 12:37 p.m. EDT January 27

HEALDSBURG, Calif. (MarketWatch)—The U.S. and its allies are working their way through another terrorist attack on our soil and fortunately, the loss of life has been minimal. Wall Street is still blocked from transacting any business, the folks at the Defense Department are not letting us in on when we can get back to trading at the actual NYSE and it looks like the derivatives market has finally, and hopefully forever, imploded on itself. In the meantime, there's another trend we should keep an eye on. Depending on which way it goes, it may prove to be the most long-lasting effect on this country and the world, far longer than the half-life of radioactive dust.

The IMF publishes a quarterly report, the Currency Composition of Official Foreign Exchange Reserves—the COFER as they call it down there at Washington headquarters, which compares the foreign currency holdings of the world's governments.

For the past six straight decades, world governments stockpiled dollars to the tune of 60% of their foreign currency holdings because of the strength and stability of our economy. This "reserve status" meant that the dollar was constantly in demand, regardless of the real underlying strength of our economy. And this strength of our currency allowed Uncle Sam to finance massive trade and budget deficits, even through the 2008 crisis.

But the growth of the budget deficit in the past decade created unparalleled risk. That combined with the continued dumping of the dollar could lead to a complete currency collapse, which will very quickly plunge the world's largest economy into depression. And on the other side of that, we're going to need a brand-new New Deal, not like FDR's but the kind imposed by the IMF on emerging markets like Argentina and Brazil in the old days.

So the recent drop of the dollar in global exchanges is only the tip of the iceberg. My old Swiss banking friends at the Bank for International Settlements in Basel tell me to watch that COFER report in the coming months. I can guarantee you that our Treasury

Secretary is, and he may not be too happy with what he'll find— *the last days of the dollar as the global reserve currency, which will permanently seal the coffin on our country's dominance of the global economy.*

Economist and author Paul Erdman is a MarketWatch columnist.

THE COMING MONTHS DID SEE the drop in foreign governments' holdings of dollars, exactly as predicted by Erdman, from 60 percent down to a dramatic 20 percent. The euro was further strengthened when OPEC took the unprecedented move of supporting the joint proposal of Venezuela and Iran to use that currency, instead of the dollar, as the quoting currency for the international price of oil. On top of which, the rise in crude prices provided a very needed lifeline for those country's leaders.

With the ascendancy of other global currencies, led by the euro, came a new wave of immigration into the U.S. But this wave was not coming in the cramped steerage of large steamers across the Atlantic, or swimming across the southwest border, or washing up in rafts on the shores of Miami. No, this wave jetted in, some in their private planes, from places like Jiddah, Tokyo, Amsterdam, Mumbai, Singapore, Shanghai, Zurich, London, and yes, even Caracas.

These immigrants were here for the fire sale of the millennium— the outright sale of American capitalism. These new immigrants did not settle in the tenement ghettos of a previous century on Manhattan's Lower East Side. Instead, this wave skipped the requisite generation of hardship and landed themselves prime real estate on Beacon Hill, Lake Avenue, Georgetown, Bel Air, Michigan Avenue, Martha's Vineyard, and Nob Hill. In another time, popular opinion would have prevented such a wholesale takeover of the country's vital economic interests. But now, facing the prospect of a new foreign boss with an odd-sounding name versus standing in growing food lines, many workers, blue and white collar alike, chose to practice pronouncing these new foreign names, with the word *Mr.* in front of them.

And along with a wave of individuals came their institutions and governments to scoop up what remained of America's blue chip stocks. Armed with their massive reserves and far stronger currencies, America's corporate titans became the equivalent of penny stocks for foreign acquiring companies whose names ended in such monikers as GmbH, Plc, NV, KK, and S.A., the legal corporate designations of their economies that now replaced America's *Inc.*

68

━┿╋┿━

SAN QUENTIN PRISON
MARIN COUNTY, CALIFORNIA
FEBRUARY 19

MA'AM, THEY'RE ESCORTING THE PRISONER out of the cell block now. He should be here in ten minutes," said the uniformed U.S. Army sergeant.

Connie Madern looked through the one-way mirror into the interrogation room where two of her CIA colleagues tested the recording equipment. "Thank you, Sergeant. We'll wait here." As soon as the young officer left, Connie turned to her companion and asked, "Are you ready?"

Kate only replied with a nod and a tense smile. She wasn't looking forward to this. Interrogating prisoners wasn't something she had signed up for, and certainly not a prisoner that had been captured through an extraordinary rendition. And because of his role as the leader of a failed terrorist plot, this prisoner was being held indefinitely. Following the Andalus Attacks, as they were now being called, this high-level detainee was transferred from Guantánamo Bay to a federal terrorist interrogation facility, newly housed within San Quentin.

The job of U.S. intelligence was to comb through every possible lead to find the ultimate masterminds of the Andalus Attacks. But given that this individual was apprehended years before, it was unlikely that he held any information that would materialize into a hot lead. Nonetheless, Kate had a special interest in being here today, despite her obvious trepidation.

"Don't worry, I've been through dozens of these since we broke up that San Francisco plot," said Connie with an air of absolute confidence. "Piece of cake. Most of them clam up anyways. Since they operate in individual cells, we haven't managed to get much out of them." Connie spoke in nonchalant business terms as she held out her hand, admiring her red lacquered nails.

Kate observed her demeanor and it struck her that Connie, someone whose career she once considered emulating, seemed oblivious to the human side of their intelligence work. These prisoners were just "intelligence assets" to her, whereas for Kate, terrorism involved real people, whichever side you were on. She had been tempered by Nebibi's words, and in the weeks since his car had careened off that cliff, they kept coming back to her: "One man's terrorist is another man's freedom fighter." What she still didn't know for sure was if Nebibi was referring to others as "freedom fighters" or to himself.

Such conjectures would be lost on Connie, so Kate focused on topics more familiar to her colleague. "Speaking of San Francisco, I always wondered how you managed to crack that plot. I never saw a single report filed on that investigation."

Connie perked up at the question. With all that had happened since then, no one had bothered to revisit the plot to blow up the Golden Gate Bridge. How the CIA managed to uncover that was now old news compared to Andalus.

"Listen, Kate, the truth is, we did squat on that. It landed in our laps through some anonymous tip. We put a whole intelligence spin on that just to get a bigger operating budget approved on Capitol Hill. That's how things really operate in D.C. The sooner you know that, the better off you'll be, career-wise." Connie was still trying to entice her to work at the CIA and thought that by bringing her into her confidence, Kate would see her value as a mentor.

But it had the complete opposite effect—it ticked Kate off. She sacrificed two friends to the pursuit of that money trail, and found and lost Nebibi in the process. Now this woman was telling her she hadn't lifted a finger on the whole Golden Gate plot—and that it meant nothing more to her than a budget approval.

Before Kate could respond, the sergeant was back. "Ma'am, the prisoner is coming in now. . . ."

Connie turned to Kate. "Now's your opportunity to shine. Since you have more background on this subject, I'll expect you to take the lead in giving the questions to the translator."

The two CIA men escorted the prisoner into his seat and secured his thin arms with leather straps to the metal chair facing the one-way mirror. He sat there motionless with a hood obscuring his face. The man who would translate today's proceedings sat at the table across from the prisoner, while the other stood vigilant by the door. Given the prisoner's weak physical and mental state, however, there was no need for all this security.

The translator spoke in English into the microphone, "The prisoner, Rashidi Hasehm, is now ready for questioning." Kate felt a shiver run up her spine.

The translator motioned for the other man to take off Rashidi's hood. In that moment, Kate doubled over, feeling like she wanted to throw up. She lost her footing but caught herself from falling by bracing her hands against the one-way mirror. The sound of her hands hitting against the glass made Rashidi look up, and his piercing brown eyes seemed to be staring directly at Kate.

"Are you okay?" Connie asked, startled by Kate's reaction.

As she steadied herself, Kate took a step back from the glass, her eyes focused on what she was seeing on the other side. *It was Nebibi!* Certainly more gaunt, and with dark circles under his eyes. Her heart wanted to believe it, but her mind walked through the logic of recent actual events. It *was* his car that had crashed off the cliff and those were *his* cuff links in his valise. She quickly thumbed through the file she held in her hand. And this prisoner, number 45297, had been in high-security custody for the past six years, under twenty-four-hour surveillance. Kate quickly kept looking through the file for something else.

"What are you looking for?!" Connie reached over and placed her hand over the open mic, alarmed by Kate's nervous actions.

"What is the prisoner's date of birth? Do we know that?!" Kate looked up at Connie with a focused stare demanding a response.

"A copy of his Italian passport is in there; but what does that have to do with anything?!"

Kate found the page. January twenty-fourth, same year as Nebibi. Nebibi and Rashidi were twins! She looked up, staring again at Rashidi's face, this time studying it more closely, trying to find clues. His right eyebrow was raised in an arch. It wasn't Nebibi on the other side of the glass; he could only raise his left eyebrow.

Connie was now glaring at Kate, waiting for her to start the interrogation. The translator tapped the mic, asking, "Can you hear me? Is this working?"

But something else was clicking in Kate's mind. She didn't want to end up jaded like Connie. She wanted something real, something human, to hang on to. And if she went ahead with the interrogation of Nebibi's brother, she would be crossing a line. She'd be saying that her time with Nebibi, both during graduate school and more recently at the Alhambra, meant nothing to her. But it did, and in this instant, she was certain of that. Now that she had lost him, love had taken over.

The feeling of nausea returned, except this time Kate knew she couldn't hold it back. She rushed out of the room and didn't look back.

69

UPPER ROCK NATURE PRESERVE, GIBRALTAR
FEBRUARY 20

THE MORNING SUN SHONE BRIGHTLY on the canopy of trees in the Upper Rock Nature Preserve, home to Gibraltar's 230 Barbary apes. Because of the car crash and security threats, tourists were still not allowed to venture up the Rock to visit the apes, which meant these animals had gone several days without illicit treats from tourists. The leader of the largest troop of Barbary apes was foraging the forest floor for any remnants of discarded morsels from days before. He came across something of note and signaled in his high-pitched scream for the rest of his troop to join him. The meeting of this Barbary ape troop was now in session to investigate the leader's findings.

On a landing just below one of the highest cliffs of the Rock were eight cylinders, the outside of which had the smell of human hands, an indication to these apes that a treat would be inside. The leader picked one up with his paw. The screw top was already loosened by the fall from above. He banged it on a rock, and he continued to do so for a couple of minutes, eventually managing to release the top. As he held the tube up, a fine particle dust fell out; some of it settled on the stone and the rest traveled on a soft breeze, landing on the bark and leaves of the surrounding vegetation cover.

The troop leader let out a sharp cry, boasting his success. Other members followed suit with the remaining tubes. Some ventured to lick the substance directly off the rocks, while others walked away with disinterest and instead feasted on their backup food supply, the bark and leaves of the vegetation of the Upper Rock Sanctuary. Within twenty-four hours, the entire prized population of Barbary apes on the Rock of Tariq was contaminated from ingested radio-active material.

A FEW DAYS LATER, the Governor of Gibraltar sat on the veranda of the Mount Barbary mansion overlooking the bay, his thoughts lost in the turmoil of the world, but thankful that it had not touched his prized Gibraltar. He had started reading the headlines of *The Times* of London, but decided to wait till after breakfast to get upset at the news. Balancing a tray in her hands, his maid was walking on the veranda opposite the pool where he sat, each and every day, with his papers.

"Here you are, Governor. Your hot tea and a couple of fresh scones with your favorite marmalade. Oh, yes, and here's the clotted cream, I almost forgot. Would you like me to pour the tea for you?"

"No thank you, Millicent. Everything looks just perfect." As she walked away back across the veranda, the governor raised the teapot with both his hands and poured some English breakfast tea in his bone china cup. Then, he lowered one sugar cube in, ever so gently so as not to spill a single drop. Nothing, not even the global headlines, could disturb the peace of this particular corner of this outpost of the British Empire. Comforted by that thought, he raised his cup to take a sip of his tea. As the rim of the china cup touched his lips, he heard a shriek from his maid and the sound of her tray hitting the stone floor. Startled, the governor dropped his cup, which cracked on the surface of his table, spilling every last drop of tea, all before he'd even taken a single sip.

He got up with blotches of tea stains on his slacks and ran to where Millicent was. She was staring at a Barbary ape that had fallen into the pool. "How odd? How do you think it got there?" he asked her.

"Sir, it fell out of the sky when I was walking back to the kitchen."

"The sky, Millicent? How could that be? Really, that's just impossible! . . ."

"Sir, I swear. The blimey thing fell right—" Before she could finish her sentence, another ape fell from a branch in the tree above and landed with a splash in the pool. Two lifeless monkey carcasses floating in the pristine pool, one broken teacup, and one screaming maid: the turmoil affecting the rest of the world had now marred the governor's idyllic setting for morning tea in this outpost of the British Empire.

Before the week was out, the Gibraltar Ornithological & Natural History Society recorded the death of all 230 of the Rock's Barbary apes. They struggled to understand the mysterious plague that had felled their prized colony of apes. Weeks would go by before they would discover that the feces of the now-dead colony registered high radioactivity. In turn, the Governor of Gibraltar had the unenviable task of informing the Queen and reminding her of the legend regarding the Barbary apes and British occupation, which held great sway with the local Gib population.

70

-+-+-+-

MR. PRESIDENT, IT'S THEIR FINAL OFFER. We've pushed them as far as we can. There's no more room to negotiate." Treasury Secretary James was on the phone trying his best to convince his boss to sign the executive order approving the deal.

"Run it by me one last time, Damion. I'm putting you on speaker." The President wanted a record of this, and the handwritten notes that his Chief of Staff and Vice President were about to make would be historical documents for his Administration's archives.

"Yes, Mr. President. The Chinese Central Bank will agree to two things: One, they'll lock in their current $1 trillion holding of U.S. securities and not convert them to euros for at least six years. And two, they will purchase another $1 trillion of our securities over the next month. They're also willing to work with the IMF on drafting an outline for our economic stability plan and fiscal spending guidelines, as long as the Chinese get more voting rights at the IMF. Then there's also that other issue. . . ."

"Geez . . ." The President looked over at his Chief of Staff, whose brow wrinkled at the deal terms.

"Sir, we need to do this to maintain confidence in our currency. The Japanese shifted half their dollar holdings to euros already and the rating agencies are breathing down my neck. They say they need to knock our sovereign risk rating down a couple of notches. We would be one notch above Russia, right next to Brazil and Chile. And if that happens, the ratings of every U.S. borrower will immediately suffer. They'll never get a nickel out of any bank, not even in Iceland. Sir, we have to take the deal. It's the only course left."

The President looked out the window of the Oval Office. A tent city had sprung up on the little park on the other side of the southern ellipse. "Things aren't looking pretty around here. Tell me, is there anybody that did their job right? Anyone? Just one person? You don't need to answer that. I already know. Not a single goddamn person did, and that's why I've inherited this situation. Even Roosevelt didn't have it this bad."

The President dug deep. He had a job to do that no one else could. It was his decision and his alone, regardless of the pile of strategy papers from his army of advisors. He picked up the brass plate on his desk, on loan from the Truman Presidential Library, and felt its weight in his hand. THE BUCK STOPS HERE it read. "Okay, Damion, walk on over with the document. I'll sign it."

"Yes, Mr. President." The Treasury Secretary didn't envy the Chief Executive in having to make this decision. His signature today would open a chapter that all thought had closed a hundred years ago. The economy of the United States of America would once again be looked upon as an emerging market, no longer the ultimate master of its own economic affairs. Now the President, and the rest of the country, would have to contend with oversight from a significant shareholder, the People's Republic of China, and their particular form of capitalism hidden inside Chairman Mao's Little Red Book. So yes, the U.S. economy was saved, but at a cost. A very high cost.

IN THE WEEKS FOLLOWING THE ATTACKS, there were grand celebrations in the mountain cave hideouts of Kandahar, but also knowledge that there would be blowback, and it would be strong. The leaders of the hobbled U.S. economic empire would make sure to focus their diminished resources on hitting them hard—aiming for extinction.

71

+ + +

CARACAS, VENEZUELA
MARCH 5

FINANCE MINISTER ALARCÓN HAD A PRIVILEGED seat directly behind
President Chávez on the grandstand. He could see the
outline of a broad smile across his President's face. No
doubt because he'd succeeded in all his goals, thought
the minister. Oil prices were up and the country's expanded social
spending budget was keeping domestic dissent to a whisper. And
today would mark Chávez's crowning achievement.

The Presidents of all thirty-three western hemisphere nations
south of Rio Grande, Cuba included, were gathered at the Aeró-
dromo Francisco de Miranda, the military airport smack in the
middle of downtown Caracas. They were about to sign the charter
for the South Atlantic Treaty Organization, SATO. Now, NATO
would have a counterpart in the southern half of the Atlantic, and
the U.S. was not invited to this party.

At exactly noon, the charter was ratified and put into effect.
These member nations would now have a forum in which to con-
sult together on security issues of common concern and take joint
action upon them. And most important, as of today, an attack on
any one of these member nations would be considered an attack
upon all SATO members.

Six new Russian-made Sukhoi Su-30MKK jet fighter aircraft
flew in formation overhead. They'd been purchased with Venezuela's replenished supply of petro euros to kick start SATO's military forces. The crowd below cheered wildly as these spanking
new jets crisscrossed the sky with their plumes.

In contrast, Cuba's contribution to this new military cooperation agreement was not widely known. It was being provided by

them behind a new fortress wall that surrounded the Bermudez Institute of Tropical Medicine. Thanks to Cuba's expert pharmaceutical researchers, the arsenal of SATO now also included a certain serum.

In another time, the U.S. would have quickly swept into Caracas with a technologically advanced military force sufficient to topple Chávez and install a friendly replacement. But now, with SATO in place, that option just wasn't on the table; that is, unless Americans wanted to ignite World War III in their own southern backyard. Besides, the costly wounds of Iraq and Afghanistan were still too fresh for such an exercise.

Not invited to any of the festivities, but nonetheless watching the spectacle from the rooftop of his embassy, the U.S. Ambassador to Venezuela was on the phone with the Secretary of State delivering the blow-by-blow scenario. His somber analysis was that the successful inauguration of SATO was the dawn of a new, difficult dynamic in the North–South dialogue that essentially marked the death knell of the long-held Monroe Doctrine. South America was no longer the U.S.'s private backyard.

72

ABOVE MANHATTAN
MARCH 9

KATE STARED PENSIVELY OUT the window as the captain of the 8:00 A.M. Delta shuttle from D.C. made the now-customary tilt of the aircraft so that passengers could get a better view of the new Ground Zero, which now encompassed most of Manhattan. Despite the bright early morning light, at this height, it was hard to see much other than the lack of traffic on either the West Side Highway or the FDR.

At the DIA, Kate had already studied classified images of what it looked like down there. Certain pictures stayed indelibly in her mind, such as the crowds of people lining up in front of their buildings waiting to be tested for radioactive contamination, the chaotic evacuation of those fortunate ones that tested negative, families being split apart, and the once wealthy and powerful now left standing in food lines after their livelihoods and pensions were eviscerated with the meltdown of the economy.

More recently, once the order of things in Manhattan began to settle into a new quieter rhythm, the Army Corps of Engineers began its work of building massive barrier walls. Twenty-foot-high slabs of concrete now separated Manhattan south of 125th Street from the free flow of traffic with the rest of the world. Due to the contamination of radioactive dust particles now embedded in stone edifices, the area south of the Brooklyn Bridge and the thirty-block perimeter around Midtown would be closed off to any human traffic for a minimum of five years.

The rest of Manhattan was left to the free rein of the military, not because of imminent exposure to radiation, but rather the panic of the population. Any resident who had managed to survive the attack on Manhattan in one sane piece, vowed never to return. Places like the Alaskan wilderness, the deep wet forests of Oregon, and the desolate sand dunes of Guam welcomed a wave of survivalist New Yorkers, eager to put their previous lives behind them, BlackBerries included.

And so the most recent pictures showed that the grid of what was once the world's most vibrant metropolitan area was now largely devoid of human traffic. In a period of months, Manhattan had turned into a ghost town. Finally, the City slept.

The world is certainly a very different place since the last time I was home, thought Kate. And this was all because the world was no longer dominated by, and could no longer rely on, America's hyper-power in matters of economics, politics, or security.

When she returned, the DIA was trying to put out fires everywhere. Lieutenant Khoury and his colleagues confirmed that every single one of the suicide bombers had taken doses of *T. gondii*. Kate's "fire" was dealing with the newly formed SATO, which was on a buying binge for all types of strategic military equipment from the Chinese, Russians, and Iran. The world beyond the quarantined island of Manhattan below was just waiting for the next shoe to drop.

Her first instinct after her incident at San Quentin was to leave the DIA and leave intelligence altogether. But Bill had convinced her to take some time off and reconsider. Out of respect for him, she agreed, knowing that a few weeks at home with her father, away from the noise of international plots, would help clear her mind.

Kate's fingers played with the pendant that hung on a chain around her neck. It was the pre-Columbian charm Nebibi had given her when they were still students. It made her think of the last time she had seen him and the shock on his face when he heard that his brother was still alive, and then the crash over the cliff on Gibraltar. They never found any bodies, but everything pointed to his death there on that rocky cliff. She looked out the window again, trying to hide the moisture forming in her eyes.

She thought about the information that had finally arrived from Herr Boeglin, minutes before the explosions. Did it prove anything that Nebibi's name appeared as one of the Califfato directors? Maybe not. But it did leave a question in her mind. Had he been an active participant or just an innocent bystander who got tangled into a violent plot?

Over the past few weeks, she had played back in her mind all the conversations with Nebibi, trying to uncover clues. Little things kept gnawing at her, but in the end she knew it didn't matter anymore. Califfato was closed and Nebibi was dead. What *did* matter was that violence had taken people close to her. She vowed to herself that she couldn't let that happen ever again.

Kate touched the pendant, twirling it once more in her fingers. One of her tears fell on the gold jaguar. This gift used to remind her of happier times with Nebibi, but now it only carried memories of death and destruction. She took the pendant off the chain, wiped the tear from the jaguar, and gently caressed it with her fingers one last time. Knowing that the time for death was done, she slipped the golden ornament into the airline seat pouch in front of her. She needed to leave it behind along with all the memories it represented. At least, she was going to try. *Onward and upward.*

TOMÁS AND HIS DAUGHTER SAT on a bench at water's edge in Tod's Point Park in Old Greenwich. Across the sound, they could see the outline of Manhattan's dormant skyline.

"Happy birthday, Kate." Molares handed his daughter a small gift, on this, her thirty-first birthday. She unwrapped it. It was a small Bible, worn at the edges. "It was your grandmother's. She'd always planned on giving it you." Tomás was thankful every day since January twenty-fourth that Kate had managed to survive the turmoil unscathed.

"Thanks." They sat there for a moment, silently staring across the water, until Kate changed the subject. "So what's the story with Royal Lane?"

"Well, we just finished unraveling the last bits of Sam's fund. We've got an entire wall of files tracing each derivative trade, showing who owes money to whom, on each one of the trades. It took two months to unravel. Problem is neither Sam's fund nor any of the counterparties are solvent, so it's really just a piece of history. The office will officially close at the end of this week."

"And where's Sam in all of this? . . ."

"He stuck around for a few weeks, but then when they had to auction off his jets and his estate, it just was just too much for him to handle. I heard he moved to some small town up in Northern California. Cloverdale, somebody told me. His wife's family had some ranch land up there."

"He's not the only one who had to downsize, right? And so what are you going to do, Dad?"

"I think I'm going to go back to the U.N. They have a lot of work ahead of them with the move and all." Since the attacks, the U.N. was working out of temporary quarters at Manhattanville College in Westchester County, New York. The General Assembly would vote next week on the selection of a new permanent site with Versailles, Dubai, Geneva, Shanghai, and San Francisco in top contention. Her father had missed that big payday from the sale of Royal Lane by a day, but at least he had the U.N. to fall back on.

"What about that Nebibi fellow, did he ever surface again?"

"The car that went off the cliff in Gibraltar, it was his. No remains were ever found, so the going assumption is that he died in the crash. Well, let's put it this way, at least the other owners of The Milestones Fund formally registered his death so they could take over management of the fund's remaining assets. So legally, he's dead." She took a breath, not mentioning the episode with Rashidi in San Quentin; she didn't want to cry now, not at this moment.

"You say that like you think otherwise? . . ."

"Well, it's uhm, more complicated than that really. . . ."

"You were close, I could see that . . . I'm sorry."

"There's something I need to tell you. It's why I came here. I wanted to tell you in person, Dad." She hesitated, which caused concern to come across her father's face. "I should just come out and say it. . . ."

"Yes . . . you have me worried now. . . ."

"I'm nine weeks pregnant. The father is, was, Nebibi. . . ."

In another time, Tomás would have hit the roof thinking about his daughter being a single mother, but now, with so much that had happened in their world, this news came as a welcome sign of new beginnings. "I'm going to be a grandfather!" He hugged Kate warmly, his heart lifted by the news.

"I'm happy, too." Just as she said that, there was a beep coming from her purse. It was her iPhone. The calendar reminder had popped up about an appointment in an hour in downtown Greenwich. Problem was, as far as she knew, she didn't have an appointment at noon. Kate stared at the appointment, trying to understand how it got into her calendar.

"Dad, can you drop me off on Greenwich Avenue? I need to run an errand and maybe I'll do some baby shopping while I'm at it. . . ."

KATE STOOD IN FRONT of the address shown in her calendar. It was Méli-Mélo restaurant. A thought crossed her mind. She remembered when Nebibi had mistakenly switched his iPhone for hers that morning in the Alhambra. I've come this far on a hunch, why should I stop now? she thought. It couldn't be, she thought. She had just wrapped her head around his death, and now this. It just couldn't be. Take it slow, Kate, don't jump to any conclusions, she said to herself.

She stepped inside, and the chef's ever-friendly wife, Evelyne, immediately recognized her.

"Hello, Ms. Molares. So good to see you again. We haven't seen you here since before Christmas. Seems like a thousand years ago now with everything that's happened. . . ."

"Certainly does . . . ," Kate responded as she looked at the number of empty tables in the restaurant.

"Well, just as you requested, we have the table by the window ready for you."

"You already had a reservation for me?" she asked.

"Yes, let's see. Yes, see here. It was made two months ago . . ." Evelyne lifted the page of the reservations calendar for her perusal. "*Venez,* I'll take you to your table?"

Kate's heart started beating faster as she walked. She stopped to look at the table, expecting to see someone already sitting there.

No one. She felt that tug at her heart and a pain in her throat. With disappointment on her face, she sat down and took the menu from Evelyne. She remembered the last time she'd sat here, back in December, waiting with anticipation for Nebibi to arrive. She looked out the window, half expecting a car to pull over in front of the entrance. *No snow this time.* A solitary bird, one of the first to venture back north after winter, was perched on a bare branch that scratched the window. The bird tilted its head, staring back at Kate, and then in an instant, it flew off.

Kate looked at her watch. *Noon, on the dot.* Evelyne returned to the table, but now was followed by a man in uniform. It was a FedEx delivery man with a package in his hands.

"I have a delivery for you. Are you Kate Molares?"

"Yes, yes I am. What is it?"

"Sorry, miss. I don't know what it is, but it came with instructions that we should deliver it here to you at exactly noon. Would you mind signing for it, please? Right there above that line." The man handed her the digitized delivery log.

"Thank you." After she signed the log and handed it back, both Evelyne and the FedEx delivery man stood there for a second, waiting for her to open the package. Instead she put it aside to signal that she wouldn't be opening it in front of anyone. As soon as she saw them disappear, she picked up the package and looked to see who sent it. There was only an address: Avenida Meritrxell, 22, Andorra.

She opened the FedEx box and pulled out a smaller box covered in velvet, with gold-stamped letters that read Van Cleef & Arpels on top. She opened it to find a necklace from their famous Alhambra quatrefoil design line. It was a long white gold chain with one Alhambra quatrefoil of turquoise set with a diamond in the middle. *It's beautiful.* There was a card enclosed with familiar handwriting. Without thinking, she placed her free hand on her belly as she read the simple message:

بيط تنا و ةنس لك / Feliz Cumpleaños / Happy Birthday

FEDEX HAD ANOTHER DELIVERY TO make today, this one in Washington, D.C. At 3:00 P.M., a package was delivered on Connecticut Avenue to the senior partner of Vann & Rossi, a legal firm that specialized in civil rights cases and was well known to the U.S. Supreme Court. When the senior partner opened the FedEx envelope, he almost fell out of his chair. Inside was a check for $20 million made out to his firm and drawn on a bank in Andorra. It was accompanied by a letter explaining the case of their new client, a certain Rashidi Hasehm, who was currently detained by the U.S. military in San Quentin. The $20 million was meant to cover the fees and expenses that would result in getting those who held him in custody to read Mr. Hasehm his Miranda rights. While the $20 million was not intended to secure his freedom, it was meant to at least buy Rashidi Hasehm protection of due process of law guaranteed by the Constitution of the United States. After that, let the cards fall where they may.

IN A WEATHER-BEATEN HOUSE sitting atop a hill, a man sat alone in front of his computer surfing the Internet and checking his e-mails. Outside, the winds of the ocean spat their mist on the wood boards of this creaky hundred-year-old house. Fall was coming to this desolate tip of Chiloé Island on South America's Pacific Coast.

The speed with which Internet pages came up on the screen was slow because in this remote area the only connection to the outside world was through the old-fashioned phone line. People who lived on this island off the coast of southern Chile were either tenth-generation fishermen or potato farmers, or looking to be lost to the outside world. And the man catching up on his e-mails was neither an expert in the feeding waters of the Chilean sea bass nor in the ancient cultivation methods of the renowned Chiloé potato.

The Yahoo e-mail address he was using was registered to a certain Abdul Rahman. But *this* Abdul Rahman was not eighty years old, and was definitely not rotting at the bottom of Lake Lugano. This Abdul, or at least the one who adopted his name and identity, was thirty-five years old, most definitely had both his arms attached his body, and was quite dry in his black cashmere turtleneck. *No saber cuff links.*

"Abdul" opened his e-mails. There was one from Banca Seguretat d'Andorra confirming the combined current value of his account. *$24 billion.* Because he had switched the original $17 billion deposit entirely into euros in January before the attacks, on the depreciation of the dollar alone, "Abdul" was now more than 40 percent richer. And maybe that money could be the cornerstone for a new path for his people, *la terza via*—the third road—that could help his people rebuild their gloried past, a future al-Andalus, without violence and destruction. Finally, he knew where he belonged and was at peace with his choice, one that left him altogether alone, but also one that allowed Kate a life not complicated by his.

Another e-mail arrived. It was from FedEx, confirming that his package had been delivered to its intended recipient in Greenwich five minutes ago. Along with the e-mail came a jpeg of the familiar signature of the recipient, Kate Molares, taken on delivery. "Abdul" smiled and touched the on-screen picture of the signature with his hand. "Happy birthday, Kate."

73

⏤◀╋╋╋▶⏤

THE SIT ROOM, THE WHITE HOUSE
MARCH 24

THE PRESIDENT SAT WITH his Vice President, the Secretary of Defense, the head of National Intelligence, and the National Security Advisor watching a scene play out on the large screen on the wall. They were looking to draw blood on behalf of the battered American public, and this was the moment for such retribution, which was being telecast to an exclusive audience half a world away.

American soldiers dressed in desert camouflage were rushing into several caves in the mountains between Pakistan and Afghanistan. After massive payoffs, in euros of course, to certain shady individuals, American intelligence forces had been tipped off about the location of the long-sought secret hideouts for al-Qaeda's top leadership. The President needed some good news, and so the event was being televised live via wireless cams on several of the soldiers' helmets. All that was missing in the Sit Room for this show was a fresh batch of buttered popcorn served in big tubs.

They stormed the inner chamber of the largest cave, expecting a barrage of terrorists defending their secret headquarters, but instead all they found were empty rooms and discarded papers. From the looks of it, the previous inhabitants had left in a rush. The commander of the raid, the master of ceremonies for this evening's entertainment, spoke into his microphone for his audience sitting in their comfortable leather chairs on Pennsylvania Avenue. "They got wind of our impending visit."

74

THE STRAIT OF TAIWAN
MAY 22

CAPTAIN XIAO YU SURVEYED the dark skies ahead of him. The young captain of the People's Liberation Army Air Force was leading his squadron of twenty Jian-10 fighter jets from their home base on the mainland. The wind currents over the Strait of Taiwan were calmer in late May, allowing them to undertake this historic mission. The first glimmer of daylight over the Pacific illuminated their target below. Captain Yu finally saw the coastline of the Pescadore Islands, the Taiwanese-controlled territory located thirty miles west of Taipei.

"Jié!!" Victory!! the captain yelled his attack signal to his squadron. For the next hour, the state-of-the-art jet fighters pounded the island with surgical strikes, taking out two strategic airfields and its port facility. The PRC's East Sea Fleet, normally stationed in these waters, were then clear to land massive amphibious forces to complete the invasion.

With this foothold under their control, additional PRC air and naval forces launched the second phase of the military campaign code-named "One Family." Within six days, the entire 14,000-square-mile territory formerly known as Taiwan flew the flag of the People's Republic of China, fulfilling the wish of all its leaders since Chairman Mao.

The swift success of the campaign was owed principally to the lack of countermeasures by the U.S. Pacific fleet, conveniently sidelined for the bargain price of $1 trillion. On the day that Taipei was captured, the U.S. President signed two documents that guaranteed military and political cover for the invading military force. The first was the unilateral cancellation of the Taiwan Relations Act, which had guided three decades of U.S. friendly relations with Taiwan. The second cemented the victory for the PRC. It was a new American-Sino Mutual Defense Treaty, which guaranteed U.S. military support for the PRC in this reunification campaign, as well as future ones they might plan in their Asian sphere of influence.

To its detriment, Taipei was surprised by this about-face in U.S. Asian policy. In the days that followed, the news of this military pact was not met with calm in Tokyo and Seoul. They understood the stakes. Pax Americana was for the history books, and the reality of the very stark Chinese Century would soon bear down upon them.

75

→+◆+←

TIBURON, CALIFORNIA
SEPTEMBER 24

55. 56. 57. THREE YEARS with him in my life. 58. 59. 60. Today's a big day. 61. 62. 63. Kate was in the midst of her ritual laps in the pool when she heard a voice cut through her concentration.

"Kate, Kate. We need to get going."

Tomás Molares, already dressed in a suit, stood at the edge of the pool trying to get his daughter's attention. In his arms, he held his other pride and joy, Tomás Molares Jr., or Tommy as they called him. Today was Tommy's third birthday and they planned to have a grand celebration late this afternoon with his classmates from pre-school. Seeing that her son was now awake, Kate stopped her laps and swam to the edge of the pool.

"I think you'd better get dressed. Remember, we have to be there early before everything gets under way." Tomás was referring to another celebration they would be attending this morning.

"Mama, Mama." Tommy's face beamed with a broad smile as he held his arms and hands out trying to reach for his mother in the pool.

"Hold on, birthday boy, I'm getting out in a sec." She turned to her father. "Sorry, Dad, I thought I could squeeze in a few more laps this morning before the little one woke up. What time is it?" Kate jumped out of the pool, revealing that her frame was fully recovered from the changes brought on by childbearing. She started drying herself off in the cool morning air.

"Six thirty, and we need to be there by eight thirty."

"Okay. I'll be ready in thirty minutes." Kate donned her robe and wrapped a towel around her head. She grabbed Tommy from her father's arms and gave him a kiss on the cheek. "And you, looks like you had a good night's sleep, my little one." His eyes were bright and ready to face this day's adventures in toddlerhood.

As the three of them made their way back in the house, Kate gazed at her young son. The instant she first laid her eyes on him, Kate knew that his face bore a striking resemblance to his father. The similarity only grew with each passing year, and so Nebibi was never far from her thoughts.

TOMÁS'S OLD BLACK JAGUAR had not made the journey cross-country, so instead he drove the small Molares clan in their new green Prius across the Golden Gate Bridge. He looked in the rearview mirror and saw Tommy waving happily at all the passing joggers. Then he glanced over at Kate sitting next to her son and they gave each other knowing smiles. It didn't amaze either of them that concern about global issues could be so easily wiped away with one smile from a three-year-old.

"That pretty, Mama." Tommy was now tugging at his mother's Alhambra necklace.

"Yes it is, sweetie. Careful though, you don't want to break Mama's favorite necklace. It's from a beautiful red city on a hill on the other side of the world, where everyone was happy a long, long time ago. When you're a little bit older, I'll take you there." She recalled that that part of Granada would be open to the public again only in another three years.

The fog was rolling out of the bay toward the Pacific, clearing the way for the sun to warm another picture-perfect fall day. Light glimmered off the peaks of the dark blue water below, which was being churned by a variety of watercraft, from sailboats and yachts to several tall ships. Cars traveled on only half of the bridge, the other half now permanently the exclusive domain of cyclists and joggers. After all, San Francisco proudly held the title of "Greenest City in America."

Tomás turned up the volume on the radio to listen to his favorite local morning program. "Good morning KGO listeners, Marc Adelman here, coming to you live. We're devoting our entire three hours to the San Francisco event of the century, the opening ceremonies for the new headquarters of the U.N. right here in our hometown. And to start us off, I have the mayor on the line right now, who we can thank for making today an official city holiday. So, Mr. Mayor, you must be very excited about all this."

"Hello, Marc. Good to be with you. You're right about that. This is gonna be *the* event of the century. We're very pleased to have the U.N. back here. The first member countries signed the original charter over at the Veterans Memorial Hall." Because of the commotion around him, the mayor was practically shouting into the microphone.

Tomás turned at the first exit after the bridge and then drove a few minutes to the main entrance of the Presidio. He'd been working for the U.N. ever since the last days of Coldsmith's fund. And when San Francisco was selected as the new site, he moved out to the Bay Area to oversee the creation of the leading-edge infrastructure that would be needed to bring the U.N. into the twenty-first century.

". . . how did the deal on the Presidio land grant come about, Mr. Mayor? That's a pretty prime slice of local real estate. . . ." The radio show was still in the background, with Marc talking about the piece of land first settled by the Spaniards in 1776, on the northern tip of the city next to the Golden Gate Bridge.

The mayor was standing on a stage facing the U.N.'s new building in the Presidio with dignitaries arriving every minute and surrounded by hordes of the international press. Overhead, the Goodyear blimp was transmitting the scene to billions watching around the world on their TVs, cell phones, and computers.

At the ceremony, the mayor continued shouting into the mic, "It's what turned it around, really. Remember, France, Switzerland, and China were all lobbying hard. Most of the world, though, wanted to keep it in the U.S. as a sign of solidarity with our new Administration. So I had a meeting with the Presidio Citizens' Committee and after they agreed to cooperate in the process, we made our bid. It was the land grant plus the city's historical U.N. link that tipped it in our favor. Hold on a sec, please." The mayor turned to listen to one of his assistants. "Marc, I'm going to have to sign off now. My people are telling me the Pope and the Dalai Lama just arrived."

Still in the car, Tomás turned down the volume of the radio and handed his ID to the guard. He turned back to Kate, saying, "We've never had so much security. No choice, though, we've got senior reps from all 192 member countries, plus spiritual leaders from around the world." The Basque Country would also be present in the official observer status it had recently managed to win for itself.

The guard recognized Tomás, and after checking the names of the other two passengers, waved them through. "You're all set, Mr. Molares."

Tomás drove to the underground parking lot and found the space with his name on it. Unbuckling her son from the car seat, Kate said to her father, "I'm glad we could bring Tommy along today. He'll be able to look back on this day and say he was here."

Tomás and Kate held on to Tommy's hands as they walked out of the parking garage toward the main hall. Throngs of dignitaries were making their way inside the single-story structure. The building's roof was covered in green grass and sloped into the natural terrain of the surrounding land, as most of the new headquarters was underground. The visible façade wound around much of the area that used to house the Presidio's army barracks and was made of natural materials, wood and red clay.

The goal of the architects had been to build the greenest and most technologically advanced building in the world. They succeeded, but more important, they made the massive ten-story structure below the most secure and impenetrable ever built. As of today, the new and improved U.N. was open for business, and would never close again, no matter the threat.

Today was more than mere ceremony, as it also signaled what many hoped was the death of unilateralism. With the heavy influx of foreign investment, the U.S. economy was all the more dependent on external forces, particularly the Chinese, and the current Administration had worked hard to frame a foreign policy for this new reality. At the same time, however, no one was any closer to breaking apart Murad's virtual global caliphate, so danger still loomed in hidden quarters.

All these factors converged at this moment in history, prompting the U.S. and most of the rest of the world to finally take toddler steps toward a more pluralistic management of global society through a revitalized U.N. And the new U.N. Secretary-General, a career public servant, the first *woman* in that role, was ready to lend a steady, nurturing hand in those first wobbly steps.

EPILOGUE

⊰+♦+⊱

RIO JARI, STATE OF PARÁ, BRAZIL
SEPTEMBER 24

THE SMALL ONE-ROOM SHACK SAT ON the banks of the Rio Jari in the heart of the Amazon jungle. The shack had been here for forty years, inhabited by a sole woman whose only sustenance was the harvesting of Brazil nuts in the surrounding dense forests. Once every three months, a slow riverboat passed by to trade the woman's Brazil nuts for other basic supplies and to relay news of the outside world, meaning only as far as the broader Amazon delta, with never a mention of issues like the "collapse of the dollar" or the "global jihad." This was the cycle of this woman's life, and as she was in her late sixties now, the harshness of the dense jungle around her wouldn't allow that cycle to last many more years.

The slow riverboat from the mouth of the Amazon docked at its familiar spot. In the middle of the river, the trader could see a patch of bubbling water, signaling a school of piranhas had found their prey. The river trader turned toward the shack and called out for the old woman and her Brazil nuts, *"Senhora Zorana!"* No response.

He looked inside her small room. A hammock was swung on one end and a crude table and chair were at the other end. A frayed picture of the Virgin Mary was all that adorned the bare wood walls. But no sign of the woman. He searched the surrounding grounds but all he found was a bag of Brazil nuts, with no sign of any other life. He assumed that the woman had finally succumbed to death somewhere in the dense Amazon, or maybe slipped into the river and the waiting teeth of the piranhas. He took the full bag and loaded it into his boat. Then he crossed this location off his map for future trading runs and, with that stroke, wiped all record to the outside world of this "uninhabited" location.

Five miles inland, quite the opposite was true. Armies and infrastructure had been reassembled here from faraway mountain caves. Under the dense canopy layer of the forest, there were full-fledged living and training quarters for Murad and his colleagues.

At the center of this complex of low-lying structures was the medical research unit. The men, the jihadists, lined up here every morning to receive their vitamin booster shots, version II of a certain serum. The side effects were negligible, and it was helping to shape the most focused army on the planet. One of the youngest of these soldiers of jihads-to-come was already being groomed for a future leadership role. He was demonstrating the tenacity that would lead his people to future military conquests. The young soldier's name was Mohamed, son of Atta.